RITWIK AND HRIDAY

Siddharth Chowdhury is an author, most recently of *The Patna Manual of Style*, which was shortlisted for the Hindu Prize for Fiction. He works as an editorial consultant for the house of Manohar.

RITWIK AND HRIDAY

tales from the city, tales from the town

SIDDHARTH CHOWDHURY

PICADOR

Diksha at St. Martin's first published 2002 by Srishti Publishers
Patna Roughcut first published 2005 by Picador India
Day Scholar first published 2010 by Picador India

This volume first published 2016 by Picador India
an imprint of Pan Macmillan India
a division of Macmillan Publishers India Private Limited
Pan Macmillan India, 707, Kailash Building
26, K. G. Marg, New Delhi – 110 001
www.panmacmillan.co.in

Pan Macmillan, 20 New Wharf Road, London N1 9RR
Basingstoke and Oxford
Associated companies throughout the world
www.panmacmillan.com

ISBN 978-93-82616-95-5

This is a work of fiction. All characters, locations and events are fictitious. Any resemblance to actual events or locales or persons, living or dead, is entirely coincidental.

1 3 5 7 9 8 6 4 2

Typeset by Manmohan Kumar
Printed and bound in India by
Replika Press Pvt. Ltd.

Contents

Diksha at St. Martin's

To Patna

Contents

Homeward Bound

It was just before Dushera and the schools were closed in Patna. The oppressive heat of September had given way to the lazy warmth of October. The evenings had grown cooler than before. Javed Ahmed Siddiqui, a high school teacher, was going home to Gaya. He boarded the 6:45 Passenger from platform no. 3 and settled down to a seat near the window. The familiar railway track smell of fresh hot shit and stale vinegary urine assailed his nostrils. The train started on its way. It was dark outside now and as the train left the city limits, the scent of wildflowers mixed with ganja wafted in with the cool air. He liked the rush of wind on his face. He was an ordinary sort of a man. A contemplative man. A man who was more often than not happy and perhaps for that reason alone a rare kind of a man. He looked forward to the week's holiday to be spent with his family. Parents, brothers and sisters, assorted nephews and nieces. Whenever he went home, the children wouldn't leave him alone even for a minute. They crowded around him all the time and tagged along with him everywhere. He would play cricket with them in the mornings and in the evenings tell them stories of all kinds, for he had a fantastic imagination, and recite for their benefit couplets of Ghalib and Kaifi, most of which he knew by heart. Most important of all, he never asked them to study. A rare and ever-endearing quality in any uncle. He taught Urdu and Persian at a missionary school in Patna. At thirty-five he had a receding hairline and the aquiline nose of a Mughal warrior and laugh lines had started appearing around his mouth. He had the beginnings of a double chin. Till a couple of years back his parents were anxious to see him married but he knew he couldn't afford a wife. At the same time he realized that some things would become much easier if he just said yes. Sex for one. Food for two. He felt he should settle down, have a couple of kids, a regular family, but he had one curious notion. He didn't want his wife to be a poor man's wife. He didn't want his bride to have the same slow, stagnant life of his mother and sisters. A life of low compromises and nil delights. An apparently stable, slow lower middle-class existence with a tentative hold on respectability. An inch away from poverty always.

He had plans for his begum. He wanted to be affluent enough to buy gifts for her whenever he wanted to: perfume, silk and gold. Meanwhile, time was running out. He had saved some money but time was running out. He would probably say yes if asked again, he thought to himself, all the time staring into the still darkness of the hurtling countryside. They hadn't asked again in over a year. He wondered whether his parents had already given up on him.

He wondered what Mirza Ghalib would have done in a similar situation but then he said to himself, 'Now that's a thought. A crazy thought. He was a rebel, wasn't he? He was a genius. How can one compare oneself to Ghalib? You can't compare yourself to Ghalib. He could do anything. If he wanted to marry someone, he would just marry her, simple. He surely wouldn't let a petty thing like poverty stop him from doing what he wanted to do. He was touched by God. He could run a gambling den in his own house. Kill a man if the need arose and then go home and write poetry so sublime that it would make the dead live again. He was a hero and heroes can do anything. You are not a hero.'

The train chugged along, on the familiar tracks past the villages and small kasbas, indifferent in its battered majesty. He wondered what it felt like to be a poet, a regular genius, to be able to change people's lives and their world with the words they write in the sanctuary of their lonely rooms. To weave words like pearls on a string to adorn a beloved's graceful neck and sometimes like a stone in a slingshot to shatter the narrow mirror in which society sees its reflection and preens in delight. What heady feelings it must induce to be able to wield such powers. But it was of a past era he was thinking about and he knew that no one read poets anymore except other poets. Even Javed hadn't read any of the younger poets except Javed Akhtar but then even he was primarily a lyricist. Javed's point of reference was of forty to fifty years past, the time of Firaq Gorakhpuri and Sahir Ludhianwi and Kaifi Azmi, the revolutionary poets of the forties and fifties. Those were his heroes but there was only one god and that was Ghalib for him. What made Ghalib what he was? What made him tick? He wished he had been born in the last century and had known Ghalib. He was sure he would have been a friend of Ghalib's. He said to himself, 'The similarity between me and Ghalib is that of the tomcat and the tiger. Only the genus is the same. He was a poet and a prophet. Sometimes drunk, sometimes dangerous but always generous. As adept with a rapier as with a quill, walking the bylanes of Chandni Chowk with the cool swagger of a local hero. Tortured yet brimming with life. Sunshine and despair. He would have been a hard man to love but I would have loved him. I would have been his friend.'

Javed smiled to himself as he thought about this. He wanted to write a critical biography of Ghalib and had been taking notes for the past two years. Mirza Ghalib was a kind of an obsession for him. For him everything that was there to celebrate in life was right there in Ghalib's poetry, in his couplets and ghazals, and one only had to immerse his mind for a couple of minutes every day and have his jaded spirits rise up rejuvenated in no time at all. He sometimes dreamt of Ghalib in his long achkan and Cairo cap, walking with Javed through some gali and they would enter a haveli after a while and then start climbing the stairs of a winding staircase. Ghalib in front leading Javed by the hand but the stairs would go on and on forever and then it would be morning and he would wake up. Now as he sat in the train looking out of the window, the recollection of that dream—it was always that same dream—made him laugh out involuntarily.

He heard a girl giggle and looked out of the corner of his eye to see a girl of sixteen-seventeen sitting opposite him diagonally, suppressing her laughs with her dupatta and having a hard time doing it. For a second Javed was surprised that there were others beside him. He had been totally engrossed in his reveries. He was embarrassed then. A middle-aged man in a dhoti-kurta who was sitting beside her looked at him and then said something to the girl. She looked at Javed and quietened down. The giggles subsided. The other passengers too checked out Javed with some interest and then looked away. This chronic daydreaming had always landed him in sticky situations. *The girl probably thinks that I am crazy or something but she is so pretty she can think anything she likes,* and as he mused about this he smiled some more but then he realized what he was doing and he stopped quickly.

The compartment was filled to capacity and some of the passengers were squatting in the aisle itself. At the end of the compartment near the door, three armed railway policemen stood around smoking. They all confirmed to a type—large, potbellied and sluggish-looking. A family of four was sitting beside Javed. The father in a khadi kurta-pajama, with a green wheel insignia pinned to the breast, looked like a grassroots-level political worker. He was close-eyed with a small nose and luxuriant moustache whose ends he chewed with his tobacco stained teeth constantly. He had the face of a minor extortionist and the blustery rude behaviour to go with it. With him were his wife who was in ghungat and who kept quiet all the time, and a little girl of ten or eleven to whom none of the parents paid much attention and then there was the son, the crown prince, who was a voluble little fellow of around four years and who talked and shouted and sang and in whom the parents delighted entirely. He sang songs from Hindi movies and the girl who had giggled at Javed found it to be very endearing but Javed felt otherwise. The favourite song of the kid was the popular 'I Love My India' from the Subhash Ghai movie *Pardes.* He sang it once and then at the insistence of the girl did an encore and then again and again. Javed thought to himself in dismay that probably his nephews would do the same to him when he reached home in a couple of hours' time.

Across from Javed, on the side of the aisle, sat a couple of young men in their early twenties. They talked among themselves most of the time. Once in a while they would fall silent and watch the other passengers. One of them with a thin smeary little moustache kept looking at the girl. As was mentioned earlier, the girl was pretty. In the first bloom of youth and aware of her prettiness and sure of the fact that what she had was something rare, perhaps transient, but while it lasted life itself would on bended knees do here very bidding. Once in a while Javed stole a glance at her and wished that she would look at him again. She was fair and had a sharp little nose with a silver nathani embedded in her left nostril and a generous mouth and light-coloured eyes that twinkled with mischief and a certain vibrant joy in being alive, taking in everything with a gaze that was both inquisitive and bold but it was her breasts, her left breast actually, that captivated Javed.

Under the tight kurta and partly uncovered from the sides by the dupatta, sidewise curved from her armpit to the folds of the dupatta, a mound of solid jelly slung low. Would she have brown areolae or pink ones? Pink nipples of course—she was so fair—with tiny light-coloured hair around them, almost invisible on her skin. If he could just touch them, squeeze them softly, roll the nipple around with his tongue. Ah heaven. *Look at me.* The girl looked at him straight on at that moment and he was startled. He turned his head towards the window hurriedly. Would she know what he was thinking? If on this visit his parents asked him to marry he would definitely say yes. This can't go on, he said to himself. Could she see it in his face? He was getting to be like an adolescent each passing day. The girl probably thinks that I am another of those middle-aged lechers but I am not middle-aged. I am only thirty-five. My god I am thirty-five!

The girl wasn't even aware that he was checking out her breasts. The left one in particular, but she was acutely aware of his presence. She thought him to be interesting and funny. When he would stare out of the window all kinds of expressions would glide across his face like silver white fishes in a dark pool. He was like one of the actors in the Ramleela troupe that visited her village every year during Durga Puja. Maybe he is an actor too but ... he doesn't look poor enough. He is too 'tip-top' for that. He would be just right for the role of Sita, though, his mouth is so pretty, and she giggled some more. If she had known that he was a Muslim she would have been mortified. Muslims were dangerous. They were unclean. Muslims were bad news. Her father whispered to her in Magahi to keep quiet and then glared at Javed again who was as usual looking out of the window. The soft prettiness of the girl, her close proximity, the smell of woodsmoke in the air, coupled with the fact that he was homeward bound had made his mind segue into a mellow poetic mode. The long stretching darkness with the occasional night fire dancing in it like fireflies in a dark room seemed to him like a simile for his own life with its routine everyday compromises and fugitive desires and it was passing him by in a hurry.

He wondered what Ghalib would think about the simile. Would he use it in a couplet? Probably not, he decided after a while.

The train reached Nadaul and some people got off and a group of five young men in their early twenties or late teens boarded the coach. After a five-minute halt the train resumed its journey and the trouble started just after that.

The young men whipped out kattas and they were joined by those two men who were sitting opposite Javed. A couple of them took the policemen unawares and they didn't put up a fight. The policemen handed over their rifles. The rest of the men started looting the passengers systematically. Nobody protested or said anything but handed over whatever valuables they had. It was the third robbery in as many weeks on that line alone. 1997 would prove to be a banner year for train robberies in Bihar. Javed felt as if a small cube of ice had suddenly been lodged above his left cheekbone and now the intense fear that he could feel rise up in waves inside his heart made the ice melt into little droplets which coursed down the side of his face, inside the skin. The little boy was quiet now, wide eyes staring into the terror-ridden ones of his close-eyed father. He had never seen him so pale and submissive before and it awed him. He did no more encores of 'I Love My India'.

Javed could see the terror all around him reflected in the faces and eyes of his fellow passengers. They all looked alike. They looked trapped but there was no anger in their eyes, just empty despair which paralyzed them totally.

Javed felt that if he stood up he would just sink to the floor in a squelchy mass of muscles, blood and bone. An open sluice of water was running from his knee caps to his feet. 'Coward,' his mind whispered back to him. As he handed over his wallet and watch he could see his hand shake uncontrollably. The man who took his wallet and watch laughed and it went like a spike through Javed's ear. It was the man with the thin, smeary moustache and shifty eyes. He didn't appear much older than many of his senior class fellows, Javed noted. 'Coward,' his mind screamed back. He felt ashamed with himself and a tiny flame of anger started flickering up in his breast. He was not a fighting man, had always shied away from confrontations of any kind but today he wished otherwise. He wished he were different. He wished he wasn't such a coward. The slow flame of anger burned higher and higher but he didn't do anything. Anger warmed him up and he felt better.

The ice was gone from underneath his skin. Something like this had happened to him only once before, a few years back, on a chilly early December evening in 1992. He had felt the same kind of terror and isolation of being completely alone. He hadn't gone to his school for days after that. He felt like he didn't have a single friend left. There wasn't anyone he could trust anymore. He had taken it personally then and he took it personally now.

The dacoits looted in a leisurely fashion. They abused when they felt like it, slapped the men around a little just for fun and touched the women. No one raised their voices. Nobody protested. No one tried to fight. The policemen, now divested of their rifles and with them of their duty, were feeling relieved. They huddled together, smoking and whispering among themselves.

Looting over, one of the dacoits pulled the chain and the train started slowing down. The thin, mustachioed man who was their leader now suddenly caught hold of the girl and started dragging her towards the door. The girl didn't shout and she didn't cry. She just didn't do anything. Her father too looked on helplessly. He was so frightened that when he tried to speak he just couldn't form the necessary words. All the other passengers looked down at the floor. It is always the recollection of the immediate past during moments of crisis, the way things were just a couple of hours back, that fuels the terror and it was that terror which reduced the other passengers from healthy, vibrant specimens of humanity to the level of soul-dead zombies. They were lucky. It could have been their own sisters, wives, daughters, but miraculously it wasn't and they were lucky. They didn't want any part in it.

They didn't want their lucks to change. If they only closed their eyes and kept quiet, the nightmare would be over in minutes and then they could pretend that it never happened. Afterwards with a sigh of relief they could resume their journeys and their lives.

A silent scream rose in Javed's heart, a scream like that of a small furry animal in great pain, as he saw the girl being dragged. His mind felt like some dank and dirty, rotten-smelling jelly-like creature had suddenly attached itself to it and was sucking out memory, love, past pleasure away from him like a virus and leaving everything blank beneath. He grew calm in the few seconds that had elapsed and he realized what he would do. He didn't feel any terror anymore but only the sense of being intrinsically violated. He could see the immediate future with great lucidity now and what he saw there didn't deter him from doing what he was now determined to do.

The train had slowed down considerably and was coming to a halt when Javed said calmly to the man, 'You have got what you wanted. Don't take the girl. Please leave her alone.' In reply the man squeezed her breasts and abused her and then said, 'Saale hero banta hai. Shoot kar is Mithun ko.' There was silence all around. The girl looked at Javed and he realized he didn't even know her name. Not that it mattered anymore. One of the dacoits put his katta at point-blank range and shot Javed through his heart and then pushed him back to his berth. The girl screamed then. A thin, piercing, knife-like cry. The train lurched then and stopped. The man released the girl, pushed her away and then scrambled towards the door in a great hurry. In a few seconds all the dacoits had got down. They left the rifles on the ground and then disappeared into the vast darkness. The policemen got down and collected their precious Lee Enfields. The girl slumped down to the floor and fainted. In a few minutes the train started to move again. Meanwhile the father went forward and picked his girl up, relief written all over his face, and moved towards the door where the policemen were standing. The girl had started coming to her senses.

The girl pointed towards Javed with her finger and looked into her father's eyes but he didn't do anything. All the other passengers picked up their baggage and moved towards the door on both the sides. They all wanted to move away as fast and far away as possible from the sight of Javed slumped head down on his chest, slowly, painfully dying. He was like a dead rat in Surat in the time of the plague. Even the sight of him would contaminate them. They didn't want any part in it. They had already erased him from their memory. They would never talk about it to anyone. Crisis now over, denial had set in. They were all honest, hardworking men and women. The common people. They were respectable people and they didn't want any part in it.

Javed? What about him? As life slowly ebbed away, drop by drop, he thought how utterly insignificant his life had turned out to be. It was not despair, just a simple realization. He was in terrible pain and was barely conscious. He saw the familiar dream unfolding before his eyes and with greater clarity than ever before. He was walking beside Ghalib down one of the alleys of Ballimaran and both of them were silent and they came to the familiar haveli with its weather-beaten facade but inside it was clean and cool and they started to climb the stairs but somehow it was narrow, steep and straight now while earlier it had been a winding staircase. Ghalib led him by the hand. There was a room at the end of it which was not there before and they entered the room. A clean and bare but well-lit room and there was a large bed in the middle with a large green sheet spread on it. Javed lay down on the bed and Ghalib sat on the edge looking at him and smiling broadly. Javed closed his eyes. When he opened them again, there was no one around. He was all alone. He died then.

As the train reached Jehanabad station, all the passengers got off and boarded other compartments. The policemen got down too. In a little while another group of policemen arrived and they took away the body.

The girl wanted to see whether Javed was alive or not but her father who was now openly crying slapped her hard and dragged her down from the coach. He would forget everything. He would forget that a man had molested his daughter right before his eyes and he couldn't do a thing, that another man had tried to save her and was shot in return. He would forget that he had refused to help that man. He would forget everything.

One month later. Early one evening the girl made dinner, served her two younger brothers and then went to her father's room and locked the door. Her mother was in the kitchen. Her father hadn't come home yet. She tied her dupatta to the ceiling fan. She tugged it hard to see if it would hold. Her fingers were clenched into fists.

Seraphim And Cherubim

Hriday K. Seraphim was the 6-B class monitor. A uniformly bright and popular lad who was also a keen cricketer. A bonafide future pillar of society. The right stuff. Being the class monitor was yet the most spectacular achievement of his young life. But it was also the source of his secret pain, one he couldn't share with anybody. Not even his parents. One which gnawed at his self-worth like a rat and left it tattered each passing night.

The reason, rather the man behind the reason, being Adrian E. Cherubim. The new class teacher who was also the stopgap Moral Science tutor. Cherubim, a slight young man in his early thirties, not very bright and with not much of a prospect for marriage except perhaps with a passing adivasi servant girl, loved cute, well-groomed young boys from clean-cut families, definitely below the age of thirteen, who wouldn't put a compass in his eye while he nibbled their succulent ears.

For Cherubim, the old bugger, it was love at first sight. The first time he saw Hriday, during roll call, he knew that the present year at this new school in the Gangetic plains with its mock-Gothic depressive exterior would turn out to be his *annus mirabilis.* That very evening he contrived to keep Hriday back after school. He announced he needed a volunteer for an act of profound piety. He needed a boy who could transcribe a passage each from the Bible, the Gita, and the Koran, dealing with the virtues of pure and austere life, on to the blackboard for the next morning's Moral Science lesson. Of course, nobody volunteered. Children are not stupid. They only seem so at times.

'For God and Country,' thundered Cherubim at the tousle-haired and shifty-eyed congregation. 'Isn't that supposed to be our motto? Well, you are too young to do anything for your country, except perhaps collectively go to the "toilet" on it, granted. But remember one is never too young to do anything for God. Since nobody has volunteered, we must shut our eyes and pray, while I confer with the Almighty as to who will do his work today.'

After a minute Cherubim gently opened his eyes, smiled beatifically and said, 'Hriday K. Seraphim'. The next day Hriday was made the class monitor. For a couple of weeks after that, Cherubim left Hriday alone. But soon he was back to his old ways and would frequently ask Hriday to stay after school hours to do 'God's humble work'. Hriday had never thought that the innocuous-looking legend 'For God and Country' which was printed on the crest of all his shirts, and one which he had treated with exemplary indifference, could suddenly acquire fangs so sharp that each morning, as he would put on his shirt, he could feel it burrow deep into his heart and deposit drops of poison in his blood. Half the time he would be in a daze. He didn't know what was happening to him anymore. But whatever it was, it wasn't good. It made him sick. He thought about telling his parents, but the shame … He blamed himself. He must have done something wrong. He couldn't concentrate on anything. The studies suffered and from a charming, outgoing personality, his became a morose and silent one.

A couple of months went by. The first-term exams approached. Hriday started resisting. He wouldn't heed God's call anymore. When the results came out, Hriday had failed for the first time in his life in History/Civics/Geography. Needless to add, Cherubim was the teacher who was assigned this paper. His parents were shocked but Hriday knew he couldn't tell them ever. For the moment he only concentrated on the fact that the approaching summer vacation would effectively put him out of reach of his nemesis. Perhaps by the time the vacation ended there would be a new candidate to do God's work. 'Please let it be Ritwik. He is such an arsehole. He might even enjoy it,' Hriday prayed fervently.

But God, as we all convent-educated buggers know, like Elvis, moves in mysterious ways. A day before the vacation Hriday's father informed him that Mr Cherubim would come thrice a week during the holidays to tutor him in History/Civics/Geography, with an additional lesson in Moral Science thrown in on the second Sundays.

'That nice young man himself came to my office and offered his services. He said you have much untapped potential, though looking at you I wonder what made him say that. He said he would do it for free but of course I refused. Judging by his clothes he could sure use the money.'

Talk about one's worst nightmare coming true. Now one wasn't even safe in one's own home anymore. Again he blamed himself. If only he hadn't spurned Cherubim's advances, things wouldn't have come to such a sorry pass. All night long he thought about it and by morning he had reconciled himself to a compromise. He would meet Mr Cherubim and be the obedient lad he earlier was, and in return he should be spared during the vacations. The thought of Cherubim in his own home nauseated him.

'Come to the auditorium after four and we will solve your problem,' Cherubim said to him during the lunch break with a wink so manic that it almost looked like a muscle disorder. By three all the 'goodbyes' for the vacation had been said and the school was practically empty. By four it was completely empty, except for Osta the ancient watchman on his perch by the portico, who couldn't keep awake even at mid-day.

The auditorium was at one end of the school. By the side of the dark pond. A full ten minutes' walk from the main building. With bowed head and drooping shoulders, tie askew, like a man condemned, Hriday shuffled towards his fate. The door of the auditorium was ajar and on the ledge inside lay the big padlock with the key, its bow sticking out of the groove like a thermometer. It was dark but the light of the green room had been switched on. Suddenly the fog in his mind cleared. The last drop of poison kicked in. A deceptively simple thought occurred to Hriday. He went up to the green room and cautiously peeked in. Yes, Cherubim was there, reading Dale Carnegie's *How to Win Friends and Influence People*, a book he carried around everywhere with him. Smug and at peace with the world.

Hriday quickly switched off the light and bolted the door. He locked the main door of the auditorium with a calmness that had all but disappeared from his persona. By the time he crossed the dark pond, the screams had grown fainter. He stopped and turned, and with all the lung he could put into it, shouted, 'For God and Country,' against the wind, and flung the key into the weed-choked pond. Then with wings magically acquired Hriday K. Seraphim flew home for the holidays.

Danasur

Once upon a time there lived a young man called Ritwik in the big city of Delhi. He was a student. A pretty decent one too but he was not extraordinary. In short he was not a world beater but a serious, stable, steady sort of a fellow. A regular guy. There are thousands of them around like him, who are our friends, brothers and other assorted strangers. People who are the backbone of our society and family life. He was one of us.

Like I told you, he wasn't extraordinary. Just a facc in the crowd but still I feel deep down that he was one of a kind and that his story should be told. Because if it can be told then perhaps his existence wouldn't be meaningless anymore and also because I knew him for a while, when I lived opposite his room in Hakikat Nagar. Both of us are from Patna and we are of the same caste too. We studied at the same school. Ritwik was a couple of years senior to me. Because of all these reasons and some more abstract ones I feel a deep, strange kinship with him but the reverse, lamentably, is not true.

It has now become a compulsion with me to give meaning to his life or rather find meaning in it for myself. So I have decided to tell his story and not let him fade into that vast twilight of lies, conjecture, subterfuge and half-baked legends that constitute irredeemable obscurity. I am not a storyteller but I have read some books. I have done English (Hons.). My favourite author is Jeffrey Archer. You must have heard of him. My sister loves him too and she should know, after all she is the intellectual of the family. She is working for Zee TV. Now isn't that something?

I will try my best not to botch it all up because there are things that are so weird which happened to him and the legends are so many that right now I feel perhaps mere words will never explain the demented quest that finally did him in. I will spread the thin patchwork quilt of his life before you, dear reader, and you can trace the story out for yourself. People may come up with different versions but according to me this is how it happened.

I will move on now and start from the past. I promise I won't be longwinded and move as fast as I can. All right then, like I told you, he was a decent student. In fact, he had always topped his class back in the old government school. The principal there had predicted great things for him in the future.

From childhood his father had inculcated in him a dream to join the Civil Services in general and become an IAS officer in particular. Ritwik nursed that dream from childhood through adolescence and into his early youth. He loved his father and wanted to make him proud but when he failed to clear the mains for two years, desperation set in. Time was running out and he also had no 'reservation'. In a couple of years he would become, in Delhi University Biharispeak, a 'danasur'. A dinosaur. He would be extinct. He knew he could not go back home again. He felt guilty and worthless, always a bad combination for the soul. He knew his whole fraternity, rather our whole fraternity, was talking about him in a flippant and trivial manner. He felt bad for his father. He felt like hell inside but he stayed back for one more year. He studied hard, working day and night (I stayed in Hakikat Nagar for a couple of months at that time); he cleared the P.T. (preliminary test) like always, took the mains in October-November and then waited anxiously for the results. He was under great pressure no doubt. One distant cousin of his had got through to the allied services the previous year. Ritwik would brood in his room for hours and at night he would wander the streets of the university. When he became dog tired he would come back to his room with the green-painted walls and sleep his dreamless sleep.

Then one fine day in late March, he walked out of his room, feeling for the first time in years happy and totally free. He walked towards Kaake Da Dhaba on the university road for a cup of tea as he had done for months each evening. The dhaba was empty but for a couple of blind students from the nearby seva kutir who sat, quietly huddled together like pups in winter, looking at nothing in particular through their imitation Ray-Ban sunglasses.

Ritwik felt light inside and his mind was clear as water. Accordingly, to Kaake he looked just like the Buddha sitting underneath the bodhi tree. Buses, auto-rickshaws and swanky cars sped along on the road towards the university. Ritwik sat there unaffected and outside of it all. He lit a cigarette and felt the cool smoke in his lungs and ordered a special masala omelette and a cup of tea. Then he closed his eyes. It was the day of salvation for him.

The tea came along. It was thick, milky and very sweet and it tasted as rotten as it always did. It was all right. There is stability in conformity. It was hot and he sipped it slowly, savouring it, sucking the thin cream on the top and cupping the thick green-tinted glass with both hands to feel the heat. It was a cool and windy evening.

The blind students started to talk in their naturally loud and belligerent manner with Kaake who was a friend, philosopher and unwanted guide to all the students who frequented his place. The blind students were very poor and dressed in old and dirty, yellowed clothes. They looked unwashed and desperate. Ritwik stared at them with curiosity as if he had discovered them for the first time but in reality they all knew each other well. They were telling Kaake some dirty joke about girls with big boobs and what they would like to do to them. Ritwik didn't hear the punchline. He had heard it all before. The blind students loved smutty jokes, he had noticed before. He felt as if everything was happening around him in a flashback.

Kaake brought the omelette over in a cracked white plate. It was hot and crisp and spicy. Delicious.

'The omelette is nice?'

'Very nice,' Ritwik answered. He usually enjoyed talking to Kaake but that day it was different. He was sure that Kaake would destroy the exquisite feeling of lightness that he felt.

'I never fry it for long; it gets hard and rubbery.'

'It is just perfect. Delicious,' Ritwik said and he knew the next line. He had heard it all before.

'The trick is in selecting the right eggs.'

'Really?'

'The selection is very important.'

'But I thought all eggs were similar. If you have seen one you have seen them all.'

'All eggs are different. They have different personalities and temperaments and to make the perfect omelette you have to find the perfect egg. Unfortunately, I myself haven't found it yet.'

'The perfect egg?' Ritwik played along.

'The perfect egg should snuggle in the gap between your forefinger and thumb. It is just one of the criteria. It should fit in totally. Every man has to find his own perfect egg. It varies from person to person.'

'Kaake, there is something very important that I must tell you.' Kaake nodded eagerly. 'You are a stupid fool.'

'No, I am a genius and you, Ritwik, my friend, are a stupid fool. One day I am going to find my perfect hen who will lay the perfect eggs and I will serve magical omelettes all around. Soft, crisp and supremely delicious. I will be bigger than Nirula's, Wimpy's, McDonald's. Standing room only.'

It was rumoured that ten years back Kaake had left his hometown in eastern UP and boarded the train for the big city to study and prepare for the Civil Services. Only he wasn't called Kaake then but had a real paan-chewing cowbelt name, which unfortunately is now lost in the annals of time. When he failed to clear the preliminary test four times in a row, his father severed all relations and with it all the money. Kaake refused to buckle down under the pressure and he took a loan of Rs 5,000 and set up his small dhaba on the very same spot on the side of the university road where he had sat down and shed copious tears each year as a monumental tribute to his shattered dreams. He did a little market research and found that most dhaba owners were called 'Kaake' and so … Now you know, and from there began his quest for the perfect egg and magical omelettes.

'So did you clear it this time?' Kaake asked him after a while.

'What?'

'You know. The mains! The results came out yesterday?' Kaake always made his statement sound like questions.

'Yes, sure, I made it this time.' Ritwik closed his eyes and said slowly.

'What?'

'Yes! Yes! Yes!'

'No! You are an IAS now?'

'If I clear the interview—it depends.'

'You have cleared the mains! No one else before has done it. At least not the ones who had my magical omelettes. You are the first. You have broken the jinx, O pioneer.'

'I must leave. I have got lots of things lined up.'

'Are you really an IAS now?' the first blind student asked him. He hadn't been listening closely.

'Almost,' Ritwik laughed and replied.

'I see,' the second blind student said sotto voce and even he started to laugh.

'I have to run. I have got so much to do,' Ritwik said to everyone present and then he started running. Kaake and the blinds cheered him from behind, 'Go man go, go, go,' and Ritwik ran and ran and ran.

According to my little brother and local legend he never stopped but ran all the way to Patna and stopped only when he reached his home and his father opened the door. Personally I think he took a train, don't you? Anyway, no one in Delhi ever saw Ritwik again. Kaake tells the story of his magical omelettes and Ritwik to anyone who cares to hear. He lives with his illusions and I don't have the heart to break them. He felt hurt that Ritwik had never come to meet him after he became an officer. He told his story to every IAS aspirant who came to his dhaba and they all listened and had his omelettes and in the evenings there would indeed be standing room only. He is not yet bigger than 'Nirula's' but he is getting there. He has opened one branch in Hudson Lines and another one across the road in Outram Lines. In Ritwik's honour he called his special omelette 'Ritwik Da Mayawi Aamlet'. A prerequisite dish for all UPSC candidates. If you don't believe me you can go and take a look. I have never eaten it myself but you can't blame me for that. I am taking the examination myself next year I must admit. I wasn't taking any chances. In this line you can never be too superstitious. Anyway, I knew the story. The ones who had it said that after eating those 'Mayawi' omelettes they felt rejuvenated and their withered spirits rose again with each delicious bite.

Meanwhile, the day he reached his home Ritwik told his father that he had finally discovered his true calling in life. 'About time, son,' his father said caustically but Ritwik let that pass and explained to him that his endeavour had to remain a secret for now because there were others working on it too but he assured his father that when the breakthrough came he would be proud of Ritwik again.

That very night he went out and bought petridishes, slides, dividers, compasses and scales and weights, and of course eggs. His head was full of eggs now. Hen eggs, duck eggs, turkey eggs, striped eggs, spotted eggs, chipped eggs, eggs of all kinds and hues, and he brought them home in brown paper bags and hid them in his book cabinet. Soon he had to throw away all his books and the cabinet became an egg cabinet. Eggs were everywhere. They took over his life. From eggs we rise to eggs we sink. He had joined the vast fraternity of egg seekers. He measured them in the morning, he measured them at noon and he kept at it all through the night. He kept notes of all his findings. He was looking for the mythical perfect egg.

One day his father entered his sanctuary after many months and passed out from the stink.

He was put in the asylum near Ranchi (Ritwik, not his father), but even there Ritwik has smuggled in his calipers. He still looks for ways to further his vast knowledge on eggs. He hasn't given up. His condition has been described as being one of acute compulsive eggomania. He has also written a thesis based upon his findings and sent it to MIT. I know that because I sent it myself. He gave it to me when I went to meet him a couple of months back. It was the least I could do for him.

If life ever for some sublime reason deposits you at the doorsteps of the Kanke asylum, do ask for ward 22 and you will be taken to a nice young man with luminous eyes who would after some time ask you cordially if you could by any chance provide him with some eggs for an experiment he is conducting for the welfare of all mankind. 'Just one truckload will do.'

Outlaws

It was a cool, sunny, December afternoon and all over Patna the winter holidays had just begun. The schools were closed. It was a happy and cheerful time for Ritwik and Subir. They lived in the old Bengali colony of Kadam Kuan and had been friends since childhood. Before them their elder brothers had been friends and in a way they were continuing a tradition. Both of them were Bengalis, both of them were fair and wore their hair long, but Subir was taller and thinner, somewhat a dandy; Ritwik the more serious of the two, the slower of the two. There was a slight similarity in their appearance—people often mistook them to for brothers. They had done everything together; learned play cricket together, to ride the bike, whistle at the girls, listen to the same kind of music, been in the same fights, and to top it all, had fallen in love with the same girls and that too many a time. They had grown up together fighting, laughing, sharing, on the same streets of Kadam Kuan.

They spent their days playing cricket in the mornings and in the evenings they looked at the girls in the marketplace and smoked as many cigarettes as they could. They had no worries and no fear. They were as free as birds. If they had wings they would have flown to the sun, surely. Those were the golden days of their friendship and adolescence.

So on that glittering December afternoon they walked to the small cigarette shop at the corner, bought two cigarettes and lit up. The cigarette shop was situated at the gate of a large mansion. Nobody except an old Bengali widow lived there. The whole thing was slowly crumbling down; more and more cracks appeared on the faded walls each year, the house worn and weary with age and loneliness—but it stood there in spite of it. Both Subir and Ritwik could remember the time when it used to be so beautiful and they would play in the vast courtyard inside. There used to be a guava tree inside the courtyard but it was chopped down a long time ago. One of their earliest childhood friends used to live there. He had left for Dhanbad eight years back. Bengalis were slowly leaving the place. Everybody was going away. Only the old remained in the beautiful old mansions. The young had moved away and soon the old would die and the houses get sold off but still the Bengali flavour remained in the air. During Durga puja they still put up the best pandal in town. There wasn't as much money as before but the heart stayed generous and proud. The cigarette and paan shop was an encroachment.

They pulled low their baseball caps over their eyes and watched out for relatives and other assorted senior citizens. They didn't want to be caught smoking. It would be a big scandal if they were caught, after all they came from such respectable families. They talked about some of the neighbourhood girls and decided they were all stuck-up bitches, not much worth talking about anyway.

After some time Subir asked the shopkeeper for some ballpoint refills which he knew the man kept at the back of the shop. As the man turned around Subir took a packet of Gold Flakes from the front rack and slipped it into his pocket.

He looked at the refills but then decided that he didn't need them anymore and both of them walked away from the shop.

'Why did you do that?' Ritwik said to him in Bengali, his eyes burning with excitement.

'Why? Because. I wanted to have them.'

'But it isn't right, is it?'

'I don't know about that but you do want to smoke, don't you?'

'Yes.'

'And you don't have any money?'

'No,' Ritwik shook his head, realizing he had already lost the argument.

'See, now the problem is solved, we don't have to buy any more cigarettes today. We have saved twenty rupees. We can watch a movie tonight at Regent.'

'But, Subir, it is stealing; we shouldn't steal!'

'All right, it is stealing but so what? Nothing matters.'

'Is it the first time or …'

'Remember all those Gold Flakes that you smoked yesterday, trying to impress the girls, yes? Well those were free too.'

'But it doesn't feel right you know. We are not thieves.'

'You are right, we are not thieves. We are uh … well we are, how shall I put it, all right, well we are just outlaws, yes, that's right, we are just a couple of cool outlaws. Don't you feel the thrill of it? Kind of like Robin Hood.'

'Robin Hood stole from the rich to give to the poor. But we are going to smoke these ourselves, won't we, dear Subir?'

'All right, we may not be Robin Hoods but we are still outlaws.'

'We could have been caught and then everybody would have known, everybody…'

'Who gives a fuck and anyway we didn't get caught.' Subir crushed the butt and smiled beatifically at Ritwik.

They walked in silence for some time, the thrill of their adventure still clinging to their walk, making Subir swagger and Ritwik slouch. They looked at the girls in the marketplace from the corners of their eyes. They were happy and at peace with everything.

They didn't want anything else. It was Subir's birthday the next day, so after a while Ritwik asked him about it, just to break the silence and start a conversation again.

'It is your birthday tomorrow, isn't it?'

'Yes, I am bored with birthdays. It makes me feel old and grey. I am too old for birthdays. I want to fuck some girls now.'

'Even old people have birthdays. You can't escape birthdays, only when you die can there be no more birthdays,' Ritwik said in a patronizing manner.

'You know, Ritwik, you make me sick. You are a bloody poet, you read too many books. You make me sick, I am positive, you make me sick.'

'And you make me sick, you thief.'

'I am not a thief, I told you. I am an outlaw. I am a sixteen-year-old outlaw. Don't you remember what Bob Dylan said?' Subir asked Ritwik indignantly.

'Sure. To live outside the law you have to be honest.'

'Yes, that's right,' Subir agreed and smiled and fished out a cigarette and lit it with as much coolness as he could manage.

'But you know what Subir, it doesn't mean a thing, what Dylan said; stealing is still stealing.'

'Now you know more than Dylan!'

'If you look at it rationally, it doesn't mean a thing. It's just stylish American crap.' Ritwik knew how much Subir loved Dylan and regretted saying it the moment he uttered it. Subir didn't seem to mind but he became more serious.

'You have to be honest; I am honest. I took just what I needed, I could have taken two or maybe three packs but I took just one—I am honest.' Subir said it slowly. He knew in his heart he was right.

'Don't do it again, all right? I am telling you.'

'I don't have to listen to you, Ritwik.'

'Don't ever steal anything, all right?'

'You call yourself a bloody poet and you don't have any understanding of life. When there is no thrill there can't be any poetry, no life. It is the thrill that is above all other things in life.' Subir took off his cap, put his fingers into his hair and pushed it back, narrowed his eyes and then pulled low his cap again.

'We don't have to steal; it's something very low and degrading, even if it's thrilling. I won't ever do it myself,' Ritwik went on and on like a stuck record.

'Then don't.'

'But you will steal like some common thief,' Ritwik said to him in mock anger and took out a cigarette from the pack.

'I don't want to be respectable, maybe you do, but I really don't give a fuck what anybody thinks, what you think. And I'm not a fucking thief. Don't you ever call me that again.'

'If you promise not to do that again, I won't,' Ritwik said to him seriously.

'All right, all right, I won't. Happy now?'

'Sure.'

So they walked silently, together, each one happy in the company of the other. Life was beautiful, magical and flowing smoothly and to them their friendship was the greatest gift of all. They didn't realize it fully but they could sense it. There was rock music and cricket and beautiful girls to make love to if only they could get the chance, but for now they were content to just talk over the phone late into the night. It was a wonderful life. Nothing ever could go wrong.

'Did you see that girl?' Subir nudged Ritwik and asked him.

'The one in the red salwar suit, right?' Ritwik said, looking at the girl in question who was crossing the street just ahead of them. She was an exceptionally beautiful girl with long auburn hair parted in the middle, with a small pointed nose, red red lips just meant for kissing, small, tight breasts that shook slightly as she walked. She was older and obviously rich; both Ritwik and Subir were smitten.

'Let's follow her,' Subir suggested and Ritwik accepted as always. Subir was the leader, Ritwik was the poet. They followed her into a music shop and Ritwik said to Subir, 'She looks old, must be over twenty.'

'Yes, nice, isn't she?'

'Nice.'

The girl, cool and oblivious to the turmoil she had caused, sauntered into the shop and flitted from shelf to shelf, touching a tape here, a tape there, reading the contents, smiling to herself, combing back her hair with her long fingers, her eyes effulgent and expectant, totally ignoring the boys who walked a step behind trying to look serious and sophisticated. Just then a man entered, tall and with a face that could only be called pretty, with long eyelashes and greenish grey eyes, red, thin lips like a slash and a long fragile jaw with a dimple wedged in the right cheek. He went up to the girl and gently tapped her shoulders as if she were a windowpane and her face lit up with a spreading smile. They walked out together.

The boys watched her go out and they felt crushed and defeated. She was so enchanting. She had taken out with her the 'something special' that was in the air, a hope, a romance, a story, an adventure, thrill…

'Bitch but nice bitch,' Subir said mournfully.

'Nice, wonderful, sexy sexy bitch,' Ritwik agreed.

Suddenly the adventure had ended and there was nothing more to do. They looked at the music tapes. Rock music was their shared passion. They read anything they could find on the subject and listened to whatever tapes they could get. They didn't have the luxury of discrimination. From the floor to the false ceiling, thousands of music tapes were stacked on the glass shelves and the reflected light from them caught their eyes. They looked at the tapes and wished that they were rich. They wished they had a hundred rupees.

'They have Dylan's *Blood on the Tracks* album, can you believe it?'

'This is a fucking classic. A real classic.' Subir laughed and looked at the tape wistfully, read the contents again, shook his head and finally put back the tape in its proper place on the shelf. He then ambled over to the other side where the Books and Magazines section was but Ritwik didn't move from his position, his hands inside his jacket clenched into fists as he continued looking at the wonderful glossy tapes and wished again that he were rich.

After some time they walked out of the shop. They were both a bit subdued now. They walked back towards their homes, back to the familiar streets, the earlier spring missing from their walk. Subir was graver, as if he had learnt something profound and unavoidable back in the shop. Then he thought about the girl and he felt light and glad inside. Both of them would never forget that beautiful girl all their lives. She would always be there. She had meant different things to both Ritwik and Subir. She had promised different things to both of them. Subir just wanted to reach home early now and lie down, watch TV or masturbate maybe, and in the evening they would go to Regent where they were showing a revival of *Sholay*. Things would be better in the evening.

'Subir, I am sorry I was angry at you earlier.' Ritwik said after a while.

'It is all right.' Saying sorry and acknowledging one's mistake was always a torturous job and the important thing was to get it over with as quickly as possible.

'You know, you were right about the thrill part and about life and poetry. It is pretty important I guess—you have to be free. What's life without a little passion,' Ritwik repeated their favourite catchphrase from a popular motorcycle ad.

'Yes,' Subir laughed and repeated the phrase.

'And one thing more, Subir …'

'What?'

'Happy birthday,' Ritwik said to him and thrust into his hands the Bob Dylan tape he had coveted so much. *Blood on the Tracks*.

'You didn't!' Subir stared at the tape incredulously.

'Yes I did,' Ritwik said and embraced him.

They both laughed and their laughter so wild and free merged into the shared laughter of many such golden friendships that were forged in small trivial moments such as this and their laughter would never die and nor would that moment. Perhaps later sadness would make its inroads and life would create fissures but for now all that could wait.

The Women

If you went straight down a certain avenue and then turned right and again after a while left, you would enter one of the oldest localities in Patna and like most old places you would find it to be extremely contradictory in nature. The place is peopled with doctors, professors, IAS officers, civil servants and other white-collar representatives but with them also live the pimps, the petty thieves, the smalltime extortionists, poets, revolutionaries of diverse faiths, shopkeepers, in the words of Faulkner, 'all breeding and spawning together'. The upper-class people high on culture, low on cash, live in old, dilapidated mansions with a portico and a courtyard inside with a guava tree in it and a mango tree in the backyard and the others make do in peculiar drab, brown buildings which seemed to have mushroomed overnight and which were made to occupy as little space as possible in terms of width. These buildings have small rooms like cells with a little window on the side for ventilation and are unavoidably hot and stuffy at most times of the year.

In one of these rooms a man sat cross-legged on the floor, brooding. A thick yellow candle burned at the end of the room and he watched the flicker of the flames and the play of shadows his wife made as she sat preparing the evening meal for him. For hours there had been no electricity in the area.

In the past one year so much had changed. The rooms appeared as if they had shrunk in his absence and the very streets had become narrower. He felt like a stranger in his own home. It was from this very place that he had left for the countryside, as ordered a year back. He hoped fervently that nobody had seen him enter the house. They were still looking for him, he knew that. They never gave up. He knew it was a mistake but things were getting unbearable. Maybe he was getting too soft. He still believed in the 'struggle' but his heart was not in it anymore. He had to see his wife and son. His wife had sounded desperate, almost hysterical in her last letter. 'It could be a trap. Do not leave, you know we can't trust anyone,' the area commander had said to him but for once he had defied the orders. He had to see her once; sometimes even the fact that he was married seemed unreal to him and only when her letters would arrive months after they were written, the piercing reality, the hopelessness of their situation would strike home and he would become deluged with guilt. He shouldn't have married and sometimes he wished that he hadn't. It was a mess.

His son was almost five years old and very shy and had refused to come near him. The boy had totally forgotten his father and the dim mythic image of his 'real' father locked in his memory refused to come to terms with this tangible reality. His son was sleeping now and he would be out of the house before dawn. He wondered if it would ever end.

'I can't stay the whole night. I'll be out before dawn,' he said to his wife in a whisper. It had almost become second nature for him to whisper nowadays.

She looked at him. The months of living like a fugitive had taken their toll on her husband's once-handsome frame. He had lost weight and his long, lustrous hair was cropped short and had become thinner over the top. She could see the whiteness of the scalp through the short bristles. Somehow that made her feel vaguely disturbed. He had shaved off his beard and didn't quite look like the man she had once loved anymore. *He has grown so quiet*, she thought. Two hours had passed since he had arrived but still she felt as if she were in the room with a total stranger. She went and opened the window and peered out into the darkness. She felt a vague sense of fear as if this cherished, longed-for intimacy could be snuffed out at any moment.

'Can't you stay a day or two?' she asked him timidly, knowing all the time what his answer would be.

'I wish I could but it is too much of a risk,' he whispered.

All the time that he was underground, moving about at nights through the villages and moffusil towns of South and Central Bihar, holding meetings in the middle of the fields in the dead of night and training the cadre to shoot and make bombs near the river edges, writing pamphlets that endorsed the 'party line', the struggle had changed from 'class' to 'caste' in reality and its very ideology he himself wasn't sure about anymore; but he wrote them nevertheless, living rough like a fugitive, and his only wish had been to spend some time with his family, but now when he was with them he couldn't wait to move out again. Fear had suffused every pore of his body and coursed down his bloodstream. He had to run again. He knew that. He felt as if he had never known her and the life they had lived earlier had perhaps happened to a different couple altogether but at the same time he wanted to stay with her, make love to her slowly like she loved, explore again the familiar comfort of her body and somehow tear down the unseen wall of silence that lay like a dead child between them.

'I hope you get the money they send?' he asked her after a while. 'Yes. They are very particular. Money is not a problem. There is more than we need. I was thinking of putting him in a school now,' she said to him. 'He is still so small,' the man replied.

'He is old enough. All the other boys of his age are in schools.'

'Do whatever you think is best.'

'You have become so thin; don't you take your meals regularly?'

'I eat whenever I can, like the rest of them. It's just that I don't seem to put on weight anymore. It is better this way, less of me to carry around.' He smiled at her for the first time.

'Have you got a woman to look after you over there?'

'I don't stay at one place for long.'

'You must have had women to care for you sometimes,' she asked once more.

'They were not important. I don't even remember their faces.'

She put his dinner in front of him and he ate in silence.

'When will you come again?' she asked, staring longingly at his face.

'I don't know. Patna is too dangerous for me. Maybe I'll call you over to some place safe if I find it.' As he said this he knew there was no way that would ever happen.

'Can't you take me with you? We could leave right now,' she said in a voice that had suddenly become quite hysterical. 'And what about our son?' he asked, taken aback a bit.

'The neighbours can take care of him for the time being. I just want to be with you. I can't bear the loneliness anymore. I can't make sacrifices anymore. Every day I get nightmares. I think about you constantly. I have seen you dead many times. I can't sleep anymore. I keep the lights on the whole night.' She was on the verge of tears and her face twisted with pain and sadness but in that sadness there was also hope for the future. Hope that he would say yes.

'You can't come with me. You know the party work. You wouldn't be safe ever. I can't take you and you must take care of our son because I can't.' They were silent for some time and then she said slowly, 'Have you ever taken anyone's life?'

'Why do you ask that?'

'I just want to know. I must know.'

He didn't say anything for a while and then he looked at her thoughtfully and said, 'No, I haven't but I have taught others to kill so I guess it is the same thing. I have seen terrible things. I was there. I have been a witness.' She could see the truth of the statement stamped on his face.

'Do you think all this is worth it?'

'Killings are never worth anything; they can't ever be part of any long-term solution. I know that but it is not as simple as that. One must fight for one's dignity, for the simple right to live as humans and in this our caste-haunted land, there is no dignity without protest. So I protest. But there are times when I do feel that somewhere something has gone horribly wrong and rather than rectify it we have messed it up some more. I am just a very small cog in a large wheel; perhaps the people in the high command have the larger picture in their mind. I hope they are sure about what they are doing but then they are hardly ever in the field. There are times when I feel that I am doing something worthwhile, when I raise a sub-human dalit to human existence, give him some pride, teach him his rights—I feel calm then. There are too many things involved now. It is not a matter of ideology anymore. It's not simple at all. Let us leave the judgement to history. Terrible things have been done to us and in return we have done the same. It will go on. But it is true I am getting tired. My heart is not in it anymore. Once I believed passionately in our cause. I am not so sure now. In my mind I have too many questions and not enough answers. So I don't know if all this is worth it or not but I know that I will go on doing it because once when I was very young it had given me a cause, something to believe in and it is very important for a man to believe in something, have faith in something external to him—I haven't talked this much in weeks!' he finished, out of breath.

'Why don't you give it all up! It would have been better if you were in jail—look at Kashyapji. You could do the same. I could visit you then. Maybe they will pardon you like they did Kashyapji. You would be safe. We could be together.'

'You don't understand, do you? He was an informer and I can't ever be that. He won't live for long on the outside. You know what they do to informers, don't you? You will starve, you stupid woman! Bring the candle over here.'

She brought the candle closer and his face gleamed in the light. There were dark circles beneath his eyes and his fair skin had darkened as if something had burnt him from the inside. She touched his fear-denuded face, running her fingers over his lips, his sunken eyes. He stopped eating and looked up at her with surprise and tenderness.

He pulled her toward himself and kissed her softly on the lips. She pulled him down on top of her and they made love. Afterwards as she lay beside him he felt an uncontrollable urge to cry, he felt a terrible emptiness. Like a bone with the marrow all sucked dry. Just then there was heavy banging on the door.

'It's the police,' he said simply while reaching for his Mauser.

'Don't! They won't hurt you,' she said to him hysterically. He looked at her and he knew.

They broke the door. He put the pistol down. His son was sleeping in the other room. He didn't want to wake him up. He wanted everything to be done quietly. There was no point in fighting anymore.

'You fool, you stupid fool,' he said to her once but in an undertone so low that it looked as if he were talking to himself. Maybe he was.

The City SP with two inspectors and ten constables entered the room. The SP was in plain clothes. He felt a curious sense of pride as he counted the number of policemen sent out to capture him. They didn't put handcuffs on him and he was a little surprised. They just grabbed him and pushed him out of the room; he looked at his wife, tears streaming down her face, and he wondered what for. Then he felt a kind of peace as if suddenly everything had been decided for him. There was no choice anyway.

As he stepped out onto the street he could feel the stillness of the night. There was no one outside but he could feel their eyes on him from shadowy rooms and darkened balconies, peering out at him, staring. He was tired. Someone grabbed his arms from behind. He was too surprised to react but he had seen it coming. They hadn't put handcuffs on him. He was struck on the side of his face with a rifle butt and he fell down, hit his face on the street and broke his nose. They shot him twice, keeping their rifles just inches away from his body. A silent scream rose in her throat. She was still at the doorstep. She tried to scream but could only mumble incoherently, then she fainted.

She filed a case against the City SP but nothing came of it. There were no witnesses, they said; there was never any witness but that was nothing new. In a curious quirk of fate, the SP was gunned down near Jamshedpur while he was returning home with his wife from a party late at night at the Beldih Club, a couple of years later.

Everything was forgotten after a while but even after the headlines die, the women live on. They could never forget the way his body would jerk up with each shot like some big fish that still thrashes around after being clubbed on the shore. They would remember that for the rest of their lives. All through the night, they still keep the lights on.

The Adolescents

'Can you please call her? It's room A-7, I think,' he said to the girl who was going into the hostel.

'Sure. A-7?'

'Yes, A-7, Mira Verma. Thank you,' he called out after her and then turned back towards the hostel gate. He heard her call out Mira's name: 'Mira Verma, A-7, visitor.' He waited down by the gate under the shade of the bougainvillea creepers as the diffused November sun filtered through the pink flowers and made patterns by his feet. In the small covered portico, which was called the 'Cage', Coca-Cola Pepsi, a small, black mongrel pup whom the girls had adopted, played with flowers. He was the guard dog.

The sunlight felt warm on the heavy flannel shirt that he wore and he felt strangely happy. It was one of those rare moments that are nostalgia before they are even over.

He closed his eyes and turned his face towards the sun and he realized that if he didn't control his impulses he would start smiling—he felt that happy.

'Ritwik, when did you return?' someone asked him in Bengali and he opened his eyes.

'Today in the afternoon,' he answered in Bengali and smiled his most charming smile which he reserved for girls like her. She was a friend all right.

'Nobody informed me that you were here, in the hostel I mean,' she said again in Bengali. She had for some time lived in Bengal and had picked up the rudiments of the language, just the basics, and she had the strange notion, which many non-Bengalis have that if they pronounced every 'a' like an 'o' the Hindi they speak will magically turn into Bengali. Maybe he was supposed to feel flattered, Ritwik thought.

'I am waiting for Mira,' he informed her in Hindi.

'Mira? Oh I thought … never mind. Shall I call her?' She switched over to English and he felt grateful.

'No, no, it is all right, I have already asked one of the girls to inform her.'

'So how are things going now, studies and all?'

'I am coasting along, nothing new,' he answered and looked at his watch.

'You know what, you remind me of Uttam Kumar.'

Last time it was some other movie actor, Ritwik could not recall the name.

'I don't like Uttam Kumar.' He felt the necessity to lie and then hated himself but it was okay. It was required.

'You don't? Are Bengalis not supposed to adore him or something?'

'Are they?' he asked softly. He wished she would go away. He looked at his watch again.

She smiled and said, 'I have got so much work to do. The college festivals are coming along; I am doing the choreography this year.'

'That's great, you must be very busy.' He gave her the cue.

'Yes, I have to run, bye. I will be seeing you some other time,' she said and walked out of the gate. Ritwik watched her for sometime, lit a cigarette and upturned his face to the sun again. It had already been five minutes since the girl had gone in.

After a while Mira's roommate came out. She was from Jharia, a small town in Bihar, and had a strange slow old woman's gait. She was doing an honours course in Psychology.

'She has gone to Kamla Nagar,' the girl said to him. She knew about him but he had a feeling that she didn't much approve of him.

'Has she gone alone?'

'No, with some friends.'

'Do you know when she will be back?'

'In an hour or so. Did she know that you were coming?'

'I don't know, I don't think so.'

'I will inform her that you had come.'

'No, that is all right. I think I will wait.'

She looked at him for a second longer than was necessary and then slowly turned towards the Cage, where the phone was. 'Thank you,' he called loudly after her, and went out of the gate, walked towards the ice-cream seller and sat down on the brown sackcloth that was spread on the pavement. He could watch the street and the hostel gate from there. It was nice to be back. The one month in Patna had been nice too but now he was glad to be back. Delhi was beautiful in November and he wanted to get on with his life.

When you want something to happen, it never happens quickly, because you are always thinking about it, and when you are waiting for something, time moves as if on crutches. Ritwik promised himself that he wouldn't think about it. He was happy sitting there, he knew Mira would be there and he didn't glance at his watch all the time that he was waiting for her.

After an hour or so, he saw a rickshaw with three girls, one fat, one medium, one lean, perched precariously upon it, as it hurtled down Chhatra Marg. The lean one was Mira. The rickshaw stopped in front of him and he crushed his cigarette under his foot and smiled.

Mira was smiling too but she was conscious of her friends; they were looking at him from underneath their averted eyes. They had suddenly become very business-like and serious. They had been laughing in the rickshaw, their hair blowing in the wind. He had seen that.

Mira came towards him smiling and wishing in her heart that she had worn something else other than the dirty black jeans. She had wanted to wash them on Sunday but had overslept.

'I've been waiting for a long time.'

'I'm sorry. I never thought …'

'But you knew I was coming back today, didn't you?'

'Yes, I got the news but I thought maybe you would come tomorrow or the day after, sometime later anyway.'

'I had to see you today.'

She was silent for a while and then he suggested, 'Let's walk.'

'Yes, let's go over to the University garden; the roses are in full bloom. I am glad that you are back.'

'And it is nice to know that you are glad that I am back.'

He laughed and she looked into his eyes and saw that he wasn't lying. They walked towards the University Co-operative Store, by the side of Meghdoot Hostel, up the incline of heaped-up soil, into the green clearing where some kids were practising kung fu. They have built big cement steps there now.

'Why didn't you write to me?' Ritwik looked at her sideways and asked.

'I didn't have your address.'

'You could have easily got it.'

'Yes, I don't know, I was not sure . . . were you expecting a letter?'

'I thought you might write, you always said that you loved to write letters, I hoped maybe you will add one more to the list.'

'Even you didn't write to me.'

'No, I wanted to. But I didn't know where to begin, what to say, all that, but I did want to. I had your address.'

'You never say anything clearly.'

'I am moody and stupid but you know that, don't you?'

'I don't know much about you but I like you, I feel comfortable with you; I think I've told you that. I am not eloquent at all.'

'Did you write anything in the autumn break?'

'Yes, two short stories, both of them are of my childhood, very simple stories really; I will read them out to you sometime.'

'You should have brought them today.'

'I don't know. I have to work on them some more. They are not very good but they are honest; I will read them out to you. When I was writing them I thought about reading them out to you.'

Some students were playing volleyball down by the side of the University garden. Some of them turned and looked at Ritwik and Mira as they passed and whistled. Mira giggled, looked at Ritwik. He smiled too.

They sat down on a wide cement bench and looked at some kids playing tag on the grass. After a while a small dog ambled over and joined the games.

The sun had gone down and the fluorescent lights came on and the whole garden was bathed in a glaring bright orange light. Couples moved among the trees and walked along the pathways with arms around each other's waists. Mira and Ritwik, oblivious to the world, talked away. They talked about many things, the films they had seen, the books that they had read, how wonderfully camp *Hum Aapke Hain Kaun* really was, the crazy new Hindi film songs, about Arvind Swamy and Manisha Koirala, about their families, common friends and finally about death, suicide, the poetry of Dylan Thomas and Guru Dutt, but never once did they discuss anything that was remotely personal as if the subject were too painful to both of them. They didn't talk about the thing that both of them so much wanted to talk about. It was already being discussed in the hostel. They knew that. Ritwik could sense a kind of darkness hovering about and he was confused. There were so many things that had no answers.

'What do your friends think about me?'

'Does it matter to you?' she asked him softly.

'Yes if it matters to you,' he said to her in Bengali.

'What did you say?'

He repeated what he had said in English.

'No, it doesn't,' she looked at him defiantly.

They were silent again for some time and Ritwik lit another cigarette.

'And what do your friends think?' she asked him.

'They think you are a bit dark,' he laughed.

'A bit dark?' It was her turn to laugh.

'Okay, dark,' he accepted.

Two constables strolled along the pathway and walked past them, then one of them noticed the couple and sauntered over to them. 'What are you two doing here?' he asked in a heavily accented Punjabi-Hindi.

'We are sitting here, talking,' Ritwik pointed out to them.

'You can't sit here; go away.'

'It is the University garden; anyone can sit here and we are students.'

'What are you two doing here then, after dark? Studying?'

They chuckled between themselves and one of them spat on the grass.

Mira whispered to him, 'Let's go, it is time anyway.' He felt his eyes burning within but he didn't say anything and he didn't get up.

'Show me your identity card,' the constable who had spat on the grass said to Ritwik.

'I haven't got it here with me.'

But Mira had taken her card out and they peered at it like the illiterates they were, for some time, and then gave it back to her.

'All right, but we know all about you "students", what goes on here.' And they chuckled again and continued on their beat.

'I feel so … I feel so … defiled,' Mira whispered to him but he wasn't listening to her anymore.

'Let's go,' he said after a while.

'We can sit here for some time now,' she said wryly to him.

'Let's get out of here. I am sorry I brought you here.'

'Ritwik, it was my idea and this is nothing exceptional.'

'But they had no right, fucking common constables.'

'Don't get angry.'

'I shouldn't have brought you here.' They walked towards the hostel slowly. Ritwik felt the warm happiness that he had felt in the evening drain out of him and now only the sharp chill remained. They walked through the trees; the path ahead of them lay dark and bare.

He looked at her—her sadness and loneliness complemented his with her warm and slightly bemused stare. She was confused too.

He draped one arm around her shoulders and pulled her close to himself and kissed her on her right cheek. She tasted of summer rain and mangoes.

'Why did you do that?'

She wasn't hurt but the question mark was there in her eyes.

'I don't know, just felt like it.'

'You are very bold.'

'I am very afraid, I am not bold at all. There are many things that I don't understand.'

She didn't say anything but walked silently by his side; his arm was off her shoulder now. It was getting chilly as the temperature dipped and cold wind ripped through the trees.

'I won't come tomorrow.'

The sadness that he felt wasn't like anything he had felt before and she remained silent and brooding. Slowly they walked down the incline by the side of Meghdoot hostel. Some PG students were sitting around, smoking and talking.

Mira thought about the empty gossip, the lukewarm evening tea and the soggy pastries, the new dress that she had worn just once, the poems that had remained unwritten, dreams that had become brittle as old pressed flowers between the covers of her heart, and said, 'I want you to come tomorrow. I want this. Let's not rush into anything but let's do this; after all, "tomorrow is another day."' She looked at him; there were tears in her eyes.

'I will wear my brown turtleneck tomorrow.' He hugged his arms and said. He felt nice and happy all over again.

They had reached the hostel gate and some of her friends were staring at them.

'They are staring at us,' she whispered to him.

'Frankly, my dear, I don't give a fuck.'

She laughed and hoped that nobody had heard him.

'I will see you tomorrow. Bye.' She turned back and went in.

'I will come at three o'clock; just be outside,' he shouted after her, making sure everybody heard him, especially her friends, then he lit a cigarette, shivered and blew at his fingers, rubbed his palms and started walking up the street, rapidly striding. He would definitely wear the brown turtleneck tomorrow, he promised himself.

A Scene from Class Struggle in Patna

We were coming back from the film society screening of *The Tin Drum.* It was after 10 p.m. and the streets were mostly deserted. Patna goes to sleep early in the winters.

Ritwik was driving the Yezdi. He is a few years older than me and was then working as the cultural correspondent of a leading Patna daily. I, on the other hand, had just completed my Intermediate in Science, and was waiting to leave for Delhi. I was seventeen years old and had no plans for the future whatsoever. Come to think of it, even almost a decade later nothing much had changed. I had some vague notion of making movies one day but all that was in the future and even the very thought at that time seemed a trifle absurd to me. I loved the movies. There were no two ways about it. I was obsessed with them. At that particular time of my adolescence, I thought I knew more about movies than anybody else in the world. I knew almost everything, all the trivia, but it was hollow book-based knowledge, good for quiz shows and impressing the girls. But it was fun and it required enormous scholarship and remember, it was the time before the satellite revolution and Star Movies and HBO and TCM and all the other movie channels which have made movie buffs out of everybody in India. At the film society that month it was the German Directors' Retrospective. We had started on Friday evening with the excellent Wim Wenders movie *Alice in the Cities*, which like all other Wenders movies of the seventies had a terrific rock-n-roll score. On Saturday we watched Klaus Kinski hamming it up as Fitzcarraldo in Werner Herzog's obsessive movie about an Irish man who wanted to bring Caruso to the Amazon. Later on when I watched *Burden of Dreams*, Les Blank's landmark documentary on the making of *Fitzcarraldo*, at the American Library in Delhi, I realized how obsessive and self-indulgent Art can become. That and *Hearts of Darkness* are a window to the soul of film-making which I recommend to anyone who is even half in love with the magic that is cinema.

I remember I couldn't sleep that night after watching *Fitzcarraldo.* Something about that Irishman had disturbed me, his manic single-mindedness, almost psychotic persistence and obsessive behaviour, in which I had perhaps seen a reflection of myself. Maybe even old Fitz was just an overgrown adolescent. You can't be that obsessive and not retain part of your adolescence in some measure. Obsession and adolescence go hand in hand. Everywhere.

I can recall only two more movies which affected me that way: one was Ray's *Apur Sansar* which is still to me the greatest love story ever made and the other was Scorsese's *Taxi Driver*, which, perhaps, has the most perfect screenplay ever for a Hollywood movie. I must have seen both of those movies over twenty times and could at that time give a shot-by-shot narration of either at a moment's notice for any poor fool who happened to be nearby. More often than not it was Ritwik, who incidentally had absolutely hated *Taxi Driver* and whom I was zealously trying to convert.

And so on Sunday evening it was Volkar Schlondorff's 1979 Oscar winner for best film, *The Tin Drum*, about which we had already heard that it had lots of nudity.

One had naturally waited with extreme excitement. I tried reading the Gunther Grass novel when I was fifteen but had found it to be too dense and couldn't ever finish reading it though of course I gave the contrary impression to everybody present that day for the show. Now that Grass had won the Nobel Prize, I thought maybe I should take it out of the carton, dust the silver fish off and put it back on my desk for all and sundry to see and have a sudden debilitating attack of inferiority complex. Nothing like an unread laureate novel for decimating humbug in one's friends. Works like poison. Every time.

The movie didn't disappoint. After the show there were a lot of red-faced middle-class housewives whose carnal knowledge, if not their minds, must have expanded exponentially that night. Ritwik and I could barely suppress our laughter. We both had thoroughly enjoyed the movie and images from it would cling to our memory all our lives. The voluminous skirt of Osker's grandmother under which a man found his salvation, the single pussy hair stuck on young Osker's tongue after a bout of honey-prospecting, his terrible hypnotic stare and drum playing, his growth stunted while Nazism grew, his mother weeping in the bedroom, being diddled by his uncle (his real father?) while the father sat reading the newspaper in the next room, the dead flyblown squid (or was it a fish?) on the beach… Afterwards we went to a cafe nearby and had a couple of kathi rolls and discussed the movie. Rather, we deconstructed it. At night Ritwik would write about it for his regular column. We talked about the camera angles and the magic realist treatment, the colour schemes and all the intellectual claptrap. We were like Rohmer and Godard in the *Cahiers-du-Cinema* office. Thinking about those days brings a wry smile to my cynical face. Those were good days. Naive, idyllic, carefree days. Then something happened. An incident. A minor one in retrospect. But one which both of us haven't forgotten to this day; it is a topic which we still invariably get around to after half a bottle of Old Monk. Well, we almost got lynched.

The Mandal Commission agitation was still going on at that time. The whole of our country stood divided like never before. And Bihar, my precious caste-ridden republic, never actually recovered from that blow. Now one was either a 'forward' or a 'backward' and being either in the wrong place at the right time could land one in serious trouble.

Patna was relatively quiet except for a few random bandhs and police firings but it was from the countryside, the villages, the smaller towns, that one heard the real horror stories. Things which started then have continued to this day. The hierarchy collapsed to some extent but beneath the ashes of the old-time feudalism, embers still smouldered. It took on a different shape and continued anew. The characters changed but essentially the play remained the same. Earlier that year, Laloo Yadav on a pro-poor and anti upper-caste mandate had ridden into town and had already made Patna the clown's paradise, which it would remain for years to come.

There were still one or two demonstrations a week. The university was closed. I, on the other hand was unaffected by all this because at that time I was totally apolitical, though sometimes fancied myself as being on the 'left'. Why? Well, because Che was left and so was Godard, and Rocha, and Saeed Mirza, and because Marxists were an anathema to my posh upper-class society. I was like Jimmy Dean. A rebel without a pause.

We entered Nala Road, laughing and talking loudly against the wind, and in no hurry to reach our homes. Ritwik was driving very slowly. Suddenly there appeared on the road a drunken man on a bicycle. He tottered comically before hitting the motorbike, lost his balance, fell and passed out on the street. A look of profound satisfaction spread on his florid face.

We too lost our balance and fell. Afterwards I crouched near the man and said to Ritwik, 'He is all right. Totally drunk but unhurt.'

'Leave him, Hriday. He will be all right. Let us move out quickly.' Ritwik's voice, usually a firm baritone, had slipped down an octave or two. Then I saw the reason. Half a dozen men had gathered from the footpath, where they had perhaps been sleeping and were now moving towards us. There were others who were watching from the dark; they would join in when the fun really began. All of them had half their faces covered with shawls. Most of them were labourers who worked as servants on daily wages in our homes or nearby construction sites.

A roar of 'maar daala, maar daala' went up and within seconds we were surrounded. One of the men, a reed-thin, wiry chap, tried to snatch the keys but I caught hold of his hand and told him that it wasn't our fault that the mishap happened; moreover the cyclist was very inebriated. Also he wasn't hurt or anything but to no avail. The mob refused to listen to reason.

As I now think about that night, another more recent night comes to mind, when a group of kids from well-heeled families ran over a couple of street dwellers in a BMW in Delhi but eventually nothing much happened to them. They went scot-free. A decade back, were we any different from these clean-cut kids who crushed to death several human beings, dragging one of them for a length of time entangled in the wheels but refusing to stop? Perhaps we wouldn't have been so cruel. So callous. But we too wouldn't have stopped if we hadn't lost our balance.

No one stops in Patna after an accident. One is taught never to do so. No one actually says it in so many words but it is there in the atmosphere and one inculcates it just by breathing.

They were in no mood to listen. They just wanted to lynch these affluent, clean-cut, high-caste kids who were callous and arrogant with no sense of responsibility; their kind couldn't be allowed to go unpunished anymore. They started abusing us but no one tried to help the man who was still lying on the street, sound asleep, totally oblivious to the commotion he had caused.

One inquired, 'Are you blind?'

The other said, 'Must be. Because they have money.'

The third said, 'Brahmins,' and spat on the ground.

Still another hissed, 'No moustaches.'

The fact that we could have been Brahmins (we were not) and were fair, had no moustaches but wore glasses and expensive clothes, had fomented such a volcano of resentment that I (intellectual to the end) remember thinking at that moment how utterly Kafkaesque all this was. In their inarticulate anger they had eloquently stated everything they held against our kind, the centuries of prejudice and repression and then the sudden half-baked empowerment called democracy which in actuality didn't mean a thing except for a blanket or two just before the elections.

No one had dared to lift their hands yet. It was still 1990 and Patna was predominantly upper class but in a couple of years the equations would change. They were waiting for a sign. No one wanted to start it but would join in gleefully once it happened. I had almost gone into a deep shock. My hands were numb, the knees shaking badly, my heart in a cage of ice.

Ritwik though still had his wits about him. He started abusing them back. At times like this retaliation is the only way out. Theatricality and melodrama, raised voices work but reasoning and logic never. Reasoning breeds counter bravado and makes even the weak feel strong.

Perhaps only a minute had passed, maybe less in which all this melodrama had been enacted and the man who was the sleeping partner to all this chaos suddenly with a groan woke up, startled to find so many people crowding over him gave a great howl of fright and in turn startled the mob. This was the opportunity that Ritwik needed and he kickstarted the Yezdi, running it over the sprawled bicycle and a couple of toes and we escaped. Someone yanked my hair from behind and in the bargain I lost a couple of my precious locks. The hair still hasn't grown back in that part of my scalp. The price some pay for wearing glasses and not wearing moustaches in Patna.

Like Osker, I wished I too had a drum to beat out my anguish. Maybe now after all these years I have finally got my drum.

Five minutes later, standing outside my home, we were back to our old smart-ass selves. Both of us refused to acknowledge that we were horribly frightened. Till then we had lived a life of privilege and plenty and nothing had prepared us for this. The cliché 'Was this the sign of things to come?' echoed in both our minds and I remember scrutinizing the face of the labourer who came to work in our garden the next Sunday very hard but of course I couldn't be sure. Earlier I had never noticed him.

Ritwik said, 'Let's make a movie about this, Hriday. A short movie. Half an hour, twenty minutes, you know something like *Zero for Conduct* or *All the Boys are Called Patrick*.'

'What shall we call it?' I asked him playing along. Those days we were always talking about making movies. We were a team. Like De Sica and Zavatini, Schrader and Scorsese, Sahir and Guru Dutt.

'How about "Patna Melodrama"?'

I thought it was corny and said so, then suggested an even cornier one. 'How about "A Scene from Class Struggle in Patna"?'

And Ritwik's face broke into a dreamy smile. 'Yes, yes, yes,' and he cupped his hand around his right eye like a viewfinder and panned to my face lighting a cigarette and then panned left towards the empty street. A long shot. The deep silence, fine mist, a construction site, a group of labourers huddled around a fire, shivering. The cloyingly sweet whiff of ganja in the air and then the music rolls out, building in tempo with the credits in Dolby sound. The light dims in the auditorium. The movie begins.

The Leader of Men

He was one of the replacement guards who came to work in our apartment building at the end of November. There are four guards in residence at all times. Two of them work in the daytime and the other two at night. They stay in poky little servants' quarters near the parking lot and are not allowed to keep their families in there. Most of these security guards are lazy, miserable fellows who are, it seems, just content to survive somehow. Most of them are illiterate and from the lower castes, and amidst the gleaming chrome of the shining cars their poverty stands out in glaring contrast.

So I was taken by surprise when I first saw Roop Singh last December when I was back in Patna for the winter vacations. He wasn't at all like the other guards. He was around 5'10", well built, had a long, sharp patrician nose and a glorious light brown moustache that covered his upper lip and curled at the ends in a defiant flourish. He did credit to his name. His uniform was always ironed and creased and the leather boots were gleaming black. He was so different from his defeated little brethren in mismatched uniforms and dusty brown keds that he was actually a revelation in the true sense of the word. He simply didn't fit in at all.

So, the first time I saw him he was at the reception counter in the lobby and was getting a dressing-down from Mr Kedia. Mr Kedia lives right across our flat in F-9 and is in his late thirties. He has sundry business interests and is reputed to be fairly rich. He has the stupid arrogance that comes with it and he wears it on his face with the same sense of pride as the hideous chunky gold watch on his left wrist and the Motorola cellphone on his right hip. He is short and stocky and going bald. His face has started to bloat from an excess of Stroh's beer. He is the kind of on-the-make, ready-to-take, upwardly mobile enterprising men who we see hovering around the periphery of our lives with alarming alacrity but then I guess it is a positive thing.

Kedia is the consummate consumer. A true child of his times. He has to buy things randomly to live, to survive, to find a purpose for his life. When he consumes he lives. Buying is his brand of nirvana. If a new car is not launched in the next six months he may simply fold up and die.

Back to the story now. There was Roop Singh standing behind the counter, Kedia in front of him shouting and another man, who looked just like Kedia, gold watch and all, gesticulating frantically and shouting in the same breath. They were both very angry with Roop for some reason or the other. Normally I wouldn't have stopped because every few days or so Kedia shouts at one worker or the other. He is the president of the owners' association and he takes his job very seriously. But it was Roop—his open, confident face and erect bearing, an innate pride in himself, a sense of defiance and wounded honour in his eyes—that made me pause and look over the scene in a new light. A totally astonishing thing happened then. Roop said to Kedia, 'But it is not my fault, sir, I was just doing my duty,' in impeccable English, albeit with a little rustic lilt. Now this is wonderful, I thought; I could suddenly sense drama in the lazy December air. Kedia was stupefied and he couldn't believe what he had heard and nor could his friend (for it had to be his friend). I could deduce it from the shock on their faces. The rights to snobbery had suddenly been reverted. I am sure Roop too could see it in their eyes. I was interested now but I realized how trivial the problem really was. Kedia was now all red in the face and bluster broke out of it like hot air from a punctured balloon.

'You talk *English* to me! How dare you talk?'

'I just said that I was doing my duty, and I am not a rascal. I do understand English,' Roop said to Kedia in Hindi.

'I will kick you out.'

Roop kept quiet at this and contained his anger but just barely.

I intervened around this time with a neutral, 'What's the matter, Mr Kedia?'

He turned and looked at me. Normally he doesn't ever acknowledge my presence but that day I could see he was glad that I was there. He thought of me as an ally against the class enemy but soon I would prove to be the contrary.

'Ah Ritwik, good you are here,' he started to speak in English but I guess better sense prevailed and he switched over to Hindi, which was worse than his English, but anyway. 'My friend, Mr Sharma (here the man smiled and I smiled back), came to see me fifteen minutes back and this idiot of a guard wouldn't let him come up to my place.'

'I come here every week and this has never happened to me before. He wanted me to talk to Mr Kedia over the intercom and when I refused he physically stopped me from going upstairs,' Mr Sharma said to me.

I felt embarrassed at being involved with something as stupid as this but still I said, 'He was only doing his duty and moreover he is new and doesn't know you.'

'He insulted my guest,' Kedia shouted but there wasn't much conviction in his voice anymore.

'These rules have been made by us, Mr Kedia, and Mr Singh was only doing what he has been told to do and it is for your own safety.'

Sharma and Kedia glared at me and then Kedia said, 'Ritwik, I am going to complain to your father. You don't even know how to talk to your elders.' I smiled at him and kept quiet. He went away hurriedly into the elevator with his friend in tow. I took the stairs.

Later on I learnt from Munna, my servant, that his name was Roop and that he was a Rajput. Munna also told me that the other guards didn't like him much and thought him to be haughty and stuck-up. He thought this was because Roop was of a 'forward' caste, all the others being 'backwards'. He generally kept to himself and after his duties were over, he read books in the guard room. All this seemed, to Munna, as subversive behaviour but even he grudgingly agreed that he was the best ever security guard that had worked at our building. He was smart, efficient and did his job quietly and competently and for this he got the princely sum of six hundred rupees a month and subsisted on boiled rice and potatoes like the other guards. All this for a mere six hundred rupees a month; my shirts cost much more than that; it was ridiculous—the sum—but it was true.

Kedia did complain to my father but my father didn't say anything to me like I knew he wouldn't. But after that incident Kedia with his wounded pride came down hard on Roop Singh. He criticized Roop for everything and anything. He called him inefficient and insolent and once claimed that he had caught him sleeping at night while on guard duty. He was bent on getting him kicked out of the place but the other residents opposed the move and so Roop stayed.

Kedia just couldn't take the fact that a poor, miserable little guard had answered back to him and that too in English. He was sure it was just to show him up in front of his friend and worse, me. He was really sore about the 'English' part.

In his blind vanity he probably never even realized that he could have been wrong. He had always been rich and the rich are always right; according to him there could be no two ways about it. Roop on his part didn't do anything that was counter-reactionary except that he stopped saluting Kedia. Whenever someone else would be with Kedia, he would salute the other person but ignore Kedia, and this galled him no end.

It was during those days that I came to know more about Roop from talking with him every evening for ten to fifteen minutes after I returned home. He felt obliged to me and later thanked me for my intervention that 'fateful' day. The other guards by that time had started to come around. Roop would read to them from the newspaper and tell them what was happening around the world; not that they were much interested. They had unofficially elected him to be their leader and I thought that it was fitting for he came from a race that were once leaders of men. His ancestors must have waged wars against the British and the Mughals and fought glorious battles amidst the golden sand dunes of Mewar. I think I am needlessly romanticizing him; his ancestors were probably as poor as he was and were simple farmers toiling hard for their daily meal, but who knows?

He was an educated person. He had studied till the Intermediate at the College of Commerce, Patna, the very same college I had gone to albeit for a short time and much later than him. I didn't tell him that because I thought it might embarrass him. His father who was a farmer had died around that time and Roop had to leave his studies and look for a job. He went back to farming when he couldn't find any job that he liked. They didn't have much land and some of it had to be sold for his sister's wedding. He himself had married when he was just fifteen and now had a wife and a son back home in the village. The income from the farm wasn't much so he left farming to his younger brother, who wasn't very interested in education anyway and started looking for a job again. Eventually he got a job as a teacher in a school near Bihta but after six months without pay and with no hope of the situation ever changing he left the job and came to Patna, drifting from job to job, sometimes working as a sales help in a grocery store, sometimes as a construction worker. Finally, around four months back, he got the job with the security agency. He would tell me all these things without even an ounce of self-pity yet I could feel the helplessness beneath his practised stoicism. He hadn't seen his family in six months and sometimes it made him deeply melancholic.

For a man of his background he was amazingly aware and well read. He often would talk to me about books that he had read and what he had felt about them. His perception was remarkably acute. I realized his was a sharper critical faculty than mine even though I am a student of literature. Perhaps because my experience of life has largely been vicarious while his I am sure has been a more 'lived-in' and comprehensive one.

Though I am not as well-read in Hindi literature as I want to be, I have some books and these I lent to him. Among the books were a collection of Muktibodh's poems, the complete short stories of Renu and Dinkar's *Rashmi-Rathi*. He returned the Muktibodh the very next day.

In the evenings when there would be no one in the lobby we would sit on the bench and talk about books and life in general; a little informal chitchat until I finished my cigarette and went back home upstairs.

Around that time, he stopped saluting me and I was glad that he did. Somehow it had always made me vaguely uneasy. After all we were not in the army.

He had one sweater that he would wear all the time. A bright maroon one that his wife had sent and he wore it with much pride over his grey uniform.

In the last week of December, he sent a letter to my father asking for an advance of 100 rupees, which should be cut from his next month's salary; he had to urgently send money home and it was a matter of survival. He had written that he hadn't eaten anything for two days and was having difficulty doing his shift. It was a short, formal, very official letter.

My father had gone out so I went down with the money and gave it to him and also sent some food with Munna for him and the other guards.

When Kedia came to know he laughed at my naiveté and called Roop a lazy freeloader. He thought aloud that Roop and the other guards probably drank at night because he had heard noises sometimes and that is where all the money went. I kept quiet. Kedia is a devout man. He gives donations to temples, organizes jagrans regularly and himself performs puja for an hour every morning but strangely enough has no faith in any other human being.

On 31st night, a big bonfire was organized on the terrace of our apartment building. Since I am not a very social type I hadn't gone up to join the party but instead I watched Michelangelo Antonioni's wonderful *Blow-up* on cable TV. My parents came home by 11 p.m., and much before the old year had been rung out and the new year rung in the party had died a cold, lingering death. Many families had failed to turn up, and like it always happens at these things, more food than needed had been ordered and was now left untouched on the tables. Great heaps of meat, biryani, paneer, kofta curry and gulab jamun with no one to consume it all. The ladies came down by 11:30 and the remaining gentlemen drunks were in no position to stand, let alone eat.

Anyway, one of the gentlemen drunks suddenly felt in his breast the milk of human kindness and said to Munna, who was there watching the antics and mixing the drinks and having a few pegs of his own, 'Munna, beta, go downstairs and bring the guards up to eat; someone has to eat these damn things.' So Munna went downstairs and the guards came up and all of them except Roop gorged on the food and went downstairs satisfied. Two of them had upset stomachs the next morning. When Roop eventually picked up a plate and started to serve himself, Kedia rolled over to him and said loudly, 'So Mr Singh, I hope you are not hungry now. You probably haven't eaten such fabulous food ever in your life, so eat carefully, don't overdo it.' And then he laughed and patted Roop on the back patronizingly. Roop felt as if someone had lit a long-abandoned fuse inside his body and that it was snaking up slowly to his brain. He quietly put the plate down and walked away, aware of everybody's eyes boring into his back. The other guards chose to ignore Roop's reaction; they enjoyed themselves to the full.

What happened next can only be called unfortunate, maybe tragic but 'tragic' has a kind of grandeur attached to it, which doesn't necessarily include the minor characters of this world. Roop was on night duty, on the 31st of December. After the party had died down and people had gone to their homes to sleep, Roop sat in the lobby and brooded about the recent events. This is all reconstruction, all conjecture on my part, because the evidence is all physical and doesn't really say anything about his mind, except that he was perhaps hopelessly melancholic and full of hurt and pain. He probably thought about his family. About his no-good brother, but a loyal one nevertheless, his beautiful wife who still looked young in spite of it all and his beloved land, his own little field of wasted dreams, on a part of which a bright red flag with a hammer and sickle had appeared suddenly one day and a small chunk of land was lost to him forever. As if by magic.

He remembered he had cried that night holding his wife tightly and that she too was crying silently while their son slept serenely by their side. It was his son's beautiful, calm face that made him go out in the morning and leave the village. It was his son's face again, around four o'clock that morning that finally upset the delicate balance of his mind. With his bare hands he ripped the lobby apart. With his fists he broke the glass revolving doors, the wooden bench where we sat and talked, the red plastic chairs and the intercom system. His hands were bleeding badly, the fingers broken in many places, and when Haripal, the other guard that night, tried to stop him, he punched him in the mouth. He was totally oblivious to pain, and only when Haripal came back with the other two guards and they all beat him up did he become quiet. But by that time the lobby was totally trashed. Haripal came to inform us and my father woke me up and we went downstairs. Some other residents followed in a little while. Roop was in the guard room. They had tied him up with a rubber hosepipe. His face was swollen and his hands were badly smashed. The eyes were blank, expressionless, like the eyes of people we sometime see in BBC documentaries in some remote corner of the world, struck by natural disaster. I untied his hands and legs but he sat there on the floor, motionless. Kedia didn't come down. Later I found out why. My father and a few other residents took Roop to a nursing home nearby. He had multiple fractures on his hands. He probably would never work with his hands again. Damaged beyond repair. We have sued the security agency. Someone has to pay for the damages, I guess.

Hard-Boiled

Outside the rain is lashing down hard on the soft muddy street and inside the steamy, sweaty room we lie silently on the mussed-up bed, breathing slowly but evenly. The windows are closed and the raindrops splash on the blue windowpane and blur the panorama. I light the first post-coital cigarette of the afternoon.

The smoke glides in and opens up like a fist in my lungs, making me hollow from inside. She always cuddles up and curls unto me like a cat after we have made love—today she is distant yet. She is reluctant to forgive me for some unspecified crime but I do not want to delve into it. I am already contrite. I want her to curl up unto me and to enter me and be a part of my everything, fill up the hollowness, bone to bone, skin to skin, tissue to tissue, heart to heart, prick to pussy, but a strange stubbornness gently binds me down. Today I want a time-out. I am not in the mood for the game. More and more nowadays, with alarming regularity I feel this way, like I am steeling myself from some dark adversity.

Why do I feel the need to protect myself against someone I love? But there you are, I do feel the need and so I don't inquire. I feign indifference. The raindrops look blue through the glass and their rhythmic tippitty-tapetty-tapettu-too add a strange stillness to our minds. I look at her.

She in turn is looking at her outstretched palms, perhaps trying to trace the fortunes of her future life through the crisscrossing lines of her destiny. She doesn't believe in these things, I know. But it is different today. She is sad again. Infinitely sad and sadness does fuck up our mental equilibrium. I can feel it. It comes out of her body like mild effluvia mixed with fresh sweat. A salty blue perfume.

I notice she hasn't done her underarms for a long time now and the fuzz has turned ochre near the roots. Tiny beads of sweat cling to it like pearls on a string. It mildly arouses me.

After a while she turns her head. The eyes are awash with tears.

She asks me slowly, her decibel level almost inaudible. I have to lip read. 'Do you really love me?' she asks and I turn my face away. She slides her head away from my outstretched arm. Do I? Love her that is. Of course. Why the bloody theatrics? We are both so happy together, aren't we? But I keep silent. There is nothing to say really except to reiterate the obvious but suddenly I don't feel up to it. Any moment now I know the tears will start to roll down, a thin continuous stream.

A sense of gloom has wafted over the whole place. A pure blue funk of ennui and despair. Her hands are folded over her breasts, one knee curled up towards the turquoise wall. All taut smoothness and dull sheen. She is beautiful. Of course I love her. But why is it today that we find simple speech so tortuous? Seemingly nothing has changed from yesterday or last week or even last year but something has, nevertheless.

Maybe she didn't have any orgasm; today she didn't even pretend to fake it. I always get cruel when I am angry and I am cruel to people I love but then that is no consolation, not to me and certainly not to her. Her mouth, lips and tongue get very soft when she nears her climax but today they retained their secular warmth throughout.

'You never seem to feel anything deeply. Nothing is important to you. Everything is a big joke. Our whole life, the future, a home, a real home, is a joke to you. You feel nothing.' She tries hard not to sound angry and defeated. The nipples stiffen from the strain, the tears flow out.

It is not true, but what can I say? I feel miserable but I also feel an intense desire to laugh out this pain into oblivion. Wipe the slate clean. But if I do that, I know she will take it as yet another example of my flippant attitude towards everything sacred in general.

I don't blame her. Anyone would feel the same. She stares at the wall.

Her back is towards me. I try to draw her unto me. Fold her into my arms, smoothen her sweat clotted hair. It makes her break out into a fresh batch of tears—the strongest hydraulic force in the world.

She feels totally alone. Abandoned. She is terrified. I can sense it because I myself have felt it many times. On some dark days, at one time or the other, we all feel abandoned, forsaken, like orphans. Then loneliness looms large like a giant octopus, its tentacles reaching every corner of our meagre world. Tears are good at times like this. At least it gives one something to do. It keeps you occupied.

'Why do you say that? Have I ever let you down? Am I not there for you always?' I ask her, half-knowing the answer, sure of my stance. I know I am not in the wrong.

'You are always so distant. Closed up like a shell. What are you afraid of?'

'Nothing,' I say and I am right.

'Let's face it. You are indifferent to everything except sex. There is not much difference between you and a quadruped. You never tell me about anything and I discuss everything with you, every single fucking thing but you ….' And here she makes a vague fluttering motion with her hands. Her hands are beautiful, slender long fingers which are soft yet surprisingly strong. Writerly hands but she doesn't write, except for memos. She weaves patterns of intricate beauty while she talks. It was one of those numerous things that drew me to her in the old days. I guess it is her turn to be cruel now.

'I tell you everything that you need to know.'

'Need to know (here she shouts); what is that supposed to mean? I want to know everything. Don't you know everything about me?'

'Yes I do,' I tell her softly, but do I?

'Then why not me? Why do you keep your thoughts a secret? Why is everything so covert? An espionage, a subterfuge, a secret venture up a dark alley?'

I smile. It is the least I can do. It is so strange how sometimes everything pure and bright can transform itself into the raw and the rotten in such a short while.

I playfully run my hand up her naked leg and she jerks it away with a look of sheer disgust. Now I am really really angry. This is taking it a bit too far. We all have our bouts of intense melancholia but that doesn't mean … no sex!

'You have five minutes to dress up and leave,' I hiss at her, secure in the knowledge that she will dissolve into a quivering column of tears and bury her head in my hairy chest. And everything will be fine. All said and done, I don't have a heart of stone. I too am a sensitive man. I wash the dishes after dinner. Sometimes.

Then a strange thing happens or maybe it is my imagination. She looks at me and the colour of her eyes changes and in them flashes across something that I have only seen once before in my life. I remember I was thirteen and I had just beaten the neighbour's cat so hard that it lay on the ground motionless. Its breathing was irregular or totally absent. I don't recall, but I was fascinated and felt proud and excited. I remember I almost had a hard-on. Out of sheer excitement I knelt beside the cat and poked her with a stick. She was dying. And then her eyes jerked open and she snarled and hissed and leapt at me. Like traffic lights the colour of her eyes changed to red from green and in them flashed something that I would see once more, in the luminous eyes of my intended, years later. Just now.

She swings her legs slowly and pulls up her panties, picks up the bra slung from the chair like a slingshot, hooks up her blouse, drapes the sari, puts on her pearls and slips on her ring, elegant and cool as ever. Within five minutes too. The stipulated time. She opens the door and on her way out closes it softly. Without a backward glance. She doesn't even slam the fucking door.

For a long time I lie there, naked and feeling increasingly stupid. Tossing restlessly, totally numb till I feel a sharp tearing pain in my backside. I turn over and feel my bum. There is something embedded in the fleshy part of the right cheek.

There is blood on the sheet. A jagged splinter of her shattered shankha. There are pieces of ivory strewn all over the bed. Fuck. The sight of blood nauseates me. I faint.

Will You Be My Valentine?

Someone was calling out her name softly and incessantly from between the hollows of a beautiful ruined tomb and tugging at her blanket but it felt like it was happening to someone else in some distant dream, twice removed from her and reality. She burrowed deep inside the thick blanket and slept on contentedly but after a while she felt the blanket being snatched from her and reluctantly she opened her eyes; she felt cold and curled up her bare legs, trying to focus her eyes on the shape looming above her.

'Wake up, angel, wake up, wake up. I have been trying to wake you for the past ten minutes, don't you want to wake up early today, today! today! today! today!' It was her roommate Ritu, Anjali could make out after a few seconds of repeated blinking-unblinking and trying to adjust to the dim darkness. She was still feeing very sleepy and now very bugged.

'Why? What is so important about today? Go back to sleep.' She squinted at her watch. 'It is only eight o'clock and really what is so important about today? It's here this time of the week every year, with monotonous regularity,' Anjali said quietly and pulled up the blanket again. Ritu sat down beside her on the bed and started doing her nails. She had already taken her bath and her long hair was all wet and shampooed and hung down to her waist in shiny thick waves.

'It is Valentine's day today, if you remember, angel.' Everyone in the hostel called Anjali 'angel' because she was very tiny and delicate and also because 'angel' kind of went with Anjali who was always very nice and sweet to everybody.

At first she used to feel very uncomfortable when someone called her that because, she explained to everybody, 'It makes me feel like a symbol of some kind or the other,' but it persisted and the name stuck and now she didn't mind it really; it was much better than being called 'Tinytoes' or 'Babyfinger' or worse still, 'Babydoll'!

'Right, Valentine's day, lovers' day, oh yes, how can I forget? Have I not been waiting all these months for today? For just this one glimpse of "today"? Of course I have been, oh yes, but still it is too early for me.'

'All right but I just thought I should wake you up; you don't want to be late for Ritwik, do you?'

'No, I won't be late. I told him I would be there by eleven; I won't be late.'

'He has sent such beautiful cards to you, really lovely ones; Ritwik is a real romantic guy. A bonafide knight in shining armour.' Ritu winked at her and Anjali couldn't help smiling. Ritu was wearing her new lace underpants and she caught Anjali looking so she wiggled her bottom at her roommate and winked again, and they both laughed.

'He is a real "cool dude", Ritwik is,' Anjali said softly and slowly she got up from the bed and the floor felt cold and slippery to her feet so she walked on her toes to where she had thrown her slippers and slipped her feet into warm fur.

Ritu had changed into a soft red and white sari. The blouse was a bit loose and her arms looked thinner. Anjali went and assisted her in tightening up the blouse with a safety pin and straightened the fall of her sari. Then she took a step back, lit a cigarette and looked at her critically.

'No, no, don't wear that bindi, that is too small, wear the big one and don't tie up your hair … yes the big one. It kind of looks more chic and bindaas,' she said to Ritu and dropped the ash on the floor.

'Nice?' Ritu asked her, not really sure of the way she looked.

'You look beautiful.'

'Really?' She was smiling now and looked radiant and it made her look prettier than she was.

'Really.' Anjali passed the cigarette to her.

'Ravi says that girls look better in saris, they look more "womanly", more grown-up and mysterious.'

It is always 'Ravi says this, Ravi says that', thought Anjali to herself, a bit amused.

'You look womanly enough, don't worry,' she said after a while.

'What will you wear? And for god's sake, don't wear that grungy pair of jeans, you look like a little kid in those. Wear something traditional,' Ritu said seriously to her and exhaled a lungful of blue-grey smoke and passed the cigarette back to Anjali.

'I have no problem in looking like a kid. I am a kid, remember? I have hardly grown up. I've always been a kid, right since childhood. And I love that pair of jeans.'

'Not today. Wear something nice, Ritwik will love it, okay, angel, okay?'

'All right, I will wear that cream salwar suit of mine.'

'Yes, do that. I must hurry, I have to get to Vasant Kunj; he is staying with his mausi and from there we will drive out,' Ritu said a bit breathlessly and looked for the last time at the mirror and straightened her sari for the umpteenth time; she wasn't much comfortable with saris yet.

'Say hi to Ravi for me and have fun. See you at 7.30,' Anjali said to Ritu who was at the door now.

'You too, and listen, say hi to Ritwik and give a big kiss to him from me. Bye,' Ritu said, out of breath again and then she was gone. Anjali crushed the cigarette on the floor and then she picked up the butt and put it carefully in an envelope filled with other butts and put it behind her books, away from view.

Suddenly she felt very forlorn and for a few seconds passed into a pure blue funk of melancholia but then she caught sight of her image locked in the mirror and she couldn't help smiling. She looked so sad and blue that it was hilarious; sadness didn't go with her face. She was still smiling when she went to the bathroom to wash.

She was in her second year studying Literature and she was happy doing that. She liked literature, liked the eternal magic of stories and had always wanted to study it and she was good at it too but when she had first come to Delhi from Patna and stayed in the hostel, it was the first time she had stayed away from home and with so many girls and she had felt out of place in the midst of their sophistication and cool. She wasn't cool, she knew that, she was just pretty and intelligent and all the other girls to her looked more beautiful, more intelligent, more aware and chic than her. She felt she couldn't compete with them, ever.

All those cool girls had boyfriends and those boys would come and visit the girls in the evening outside the hostel and she would look at them and wonder how these girls had met these boys. Some of the boys looked really cute to her. She went to many college festivals, to seminars, to plays, where her new, more experienced friends had hinted she could meet boys but nothing like that happened and so after a while she was reconciled to the philosophy that 'there must be some magic, some mystery in it that is totally beyond my range.' She was content with the explanation but then one fine day after the last summer vacation, Ritu, who was her best friend, a year senior to her and her roommate-cum-soulmate, came and let it drop as unobtrusively as a fox in a chicken coop that she was wildly in love. She had fallen in love with a guy called Ravi back in her hometown during the vacation. He was studying at IIT Kanpur and she showed a snap of the boy to Anjali. He was good-looking, very handsome in fact, Anjali had to admit.

Ritu, who had always bitched about those girls who had boyfriends and had a kind of condescending attitude towards them, had herself gone ahead and fallen in love. Anjali felt a curious sense of dismay over this and then she had felt guilty about it.

Ritu would read aloud all her love letters to Anjali when they would arrive and moon over Ravi's snap at night. She kept it underneath her pillow. In Ritu would her cupid-induced stupor tell her, 'You should fall in love too, angel, you don't know what you are missing.' Life got unbearable for Anjali but she smiled on, like always.

So when she went home for the autumn break, there in the sanctuary of her room, she created 'Ritwik'. She had always liked the magic of stories. She worked hard on Ritwik. She made notes on him and carved him out solid and real from the limpid block of her fertile imagination.

1. Ritwik should study at JNU and be 2–3 years older than me.
2. He will be a close friend of my cousin Hriday.
3. I met him at my cousin's place during the vacations and it was kind of love at first sight for us.

Ritu would like that, she liked love-at-first-sights. These were the main points and she added little bits of detail to go with them. She selected a snapshot of Hriday standing underneath a tree with some of his friends, laughing and saying something and there was a guy sitting indolently on a black Yezdi mobike, looking away from the camera. He had a remote quality and it struck the right note for Anjali. She picked him to be her Ritwik. When she asked her cousin what his name was, he wasn't sure because that guy wasn't such a good friend of his. So Anjali called him 'Ritwik' because it kind of went with the image she had of him and also most importantly she had no idea what Ritwik really meant. It was okay, it wasn't a great characterization but it would do.

So when she came back from her vacations, she acted a bit mysterious for a few days and when Ritu and her other friends were sufficiently riled, she coyly confided in them that she was in love with a JNU intellectual named Ritwik and showed them the snapshot. In a few days the news spread like wildfire in the hostel and the girls smiled at her and gave her meaningful looks. She liked that. Like all artists she loved applause. Everything was fine now and even Ritu didn't moon that much anymore. Once in a while Anjali disappeared for a day and spent it watching movies at Priya and came back by 7:30 to announce in a cool manner that she had lots and lots and lots of fun with Ritwik.

She looked at her watch; it was 9:30. 'Time to move on,' she said to herself. She pulled on her 'grungy' pair of jeans and a black turtleneck sweater, combed back her short hair and put on her glasses and went out.

The college wore a festive look. Most of the girls were decked up and had bunches of roses in their hands and their faces were shining with excitement. The whole university was alive to the beat of lovers' hearts. Hunks with slicked-back hair and sunglasses moved around in shiny cars in a desperate manner and girls were bunched in groups outside the colleges, cool and waiting to be plucked. It was a festival on par with any of the traditional festivals of the city, perhaps now more important than them. Anjali felt nauseous with all the gaiety flying around unchaperoned mixed with exhaust fumes. She caught the bus to Priya. One really good thing had come out of this charade: she had become a serious movie buff. Anjali always found silver linings where there were none.

She reached Priya round 11:15 and got a ticket for the afternoon show. They were still showing *Alladin*; she had already seen it thrice. The crowd of happy people was there too and she realized it wasn't such a great idea to visit Priya on Valentine's Day. Some of the girls from the hostel could be there or worse still, Ritu and Ravi could drop in. After all Ravi was visiting for a few days and would surely like to see *Alladin* and on what better day to watch it than Valentine's Day, right?

She was one of the first to enter the movie hall and settled comfortably in the back well before the movie started. She liked Alladin. He was very handsome and had beautiful dark eyes and she would have loved to be his princess.

At the interval when the lights came on she got the shock of her life. Ritu and Ravi were sitting just three rows in front of her. There was a big group of kids with them. Probably friends of Ravi, thought Anjali, crouching low in her seat and heaved a big sigh of relief when the lights were turned off again but she couldn't enjoy the movie any longer. The pizza she had eaten before the show sat in the middle of her tummy like a big sticky mass of lump.

Just five minutes before the ending the group got up, three girls and two boys and Ravi; only it wasn't Ravi, Anjali could make out in the flickering light. It wasn't Ravi at all. The group went out and Ritu was still sitting there, her eyes glued to the screen.

That guy wasn't Ravi. From a distance in her excitement he had seemed—

Now everything became clear to her.

When the movie ended and the crowd moved out, Ritu was in the front, walking a little awkwardly in her beautiful red-white sari, getting curious stares from the cool kids. She looked so beautiful and alone that it broke Anjali's heart. Some of the magic died for her then.

At night after dinner, Ritu came into the room. She looked serene, calm and satisfied. Anjali didn't look at her. She was staring at the ceiling.

'Why didn't you come to the mess for dinner?' she asked Anjali in an offhand manner.

'Just didn't feel like eating.'

'Ravi and I had such a great time. He was really romantic and beautiful today. We went to Surajkund,' she said to Anjali calmly while brushing her hair and Anjali suddenly realized that Ritu wasn't putting up an act. In her heart of hearts she wasn't lying.

'Even we went to Surajkund.'

Ritu's eyes flickered once and she turned and looked at Anjali and smiled.

'Really? It is such a pity we missed each other; the place is always so crowded. We could have had such a great time together. Me and Ravi, you and Ritwik.'

'Yes,' Anjali whispered.

Aren't we lucky we have someone we can hold on to, someone who loves us as much as we love them?' Ritu said and smiled a truly beatific smile.

'Yes,' Anjali accepted and lit a cigarette.

The Unbearable Loneliness of the Short Story Writer

I have measured out my life in large Patiala pegs, and frankly, my love, it sucks. I sit here day after day with a pen in my hand, a blank virginal page staring right into my eyes, unable to come alive and I think it has all come to a waste. The slide from the land of gup to the land of chup has been swift and definitive. There are no stories anymore to tell. I despair—but a tiny voice at the back of my mind pipes up now and then with an 'It's not true, not true at all'. There always will be stories as long as there is life but somehow it all comes out stillborn. Dead on arrival. The last story I did was a couple of months back when we were together. When I would just pick up a pen and point it to the page and a world all tangible and new would appear and we could escape into it and be safe from the encroaching reality. My love, come back to me. I know I have sinned. I am consumed with remorse. Be an angel and grant me absolution.

Each dawn I awake, and for half an hour I lie back on the bed, eyes open, staring at the ceiling fan unable to get up—no drowsiness or anything but just the complete lack of will to get up and face what I dread to face. I do the mandatory fifty pushups and crawl to the table. It is piled up with books, many I haven't touched in weeks, maybe months. Large tomes of wisdom no doubt but even these do not alleviate the utter sense of desolation that I feel. I sit in my chair, pick up the pen that you had given me, a silver Mont Blanc long ago (I remember it like it was yesterday), right here in my little barsati with the dark green walls. You remember that, don't you? It's the same pen with which I write today this lament to my soul. The notepads are there, expensive and blank, the finest money can buy; at the corner squats the old Remington.

Above the table on the wall hangs a lithograph of a man who was once to me the embodiment of all that I wanted to be, in his eyes freedom and rebellion blaze like slow fire, the face undeniably angelic with the prettiest lips on any man that I have seen. Prettier than Presley, a tougher Montgomery Clift with the same brooding sadness; and what glorious talent while it lasted. It is old Jack Kerouac who looks to me from the wall every day but St Jack, kind Jack, free Jack, has no accusation in his eyes. Jack, hey Jack, thou prince of the beat and the beat-up, thou saint of love and loneliness, help thine acolyte mired in misery, wallowing in wine, soaked up with self pity, miserably maudlin to boot. Just show me the open road, mate and I will go. The backpack is ready. It is also empty. But he with his beatific smile can't help me anymore, he has been dead for thirty years, a drink-sodden death, straining at the toilet seat … no sorry, I apologize, that was Elvis. I am getting my stories confused. Jack died watching the tube, washed up and dead for years when he died. You frighten me Jack but still I love you Jack. I wanted his freedom, his words, his mind, hell I wanted to be a rebel too. I longed to be alienated too. He was poor and I was rich, he hated his father and I loved mine, he had a chip on his shoulder and I wanted one too. Till one day as the mist cleared, I met you and wanted to conform to everything that you projected. You brought out the bohemian beneath the bourgeois, the snake beneath the skin, the artist behind the thick-lensed dullness in me. Jack with the pack on his back, a smile on his lips and a backward glance and a wink that said, 'You are in good hands brother, just hold tight,' went up the lonely road; *Pather Panchali* playing upon his tongue unforked. I didn't complain, I had you and I could write. It was heaven. All those years I would always think of writing about you. Construct a veritable home movie of a story about you but never could because for one I had other things to write about. You opened the floodgates of my mind and stories, poems, haikus came rushing out like vomit and there were only so many I could mop up; many spilled about everywhere in alcohol and friends and foolishness but I couldn't care less about it then. I was sure there would be more to follow. You were too real to write about. I couldn't ever distance myself from you. You were on my back like wings and in my side like Eve in Adam's rib. There was no getting away from you. You were the one thing that I kept just for myself. I couldn't have shared you with the world but I should have. I know that now. I should have bound you in words, never to let you depart. I should have paid attention to Donne. I should have listened to him and you could still be here beside me watching the bloody sunne rise and go down again in the evening, drinking beer, comparing Larkin's 'Aubade' to Empson's. But I can start now and retrieve lost ground. I could write about the time when I first met you. Remember the fair? The stupid fair? The eternal fair? The book fair. Do you remember the two adolescents young with lust who could barely keep their hands off each other and wished to melt away together far away from the madding crowd—and they did. You remember that, don't you? I should have written about that. About your hair auburn and straight, uncombed and loose, symbol of disorder, 'chaos', my literary friends perhaps would call it, and which I would shampoo and comb back from your high forehead but never braid. Even when you would come with your hair tightly bound in a bun I would close the door and take out the pins. Or your toe ring shining with silver sweat or the toe itself. The small left one. If not a short story, perhaps a haiku:

Your bloody toe
in my mouth
taste of salt and sour metal

See, now I do it and it comes out all wrong. Remember the time I came piss drunk to the hostel? I had published my first story and was delirious with joy. We had just met the other week and here I was on my knees, laughing and crying, all at the same time, and your friends were horrified but you had laughed when any other girl would have died of social apoplexy. Later on that night in the hostel, your roommate envious and scandalized, asked you, 'So he writes. That's all very well but what does he plan to do exactly or is he as vella as you are?' and you replied, 'Well you saw, didn't you?' and laughed some more.

Rifat, come back, I still love you. Do you still keep the copy of my story on your desk, like you did when we were together or have you flushed it down the toilet with the photograph and other memories?

I should have written about that, about finding in that laughter an affirmation of our oneness. We understood each other totally. We communicated silently, our fingers intertwined bashfully, walking together in the November chill, coffee in styrofoam cups from the hostel, the moon dirty and weary coming out behind us at five o'clock in the evening. Your friends suspicious and protective and mine frankly bewildered—but we didn't care, did we? We talked about Art and commitment and all that jazz but more often than not we talked just about literature: Agyeya and Muktibodh, Barthelme and Carver, Rushdie and Marquez. We spent endless evenings discussing magic realism, dirty realism, neo-realism, oblivious to the world. Sometimes comparing Hughes's crow to Laxman's series on crows and sometimes the dichotomy of Garfield's sloth and Macavity's feline stealth. One of those early courtship days I brought you a copy of *Gone with the Wind* because you mentioned that all your friends had read it umpteen times and you wanted to see what the fuss was all about; but you could never finish it though you kept trying intermittently over the years. I never realized how much you hated the book until the 'incident' a couple of months back.

You would always wear those frayed black jeans of yours, the ones I totally detested, and a grey college sweatshirt with the hood pulled over your head which made you look mysterious like Orco. It would be very hard to kiss you—I had to pull the hood down every time. Did you use your hood as a ghunghat, silly girl? Come seven o'clock and you would say goodbye and I would protest, 'We have half an hour more at least,' and you would always say, 'But I have a tutorial tomorrow.'

Or of the time we both met Arundhati Roy at the Delhi School of Economics cafeteria when she had come to lecture on *Bandit Queen* and how it was such an exploitative movie. She wasn't the goddess of all things then but just as lovely as ever and how I had made a fool of myself by disagreeing with her, making her angry in return, and I had not even seen the movie then; well, nobody had. It hadn't been released yet but in retrospect I was right. You laughed all the way back to the hostel but you see I had to impress her. She was so enchanting, so fit, though I agree she didn't take my words too well.

Once you won five hundred rupees in a poetry contest and we went to see *Death and the Maiden* with Bhaskar Ghosh in it. We bought the most expensive tickets available and later on had dinner at a Mexican restaurant and didn't have any money left for the auto fare. It was ten o'clock in the night and we caught the 901 to the university. I had a fight with a couple of inebriated louts when they tried to act fresh with you.

The prudent thing to do would have been to get down and catch another bus but something made me fight. I wasn't scared then but I was afterwards. When at home that night you said to me, 'I was so scared, man,' and buried your face in my chest, I burst out crying myself. I was embarrassed later and said to you, 'I am just not the macho type,' and you said, 'I would hate you if you were.' The next morning we had a good laugh over it with our morning chai and then you left because you had a tutorial.

We could laugh at anything then, love, happiness, sadness, humbug. We used laughter like a machete to level anything and everything. You had the bright idea to write a short story about it in collaboration with me, and as we spun it yard for yard it became in a short while a fit treatment for a movie by Mrinal Sen on a bad wicket. Remember *Calcutta 71*?

My eyes lost focus for days after watching that. It is good that I didn't write anything about it seriously because it never would have come out the way it happened. It would never have been a story but at best only an anecdote like it is now.

Once after reading *Ulysses* in two days flat I went blind the next morning and panicked as I also had a high temperature and my only thought was to have you by my side and my old landlady, that sweet old lady, called you and you came running though you had a tutorial that day. You cooked for me, looked after me, took me to the doctor, brought the medicines and generally with cool efficiency took over and made me as good as new in only a couple of days' time. Can I put that in a story and still tell you how blessed, how loved I felt? It is good I never wrote about that because, perhaps, then I would have destroyed it but I remember everything. Since you have gone I have suddenly got the curse of total recall.

One time we went to the Alliance Française to see *Jules et Jim* but of course we didn't have the passes, still we knew we would get in and we did. We begged, we cajoled, we pleaded and flashed our college identity cards, did our 'but-sir-we're-students act' and got in at last but since the chairs were all taken, we sat on the steps. Rich matrons in pearls cast us curious stares but we didn't mind. Later on I made you jealous by going on and on about how fascinating Jeanne Moreau really was and I only stopped when you cried. I never thought I would miss you so. The only comfort these days are those memories. They are with me everywhere, when I go to the library in the morning, when I am working on the stupid dissertation, at the dhaba nearby where I have my lunch every day, and back home in my room from where it seems you have never left. At the corner of my table, beside the typwriter, the manuscript of your book of poems is kept. How well you write; I get jealous sometimes. Your poems are a great comfort, they speak to me in your voice and remind me of your wit and charm and dear comrade the last seminar we attended together. It was spring and Al MacGuffin was giving a lecture at St. Stephens on 'postmodernism'. The mic was perhaps a bit faulty and MacGuffin, the klutz incarnate, tried to position it right and in the process demolished it totally. A new one had to be brought and horror of horrors, in that snooty, august gathering, your high-pitched laughter, proletarian, suddenly rang out. I couldn't control the giggles myself. We were both thrown out. Later on you said, solemnly, as we sat in the coffee house, that it was the single most defining act of 'deconstruction' that you had ever seen. Ah if only I had thought of it first, but as usual you beat me to the gun. We had the big fight a couple of days after that.

The only time my memory fails is when I think about that fateful day, about that stupid fight we had and everything comes through a wall of perforated mist; words, phrases and some actions are missing at times and my memory unspools through many jumpcuts. All I remember is that I played Othello to your Desdemona with my mind at its scene-stealing best as Iago. All I know is that I am sorry. I was a fool to suspect you of infidelity but you did praise Ritwik's story much more than mine at the café and he kept giving you those adoring looks of his while I burned up inside. His stories are better I agree now, but I was consumed by envy then. And you shouldn't have shouted and thrown *Gone with the Wind* at me, smashed my glasses and I shouldn't have punched you and split open your lips and then for an encore given you a black eye, to say nothing of your hair, a tuft of which somehow came into my hands in the end. I sincerely hope it hasn't made you bald in the back. My fingers have atrophied since then, withered and scaly-white like chanticleer claws, though I can still hold a pen and write, like I do now, the blood has dried up and believe me, even as I hit you, I realized that perhaps this time I had gone too far. But I didn't hit you out of spite or anger or to teach you a lesson but only out of artistic curiosity. Now I believe at the back of my mind the burning question was whether I could ever hit you or not. And how would it feel to hit? And to watch your face and gauge your emotions after the act closely so I could write about it later on. It was just an experiment, darling. My anger had died out the moment before I had hit you. Just an experiment for my art, you see; I had never hit a woman before. I really never thought you would take it so badly and disappear totally from my life. I realize the enormity of my act and am now penitent. I am down on my knees and *begging baby please,* but I didn't do it for pleasure. I did it for art and as an artist you too can understand the importance of investigation and experiment when it comes to method writing. Perhaps by now you too have written a long poem about it. You are my Beatrice, my Banalata Sen, my Layla. You are my own little private goddess of all things. Come back, little Mira, come back to daddy, come back back back or let me do my Jimmy Dean in all my petulant surly mouth sorrow: 'You're tearing me apart, you're tearing me apart!' That was always good for a laugh, wasn't it, darling? Back in the good old days but now it has become excruciatingly real and cuts right to the bone.

Mira at 24

I am twenty-four years old today. A beautiful, wild, cheerful twenty-four. The breasts are still firm. Upturned and perky. The tummy tucked and poster-smooth. Hips delicate, made of glass. I am proud of my body. It is all class. The legs long, supple and strong. The heart a tired leonine. Why tired? Ritwik. That is why. I wish he would do something soon.

Anything. Earn some money. Settle down. So I can marry the slippery little bugger finally. For a certified intellectual he is incredibly stupid. No sense of reality at all. I want to mate now. The time is ripe.

Moreover, I am bored. It would be a change, don't you think? There would be responsibilities no doubt but I am old enough, am I not? I can take care of anything. I have got a couple of baby cacti on my desk and they haven't died in weeks. Also a nine-month-old dachshund who is living yet.

It is early morning. Still dark with a hint of rain. Here in paradise.

Just kidding, of course, but on some days it really is like paradise. On those days we all love each other very much. Mama, Papa, Adolf and Mira. On other days it is like any other normal home. Then it is not fun at all. But then nobody ever said that parents were supposed to be 'fun' and families 'cool', did they? They are asleep, my parents. I have one clear hour of uninterrupted privacy yet. Before they awake.

I won't work on my dissertation today but in the afternoon go to the library and treat Ritwik to some magical omelettes and cold coffee at Kaake da Dhaba. I wish I could treat him to a nice juicy double cheese pizza with sausage toppings. Well, that will have to wait for now. The one good thing about Ritwik is that he eats anything. He is omnivorous. He consumes everything. Never complains. Just like Adolf. My sweet little portable liver-breath sprayer. The only difference is that Ritwik smells better. Tastes good too. Well, if he wants anything juicier than an omelette he can always suck on my tits later on behind the reference section. He tastes of jaggery, Ritwik does. Jaggery with a twist of lime.

Before I knew Ritwik I thought the human body only smelt of abstract things at different times of day. Of security and concern like my father's hands in the evening when he would come home from work tired and soft, of loneliness in my armpit hair after another unending college 'social', of despair and fear on my mother's lips when on some empty sun-filled winter afternoon she would kiss my forehead and cry. My parents don't like Ritwik much. I don't blame them. He is a bit of an oddity really. An acquired taste. But I love him, don't I? That should be enough for them. That is if they really are my parents and haven't adopted me from the nearest orphanage. I don't look anything like my parents so you never know. That is one of my ever-recurring nightmares, really. On the other hand, I think it is simply an overdose of the golden era of Hindi movies on the late-night channel. The 70s. I have such a nostalgic thing for the 1970s. Perhaps it is because I was born then.

Love those printed polyester shirts, bell-bottoms and dog collars. Long hair, sideburns, and handlebar moustaches. Zeenie baby on a slow burn doing 'dum maro dum', kumbh ka melas, Manmohan Desai, and lost-and-found themes. Ah the 70s! It was the time when even God wanted to look like Amitabh Bachchan and often did. At least to me. Now not even Amitabh looks like Amitabh anymore. Talk about losing face. Literally.

'Mira, he doesn't have much of a future,' my mother told me once and I didn't talk to her for a couple of days. She got the message. Loud and clear. Mama, dear sweet Mama, you don't leave anyone for something as slight as not having 'much of a future', for being of a different caste or community or religion, for being poor. It is almost like killing an infant in Rajasthan for turning out to be a girl.

It is deliberate cruelty. And like Blanche I won't ever be condemned for that. Perhaps his parents think about me in the same way. A klutzy, anorexic girl full of intellectual pretensions come to whisk away their gorgeous golden son. Parents! They are mostly right, of course. Because of hindsight. Because they too did some wrong in their youth. They call it experience. In one's youth, the right to wrong is a fundamental right. I do not want to be deprived of my share. Perhaps in time Ritwik will turn out to be my tragic flaw. My 'hamartia'. Tell you what? I will take my chance for now.

The birds sing the aubade outside on the windowsill. The house is stirring. I hear my father piss in the toilet bowl. He will come and wish me afterwards. Sweet sweet daddy. Mother is making coffee. Ah, the lazy, bleary-eyed smell of strong espresso in the morning. And no one makes it better than my mother. She mouths a silent 'Happy birthday, darling' and blows me a kiss.

Mira blows it back. I will do my yoga now and sing the body geometric. Must keep it supple and smooth for Ritwik. From the corner Adolf lets out a delicate fart and then ashamed, pretends to be asleep. Just like Ritwik.

The Writer's Wife

Monday came at last, and with it, the letter. Finally. The verdict had been out since last week. But Mira had somehow restrained herself from calling up the magazine. She wanted the letter. In writing. Whether she had won or lost. The short story competition, that is. For posterity, it could become an important document. Like the Birth Certificate. The School Leaving Certificate. The Death Certificate. It would change the course of her life, so she wanted it in writing. She had plotted it that way. If she won, she would leave Ritwik. Her husband. If she lost, well she would simply wait till the next contest. In the past one year she had already lost three. She closed the letterbox. Let the letter lie there like a rattler. She would wait. Yet.

She was the writer's wife. That is, her husband was a 'writer' or rather thought that he was a writer. He was actually just a middlingly successful book reviewer and society columnist who once in a while still wrote the occasional unpublished poem. For the last seven years he had been Casaubon-like, working on the great Indian postmodern neo-magic realist novel, tentatively titled 'Magnum Opus'. The old broken-down refrigerator was already filled to bursting point with shrink-packed yellow manuscript pages. He had started the novel on their honeymoon. In fact, the first line had been written on Mira. Literally on her. From her belly button to her breasts. *It was a dark and stormy night.*

Ritwik the writer. The boy whom all her friends had found darkly glamorous. In the final year of college. She wondered now if it had been a conspiracy all along. On her friends' part. Her friends found him to be good-looking, so Mira too decided that he was handsome. Her roommate found him interesting so Mira too started taking an interest in him. Then her best friend fell in love with him and Mira had no choice but to claim Ritwik for her own.

To be fair to Ritwik, he actually did have a modicum of subversive charm in those days. He was different. When all the other boys were preparing for an MBA, he was writing poetry. On her. She should have known then. By the end of the first year he had published his first long short story in the noted *Little Magazine*. He graduated, got a job with a newspaper and published his first very slim anthology of poems. They got married. He started work on the Novel. Things started getting fucked up after that. The short stories stopped getting published. The poems limped back home rejected. The 'Little' magazines, the 'Slicks', all turned their backs on the golden boy.

Love went out quick and clean from their marriage after that. It wasn't as if he was constantly abusive. He only hit her about once a week. After a while it just became hard for Mira to take on all those rejected stories and poems. She felt all those millions of words floating around her, slowly sucking out happiness right from her life. He wasn't even good-looking anymore. She never forgave him that. That he was untalented she could somehow rationalize but the fact that he let himself get fat, lose all his hair and with it his erection, galled her no end.

He would get drunk every second day and would chastise the literary world for the injustice of it all and cast aspersions on the critical acumen of all the editors in the trade. After the sixth peg he would start on the novelists: 'Ah Rushdie, now there's a bugger with no…' and Mira would clamp her hands over her ears. Ritwik would hit her then. A backhand cross-court. But the worst was that he would then cry the whole night and not let her sleep. Like most literary-minded married women all over the world, Mira too couldn't fathom how the golden boy straight out of F. Scott Fitzgerald that she had gone to bed with somehow turned into a Stanley Kowalski in the morning. Worse, he didn't even look anything like Brando. She decided to leave him in the end. But she wouldn't go gently. She would wound him first. She would be successful where he failed.

She started writing and found to her surprise that it came naturally to her. Mira started sending contributions to short story contests, and when the letters would come she would leave them unopened in the letterbox. She would watch from behind the curtain as Ritwik opened the letter and read. The reaction on his face would decide his fate.

At four o'clock and the doorbell rang. Ritwik scuttled in. 'Ah, a letter for you,' he announced and tore the envelope open. His sense of propriety was nil. His thirst for information enormous, unlike his member. He was the Novelist. To use a cliché, Mira with her heart in her mouth watched him closely, waiting for the laughter to explode but Ritwik after a few millennia-like seconds just clutched his heart and sank to the floor. The lethal piece of paper slid out of his long writerly fingers and Mira caught it in mid-flight. It read: 'Dear Mrs Ray, we are delighted to inform …'

The Niyogis

Even at the age of seventy-one, Mr Niyogi gave the impression of corded vigour and vitality. Rather, he had the look of a much younger man. He was tall. His hair, grey as steel, was thick and brushed back from his wide forehead in a wavy flourish. The teeth too, slightly nicotine-stained, were still all there. Every morning he walked for a mile to the post office and back again. Every so often Mrs Niyogi would accompany him but after a while she would feel tired and plop down on a bench in the neighbourhood park. Her husband on his way back would pick her up, and then together they would go to the vegetable market, the grocery store and back home to their flat on the fifth floor of a large apartment building in South Delhi.

In contrast to her husband, Mrs Niyogi was tiny, barely touching the five-feet mark. Frail and fair, she looked the part of the much-loved Bengali grandmother, down to every spunky inch of her diminutive frame.

The Niyogis had one son, Hriday, who was a senior executive in a foreign bank. Hriday was in some ways the mythical perfect son. Reverent and solicitous and only sometimes mildly critical. He wanted to provide for his parents all the comfort and security he had received when he himself had been a dependant. In this endeavour he was extremely successful but perhaps for this the real encomiums should go to the lady of the house, Hriday's wife Charu, who in spite of her busy career as a copywriter took care of her in-laws as if they were her own parents and never let them feel the neglect which is sadly the lot of most elderlies in the autumn of their lives.

On their part, the Niyogis gave Hriday and Charu ample breathing space and privacy. They were never meddlesome and only volunteered advice when specifically asked for it. There were things that they did not like about their son, such as his excessive drinking, his late-night parties, but they never voiced their concern because they knew that the young must live their own lives and that their son was a fine young gentleman, much respected in his own circle, and so must be allowed to do his own thing as long as he kept playing tennis in the mornings and generally kept himself fit. Likewise, they also felt that Charu was sometimes too strict with their son and most importantly their grandson Tanmay, or Tanu for short. Charu was perpetually worried about her ten-year-old son's future and the son, though academically bright, was perpetually worried about his batting technique. Whenever Tanu came home late from the park in the evening he would get a tremendous scolding from his mother, but that did not bother him much. He would go and routinely complain to his grandmother, and after wheedling out the requisite sympathy, try to wheedle out some money for comics and succeed every time. Though the senior Niyogis thought that their bou-ma's behaviour towards Tanu was a bit obsessive, they wisely kept quiet about it. At night sometimes, grandmother Niyogi would say to her husband, 'After all, he is her son and the boy does study very little. We must not spoil him.' Mr Niyogi would nod his head like a sage and look at this simple woman who had been his wife for the past forty-five years, his beloved, his strength, his backbone and feel in his heart love and tenderness of such adolescent intensity that he would pull her towards himself and kiss her full on the lips. She would kiss him back. Then one morning grandma Niyogi died. She had had angina pain around midnight but had kept quiet about it, and only when it got unbearable and she was about to lose her consciousness did she wake Mr Niyogi up. It was too late by then. She died a couple of hours later in the ICU of a reputed nursing home. The son lost his mother, Charu that rare commodity, a loving mother-in-law, and young Tanu his 'bank', but Mr Niyogi as good as forfeited his life. The shock of her absence was simply too much to bear for this retired Don of literature, late of Patna University. Keats and his 'Ode to a Nightingale' became his theme. He lost his will to live and wished each night that life should curl up into an iron ball and roll out of him. Old Mr Niyogi, to whom once Byron was the greatest of all the Romantics, and whose reading of *Don Juan* was attended by packed classrooms, young men and women imbibing from his lips the vitality which flowed from

Byron to him in a continuous stream, now only had ears for the tender strains of the ever-melancholic Keats. In Keats' lush, lachrymose lines, his loneliness found a voice and in the evenings he invariably sat with a volume of the great man's poems. He did not venture out anymore. Sometimes he would go to the marketplace but even so little an exertion would put him out of breath. He did not say much to anyone but they all watched his condition with growing trepidation. Hriday and Charu would relay to each other their growing fear ('Baba is literally willing himself to die.') every night but even after discussing the conundrum for the whole night, no solution would be forthcoming at dawn.

Tanu too watched his dadu with curiosity and could not fathom how so much effervescence could suddenly retract into a tower of silence. He did not like this silent, morose dadu, who would not even discuss with him the ever-fluctuating fortunes of the Indian cricket team or the latest catchy Hindi film song or whether his English 'miss' was prettier than Kajol. While the earlier dadu … ah, he was something else. He was fun. But even Tanu would sometimes catch the sadness in the air and on those days he would not go out to play but sit with his dadu quietly. He prayed that his dadu would return to his old playful persona. He prayed that his grandfather would smile again. And he said to God one day in exasperation, 'Just make him snap out of it, will you? Enough is enough!'

But it is never enough. Mr Niyogi could not get enough of sadness. He did not pity himself, he did not damn God but he did crave for ever more sadness. He punished himself for all the happiness that had come his way and he wanted his body and mind purged of all the laughter, the good times, love, the memory of his wife, her voice, her smell, her body.

The epicure started starving himself. He started keeping random fasts. He abstained from his mandatory glass of scotch which earlier Mrs Niyogi used to fix for him every evening before dinner. He threw away all the pouches of expensive pipe tobacco that Hriday regularly brought for him, and, on top of it all, one day he even stopped eating fish! He pushed the dish away from himself with a feeble hand; the sight of the clean white flesh in a rich yellow gravy of mustard made his face visibly pale with nausea. Charu could not stop her tears, Hriday just shook his head very slowly, and Tanu's chin hit his chest in a downward curve and stayed there for the rest of the meal.

The memory of Mrs Niyogi clung to him like a fine mist. He never could shake out of it, it chilled his spirit of all vitality but it was also a comfort to him in a languishing sort of way. He remembered the time he first saw her, on their wedding night, in the mandap, realizing how tiny and fragile she was, like a bird made of porcelain. Her eyes, kohl-rimmed, looking up at his with a bold impishness and her muffled cries of pain as they made love for the first time. The pain of his penetration brought tears to Mr Niyogi's eyes forty-five years later. Back then it had only brought pleasure.

His hair started thinning over the top, making his pink scalp peek out in despair. The skin too looked thin and papery and one day he asked Hriday to bring him a good walking stick.

At night when all were asleep he would close his room, remove all his clothes and stand nude before Mrs Niyogi's dressing table and look at his reflection with a critic's eye. He would then run his hand over his now sunken belly, the thin, hairless legs, over the muscles that had lost their definition, the hollow cheeks, and wrinkled neck, the spare pubic hair, and would cup his balls, the size of grapes, hanging loose in their wafer-thin sacs, almost transparent and he would look with profound satisfaction at the startling metamorphosis he had achieved in only a couple of months' time. He would then intone loudly. 'At my back I always hear time's winged chariot hurrying near,' and wake Hriday and Charu sleeping in the next room, without fail.

He never used the walking stick. It remained propped against the dressing table and once in a while Mr Niyogi would pick it up and swing it around like a sword when he thought no one was looking, but twice Tanu caught him and promptly reported the matter to Charu, who thought wisely of saying nothing to her husband. It seemed that some amount of vanity still remained embedded in the old bones. Thus all was not lost. Till there is vanity, there is hope.

Six months after the death things began to change. The weather started to clear. Life still seemed like a burden to Mr Niyogi, but he had started reading the cricket scores again. He started talking with Tanu again and would listen patiently to his animated patter about school life.

When his old cronies would come, he would not shoo them away like before but offer them tea and sympathy and listened to their cynical diatribes about family life. Scotch and tobacco were still taboo. Ditto with fish.

Then one day in the afternoon, for the first time in so many months, he went up the staircase to the roof of his apartment building. When Mrs Niyogi had been alive, they had always strolled together, hand in hand, the old lady chirping away continuously, each evening.

That day as he walked out into the open air, he felt fresh and clean and was not thinking about his beloved anymore. He was not thinking about anything. He felt at ease with the world and miraculously that did not make him feel guilty. He stopped by the side of the flower pots and looked at the flowers in full bloom, the marigolds, the daisies, the dahlias and some long-stemmed burgundy roses, and they gave him the same lush pleasure as before. He walked around, looking at the neighbouring buildings, the diminutive people walking on the streets below and suddenly he noticed a familiar figure in the corner on the other side of the apartment building.

It was young Tanu, totally lost in himself, looking at something with rapt attention on the other side, over the edge, standing a little away from the railing. Mr Niyogi was surprised to see Tanu because by that time, usually, he was out playing cricket in the park.

Intrigued, he too went and stood behind Tanu and peered over the edge. The boy did not notice anything, such was his concentration. In the next building, inside a top-floor bathroom, a magnificent young woman was taking a shower. Her strong, firm flesh seemed moulded out of white porcelain. The sight of it was like a hot white light in Mr Niyogi's eyes. It blinded him for a second. His faculties starved so long for beauty were sharper now for neglect. Like an adolescent he felt as if he had discovered the beauty of the female form for the first time in his life.

Then memory fed him the sensual images of his beloved, which he had denied himself for so long. The image and the reality collapsed into one another and became one. For a second, he felt like a dirty old man but the next moment he felt gloriously alive and strangely enough, in a flash, a line from a classic Jibanananda Das poem came to his lips in a silent prayer: '… and a touch of peace came to me/once the tiredest of all men/the gift of a village-girl of Natore/Banalata Sen.' He watched her for some time in complete silence and then he gently tapped the kid on the shoulder.

'Do you know who that is, son?' And Tanu, startled, red-faced, looked at his grandfather in fear, sure now that he was in the worst jam of his short career as a bird-watcher.

'I do not know what you are talking about.' He tried to get away but Mr Niyogi caught him and made him look at the girl again, now towelling herself in a languid manner. 'The girl, look at the girl, do you know her name? Because if you do not, you must.' And Mr Niyogi laughed his full-throated laughter for the first time in months.

'No, I do not know her name,' Tanu said, eyes downcast, still red-faced.

'She is Banalata Sen, my son. She is Banalata Sen.'

'Come on, dadu, she is not a Bengali, she is Dolly Makhija, my friend Andy's sister.' Tanu tried to put the matter straight.

'So, you do know her name?'

'The whole colony does,' Tanu replied, making his stand clear.

'No more of this from tomorrow, one must take one's cricket seriously.'

'Yes, dadu, but you won't tell ma, will you?'

'Of course not,' Mr Niyogi said and gave Tanu a reassuring wink.

And Tanu made a mental note to congratulate God on a job well done.

Hand in hand grandfather-grandson walked down the stairs to the flat, where Tanu started practising square cuts in front of the mirror.

Mr Niyogi lit his pipe, put the volume of Keats back into the almirah and took out his much-thumbed copy of *Don Juan* and held its brittle sepia-toned pages to the light which suddenly seemed to have flooded the room.

River of Dreams

I am going back. I can't work anymore. Each day it is getting harder and harder to breathe. All the fields must be green and really beautiful by now and the sweet scent of rain and soft kneaded black soil would be in the air and the small ponds all filled up and the canals too, and I know, right this moment, all of them are snaking in and diving and splashing like silver-brown fishes in the water, playing with the dung-encrusted buffaloes who roam near the water banks of the pond and a little later when the sun goes down and the pale moon comes to watch over us, they will be near the railway tracks throwing pebbles and running alongside the evening trains which pass through the village like strangers, without a sideways glance or a tender smile, in complete detachment born of rapid monotonous motion.

I wish I was with them, near the tracks. The tracks feel so cool and lonely in the evenings, and when you put your ear to it you can hear the rumblings of its ancient soul echoing the future that will be past us in a few quick minutes. My mother would be making the evening meal in front of our hut, her head covered with her sari and bent over the stove and smoke from the dungfuel making her eyes burn. Every once in a while she will wipe her watery eyes and stare into the disappearing darkness and call breathlessly, 'Ram, Ram, Ram, come home, son.'

Ram came to work for us about four or five months back and for days I barely noticed him. He was of a very slight build, very quiet and used to jump when the phone rang. Later on when I came to know that he was fourteen years old, I was surprised; he didn't look more than ten or eleven to me. I guess something deep inside him was pulling him down, wasn't allowing him to grow. He was thin, really thin, all his ribs could be counted easily, but he ate okay, in fact he ate too much and his hair stood on his head like spikes on a steel coatbrush, and one more thing, he barely ever smiled. His uncle who was two or three years older than me and worked for us for a long time and was now married with two kids of his own, brought Ram to our place because, I guess, they really needed the money and feeding him in the village was burning a big hole in their budget. But he refused to do any work. 'He roams around the village like an idiot and his mother fears that he will drown one day or be crushed under some speeding train,' his uncle informed my mother. This uncle of Ram is a real piece of work. Around the same time, the plague scare broke out all over Patna and do you know what he did? Of course you don't. He tied an old tomcat on a string and went visiting the scared rich all over town to ferret out rats and kill them for a fee—and you now what? I think he carried with himself a ready supply of rats too, caught from the gutters! He is one hell of an enterprising man. He charged Rs 25 per kill and in a week he had made over a thousand in cold hard cash. Now they are saying it wasn't caused by the rats at all, but as far as Munna (Ram's uncle) is concerned, the plague was just fine; it should come at least once each year.

At Rs 500 a month, Ram was taken in and his job was to clean, wash and dust, help Mother with the cooking and generally do everything that was asked of him. He barely said anything ever, and whenever he did it was with such a thick 'over the Ganges' accent that it was hard to make out what he said anyway. Everything surprised him: the phone, the doorbell, the elevator, which I suppose was the only thing that really delighted him in those first few weeks, and he would go up and down and up again and press all the buttons and be generally happy in that enclosed area of his freedom. But then one day another small servant of a neighbouring flat in our building got stuck in the elevator and after that everybody became apprehensive. What if their own beautiful brat-angels got stuck instead? I am sure the thought must have pierced their hearts like a sabre. So a 'bill' was passed that no small children or servants should use the elevator unchaperoned. So that was that, but a ride in the elevator till the end remained a thing of wonder and joy for Ram. The TV became another of his pleasures and after finishing work and later on even between chores, he would go and sit in front of the screen and watch everything with a brightness in his eyes that was missing at other times, and sometimes in the silence of the afternoon when everything would be still in the oppressive heat of Patna, I would catch him sitting cross-legged and solemn in front of the unlit TV, on the screen nothing except a thin film of dust—totally blank—but there Ram would be sitting like the proverbial Buddha under the bodhi tree. I just couldn't figure it out.

In the afternoon my friends would come and then we would all go out barefoot into the fields of mustard, feeling the moist black soil with our soles, wading through acres of the green-yellow land and on to the canal where we would ride the bullocks into the muddy waters and then dive with eyes closed and long fingers clasping the nose and sink down into the brown spreading softness. They will laugh at me if they ever find out what I really do out here; if they ever find out that I wash and clean the clothes and do the cooking like the girls instead of working as a fruitseller as I have told them, I will die of shame. I won't ever go back to the village but what will I do? I can't stay here, I can't even breathe this foul air, sometimes when I breathe I can't even exhale, the air inside contracting my lungs, choking me. I can't sleep and all night the wheel turns overhead and one day it will fall ...

One day, a week or two after his arrival, I noticed him picking up the phone as it rang and after a few seconds he hurriedly put it down as if it were some repulsive reptile. I was surprised that he had even picked up the phone because he wasn't supposed to, but on the other hand, I had always noticed the expression of intense curiosity on his face whenever it would ring. 'What happened, Ram?' I called out to him. He turned towards me slowly, his eyes were again their dull, fused-bulb selves, but his mouth was slightly open, his nostrils flared and the hair on his head stood like millions of bright black needles. He looked positively angry. 'What happened? Why did you –'

'He knows me, he calls out to me,' he said slowly and I realized then that he wasn't angry or anything but just confused and perhaps a little scared that a strange green contraption could curl up around your ear like a snake and blow weird sounds from nothingness like 'Hello, Ram?' Later when the phone rang again, I came to know that Father had called up from his office, and recognizing Ram's voice, had uttered his name and Ram had put the receiver down; even my father was confused. He thought maybe he had got the wrong number. I tried in vain to explain the way the phone works to Ram but something told me, perhaps the look of total distrust in his eyes, that he wasn't much convinced—he probably thought it was possessed by the devil or something. He didn't go near the phone for a long time after that. But he smartened up quickly and would spend much time in front of the mirror trying to flatten his punk hairdo, much to my mother's exasperation. My mother found him to be infinitely lazy—his ability to do nothing all day was just awesome—and she was right too, because he was always listless and would dust a single stretch of window panes for hours or at any given opportunity disappear into the toilet and stay there for half an hour at a stretch. God knows what he did in there! No amount of scolding could make him see the light. He would, in the evening, stand in the balcony and stare at the stretching sky and keep on staring, his long fingers gripping the iron railing, though, mind you, sometimes the sky would be as bare, starless, devoid of light as the unlit TV set. But he would still keep on staring at it, charting, perhaps, the course of his uncertain life through the unknown sky. Some people wish upon a star but maybe his dreams were hinged on nothingness or maybe he just didn't have anything better to do. But at those times I almost admired him, his innate ability to stay aloof from everything, although deep down inside I just couldn't figure him out. I was four years elder to him and on a whim I tried to make him study. He was literate, he knew the alphabets all right, he could write his own name but his interest died right there. Language, literature, education, were no use for him, as far as he was concerned. It was futile trying to educate him. He would look listless and one day he literally dozed off right in the middle of a lesson—so much for education and my humble efforts. But Ram was all right in a way, I guess. Once he caught me smoking in my room. Well, he didn't catch me or anything but he just barged into my room (he didn't care much about knocking), and there I was, sprawled on my bed with pillows stacked high, celebrating my few hours of freedom (my parents had gone to a party), the stereo blowing 'River of Dreams' and smoke slowly curling away from the cigarette in my hand, but I made him promise not to tell and he kept the promise. He had come in because he liked the song, he informed me and stood there listening to Billy Joel's sweet cool voice, and when the song ended he went away, without a backward glance. He had integrity I must admit, and in return I would turn on the TV for him when there was no one at home.

Here at night even the stars don't shine. They are like small bulbs in the sky which go on and off in the darkness but in my village the stars look so big and bright and happy watching over us and showing us the way through the fields and into woods, shining through the yellow-green leaves of the mango trees, but here all is indifference; even the moon forgets to look beautiful and comes out unwashed and ugly. At nights I lie awake in the darkness and hear frogs croaking near the pond and the sweet night sounds of my village, which lull me to sleep sometimes, but when dawn arrives I am still here, trapped, and there is no escape.

Sometimes I would send him out to fetch me cigarettes and he would dash off in a hurry as if he were a mouse released from the mousetrap and I would watch him from the balcony, negotiate his way cautiously through the heavy afternoon traffic, Ram slow and diffident amidst the rush, his walk incongruous on the hot black coal-tar-paved street, his feet going clomp clomp clomp as if he were walkingon the soft mud soil of the wet rice fields of his beloved village (whose beauty he sometimes described to me) instead. I guess I had won his trust and I trusted him too so it came as a real shock when he finally did what he did.

Everything is slipping away slowly from my memory and like the train slowly leaving the station and people receding into the background like trivial dots, I am slipping away, going down into the darkness; my home, my mother, the little lemon shrub which my father had planted before he went away, everything is slowly slipping away like these delicate white teacups that I am rinsing under the tap; they too float away and crash and burn, shatter in the sink of my dreams. Did you hear the crash? Tell me can you listen to my heart. CAN YOU HEAR AT ALL, ANSWER ME, YOU …

A couple of weeks back I reached home around eight in the evening after hanging out with my friends for a few hours at the marketplace, smoking and telling jokes and whistling at the girls, and they looking at us with their shining eyes from beneath their eyelashes, appearing cool and unaffected, generally having a great time. The backslapping, eye-winking, elbow-nudging rites of our innocence. I am at my happiest when I am with my friends doing what everyone else is doing—nothing. My mother and a lady who lives in the flat across were standing outside our flat. Mother looked a bit flustered to me. 'He is not opening the door,' my mother said to me.

'Who's inside?'

'Why do you always ask such foolish questions, Ritwik? Ram is not opening the door.'

'Why?'

'Why? I don't know why.'

'What happened really?'

'Half an hour ago I went to the terrace and told him to lock the door and that I would be back soon and now he is not opening the door and he has got the TV on too.'

My mother was correct, as usual. I could hear the faint strains of wild guitar riffs coming from inside and started to bang on the door loudly but to no avail.

'He is insolent and lazy; he just won't listen to anything I say. Today he also broke my precious tea set, all the twelve cups and saucers. I just could not believe it and last week he smashed my flower vase; this is deliberate cruelty. I got angry and really scolded him hard but he just stood there like a tomcat, indolent and slouching. I don't know what to do with him and now he is sitting in there, watching TV,' my mother said to the lady who wagged her head in a dutiful manner.

'He is watching MTV.'

'Does it matter what he is watching, Ritwik? I have been standing outside for the past ten minutes, so do something constructive for the first time in your life.' My mother was all worked up and I was getting a bit worried too. Strange thoughts started coming to my head. What if he smashed my stereo or tore apart all my precious books out of rancour? God, I would die. I loved my stereo. Or maybe my stash of *Fantasy*, *Debonair*, *Fun*, which he knew I kept underneath the mattress. Oh my god, what to do? I rang the bell and kept it pressed till it ran out of steam and whined faintly.

'Perhaps he has hurt himself,' the lady suggested to my mother.

Now my mother was really worried. Other people, neighbours and assorted strangers, started showing their really concerned faces around our door and advice started pouring in like thick raindrops.

I went downstairs and called my father. The matter was getting out of control and I realized I was no good in a crisis. I am a civilian, I belong in peacetime. My father said he would rush back quickly, returned within twenty minutes, and by that time mother was reduced to tears and I don't know why some of the other ladies too were dabbing their eyes with their hankies. Some children and a small dog were also there, playing and howling (the brats were playing and the dog was howling), and I almost lost my mind and for the first time in my life I felt my brain melt and evaporate into nothingness. I felt so empty that I stopped sensing anything and just went and sat down on the stairs—detached from the chaos, staring at the dog. He was a small brown mongrel with a real sweet-sad expression on his face. Perhaps he was going crazy too. I am sure even he wasn't there of his own accord and like myself would have much preferred to have been elsewhere—anywhere else in fact. My father suggested we break open the door and everybody enthusiastically consented. Somehow we managed to break it open and my father and I rushed inside. Everything was still and silent and dark as no light was on anywhere except for a thin ray of light that came from the sitting room mixed with faint echoes of rock music. We pushed open the door. At first we couldn't see anything as the room was dark and the only light that came was from the flickering TV screen. Ram was lying on the carpet face upwards, staring steadily into nothingness. There was no movement in his body and for a second I thought that he was dead. He turned his head slowly towards us, saw us, and I am sure we must have looked pretty ridiculous standing there. Then he started laughing, really wild and out of control. I tried to calm him down, before my father did something terrible to him, but he hit me across my face and grabbed me. There was so much strength in those thin arms; a low scream like a call of a trapped small animal in great pain came out of him and big tears came streaming down his face. Father tried to free us but he just hung on to me by my shirtfront and in the end my new t-shirt was ripped to pieces. I looked into his eyes for the last time. He was sent away right then and there with our driver back to his village.

Why did he do it? He had everything here. I mean, I just couldn't understand it at the time. A week later Munna came by, said he was sad but that everything would be all right and the very next day he brought another of his protégés; this time a cousin of his. So everything is fine now and life goes on as usual. Everybody acts as if nothing has happened and I guess it is fine by me too. But still when I am alone sometimes, sitting and brooding in my room at night, I can feel his long fingers grabbing and tearing my t-shirt and the look in his eyes, a look of rage mixed with helplessness, anger dipped in tears, a kind of betrayal, yes, that's what it was, the look of complete betrayal—that shrill, low scream of pain violates my ears like thin, sharp needles and goes on and on and on until I can't take it anymore. I crawl on my knees to my stereo and put on some rock music and pump up the volume to the limit to drown out his scream and more often than not I play 'River of Dreams'.

Diksha at St. Martin's

Let me warn you at the outset: Scorsese to me is God. A tiny (five-foot-nothing) private God whose image I carry locked in my heart, ready for impromptu worship anywhere at the drop of a cigarette butt. He is my own private personal Ganesh. The conflict-ridden God of both good and bad tidings. A source of hope and inspiration at all times.

Growing up in the late eighties in the tough Bihari-Bengali neighbourhood of Kadam Kuan, Patna, I saw *Mean Streets* for the first time and immediately recognized those streets, the milieu, those small time 'wiseguys', to be mine. The streets, galis and nukkads of Little Italy, New York, seemed superimposed on the parallel ones of Kadam Kuan. So that afternoon, at age fourteen, I got my 'diksha' from St. Martin in a rickety, scabrous illegal video parlour with wooden schoolroom benches to sit on and such poor acoustics that one never got the dialogues ever. In time one learnt to lip-read or perchance blessed with imagination, made up the dialogues oneself. I had simply learnt to switch off my ears whenever I went there and in a sense all the movies I saw there were silent ones. Only the images remained stuck to my mind like postage stamps. So only 'moving pictures', which actually 'moved', had any impact in such trying circumstances. Merchant-Ivory could have died and gone to heaven and nobody there would have noticed. Ditto with St. Martin's *The Age of Innocence* (1993), one of the few chipped clay toes of my God.

Fifteen minutes into the movie and the audience had thinned out. Most of the 'gentry', cursing Ghosh-da for showing a movie which was 'ekdam faltu' (meaning nobody yet had fucked their brains out on the screen), had walked out. It was a miracle Ghosh-da didn't get shot; people had died for much less in Kadam Kuan. For Ghosh-da it was the year of living dangerously and the very next week he showed *Apocalypse Now*! God bless him. The video parlour closed down the next year and Ghosh-da opened a 'Chinize' food joint which the 'gentry' again ruined for him by congregating there each evening. He now runs a cyber café at the same spot.

As for *Mean Streets*, for the first time in my life I was watching something close to my own reality (perhaps at that very moment a young boy in Bolton or Vermont watching the *Apu* trilogy was feeling the same way) and which from cinema I had never got before. From the opening drum beats of the Ronettes' 'Be My Baby' to the shootout at the end (Scorsese himself putting in a cameo as the diminutive hitman Shorty). It was the attitude that said 'coolness is all' which grabbed me by my bandana (I was a frightful little punk in those days) and dragged me into a world so unlike my own, yet so recognizable and immediate. The petty crooks and extortionists, the grassroot-level political activists, small-time scamsters and dreamers, the camaraderie and the little betrayals. People getting born and dying in the same place, never venturing out beyond a thirty-minute radius around their homes in their entire lives. The quiet desperation of young men with limited education and choices for whom aping the ways and lifestyle of a mythic local 'Rangbaz' of the moment seemed infinitely more profitable than finishing college and getting jobs. Well, there were not many jobs in Patna anyway. For them, a simple nod from that selfsame Rangbaz, something or the other 'da', would make their days completely memorable. That nod would give them identity and add swagger to their walk. After the nod would come a pat on the back, next the handshake, and the katta would change hands. A diksha of a different kind. There would be no going back then. Their glory would last a few months, a year at the most till some younger kid with more desperation and less to lose would come and end their misery. A single shot at the back of the head while pissing at the street corner, one warm Sunday evening.

The Godfather was mythology. This was real life. The garish orangeish-red lights of the nightclubs and the intensity of the fistfights, which actually looked like fistfights, not some synchronized ballet where the people had hands which were 'open' (haanth khola) and actually took their time, aimed and hit the face. The thing about a fight is that you must always hit first, your hands shouldn't ever be like those of Hamlet's (they must be open and quick), because in a little while (a minute), people could come and try to break up the fight anyway. Never slap because that wouldn't do any damage, adding to the fact that it would be an insult, making it more dangerous in the long run. Also do not call anyone a 'mook'. Ever. The suddenness of the fights erupting over trivial matters, the macho honour thing over somebody's sister (Ritwik's fucking her, I want my share too. Fuck Ritwik.), over street corners (I saw Ritwik pissing against your pole. Fuck Ritwik.), over a cup of tea, or not being offered a Charminar gratis by the paanwallah (Fuck Ritwik anyway!).

Instant connection. In Johnny boy's (Robert De Niro) almost psychotic irresponsibility I could see the reflection of a childhood friend who even then I knew would turn out to be trouble (he was shot a couple of years later while grabbing booths, by the police in Danapore). Birju survived but now has one foot a couple of inches shorter than the other and which he props up like a trophy on a table which is kept especially for him in front of the cyber café, as each evening he holds forth on the future course of Lalooland. The boys who sit listening to him awestruck, staring enviously at the stump ordering tea and Charminar, get younger and younger each year. They graduate and go away but my friend sits there each evening, reworking his stories, finding new narratives, adding lines, deleting some, his only concern being: 'Will it be good for Charminars and a cup of tea next season when the new batch enrolls?' Diksha again. But perhaps then he sees his stump, pats it lovingly and feels reassured. Like a beggar he knows the stump is his meal ticket. Until the day a man with an eyepatch as well as a gimp fades in through the mist, my friend needn't lose his sleep.

If *The Godfather* (1972) in an ironic way was about family values, then *Mean Streets* (1973) set a couple of decades later is about the neighbourhood, the 'mohallah' or 'para', a tale of growing up, a tale of friendships, of not fucking up, about survival and responsibility, an intensely autobiographical movie, which Pauline Kael in her landmark review, furthering the cause of the yet unknown Scorsese, called 'a triumph of personal film-making'. In a mohallah, one is responsible for everything, for oneself, for the family, for friends, because there is no getting away from it. It is part of the culture. One imbibes it just by breathing. It is like living in a constant fish bowl. The individual doesn't matter, the community or the group does. Charlie (Harvey Keitel), weighed down by Catholic guilt (incidentally Scorsese wanted to become a priest when he was in his teens), realizes that. He can't disown his friend (though conventional wisdom suggests he should) Johnny boy, even though he knows that the kid is bad news, will foul up big and get him into even more trouble and jeopardize all his plans of upward mobility. But one doesn't abandon a friend because he will bring trouble (friends are bound to do that anyway). The code doesn't allow that. One is implicated by association. Look what happened to poor George (not of the Jungle but from a similar place). There is no getting away from it. Charlie knows it and he realizes that Johnny boy is his responsibility and he has to look out for him. Johnny is one of those 18-till-I-die fellows who, in all the time they are alive, cause any manner of trouble for all concerned. We have all had friends or relatives like that, and there is little one can do about it except hope for the best, that he will settle down after marriage and instead wreck some poor, simple-minded young woman's life who has had the singular misfortune of getting hitched to him. Generally, it has been noted, things work out fine after that.

Charlie is answerable for Johnny boy's refusal to pay back Michael the loanshark (Richard Romanus in a standout performance), and in the end will pay dearly for it. Johnny will never realize it and if he survives, would do the same thing again. Like the scorpion he just can't change his nature. He has no sense of responsibility and is the eternal younger brother. In many ways, it is the story of two brothers, with all its attendant jealousies, rivalries, concern and care. A theme to which Scorsese would return again in *Raging Bull* (1980), in his portrayal of the La Motta brothers (Joe Pesci and De Niro) and in *Casino* (1996) where Ace Rothstein (De Niro) and Nicky Santoro (Pesci) play childhood-friends-turned-enemies. If Charlie and Johnny boy survive into maturity, they will perhaps turn into Rothstein and Santoro of the later movie. The one always in control, the other unpredictable and violent. Women are incidental in most Scorsese movies, notable exceptions being *Alice Doesn't Live Here Anymore* (1979) and *The Age of lnnocence* (1993), and one more chipped clay toe *New York, New York* (1977). What they do is basically light the fuse. Cathy Moriarty's bitch goddess in *Raging Bull*, Betsy (Cybil Shepard) the uptown cock-tease in *Taxi Driver* (1976), and the confused high-class hooker Ginger

(Sharon Stone) of *Casino.* Even in *Mean Streets*, the one woman character, Charlie's epileptic girlfriend Teresa (Amy Robinson), is under-fleshed, though she brings out the tender side of Charlie's personality and whom he will probably give up because, according to the resident wise guy Uncle Giovanni (Cesare Denova), she is not right 'in the head', thus cursed by God and what's more? 'Honourable men should go with honourable men.' Marrying her wouldn't further Charlie's ambition of breaking into the inner circle of the mafia and becoming a 'made guy'.

Charlie is in many ways a conformist, alternatively heroic and weak, an upwardly mobile lower-middle-class man who just wants enough so he can live with dignity and enter his own home justified each night to a loving wife and a bambino or two. In the end he too wants to settle down, to put down roots and be a perfect representative of the bourgeoisie and attend PTA meetings.

Years later, just before he got shot and acquired legendary status, Birju Pandey and I were sitting in a tea shop near Hathwa Market, eyeing the girls, when suddenly he had a Joycean epiphany as an exquisitely beautiful girl in a chiffon sari chattering in Bengali passed us by with her mother. Pandey turned and looked at me and said, 'You know what I really want in life? I want a wife who goes to kitty parties.' He could have been joking but I wouldn't put my money on it. Like his brethren in Little Italy, he too knew that the inherent futility of dreams shouldn't ever stop one from dreaming them.

It is not an easy movie to watch. You can't do it while flipping a magazine or having 'Chinize' food. Scorsese isn't Spielberg.

He demands your undivided attention and more often than not you give it willingly. Those who can't, have no option but to leave, like all those friends and neighbours of mine who had walked into the showing of *Mean Streets* thinking it to be an 'adult movie'. Unfortunately they were all underage. I was to witness a similar situation in Delhi in 1996 during a matinee of *Casino* at Priya. There were a lot of miffed girlfriends angrily sucking on a soda during intermission while the boyfriends looked funked out, not knowing what had hit them. Scorsese is bit of an endurance test; moreover, he doesn't take kindly to ignorance. Now a word of advice: If you are going out to pay your respect to St. Martin, leave the girlfriend at the altar. She might love the movie (a long shot), but on the other hand, why take the chance? The saint ain't easy on relationships either. He is married five times over and probably still hasn't got it right. Two more and Liz Taylor would start feeling threatened. While De Niro's high-octane portrayal is something to behold (Coppola saw this performance during post-production and immediately cast De Niro as the calm and controlled Vito Corleone in *The Godfather II* (1974), which incidentally won him a best supporting actor Oscar), Keitel, another Scorsese regular (he has made six movies with him right from the time of Scorsese's first feature *Who is That Knocking at My Door* (1968)), is dignified, compassionate and in the end heroic, anchoring the screenplay with his presence and giving it the requisite solidity. De Niro's is the explosive, flashier performance but it is Harvey Keitel, aka Mr *Bad Lieutenant* (another gem of a movie with strong Catholic overtones), who is the actual revelation of the film. The screenplay by Scorsese and Mardik Martin is as tightly sewn as a baseball and the influence of its 'chatty' style on Tarantino's *Pulp Fiction* (1994) is all too evident. *Mean Streets* was the breakthrough movie for all three concerned, Scorsese, De Niro and Keitel, and made their bones and their reputations in Hollywood.

As I walked out drenched in sweat from the parlour in the evening, the shirt unbuttoned, the bandana around my neck dripping wet, I probably looked like someone who had just run a marathon and still had the crazy bright gleam in the eye, testosterone kicking in constantly. In many ways, that afternoon I had run a marathon of the mind and had left my surroundings, my friends, far behind. The video parlour had a tin roof. A hot tin roof. I was the cat who jumped off it and kept on moving, past my friends at the park playing cricket, past some '-das' at the teashop, who as usual called after me but I didn't hear them anymore. I had switched off my ears again. Years later when I was eighteen and had suddenly decided to be a writer, I would write my first short story with St. Martin as a motif, which the *Sunday Observer* in 1993 serialized for six weeks. The story was called 'Any Fan of Martin Scorsese is a Friend of Mine', and you know what, mate, the title still holds true.

Acknowledgements

I would like to thank the editors of *Debonair*, *The Brown Critique* and the *Tehelka Literary Review*, where most of these stories in a slightly altered form were first published.

To my parents for their unflinching support to a wayward son.

My brother Sanjay for keeping a well-stocked bar. My sister-in-law for letting me use it.

My young philanthropic nephew Sreyash for finally deciding not to feed the manuscript to the neighbour's Doberman Pinscher.

In the end, Pragya—muse, lover, comrade, wife—for believing all my lies.

Patna Roughcut

To my parents

Contents

Kadam Kuan, Patna

Dreams are like cut-glass carafes. They are fragile and expensive and they disintegrate at the very first impact with cold reality but cut-glass carafes only look beautiful on the sideboards of the rich because if a particular dream suddenly shatters, they can always buy another. The poor shouldn't dream. They can't afford it.

Even Harryda couldn't afford the price of his dreams but then he never let a small thing like that deter him from dreaming. He once said to me that he used to see his dreams in technicolour, the garish bright colours would suffuse his mind with larger than life images, like on a 70 mm cinemascope screen, and in the morning he would wake up all fresh and cool as if he had just walked out of Mona Talkies after the latest showing of his favourite spaghetti western *Once Upon a Time in the West.* Personally I have never known the colours of my dreams but then probably they are in black and white anyway.

My name is Ritwik Ray and I am a reporter with the Patna edition of a national daily. I am of average height, average looks, the hairline receding at the forehead from the sides makes me look older than I am. I am not one of those big shot political analysts and investigative reporters who ferret out important things about life and corruption. I write about minor cultural happenings around town and if Patna had a vibrant cocktail circuit I would be what you call a society reporter. A page three hack. I also write about old buildings and minor historical sights around town, landmarks of forgotten glory. Sometimes I do human interest stories like the one I did last month about a young man from Madhubani, a carpenter by caste who was found dead inside Golghar, a huge black pyramid-like structure built by the British to store foodgrains by the side of the Ganges and now one of the few tourist sites in town. A huge coiled staircase runs the full length of the outer walls, right to the top, and from where one can have a bird's-eye view of the entire city.

The body, in a highly decomposed state, was found inside the granary during one of the periodic inspections. The face and neck had been picked clean by the rats but from a letter found by his side, the story came to light. It was a suicide note, which stated that he was going to take his life by jumping from the top of Golghar, as his wife of two months had been abducted by her parents. She was a Bhumihar and of the upper castes and they didn't approve of her marrying a backward. He had lodged an FIR, made the rounds of politicians, but nothing much had come of it. Now in desperation he was going to end his life. No doubt a familiar story in Bihar. But he never got to the top of the staircase and how he got inside the locked granary, unused for years, remains a mystery. A marriage certificate perfectly folded in four was also found amidst puddles of rat piss.

I also write short stories on the side and fancy myself as some kind of a writer. My stories, mostly autobiographical, are about the minor characters of my childhood and adolescence who sometimes drop by unannounced in my dreams and want to have their stories told. The stories rarely get published and earlier it didn't bother me. I was happy that I could write them in the first place. Ambition has never been one of my strong points. 'Watching the Wheels' is my theme song. But lately I have begun to despair and almost in tandem Harryda started appearing in my dreams. He fades in through the mist and walks towards me with his sunken face, thinning hair, maroon terylene bush shirt and white gabardine bell-bottoms with 34-inch mohri, frayed at the knees but clean and creased and the black patent leather pumps (smuggled from Kathmandu in the seventies) gleaming in the sunlight, and he raises his hand in salute and with a flourish touches two fingers to the forehead and whispers, 'Hello Ritwik, life's wonderful, isn't it?', and then he fades out, stylish to the end. I wake up then.

Harryda or Harvinder Rai was a central figure of my childhood and adolescence and in many ways his story is irretrievably linked with mine. So, dear reader, here it goes.

Last year, after my master's from Delhi, I returned home to Patna with a job waiting for me at the newspaper office. Since I had a job so early suddenly I was somebody worth knowing in Kadam Kuan, where nobody starts working until he is at least twenty-eight. When he reaches thirty he gets married and by thirty-two he starts having the mandatory kids and settles down. It is a set pattern and very few digress from it. But the funny part is that even if given an option nine out of ten neighbours of mine would choose this 'settled' life over anything else. The first twenty-eight years of their lives they while away amidst laughter, cricket, razor-blade fights, heartbreak, harsh Charminar smoke, Old Monk with Thums Up and half-chais each evening at the eternal adda at Annapoorna Café run by Sanyalda by the side of the now defunct offices of the *Magadh Times*.

So, one evening after I was at home for a couple of days, I walked towards Annapoorna Café which had been my haunt too for a year or so before my father packed me off to Delhi. Since Delhi and Patna are twin cities, separated by 500 miles, it was as if I had never left the place. The weather was identical and so were the names of the old localities. All those Ganjs, Dariya, Sultan, Andrews and Baker. The only difference being while Patna had Baghs like Kankar and Gardani the big brother had Gardens like Dilshad and Rajouri. Since both were imperial towns of yore on whose fertile fields the fate of India had been decided many times, the public utility system was of the utmost importance. So while Delhi had grand-sounding Sarais like Kale Khan, Katwariya, Sheikh and, my favourite, Julena, Patna on the other hand had to make do with proletarian Kuans: Agam, Makhaniya and, of course, Kadam Kuan.

I was eager to meet all the characters, all the 'das' with whom I had spent most of my life playing cricket and eyeing the girls and eating bhog from the red clay chukkars sitting on square chowkis at Hriday Kutir during Durga Puja and catching up on the local gossip. I met Rajuda at the corner, a tall heavyset man who once opened the bowling for the Patna district team and still played for Patna College occasionally as a 'borrow' player. He waved to me and I waved back and walked towards the entrance where Paltu, Chotu and Sudama Pathak were laughing together and eyeing Smriti Sahay who was the youngest sister of their childhood friend Diwakar. The last time I had seen them, they were in navy blue half-pants, white terry-cotton shirts and Naughty Boy shoes. They lowered their Charminars when they saw me enter.

Sanyalda had grown balder and now was very fat and his belly hung over the tight belt like a sack of flour. 'Sanyalda, how are you?' I smiled and asked him in Bangla. He came around the counter, face lit by an artificial smile and hugged me.

'Saala, Ritwik you look so grown up and mature. I also hear that now you have a wonderful job too. You are now a writer, an intellectual. It is so hard to believe, seems only yesterday that you stood on this very same counter in your red nylon Muhammad Ali T-shirt and pissed all over. How verily time flies. You were an A-1 bichoo those days. Do you remember it?' Sanyalda's eyes got all misty as his decrepit mind took a detour through the dusty streets of nostalgia. 'How can I forget? The whole place stank for a week afterwards,' I replied, overcome by emotion in spite of myself.

Rajuda walked in with Rudrada and Sanjuda. All of them perennials at the Café right from the time I could first remember them. They were the stalwarts, pioneers who had opened the territory. They had kids, fat wives and the regulation beer belly. Though not necessarily in that order. The sight of Rajuda running in to bowl from the Aam Bagan end with his belly preceding him by a minute is something no one ever who has seen the spectacle will forget in a hurry. Most batsmen, mesmerized by the obscene undulations, would fail to offer a stroke and get clean bowled. Rajuda claimed that his open-chest action was modelled after Jeff Thomson's, a claim not entirely untrue but between Sydney and Kadam Kuan, Patna, kilometres of pace were mysteriously lost. Since Rajuda had never seen Thomson bowl and had copied his action from grainy photographs in *The Searchlight*, he usually ended up giving a rousing kick to the officiating umpire's backside at the point of delivery. After that inaugural kick, umpires literally gave him a wide berth for the rest of his spell.

'Look who is here, our very own Michael Madhusudan,' Sanyalda said to them. I cringed inwards but still I laughed. It was required. 'I met him at the corner, saala, he has become a total hero,' Rajuda said affectionately and patted me on the back.

'I am not a small-town boy anymore. Delhi-returned.' I played along with them.

'Yes, yes, here, have a Charminar, don't worry. We know you smoke and anyway now you have grown up, become a man. Fucked any Punjabans lately? It is rumoured that they like it up their arses? What with their huge backsides. Is it true? Don't look shocked. Sex is extremely important. Don't worry, you too will get your share, we all did. Just get married.' This was Rudrada, our resident Socrates. An arsehole by birth, a philosopher by conviction.

I lit up and dragged the vile smoke into my lungs and felt calm and satisfied.

The conversation veered towards the various 'happenings' which had occurred while I was away. Sutapa had run away with her chowkidar and they had got married in Nepal and when they came back after two months, broke and desperate, Samitda (Sutapa's elder brother) along with Rajuda and co. had beaten up the Gurkha so badly that they ran away together again. Chokon was moving up in life and had opened a beauty parlour where women cut men's hair and it was rumoured, for a few hundred rupees more, would also give a 'full body massage'. Prakash Singh's mother had died and Probirda's wife had tried to kill herself because she caught Probirda and the rich widow in whose house they lived rutting like dogs on her kantha bedcover one evening as she arrived early from the Ramakrishna Mission. Paplu's father (a drunk and a gambler) had run away for the tenth time. They found him in Bakhtiyarpur Station eating jalebis and looking very content with life. Rudrada's younger sister, who once upon a time Chokon claimed he had seen sucking Rudrada's cock, was getting married in November and I was invited and I must be there for the parivasan of course. Birju Pandey, my childhood playmate, had had his left foot shot off by the police while grabbing booths during a recent election and another childhood friend taking a diametrically different trajectory was now at Oxford on a scholarship reading politics. Then Rudrada laughed and said, 'Raju, you haven't told him the main news,' and sniggered some more.

'What news? Saving the best for the last?' I asked jocularly but a tinge of weariness had crept inadvertently into my voice. I knew what the main news would be like, some atrociously far-fetched gossip, like somebody's father caught humping somebody's aunt or if the imagination was as refined as Chokon's then it could even be the aunt's cocker spaniel. It could also be about some upcoming local lad with lots of 'daring' like Manager Sharma who had sliced a Marwari's ear off for asking payment for a suit length he had chosen, now out on bail.

Rajuda got the drift and he too laughed and said, 'And Harry got set.'

Harryda is working! After all these years? He said he would never work. A Harry Rai never works. I felt vaguely disappointed.

'No, no, I mean he is "set" for life. He died.' And then they exploded into another thunderclap of laughter and slapped each other's back.

'He was only thirty-six,' I said slowly, feeling hollow inside. Seeing the shock in my eyes they quietened down. The laughter slowly left their lips. They lowered their eyes and dragged on a Charminar.

Harryda was a man who loved style. The good things of life that a little money can provide. He believed that to be poor and to look poor were two different things and to look poor was a crime because the former condition one couldn't avoid but the latter could always be rectified provided one cared. Harryda cared. From childhood he had seen the disdain with which the rich treated the poor, the shabby and the weak and he didn't want any part of it. He knew he had more taste, intelligence and good looks than any of his Bengali-Bihari upper-class neighbours and he took a lot of pride in that. The rich might look down on him but their daughters would always look up to him as he stroked their hair. That was the equalizer. He probably thought of himself as a feudal lord or something. A fallen aristocrat, like Mrinal Thakur-Chowdhury, erstwhile zamindar from Manbhum and my next-door neighbour and kinsman. A lord without a paisa to call his own but a lord nevertheless. Having been born and raised in a place with such a rich feudal ambience, he couldn't have been anything but what he eventually turned out to be. He appropriated a dream that wasn't meant for him in the first place. Little by little it whittled him down to the one-note cultural joke he became at the end of his life. Right man, wrong dream.

He liked literature, music and beauty all around, good clothes and Hollywood movies, and he never worked for a living in his entire life. It wasn't as if he was inordinately lazy or a shirker but his dreams were just a tad too fragile and beautiful to include the harsh realities of a routine nine-to-five job. No one who is as poor as Harryda was can ever be lazy. Laziness is the prerogative of the rich. Many times in his life his friends, relatives and other good Samaritans of our locality got him a job or two. Sometimes as a salesman for unbreakable teacups, or as a helper in an antiquarian bookshop, proof-reader in a printing press and he left every one of those jobs within a week.

He once told me that something cold, pure and light inside his heart stopped him from working. It whispered to him never to despair. Things would get better, hope, like an open manhole, was just around the corner. One right step and everything would change. Just keep cutting the corners.

When Harryda was twelve years old his father, who was a small-time bookseller with artistic pretensions, suddenly left one day for Calcutta. There he married again and raised another family. No reason was ever given nor was one sought. It was taken as yet another example of the profound whimsicality inherent in Lord Krishna's nature by all concerned. An old Burma teak almirah full of books—Shakespeare, Gogol, Eliot, Sherwood Anderson, Premchand, Tagore, Wilde, Hemingway, Saroyan, Conrad, Camus, Nirala and many more—was all that was there for young Harry to remember his father by. Every month the father would send some money and Harryda's mother, though uneducated, also had some money. So, the household survived. In front of his house, just outside the front gate there was an electric pole. The KKRD 16522. Beside the eponymous pole there was a chabootra where he spent all his free time, reading. Once in a while he would glance up the electric pole, looking as if for some signal.

It is said that after the tragedy Harryda didn't utter a word for over a year. It seemed as if he had taken a vow, rejecting language as a viable mode of communication. He only spoke through gestures and that too minimal. He withdrew from the world that was around him to the one locked in his mind. From all available sources, it seems he was happy there. But his behaviour did raise some alarm among the neighbourhood elders. As usual no reason was ever given nor was one sought. Needless to add, young Harry didn't have many mates to play chor-sipahi with at that time. Then one day, like it happens, fate intervened in the form of little Keya Sarkar who moved in across the street.

One evening as Harry was returning from the market, eyes downcast, with bags of groceries in each hand, a stone flew in with some velocity and struck his mouth, accompanied by a gentle rolling laughter. Startled, Harry dropped the groceries and his eyes fell on Keya Sarkar, who promptly threw another stone which fortunately missed the target. Now this is a historic event, one of the defining moments in Harry's life and one which he recalled with rapturous intensity to the end of his life. The vision of young Keya in her wine-coloured frock with short ruffled sleeves, white socks and buckled shoes moved him so much that he felt the need for language once more. He said, 'You laughed at me, why?' A basic question and Keya the practical Bengali coquette that she was gave a basic reply. 'Because my mother says you are crazy. A Dumbo.' 'She is right,' Harry replied, and then he too laughed and it was terrible because his voice had started to break and he laughed on and on. The tenebrous silence of one year suddenly giving vent to the unexpected happiness of the present.

According to Rajuda, Madhubala, Boodhan Dhobi's donkey came running over and fell at Harry's feet and close in pursuit came Boodhan's six-year-old daughter Jamuna. Madhubala started to bray and dear Keya ran away. Only Jamuna remained, staring at the laughing Harry with teary eyes, awestruck. Harryda's mother rushed to him with tears in her eyes and hugged her son. She thanked God for his mercy and all the elders too said the same thing and crept back to their respective corners satisfied, their faith in the divine intact.

It was young Keya Sarkar of the luminous kohl-lined eyes, with the crooked-tooth smile, who had done the trick, and Harry was in love. Every day after school he would wait for the clock to strike four so Keya could make her appearance and play looka-churi and chor-sipahi with him till sundown. Those were days he never thought would end. He was happy, content and there wasn't anything more he craved from life. But all good things do come to an end. Just when they were graduating from their childish games to that very enjoyable game of childhood sexual proclivity innocently called 'doctor-patient'—Harry was caught sniffing Keya's pussy one evening behind her house by Rudrada's elder brother—Keya's father, a senior manager in a pharmaceutical company, got transferred, and Harry was left heartbroken. The night she left she kissed him for the first time.

Rajuda once laughingly told me, that night almost twenty-two years back Harry had entered his room through the window and had cried for a long time and had also shown him a poem about Keya. This Rajuda had found to be absolutely hilarious. Those days in some quarters of Kadam Kuan, in a certain age group if you liked poems or worse still if you actually wrote them you would also according to popular opinion love to have your arse fucked. Ironically, a lot of academicians and writers used to reside there. Rajuda's own father was a professor of Maithili who a year before his death had published a slim anthology of poems in Bangla written in his youth which was very well received. Needless to add, Rajuda thought his father to be totally useless. Even Phanishwar 'Renu' for a time lived just down our street in a corner house in abject poverty. A thin dark dignified dhoti-kurta clad prince with features as sharply etched as his stories. Those were difficult times and they haven't improved much even now. Patna, though more sinned against than sinning, is simply a place with no literary traditions and whatever few writers, poets, novelists that have emerged are not because of it but in spite of it.

Breathing the complacent slow poison air does inculcate a kind of security, a sense of community in all of us, but I have realized now that it is false. Beyond a certain point there is never any security and only if one is perpetually blind or has accepted defeat and made his peace can he survive. Even then only by ignoring prejudice and the inherent meddlesome provincialism of the place. Like most of my upper-caste Bihari-Bengali neighbours I too have learnt the art of averting my eyes and going on with my somewhat privileged life, with its steady rhythms and comfortable ennui. Just one thing redeems it from total literary oblivion and that is there is always an abundance of stories crying to be told.

Harry didn't let the derisory laughter of others bother him. He knew early on that he like Cavafy stood at a different angle from the rest of them. Even his relationship with God was one of mutual indifference. He used to read quite a lot those days and by the time he was fifteen he had finished all the books that his father had left behind. He would borrow books from anyone who would lend him one and was a member of all the public libraries. He read everything. He never discriminated.

Two momentous things happened when Harry was fifteen years old. The first was that he saw Charlton Heston in a revival of Cecil B. De Mille's *The Ten Commandments* at Veena Talkies and he realized that cinema was his destiny and De Mille his new God. Sometimes I wonder if only Harry had seen a De Sica first, perhaps then his life would have charted a totally different course. After all it is always the question of seeing the wrong movie at the right time, isn't it? He ate, slept, talked, breathed movies from then on. It changed his life.

Around that time while in another part of Asia the Vietnam War raged on, Bihar was ravaged by severe drought. Prices were up three hundred times. The ground had no moisture to attempt even a winter crop. The poor in the parched villages died of hunger and thirst. For the untouchables there was no water and no wells in the villages and money was needed for relief work. Like it had happened so many times before and after, when things got really bad for Bihar there was but one man who would set things right every time. Jayaprakash Narayan. JP organized the relief work and among other things opened 'feeding kitchens' all over the famine-affected areas. Each kitchen had the capacity to feed five hundred people a day. Along with a million blankets various articles of clothing were collected and distributed among the needy.

So even Harry heeding the call of JP like thousands of young people before and after him, recruited his friends Raju, Rudra and Happy. They would walk around town singing and playing music, imploring the heartless to part with a little of their money. Rudra would play the dholak, Raju the harmonica, and Harry blessed with a baritone would sing the bhajans of Meerabai that he had learnt from his mother. Devoid of any musical talent Happy just happily collected the money.

Yes, I know, Meera's bhajan sung in a baritone accompanied with a harmonica wielded by none other than the Jeff Thomson of Kadam Kuan. Come on get off it! Well, that's life. No explanations are given and none were ever sought. This is when the second momentous event in Harry's life took place.

They would sing at all the places, at Patna Market, Hathwa Market, at the railway station, the secretariat, in front of schools, on Ashok Rajpath where the Patna University Colleges are located, at the bus terminal near Gandhi Maidan and the aerodrome. It was at the Patna aerodrome one evening while they were performing, an athletic looking man with a beautiful face and intensely brooding eyes, a foreigner in a tight T-shirt and khaki shorts came over and started shooting their performance with the super 8mm that he carried. After the performance he gave Happy Rs 500, quite a tidy sum for those days. Then he shook hands with each of them. He looked at Harry for some time and then he mumbled, 'I like your eyes. They are just like mine used to be. You should be in the movies.' And then the man famous the world over, among other things for his studied under-articulation, walked away leaving the motley crew of boys speechless and very happy indeed. That very weekend Harry watched *The Wild One* at Pearl Movietone and he realized that the man who shook hands with him a couple of days back had been none other than the legendary Marlon Brando himself. Harry didn't walk straight for months after that. He slouched like a cat, just like Brando in that historic flick.

People say that as Harry grew older he became very good looking. At eighteen he had broad shoulders, a slim waist and a face carved by Michelangelo's chisel framed with luxurious shoulder-length wavy hair.

That year he finally matriculated on his third attempt from Sir Ganesh Dutt Patliputra High School and bid a final adieu to the world of academics. He'd had his fill of it. He rationalized to me that to make *The Ten Commandments* or *Ben-Hur* or *Spartacus*, even *Gunga-Jamuna*, one didn't need formal education but vision and talent and most importantly an ability to dream: correctly so I think. According to Sanjuda, Harryda those days would go over to Gandhi Maidan in the mornings and write scenarios for movies all day and in the evening read them out to his friends over cups of half-chais and shared Charminars at the Annapoorna Café.

As Rudrada explained, the stories though written in Hindi were always meant for a Charlton Heston, Burt Lancaster or

Robert Mitchum, never for a Dharmendra or Rajendra Kumar. Though he had a healthy contempt for the majority of Hindi movies and its stars, still he would watch them avidly and wanted to direct and act in them. His friends Rudra, Sanju, Happy and Raju, perhaps out of inherent malice or all-consuming boredom, just for 'time-pass' suggested he should crash Bollywood to try his luck. So one fine day he took them at their word and left home for Bombay.

Over there of course no one gave him a role and no one bought his scenarios and one night as he returned to his hotel near Matunga, he found it alight. Some sons of the soil had set it on fire as it was owned by a Shetty from Mangalore. Harryda lost several of his precious scenarios in the fire along with all his clothes. So the prodigal son took this latest catastrophe as a sign and returned to Kadam Kuan, Patna, after nine months, hungry, in dirty clothes, totally broke and desperate. He bought a pint of Solan No. 1 that very night, got drunk and staggered home and there right in front of his house was the electric pole with a poster of '*Dastak* Coming Soon' pasted on it. Harryda wrapped himself around the pole like he were humping it and cried, shouted and railed at the injustice of it all. Then he vomited. His mother dragged him inside. By the next morning he was fine again, busy organizing a cricket match at the Sakha field in Rajendra Nagar. One of the attractions of playing in the Sakha field even in my time was that one could always pelt stones at the sorry middle-aged buggers in khaki shorts and white half-shirts doing calisthenics with bamboo sticks for diversion when one's home side were trailing or when play momentarily stopped as yet another umpire retired hurt courtesy Rajuda.

In Kadam Kuan every year during Durga Puja, a big pandal which Bengalis invariably pronounced as 'pandle' would be erected at Hriday Kutir, the Thakur-Chowdhury mansion, where for four days the whole neighbourhood would congregate for festivity and fun. For those four days everyone would be happy and relaxed and Harryda and co. would be the active members of the organizing committee right from serving prasad to the devotees, making the barricades, policing the crowds, announcing the lost and found items to the children's play which Harryda would direct on Vijayadashami morning to the Visarjan in the evening.

Ae ho!

Ka ho?

Debiji ki?

Jai ho!

Even though Harryda was not a man of faith, he intensely loved the pomp and ceremony of the proceedings and for those four days at Hriday Kutir he would be totally in his element. It was on one of those puja days that I formally met Harryda for the first time. On short notice he had selected me for a very important role in Tagore's play *Kabuliwala*. I played the servant of Mini. Mini was played by Iladi, Mrinal Babu's niece, with a petulant charm all her own, and Harryda of course was the Kabuliwala. I was also the prompter. So a close friendship with Harryda was forged from that day onwards.

Harryda used to play the dhaak in the mornings during aarti and in the evenings he would dance the dhunoochi. It used to be the highlight of the evenings and people, especially girls, from all over Patna would come over and the pandal would be filled to capacity. And Harry before the idol would dance like a man possessed. Long clotted hair flying all over the place, the torso bare gleaming with sweat, eyes teary and red with smoke, and each time some of the burning embers singed his body, the Bengali girls would go, 'Aah maa go'. Each year many girls would come and watch him dance and play the dhaak and invariably lose their hearts to him.

At one of these events he fell in love for the second time, with a very beautiful girl called Laboni Bhattacharjee, and I remember during the distribution of the bhog we were all seated on big square chowkis and his friends were teasing him about Laboni who couldn't keep her eyes off him all through the other night's dance and Harry laughed and looked very pleased. He ate a whole bucketful of khichuri and subzi that day.

They would meet outside Patna Women's College, where Laboni was enrolled in the home science graduation course and from there they would go to the botanical garden which was nearby and secluded. There they would sit around and talk, that is only Laboni spoke and Harry listened. Once in a while they would stop talking and kiss frantically. He read his stories to her and though she wasn't much enthused, she listened patiently, waiting for him to finish so she could pull his head back to her breasts. And there one afternoon under the banyan tree—years later Harryda in his cups told me—'I fucked her till she wept. As I came, I looked up and saw the name tag high up on the bark. Ficus Benghalensis. What a magical name. Like a mantra I still remember it.'

Sometimes the lovebirds exhausted after their lovemaking would catch a Hindi movie at Veena Talkies or Regent, which Laboni adored. Harry must have been around twenty-four or twenty-five at that time and Laboni a couple of years younger. She was eager to get married and flee her home as life was unbearable there. She used to pester Harry to get a job of some kind and so Harry very much in love tried and finally landed his first job as a door-to-door salesman for Acme Unbreakable Teacups. After shattering ten sets of teacups, he left it. 'I couldn't stand the humiliation,' Harry explained to Laboni that evening. Her patience already running low she cried, and shouted, 'And I can't stand you, you are pathetic.' She then slammed the door of her heart on his face and left him to meditate under the banyan tree. Ficus Benghalensis.

Anyway there were objections from her family too. Laboni's parents were totally against the match. They were after all Kulin Bengali Brahmins and they couldn't have their girl married to a Yadav, could they? On top of it all Harry was unemployed and wasn't much inclined to be employed in the near future. He wants to make *Ben-Hur* in Hindi. Have you heard of anything more immoral Sinha sahib, tell me? Her father would ask his next-door neighbour and Sinha sahib would wisely shake his head and look heavenwards.

In time Laboni too saw reason and got married to a leather merchant from Calcutta. A mochi Harryda called him and got uproariously drunk on the night of her wedding, playing Devdas to the hilt. Nowadays, he drank the local stuff. He cried, he shouted, he railed against the injustice of it all and generally repeated his routine with the electric pole. His mother dragged him inside. By the next week he was fine again. By this time his friends had started to avoid him and would only listen to his stories if he paid for the half-chais and Charminars at Annapoorna.

Every evening at six he would don one of the two maroon terylene bush shirts that he had and which he had washed and ironed in the morning and the white gabardine bell-bottoms with 34-inch mohri and the spit-cleaned, gleaming black patent leather pumps. He would then walk slowly and with dignity like a duke on his way to his club, over to Annapoorna Café. He would stay there till closing time and then walk back with Rajuda and co. the same way. Some years had passed and his hair had started thinning over the top and most of his friends had now got jobs and they didn't have much time for him anymore.

Cricket was another of his numerous passions and in the cricket season, starting from September, to February, every weekend he would organize net-practice and on most Sundays we would play matches with other teams at Gandhi Maidan. Our team was called 'Kings Eleven' and Harryda was the skipper. He was the skipper when my cousin older to me by seven years was the wicketkeeper and he was still the skipper when years later I carried the kit-bag and rolled out the mat as the perennial twelfth man. Boys came and went, passed their matriculation, then graduation, drifted into government service, got married and their nephews or younger brothers would join the team and then they too would leave but Harry and his deputy Raju (Thomson of Kadam Kuan) remained constant fixtures. Harry used to be a stylish leg-spinner who on green matting wickets could make the ball do cartwheels right through the innings like Jasu Patel. For a spinner he had the temperament of a fast bowler. He would run in to bowl from ten yards and with a wild flailing of the arms release the ball. More often than not he bowled beamers but once in a while when the ball pitched, the batsman generally got out.

One of the most glorious days of that period if you remember was the day India won the Prudential Cup, beating the then almost invincible West Indies in the final at Lords. Those days everybody in the neighbourhood watched TV at Hriday Kutir as it was the only house which had a colour TV. The TV was installed in the mandap where during Durga Puja the idol of the goddess would be kept. In the courtyard where during the puja Harryda would dance his dhunoochi a big durree was spread and we all sat down to watch the match. The excitement was palpable; we were all out of our minds with joy. That India would reach the final was unimaginable even a week back. It was an unprecedented event and in my book almost as important a day as 15 August 1947.

Harryda sat on a chair because he didn't want to crush the creases of his white but now frayed bell-bottoms and he promised that if India won then the next day everyone was invited outside his house to consume as many rosogollas as one possibly could and Srikkanth having heard Harryda bent low on his knees and square-cut Andy Roberts to the boundary. A loud cheer rent the air. The next day we all trooped down to Harryda's place where, outside on the chabootra six huge clay containers covered in pink muslin, full of rosogollas and mishti doi, were kept. We all quaffed as much as we could. I was force-fed twelve rosogollas as I was the twelfth man. Later on Happyda produced a bottle of Old Monk and livened up the proceedings a bit more. There was an air of gaiety all around and it was something that I haven't seen since. Everyone was happy, even Laboni's father, Mr Bhattacharjee—about whom the rumours had it was last seen to have smiled exactly a day before his marriage some forty years back—came, had a rosogolla, liked it, had one more, smiled a great big Binaca smile and then as Rudrada unfurled the Old Monk quickly left. For six months afterwards Harryda didn't smoke or drink and couldn't watch his favourite Hollywood movies every weekend. He simply couldn't afford it anymore.

It was around the same time that he fell in love again. This time with the young wife of an IAS officer who had come down to Patna from Calcutta. He had seen her once sitting on a rattan chair sipping lemonade in her balcony, a cocker spaniel licking her bejewelled feet. She had smiled at him and she was so beautiful that Harry fell in love with her all over again after twenty years. This young lady now called Mrs Ajoy Bose was at one time known in Kadam Kuan as the pert and naughty Keya Sarkar. The love of Harryda's life. He believed fate had sent his first love back to claim him. He believed that. An eternal romantic, he believed anything.

Keya was now married and held a high position in the Patna social circle and anyway she loved her husband too much to think otherwise. So when she got the first letter from Harryda asking her to run away with him, she was amused. She remembered him, remembered the carefree childhood days, the games they would play, the pussy-sniffing and the first magical kiss, the vows of eternal love they had pledged while parting. That was all. It was the past and the picture was a bit hazy in her mind. Too many jump cuts. When the next letter arrived she was exasperated and from her balcony she would see a thin balding man in a maroon terylene bush shirt looking up to her. Everyday he would be there. In the same uniform and the same hangdog expression on his face. When the third letter within a fortnight arrived she became very afraid and went to her husband with it. That night around ten o'clock three constables from the local thana came to Harryda's house, dragged him out on the street and beat him mercilessly with batons. He didn't cry or shout or rail that night, arms as usual wrapped around the pole, with the batons coming down regularly on his thin frame from up high. Behind darkened windows everyone watched but no one came out. His mother dragged him inside.

This incident broke him from inside. He suddenly became a very old man. In his early thirties he looked like a man in his late forties. The hair, whatever was left of it, turned white within months, the eyes sunk in deeper, the famed looks were all gone. It was a face denuded by grief and loneliness.

In the evening he would still walk down to Annapoorna Café but now he didn't enjoy all those jokes which were legend about him and he started avoiding the place. He also became totally disillusioned with his friends. After Indira Gandhi's assassination, the anti-Sikh riots started in Patna. Though there weren't many killings, most of the Sikh houses and business establishments were looted. In Kadam Kuan there lived only one Sikh family, who owned an electronic goods shop right next to Annapoorna. Happy Sardar who owned the shop was a childhood friend of Harryda and co. On the third evening after the assassination as Harryda and I sat chatting on the chabootra outside his house, we saw Dular Mandal, a small time chain-snatcher who lived in the Daldali slums and owned a dhaba there, coming towards us with a big Weston colour TV in his arms. We caught hold of him and after Harryda slapped him couple of times he told us that Happyda's shop was being looted. We took the TV from him and put it in Harry's home and then we ran towards the main road. I saw several young boys running, thirteen-fourteen-year-olds from affluent upper-class families with transistor radios around their necks. As we reached the corner Chokon and his father passed us by on their Lambretta, Chokon balancing a Telerama TV on his lap. We tried stopping them but couldn't.

At the shop we saw the shutters were ripped off, the display windows smashed and a motley crew of twenty looters inside helping themselves to the goods. Rajuda was there, so were

Rudra, Sanju and Sanyalda. Harry lost his mind then and livid with anger caught hold of Sanyalda by his collar and thrashed him. I had never seen Harryda so angry before. When Rudra and Sanjuda tried to overpower Harry; Rajuda reluctantly stepped in.

When Rajuda put back the National Panasonic VCR and a Philips record player, the looting automatically stopped. As the looters reluctantly left the shop, I saw Laboni's father in immaculate white dhoti-kurta trying to shuffle off undetected with a walkman. I snatched it back from him and suppressed with difficulty an innate desire to kick his plump arse. I along with Harry and Rajuda put the broken shutter in place.

Later Harryda went to Happy's house and brought Happy and his mother to his own home and there they stayed for a fortnight till the troubles subsided. His faith in his friends and neighbours shaken beyond repair, Happyda left Patna soon after with his mother for Delhi. Overnight he sold his shop for a pittance to Dular Mandal. In a portion of it later a colourful character called Manager Sharma opened a very popular liquor shop.

Harry never spoke to Sanju, Rudra and Sanyalda again.

I would meet him during my vacations, sitting by the side of the chabootra in a maroon lungi and vest, Charminar dangling from his smile like always but now the smile didn't light up the eyes anymore. During Durga Puja he would sit in a corner at Hriday Kutir brooding and melancholy, listening attentively to the dhaak players. Two years back when I was home during the autumn break I heard that Harryda had got married.

Later Sanyalda clarified, 'He is not married or anything. Just living with Boodhan Dhobi's daughter Jamuna. He has turned totally crazy. He was always crazy no doubt but now he has just completely lost it. All day he stays in the jhuggi with her but at night comes back home to his mother, disgusting.'

I felt strange and confused when I heard this and later my confusion hardened into anger. How could a regular person and more importantly someone whom I knew personally do such a base disgusting thing? Living in a jhuggi with a low-caste washerwoman? And that too a man who loved style, beauty and poetry? Would she ever know who Cecil B. De Mille was or Sherwood Anderson for that matter? Would she care? How can someone negate every social decorum that has been there for time immemorial, just like that? How can someone be so monstrously callous?

Too many questions and very few answers I must admit and all around there was ridicule and sarcasm masked as neighbourly concern and very little sensitivity. Even I, a true child of Kadam Kuan like the others, became affected by it. He had no friends now and sometimes I wonder if he ever had any? People avoided him on the streets and you know why? Not because they were angry with him like me. No one cared about him much. He was an eyesore, just a joke to them. They avoided him out of fear, fear of failure. We all saw him as a failure, a man who didn't do anything worthwhile in his life and had sunk deeper and deeper into drink and debauchery. Failure is like the common cold. It is contagious. It is that simple. I hope you get my drift. Even I started avoiding him around that time and once I remember he hailed me from across the road and I turned and walked quickly away. I didn't want anyone to see me talking to him. I couldn't sleep that night. I realized the enormity of my ingratitude towards the man who had always treated me with affection and had opened before my adolescent eyes the wide vistas of literature and cinema and the beauty inherent in them. Moreover, he had always read my dumb stories and never once complained. I still had the dog-eared copy of Sherwood Anderson's *Winesburg, Ohio* that he had given to me as a gift after he had liked one of my stories many years back. The story is lost now but the book was still with me. It had belonged to his father.

I just couldn't sleep. I realized that I had to atone for my sin. I had to ask his forgiveness. Early in the morning I went to his home but he had already left for Jamuna's house. His mother gave me the directions and I reached the narrow five-feet-wide gali smelling of pig shit and intense poverty and finally located the place and called out Harryda's name. Jamuna came out and was perturbed to see me. Her neighbours, among whom I found our maidservant, were openly staring at us. Jamuna's face was half covered with ghunghat but at close range I could see how attractive she really was. She had the full rounded body of a deity and she took me inside. The room was dark but clean and there was in the air the smell of burning incense and stale marigolds. By the side of the door sat Harryda on the cot. He was reading a dog-eared copy of Lawrence Mowbray's last novel *Darkness Visible* and drinking arrack from a steel tumbler. I asked him how he was and he didn't answer. Jamuna came and sat beside him, holding him, shielding him almost. I said I was sorry about yesterday's incident but he still didn't say anything so I rambled on about the old days and the people we knew, about cricket and really stupid things just to stifle that unnatural stillness which pervaded the room. He went on drinking, ignoring me totally. I said I would always be his friend and then I stopped.

There was nothing to say anymore. He spoke for the first time then. 'Ask him to go. I want to sleep.' He put down the glass and lay down, his head in Jamuna's lap. An act which at the time seemed extremely off the wall but now has different connotations for me. Harry then raised himself slightly and let out the biggest fart that I have ever heard in my life. It set off like a siren, a thousand bells tolling at once and it continued forever, not slackening either in pace or volume even for a second, until the whole room reverberated from it. The smell was so intense that I can still feel it in my nostrils sometimes. I went out of the room gasping for air.

So his death didn't come as a surprise to me but I was shocked by it. I still haven't lost the ability to be shocked I guess. Ten days before I arrived in Patna after my graduation, Harryda as usual came home drunk. In the evening he had watched Mrinal Sen's *Calcutta 71* at the Indian Medical Association Hall where the Patna cine-society shows were usually held and had a splitting headache. He leaned against the electric pole with one hand and started to vomit and slipped and fell with a deafening thud on the side of the chabootra and cracked his skull open. He lay there trying to breathe and after a while his mother came out and carried him inside in her arms. He was now as light as a baby. He died during the night. In the morning Jamuna and his mother took him on a thela pulled by Madhubala to the electric crematorium at Baans Ghat. His friends were nowhere to be seen. Probably they were still laughing at him and his life and what an appalling little joke it had been. Soon after that Jamuna shifted to Harry's house and started living with his mother and there after eight months gave birth to a boy. I went to see the baby and he was beautiful and kept smiling always. As per Harry's wish he was named Mrinal. I left *Winesburg, Ohio* by the side of his cradle. I went home then.

Required Reading

Once upon a time in the early eighties there took place in Kadam Kuan the strange baffling case of Babu Mrinal Thakur-Chowdhury—erstwhile landlord from Manbhum, bon vivant, patron of the Indian National Congress and the art of body-building, conqueror of the English Channel, former owner of collieries, mango and litchi orchards, Pierce-Arrows, Arabian steeds, French concubines and in whose silver-grey Bentley convertible Pandit Nehru with a cigarette stuck at a jaunty angle drove around town with much élan during a state visit to Patna in the late forties—who simply disappeared one moonlit night from Bankipore Club, one of whose earliest native presidents he had been.

Each night at nine his faithful retainer Saifuddin Durrani, Saifu Mian for short, would pick Mrinal Babu up from the very same club in his cycle-rickshaw from which just a couple of decades back he had driven dignitaries home to Hriday Kutir from ballroom parties, where Anglo-Indian bandmasters in white linen tuxedos with no lining, brylcreemed pompadours and Errol Flynn moustaches had done encores of Bing Crosby and Nat King Cole classics, in the master's mint green Pierce-Arrow.

In the early forties Saifu Mian, an orphan reared in a madrasa, had arrived from Dehri-on-Sone and joined Mrinal Babu's Jharia colliery as a miner. A squat, well-built Pathan, in no time he had won the heart of every labourer, loader, cutter and foreman by his unquenchable thirst for hard work and all-round cheerfulness. In the shaft, of a depth of 400 feet, bending double for half a mile crawling for coal, a smile would still light up his coal-dust blackened face whenever a fellow miner shone a safety lamp. He was looked up to by all the coal miners and they had appointed him as their unofficial leader. In less than a year he was put in charge of one of the two Lancashire boilers which powered the lifts in the shaft. A fact which was resented by Raghunath Singh, day foreman of the gang of twenty-five miners of which Saifu Mian was a member. A Rajput from Ara, Raghunath was built like a wrestler and had the bluff blustery manner of a born bully. After all, *Ara Jila ghar ba, To kaun baat ka dar ba,* an aphorism he would repeat ad nauseum each day after a reassuring twirl of his silken butter-fed moustache. It was also rumoured that Raghunath Singh siphoned off coal and sold it to small traders in and around Jharia and Raniganj.

One day in the evening, about a week after Jinnah's Direct Action Day of 16 August 1946, when lakhs of people were killed in Bengal and Bihar, mostly Hindus, Saifu Mian along with couple of his miner friends walked into the local toddy shop they patronized. It was full of soot-smeared miners stopping by for a reassuring glass of toddy or mahua before they went home after the day shift. The shop, which was just a bamboo and dry grass shed actually, swirled with condensed heat, sweat and the fumes of fried kaleji mixed with the stale vomit smell of fresh mahua.

The conversation at all the six long benches where the miners sat hunched, their elbows on slightly taller tables like they were in a village pathshala, was of the horrific Calcutta riots and the killings that were still going on.

At the back sat Raghunath Singh in his usual place with four of his cronies. He had been drinking steadily since late afternoon and was pretty sozzled by the time Saifu Mian and his friends came and sat at the adjacent bench.

'Arrey katlu,' Raghunath Singh called out to Saifu Mian. Saifu Mian kept his back turned and pretended that he didn't hear Ragunath Singh. He knew he was the only Muslim working in the colliery and that Raghunath Singh often behind his back disparagingly referred to him as a 'katlu'. He kept quiet. He didn't want to fight. Even though he wasn't especially bright he didn't want to do anything that would change his life. He liked his life and was happy with it.

'Is madarchod ko Pakistan chahiye,' still spoiling for a fight, Raghunath Singh, sure of his 99 per cent Hindu and adivasi support in the toddy shop shouted at Saifu Mian. Conversation stopped, decibel level dropped to a murmur. Most of the miners averted their eyes and kept steadily drinking. Some left the shop after hurriedly paying their fare.

Saifu Mian got up to leave and as he passed by, Raghunath Singh grabbed his hand and swung in an arc the leather riding crop that he always carried about his person even though he didn't own a horse. Saifu Mian ducked and caught the blow on his left elbow and then swung a right hook that would have done, Mrinal Babu once told me, even Jack Dempsey proud. As Saifu Mian's massive fist connected with Raghunath Singh's thick forehead, it lifted him clean off the floor and on to the greasy wooden table, shattering half a dozen glasses and a jug full of frothy toddy. He was out cold. He regained consciousness about an hour later in the local dispensary where some of the miners had carried him to.

The very next day the young Irish manager of the colliery, fresh out of Trinity College, Lawrence Lytton-Mowbray, who had joined just a month back, fired Saifu Mian. As Saifu Mian would recount the story, Lawrence Lytton-Mowbray didn't have an option as Raghunath Singh was the foreman and Saifu Mian much junior to him in rank. Lawrence had to maintain discipline. But the other miners protested and asked for Saifu Mian to be reinstated and instead Raghunath Singh to be kicked out. But once Lawrence Lytton-Mowbray had taken a decision he wouldn't budge from it. The miners went on a strike. For three days the impasse continued. All through it Saifu Mian kept quiet and stayed in his hut and stared at the mud walls.

On the evening of the third day Lawrence Lytton-Mowbray's patience finally gave way and he drove in his new Triumph 350 to Giridih where Mrinal Babu was camping with some of his friends. On the way back Mrinal Babu drove the motorcycle and they did the journey in a little less than an hour.

On the front garden of the colliery rest-house, Lawrence Lytton-Mowbray's Burma teak writing table with two chairs was set. A Petromax was lit and placed on the table. Mrinal Babu with an imperious wave of his massive right hand gestured to the miners who had spent the previous three days on dharna in front of the rest-house to sit down. He asked a few of the old miners to come forward individually and recount the turn of events on that fateful day. All the while he sipped Glenfiddich from a thick cut-glass tumbler, but which appeared no bigger than a shot-glass to the miners viewing it through his jewel-encrusted fingers.

Raghunath Singh and Saifu Mian were then called. Raghunath Singh with his swollen face and one half-shut eye told Mrinal Babu that Saifu Mian had always resented him and that day had attacked him because earlier on a couple of occasions Raghunath Singh had caught him drunk in the shaft and had thrown him out. Saifu Mian didn't offer any explanations, looked indifferently at Mrinal Babu and proclaimed, 'The next time that I hit him, he will die. I like the mines. I am not going anywhere.' Mrinal Babu looked into the eyes of the upstart young Pathan and could detect no fear in him, only cold hard rage. The miners edged closer, transfixed by the light of the petromax like moths.

Mrinal Babu didn't say anything for the next five minutes, just soaked in the atmosphere. A peon refilled his glass of whisky, topped it with a handful of crushed ice. Mrinal Babu took another leisurely sip, looked at Lawrence Lytton-Mowbray with eyes that suddenly lit up with oriental mischief. Lawrence was watching all the drama—the silent expectant mob of miners, the Petromax, a smouldering Raghunath Singh in one corner and in the other a brooding Saifu Mian and in the midst of everything the patriarch Mrinal Thakur-Chowdhury drinking Scotch as if he were at a Bankipore Club soiree—with an impatience which was barely repressed on his young face.

Suddenly Mrinal Babu playing the feudal lord that he was to the hilt leaned forward and bellowed, 'Saifuddin Durrani, you seem to be a very strong man. With one blow of your right hand you knocked out Raghunath Singh, the pride of Ara. You must be very proud of your prowess. I will reinstate you and no action will be taken against the other miners but we will have a little contest before that. You seem to be a sporting man so we will have an arm-wrestling contest. If you beat me you can stay.'

And then the legendary arm-wrestling contest of which Iladi and I at innumerable times in our childhood had heard the narration from Saifu Mian took place. To cut an already long digression short Mrinal Babu won the contest, his great sinewy green-veined Cambridge Blue arm almost crushed Saifu Mian's somewhat proletarian hand, fracturing his right index finger in the process. His point proved, Mrinal Babu then pardoned Saifu Mian. The miners after the show returned to their homes satisfied. Peace and honour all around was restored.

But the story doesn't end here. After watching the outcome of the contest Raghunath Singh slunk off into the night, not to be seen in those parts for years. He gave up alcohol, women and gambling. Started wearing the janeu again which he had discarded after his wedding. He became a devout Hindu who began each day with an incantatory chant of the Gayatri Mantra.

Om bhur bhuvah swah
Tat savitur varenyam
Bhargo devasya dheemahi
Dhiyo yo nah prachodayat

No doubt after a reassuring twirl of his silken butter-fed moustache. All this tapasya finally bore fruit and he would return to Jharia a few years before the nationalization of coal mines and with sheer hard work and single-minded ferocity become the most dreaded coal mafioso of all time, controlling half the trade unions in all the coal mining towns of the erstwhile Bihar-Bengal border. Giridih, Madhupur, Jharia, Baghmara, Dhanbad.

I remember vividly the daily spectacle of Mrinal Babu coming home to his now quietly crumbling mansion, with its giant green shuttered windows on the first floor and chipped marble steps leading up from the covered portico where the blissfully rusting mint green Pierce-Arrow was still parked; in a white pin-stripe double-breasted seersucker suit with broad lapels, blue oxford fil-a-fil shirt with cutaway collars, the old Harrow tie askew flying at half-mast, slid on to the steel footrest of the rickshaw and then being helped up the stairs by Saifu Mian to the now impoverished sitting room with its two backed divans and faded tartan bolsters, threadbare bear and leopard skin rugs which stank throughout each monsoon, deer heads with chipped antlers on walls alongside Company reproductions and Patna School lithographs; where under a dusty unlit chandelier mail-ordered from Harrods in the twenties Ila and Ritwik sat listening to Rosemary Clooney sing 'Mambo Italiano' from the Murphy radiogram. It was the late sixties.

Ila Lytton-Mowbray, daughter of Mrinal Babu's younger sister Runu and Lawrence Lytton-Mowbray, abandoned to her uncle's care by both the parents who had gone their separate ways. Runu Debi to a new husband in Chicago after a string of lovers in Calcutta, Bombay, Zurich, London. Lawrence to the wilds of Purulia where he set up home with a Santhal woman, ate begun-pora and drank mahua religiously each evening. There he wrote a pioneering series of detective novels about a blind Santhal medicine man named Milton Tudu and a young Diku girl Melo who he had adopted. Mostly they would solve petty crimes in the community such a fowl-filching, cattle-poisoning, stolen Petromaxes and, increasingly as the series progressed, kidnapping and murder. The novels, picaresque in structure, were less crime procedurals and more of a cultural treatise on tribal values and the need to preserve them. There were five in the series.

In the first novel called *The Foundling* Milton Tudu befriends a six-year-old Melo abandoned at Purulia station and takes her home to his village near Garh Jaipur. In the second one, *Disposal of the Dead*, Milton and Melo investigate the brutal murder of a Bania moneylender in a village near Jamtara in Singhbhum. In *The Human Angle* Milton and Melo solve a case of serial cattle poisoning in Chandil and also help a Santhal boy get married to an Oraon girl. In the fourth novel of the series a young girl is found murdered after a dance during the Phagua festival in an Oraon village. It was called *Last Rites*. The novels lovingly describe the topography of Purulia and neighbouring areas in Singhbhum like Chandil, Chaibasa, Jamshedpur, and are today studied more by anthropologists than mere readers of private-eye fiction.

Iladi's favourite novel in the series was the last one where Milton and Melo leave the tribal areas of Manbhum, Singhbhum and Palamu for the first time and descend to the plains. They arrive in Patna in search of a young Santhal maidservant who had disappeared and not visited her home in two years after she was contracted to work for a rich family in a colony which is a mirror image of Kadam Kuan in Patna. It was called *Darkness Visible* and was dedicated to Kalikinkar Datta, the noted Patna historian whose seminal work *The Santhal Insurrection of 1855-57* was one of Lawrence's favourite books and with whom he carried on a lifelong correspondence.

Iladi would read the novel aloud to me and when we would go out show me the houses and landmarks in Kadam Kuan that Lawrence Lytton-Mowbray had used in an altered way. Annapurna Café where all the local gallants hung out, Peshawar Sweet House where Milton and Melo have gulab jamuns, Buddha Murti roundabout, the S.T. Martin's High School (the S.T. stood for St. Sharma and St. Tiwari, the proprietors), and a silent young boy who throughout the novel keeps a watch on the world from his perch on a raised chabootra under the electric pole numbered KKRD 16522 and helps them trace the girl by literally pointing in the right direction. The boy is clearly Harryda from whose father Lawrence would order books whenever he was in Patna.

When Ila was seven years old Lawrence died in his sleep in his village in Purulia. To this day he is famous in those parts, in Garh Jaipur, Chandil, Jamtara and neighbouring Baghmara as the Lawrence of Purulia.

Those five novels of Lawrence were Iladi's most prized possessions and she wouldn't even let me touch her personal copies though she had read them to me so many times that I knew all the stories by heart. The novels were self-published and distributed in north India by A. H. Wheeler and in the south by Higginbothams. They were printed in Demy octavo hardback by P. K. Ghosh at Eastend Press and had wonderful woodcut illustrations and a cover designed by a then young visualizer called Satyajit Ray.

Years later while making an inventory of her library I would come across those copies of the novels again and as I opened each page I found Melo's name meticulously erased by whitener and in its place Ila's name printed with her own Parker 56.

Both parents, except for a postcard or two, never bothered much about young Ila, who with a single-minded determination to thwart fate grew to a maturity and wisdom at thirteen very few women attain even at menopause.

Mrinal Babu, who had never married, had no legitimate heirs, brought Ila up from the age of six like the daughter he never had and lavished on her all the care that he could muster in his now straitened circumstances. The fields in Manbhum were all sold by the mid-sixties, paying for the living expenses of Runu Debi and Mrinal Babu, with half of them taken by the government in 1952 after the Zamindari Abolition Bill.

While most other prescient upper-caste landowners of Bihar were busy thwarting the law by rotating their tenants from one field to another in their papers so that none of them could claim that they had tilled continuously for ten years a single field which by law now could be theirs, Mrinal Babu was taking the air in South of France on a holiday with Francoise Berlemont, his old flame. By the time he returned six months later he had lost 500 bighas of land. 'I will write to Jawahar,' he said to Saifu Mian as he got off at Patna Junction after his sojourn. Perhaps he did, but of course nothing came of it.

With the nationalization of coal mines Mrinal Babu's only income was from the rent of a couple of shops and houses in the Subzi Baug and Mehendroo Ghat localities of Old Patna. Rents of which had remained unchanged since the early fifties.

Ila switched the radiogram off stopping Rosemary Clooney in mid-flight. It was time for me to take leave and go home next door across the high, broken-glass encrusted boundary wall, to lie on my narrow cot and dream about her. This was the pattern of our childhood. Unchanged for years. In the morning Saifu Mian would drop her off at St. Joseph's Convent after I got off at St. Xavier's across the Gandhi Maidan, near Golghar. We were distantly related. My father, a senior advocate in the Patna High Court, and Mrinal Babu were second cousins. My father when he had come down from our ancestral village near Baghmara to study law in Patna had stayed in Hriday Kutir for the duration in the mid-forties. One of the guests with whom my father shared a room for a while was the great revolutionary and associate of Bhagat Singh, Batukeshwar Dutt, who after he was released from the Cellular Jail in Andaman in 1938 was barred entry into Bengal, U.P. and Punjab.

Many of Mrinal Babu's kinsmen from all over Manbhum would come and stay at Hriday Kutir for their studies or jobs in Patna and there were large rooms near the back courtyard overlooking the guava orchard with four beds in each room just for them. Occupancy was always full till the early sixties. My father had seen Hriday Kutir in its last gasp of splendour. The land on which our house was built in the early sixties was a wedding gift to my mother from Mrinal Babu.

Iladi would straighten my tie each morning as I got down from the rickshaw. Ila Lytton-Mowbray (she made me practise to say her name aloud, like a mantra), the unattainable princess with dark green eyes older to me by five years (though at the time it seemed like centuries), half Vaidya, half Irish and full-time object of my affection and awe.

She was the first person in my life who taught me that there was such a thing as a secret world of the mind and imagination which could be more real and enriching than the mundane everyday reality of our meagre existence. She was the pioneer. Later there would be Harryda, the doomed leg-break bowler, intrepid litterateur, eternal dreamer and mentor at-large but that, dear reader, as you would know is another story altogether.

As Ila grew up, her cheekbones cut through the regular plumpness and rearranged her features into a strikingly beautiful one. It was a face where passion and austerity jostled for supremacy and more often than not austerity won. It was a face which did justice to her name and yet there was no vanity and none of the preening of the regular Bengali coquette in her.

Good at studies, always sunk deep in books, bereft of friends, in me she had found a perfect Sancho Panza. She was the first member of the Thakur-Chowdhury family who really put to use the massive library in Hriday Kutir which, again like the chandelier, was ordered from England sometime in the late nineteenth century, and till the time of Mrinal Babu's father new books by the yard would be added each year. Mrinal Babu, on the other hand, inveterate rider of horses and women in his youth, champion swimmer and body-building enthusiast, never had much time for reading. He himself candidly admitted that the only book he ever read in its entirety was the elementary school Bangla primer *Varna Parichay*. It was from his copy of *Varna Parichay* that Iladi would teach me the Bangla alphabets each weekend when we were young. No wonder I could not ever learn to write and read Bangla properly.

According to my father, even in the ten years Mrinal Babu spent in England, where he got his education, first at Harrow and then Cambridge, from where he was sent down, he spent most of his time travelling, socializing, swimming and 'riding', the contact with books being perfunctory at best. But he was generous to a fault with anyone in Kadam Kuan who wanted to use his library and many people would come on the weekends to read there. Teachers and students from the English department were regular visitors and the Hriday Kutir library was, along with the Sinha library, the best private library in Patna till the sixties. I remember Harryda was a regular visitor. He usually read the Russians.

By the age of fifteen Ila had read all of Dickens, Thackeray, Tolstoy, Turgenev, Emily Dickinson, Austen, Kipling, Flora Annie Steele, Dostoevsky, Byron, Tagore, Swinburne, Flaubert and Michael Madhusudan Dutt. She narrated to me the life of Michael, the young fiery poet, who one fine day left his rich feudal mid-nineteenth century world of comfort for his own beliefs and penury, converted to Christianity, perhaps just to spite his father, and in time composed that masterpiece of modern Bengali poetry *Meghnad Badh Kavya*.

The episode which really impressed me in Michael's story was when he once composed and dictated three different works of poetry in Sanskrit, Bangla and English to three amanuenses at the same time while he walked to and fro in creative frenzy about his salon. To me at that time it was the epitome of creative genius. But ever since I learnt that Erle Stanley Gardner could dictate five different Perry Mason novels at the same time, I must admit much of the sheen has rubbed off Michael's feat. Moreover I have realized now in my extended literary apprenticeship that it is perhaps not the ideal way to compose serious poetry. But undeniably there was glamour attached to his name for me.

'Michael Madhusudan Dutt' could conjure in my mind for a long time what an artist should always be: defiant, dissipated and disrespectful at large.

'For a cause one must suffer, to give light one must burn,' Iladi after narrating Michael's story for the umpteenth time would say to her ten-year-old knight errant and Ritwik with tears in his eyes, overcome by Michael's genius and fate, would nod in assent.

Apart from the literary initiation, the great educator that Iladi was she also instructed me in the world of emotions. Happiness and sadness I already knew but cold, solid as bone jealousy I understood fully one November evening as Harryda in his maroon terylene shirt and white bell-bottoms swaggered past on the street below and did his famous two-finger salute thing. Iladi said to me on the terrace from where we were looking down, solemnly, 'I would like to kiss him someday.' 'But he is not a bhadralok' were the only words that squeaked past my lips after a while.

But perhaps the greatest influence on her life was of the complete multi-volume gilt-edged Marx and Engels set bound in rich Morocco leather. Here she found her life's mission and by the time she entered Patna Women's College for her Intermediate in Arts, even I could enunciate with clarity what 'Dialectical Materialism' was. She became a member of the Patna Chapter of IPTA and rehearsals would take place in the back courtyard of the Thakur-Chowdhury mansion all winter. Sometimes I would go and watch her perform *Mother Courage and Her Children* from behind the latticework window in the corridor. Saifu Mian's broken down phaeton was used for Mother Courage's rolling stock provision store. Her friends who were all older than her, would be there, the men, thin and bearded in white cotton shirts and blue Doj jeans smuggled from Kathmandu and gabardine jackets with maroon and black mufflers; the girls in Cottage Emporium red-bordered cotton saris and cardigans.

Sometimes after the rehearsals were over I could hear them sing 'The Internationale'.

Then Comrades, come rally
And the last fight let us face
The Internationale
Unites the human race.

The rehearsals and play-acting stopped for a while when Samar Sinha, a friend of Iladi's, got shot in the leg by the police in front of Patna College during a student demonstration against Mrs Gandhi and her Congress bootlickers. It was 1974 and the start in Patna of what the Sarkari Sant Vinoba Bhave would memorably call 'the epoch of discipline'.

Samar Sinha at nineteen was an intense young man, regulation thin and bearded, with thick black prescription glasses which made him look like Dinesh Thakur in *Rajnigandha*, and who along with his studies at Patna University also covered the campus beat and wrote features for *The Searchlight* newspaper. I absolutely loved him. He was the only person in Patna then to possess Creedence Clearwater Revival and Velvet Underground

LPs, which he would bring over and play on Iladi's old Murphy radiogram. He taught me to sing 'I Put a Spell on You', which I would usually screech after clambering on top of the dining table aping the incomparable John Fogerty's sweet gruff vocals. He also taught me two red haikus. It was a little routine that we had developed.

The first one went like this:

Ritwik: Amar Naam
Samar: Tomar Naam
Ritwik (stamps his foot and gives the red salute): Vietnam!

Here's the second one:

Ritwik: Amar Bari
Samar: Tomar Bari
Ritwik (stamps his foot and gives the red salute): Naxalbari!

A day which I remember very clearly from my childhood is when Samarda took Ila and me to a matinee of *Enter the Dragon* at Rupak cinema hall for which I had been pestering Iladi for weeks. Every once in a while the audio would fade in that rickety hall and all the audience would shout 'Sound!' at the top of their voices. The audio would then come back on its own. Two rows below us sat Harryda with Laboni Bhattacharjee and just as I was about to shout his name in my excitement Iladi clamped her hand over my mouth and whispered in Bangla, 'chup thhak'.

Later in the evening Samar took us to Bharat Coffee House on Fraser Road where we had mutton cutlets and black coffee. At the next table sat a middle-aged sharp-featured man with extremely long hair like a rock star, which back-brushed from his forehead fell to his shoulders in a thick unruly mass. It was the writer Phanishwar Nath 'Renu', the finest novelist in Bihar then and one of the stalwarts of Nayi Kahani Movement. He was actively involved with the students' unrest then. There were a couple of people sitting at his table. A girl was reading out a story in Bangla from a thick manuscript that she carried in her lap. After she finished reading, Samarda went over and invited Renu to our table where we sat and listened to him awestruck as he regaled us with stories of B.P. Koirala, the Nepal revolution of 1950 and their guerrilla leader, the incomparable Bhola Chatterjee, over cups of black coffee. As we said goodbye to him that evening near Tricel Bookshop, that was the last anyone saw of Renu for a year and half in Patna as he went underground and resurfaced only after the Emergency.

After Samarda got shot I remember visiting Kurji Holy Family Hospital near Digha with Iladi to see him. He was in a corner room with green curtains on a white painted steel cot, his left leg in plaster with all sorts of messages scrawled on it. Iladi wrote:

My candle burns at both ends;
It will not last the night;
But ah my foes, and oh, my friends
It gives a lovely light.

Years later when I was in Delhi University I would meet Samar Sinha again, he was then one of the stars of the History Department, back after a doctorate from Balliol, his subalternist history of the JP Movement and the Emergency already being talked of as a classic. In his room at Gwyer Hall, in a glass case the plaster cast with all the messages scrawled on it was displayed. It was the stuff of legend now. Like the Maltese Falcon. Young subalternist girls from all over the world came to see that modernist relic and the really devoted ones were even allowed to kiss it. Later Samar Sinha would leave DU after he got tenure at Columbia.

Before we left the hospital room Iladi leaned over and kissed Samar on the mouth, as he squeezed her arse gently with his left hand.

Much later when Mira Verma, the love of my life, one February evening outside the Miranda House back gate, after planting one of her special swirling-tongue Patna kisses on Ritwik's ever eager lips declaimed the very same lines, the image of Iladi kissing Samar and, later in the rickshaw, of the tears coursing down her face flashed across my mind. What is it with adolescent Patna convent girls and Edna St. Vincent Millay, I wonder sometimes.

Like it usually happens, as Iladi blossomed into womanhood, we somewhat drifted apart. Rather her life had grown too complex for my childish attentions. Yet for my thirteenth birthday she gave me the Sushobhan Sarkar translation of *The Communist Manifesto*, recently reissued by Moscow's Progress publishers, and which my mother promptly confiscated. It was the time of the Emergency. As Jayaprakash Narayan's house was only a five-minute's walk from my home, many times I had tagged along with Iladi and Samarda to hear him speak. JP still in his early seventies was an exceedingly handsome man, fastidious about his clothes and supremely aware of the spell he cast over young men and women at first meeting. The movement to which he gave a rudderless legitimacy caught the imagination of the whole country and would in the coming decade prove to be Bihar's undoing, making it a fit case for secession unto Gabriel Garcia land, complete with widespread sectarian violence, caste senas, kidnappings, extortions, illiteracy and a magic-realist chief minister who regularly ate cattle fodder for breakfast, among other things.

Iladi went off to JNU after her graduation and continued with her agit-prop nukkad nataks over there. She was writing her own plays now which she would read out to her new set of bearded friends over shared Charms and chai at Ganga Dhaba. Five-ten-minute skits which she and her troupe would perform with guerrilla precision. I would get to hear about her from Mrinal Babu who sometimes in the evening after pouring himself a Solan No. 1 from a Cartier decanter would read from Ila's latest letter. She wrote infrequently and only on postcards, giving a meagre sketch of her life. Her few letters to me from JNU only contained assorted reading lists which I was to assiduously follow. The perfunctoriness of the letters at that time broke my heart. Ila never returned home from JNU.

She died while performing her protest play *Girgit* outside an old sixteenth-century mosque on the Delhi-Haryana Badarpur border which a then banned Hindu fundamentalist organization called the Hanuman Dal wanted to demolish since they claimed that Lord Krishna had sat and pared his toenails for a fortnight on a huge sandstone boulder which was inside the compound on his way back to Dwarka from Kurukshetra and the presence of a mosque at such a hallowed place was a slur on all of Hindudom.

As Ila and her young college friends performed the play for a motley crew of shopkeepers, school children, truck drivers and disinterested peasants that cold January morning, some dozen men armed with steel rods, guptis and motorcycle chains suddenly arrived in Matador vans, surrounded them and started hitting them indiscriminately. They singled out the young Christian-sounding Anglo heretic Ila for special treatment. Her skull was cracked open from two places. Samar Sinha found her blood-splattered form in the late afternoon in a by-lane behind the mosque where her assailants had chased her to. She died two days later at Lok Nayak Jayaprakash Narayan Hospital, reportedly of respiratory cardiac arrest.

Mrinal Babu, my father and Saifu Mian brought the body back to Kadam Kuan and I remember watching from my room, numb with grief as the body was unloaded from the hired Patna Medical College Hospital hearse and carried to Hriday Kutir, the head tightly bandaged had made her face puffy and unrecognizable. My mother fainted when she saw Ila but later with tears streaming down her face she dressed Ila in a magenta

Benarasi sari and made her as beautiful as she possibly could for her final journey. Long back once from that very room I had watched a young boy get beaten to death for stealing a pair of shoes and it had changed me in some fundamental way. Ila's shattered face reinforced that change.

Mrinal Babu, Saifu Mian, Harryda (who was always the first person to arrive when anybody died in Kadam Kuan) and I, along with hundreds of other people, carried Ila on our shoulders to Baans Ghat by the banks of the Ganges where her cremation took place. All through the thirty-minute walk Mrinal Babu refused to be relieved of his burden.

The only time during the entire ceremony I saw emotion get the better of Mrinal Babu was when he was supposed to bring the lit torch closer to Ila's ghee-smeared face during mukhagni and his hand shook uncontrollably.

They named a street in Badarpur after Ila in the next fiscal year. She was twenty-one. To give light one must burn.

For Mrinal Babu, life after that gradually became unbearable. The night he disappeared, as usual he had his quota of four large whiskies and according to the bearer Sarju, who served him, he seemed for a change to be in good cheer. He asked Sarju about his family, bantered about the old times and as he looked at the large barge-like boats plying sand from the diara which Ila and I in our childhood had named Gaipajama, on the Ganges which flowed a muddy alluvial brown, he recalled the steamer parties he had given in the past which Sarju too remembered vividly, especially the memorable one for Sir Edmund Hillary, at which Sarju had followed the famed mountaineer all over the deck with a bottle of Coca-Cola and with an incantatory chant, 'Hillary Sir-cock sir, Hillary Sir-cock sir,' in an opium-induced fervour till he had to be thrown overboard for a while by Saifu Mian.

After he downed his fourth whisky, Mrinal Babu walked to the edge of the courtyard and stood by the railings and stared at the water for a long time. Perhaps he saw a half-burnt body float past as I once did standing at the same place. Perhaps he remembered the icy cold water at Dover as he stepped into that narrow sea. Francoise Berlemont looking like a young Charlotte Rampling with bobbed hair kissing him luck, the flashbulbs going off, before he started his historic swim. From Dover to Calais. It is said that Mrinal Babu proposed marriage to Francoise five times but like Caesar each time she refused. Francoise shouting to him encouragement from the boat which followed on the heaving water, holding on to her trilby in the strong wind. Ila once told me that Mrinal Babu didn't actually finish that swim but had got into the boat much before Calais. The water had grown too cold. What is it with Bengalis and the English Channel I wonder sometimes.

Mrinal Babu unlocked the small iron gate that led to the steps which continued down to the edge of the Ganges. Sarju watched all this from the other side of the courtyard. That was the last anyone ever saw of Mrinal Babu.

He stood at the edge of the holy river unaffected by the early November chill and then the famed mighty swimmer at the age of eighty perhaps once more plunged into a swim to the other side.

To this day people in Kadam Kuam speak of Mrinal Babu's disappearance as if it happened only yesterday, though in reality decades have gone past and in the intervening years there have been many sightings, in Howrah, Benaras, Allahabad, and further upstream, in Paris, and London near the Thames, but none conclusive and all adding to the legend. For a time it seemed wherever people from Kadam Kuan migrated to Mrinal Babu would magically follow and then disappear just out of ken at the next street crossing.

I myself saw him last Sunday at Allahabad Station around 1 a.m., as the Patna-Delhi Magadh Vikramshila Express slowly chugged out of the station. He was standing at the A.H. Wheeler bookstall, reading a book in his white double-breasted seersucker suit. Just a momentary flash and then I dropped back to my heavy Old Monk-laced sleep. In the morning when I thought about it I laughed out loud and rationalized that it couldn't have been him. Mrinal Babu never read books.

I was on my way to Delhi to collect the advance copies of my first book, *The Autobiography of Sudama Pathak*, from a mainstream publisher.

Conjunctivitis

'Come on Ritwik, open your eyes. Does it hurt much?' He heard Dr Mishra's reassuringly warm voice, one that had soothed the frayed nerves of generations of Patna parents, but still kept his eyes closed. The tears continued to seep out.

'He has been like this for the past two days. Crying all the time and running such a high temperature. We have been so worried. As soon as the curfew was lifted in Kadam Kuan we called you.' He recognized the tiredness in his mother's usually ebullient voice.

He felt someone trying to pry open his eyes. Ritwik resisted but then Dr Mishra pressed gently underneath the left eye with his thumb and succeeded in slowly popping it open like that of a doll. Only the eyes were not blue but red.

Father standing at the foot of the four-poster bed looking anxious and tired, Dr Mishra looming large over him, Iladi in her peach-coloured pinafore clutching a red Morocco collector's edition of *A Tale of Two Cities*, smiling but managing to look troubled at the same time, and Mother in her red-bordered sari sitting by his side, her hands gently pressing his arms. Ritwik saw all of them through a perpetual red haze.

'The eyes are so red. So it is Joi Bangla, is it?' He heard his father ask in Bangla, the cigar-gruff voice shaky and uncertain.

'Ritwik, why didn't you open your eyes when I asked you to? Do you feel any pain? Certainly looks like Joi Bangla, the redness, the stickiness.' The light from Dr Mishra's ancient steel torch blinded him for a second.

Ritwik kept quiet. He heard the word 'eyes' but he knew he couldn't make them understand ever. The tears started again.

'Why doesn't he speak? It is so unnatural. Usually he just can't ever keep quiet. Talks incessantly. A regular chatterbox.' Mother asked anxiously.

'The Fakir was tall, stooped and had a red beard. He wore a black tunic and his hair was matted with ashes. He kidnapped bichoo boys and sold them later on. The eyes were blazing red, like that of Mahisasur, and he had one on his forehead that was always closed. They pierced his eyes and left him to die. Ritwik stood there and watched. The third eye opened and a solitary tear dropped.'

'What is he mumbling?' Father came closer, straining to hear clearly.

'Something about a fakir,' Dr Mishra offered.

'A fakir?'

'A fakir with a red beard and three eyes. Must say, he is quite an imaginative lad.'

'Not really. Basically the pirate Red Beard from *Phantom* and bits of Homer. I made it up to keep him in line so he won't write 'Ritwik Ray' all over my precious books in crayon. Seems to have worked. Poor duffer.' Iladi set the record straight in her usual imperious manner.

'Homer?'

'You know, *The Odyssey*, *The Iliad*.'

'Right, of course,' Dr Mishra replied somewhat miffed at Ila's impertinence but years of experience with children also made him see the unalloyed brightness of her mind.

'Ila reads too much and should now go home,' Mother offered as a way of explaining everything.

'Right Mamima. Good show duffer. Will read to you *A Tale of Two Cities* tomorrow morning. Get well soon or I will have to visit Gaipajama alone this Sunday.'

'That's Mrinal Babu's niece, isn't she?' Dr Mishra inquired.

'Yes, she is very attached to Ritwik. Very bright but somewhat strange but then the whole Thakur-Chowdhury family is strange,' Mother replied to Dr Mishra's query.

'Such an aristocratic family but then inter-caste marriage will always bring about ruin,' Dr Mishra put forth his firm belief in the perils of miscegenation.

'Yes, of course, but what about Ritwik?' asked an exasperated Father.

'He is in delirium. Because of the high fever. I guess he has been frightened, rather shocked by something. Can't be Ila's 'bogeyman', fakir, Homer, whatever. Did he by any chance witness the boy get killed?'

'We were not at home. Spring fair at the Bankipore Club.'

'Well, cold compress and medicine will take care of the fever. The eyes are swollen and red because of the conjunctivitis. It is fairly common right now, nothing to worry about, but highly contagious. Can't explain the crying but the ointment should take care of the redness and swelling.'

'Turns out that the boy was a refugee from East Pakistan. Not a Hindu, mind you, but Muslim. They should have been more careful. Just broken his legs perhaps. That would have been adequate,' Father said after a while.

'Ray sahib, these people are totally different from us. They can't integrate and frankly neither can I. I have a few Muslim friends and have drinks together at the club sometimes but I never have food at their homes. I always say I have some fast or the other to observe.'

'Well I can have their kebabs and kormas but never the vegetarian food, dal, salan, served in Muslim homes. Once I had some at Professor Khan's place and I almost vomited back on to the plate. It was very embarrassing.'

'They won't ever go back. It is already six months since the war ended but they still keep coming in. They have their own country now but I tell you they will keep coming in and multiply and in a few years in the border towns like Kishanganj there will be total demographic change. The crime rate will go up. We were shortchanged at the time of the partition. Same is happening now.'

'You are right, Mishraji, Mrs Gandhi should seal the borders and send all the bastards back. All this 'Garibi Hatao' and nationalization of the banks can wait. You know I sent Rs 1,001 for the Muktibahini but not for this. Let's go to the drawing room. Runu Debi has sent a box of Churchills from London. The 'fasting' excuse is very good, perhaps I will try it out the next time,' Father said to Dr Mishra and then both of them went outside, leaving Mother looking at Ritwik with deep creases on her forehead.

Ritwik felt a terrible pain in his eyes, as if someone were sticking pins in them and his whole body was on fire. The Fakir had looked at him, they couldn't destroy his third eye. Ritwik kept his eyes closed and the image receded gradually.

He recalled everything now, just as it had happened two days back. He was alone at home. Doyamoyee, their old brahmin cook from Baghmara, was making the dinner. Parents had gone to the Bankipore Club and would be home late. Earlier in the evening Iladi had come with her Tintin comics and they had both read *Cigars of the Pharaoh* again. That was their all-time favourite as Tintin visited India and met the Maharaja of Gaipajama, which Iladi had assured Ritwik was just across the Ganges from Patna. In fact it was the small island-like expanse of sand visible when the fog lifted in the winter from the ramparts of the Bankipore Club, and where even the cows were so holy and modest that they wore pajamas. All this while Iladi sipped her coffee (black) and Ritwik his Bournvita.

Then Saifu Mian came to take Iladi to the akhand kirtan at the Maithili scholar Ram Lagan Jha's house, at the back of which was a small shallow pond where goldfish swam along with the rohu, katla and bhetki of daily consumption. Professor Jha's daughter Shreya and Iladi were classmates at St. Joseph's Convent. 'Ritwik, you also come with me. Doyamoyee Devi, bring out a clean T-shirt for Ritwik to wear, one preferably without Bournvita stains.' Iladi let her wishes be known to Doyamoyee Devi.

'Ritwik will do no such thing. He will have his dinner then we will listen to *Binaca Geet Mala* and then he will go to sleep. He is not going anywhere and Ila, never use that tone with me ever again. I spanked your mother when she was little and I can spank you too.'

'She is right,' Saifu Mian smiled and said to Iladi. Ritwik could hear his hopes crash and shatter.

'Kaka you always take her side just because she feeds you paan in the evenings when there is load-shedding.' And then Ila di turned towards Doyamoyee Devi who was laughing and said, 'My mother would have hit you back.'

'Yes she would but Runu always cried and made up later on. She was a dear.'

'Well, neither would I cry nor apologize. The duffer can stay with you. Off I go.' Iladi along with Saifu Mian made her exit.

The evening passed as per Doyamoyee Devi's schedule. Ritwik had his dinner and then became drowsy as Ameen Sayani's soporific voice dipped in thick chocolate washed over him. After the *Binaca Geet Mala* ended Doyamoyee carried a heavily sedated Ritwik to his room upstairs and put him under the mosquito net.

He woke up sometime late in the night. The continued hum of the kirtan was pierced by a loud wail. Ritwik shuffled over to the window rubbing his eyes and saw Saifu Mian pin a boy of fifteen or sixteen against Professor Jha's house and hit him across the face with the shoe he was holding in his hand.

From what Ritwik could gather the boy probably was trying to make off with a pair of shoes from the front verandah of Professor Jha's house and was caught by Saifu Mian as he tried to run away. The kirtan stopped. The devotees, among whom were all his neighbours, rushed out. The boy was whimpering now and trying to touch Saifu Mian's feet. Ritwik heard Saifu Mian explain to Professor Jha the situation. The boy was now being held by Rajuda, Professor Jha's son.

He heard Professor Jha tell Raju to let the boy go but then Mr Bhattacharjee who ran a medicine shop around the corner suggested the police must be called. Others joined in and shouted that an example must be made of the thief, a message sent out to the slums which had rapidly come up all around the colony. Among the 'gentry' Ritwik could make out Professor Sen, Justice Sharma, Dr Sinha, Sanyalda, Rudrada and assorted drivers, servants and retainers.

Bhattacharjee caught hold of the boy by his hair and punched him on the mouth. The beating started in earnest then. It was as if the crowd were waiting for some switch to be thrown that would cut off any inhibition, kindness and humanity which otherwise would come in the way. The boy lay curled up on the street, trying to protect his face and groin, the trouser torn open at the waist, blood dripped from his mouth and nose as he was simultaneously kicked by ten to fifteen people. Saifu Mian now tried to intervene but he was pushed back and asked to leave by Rajuda. The boy kept crying 'Ah maa go, Ah maa go', but nobody listened to him. The atmosphere was that of a carnival, men were laughing and smoking and women and children watched fascinated from their terraces, some of the older children were out on the street with wickets and hockey sticks waiting for their turn.

Ritwik saw Saifu Mian go silently into Professor Jha's house and after a while come out with a sleeping Ila in his arms. As he passed below on the street he looked up and saw Ritwik and gestured with his hand violently for him to move away from the window. He then latched the gates of Hriday Kutir and climbed up the marble steps, the arms of Ila like that of a floppy doll around his neck.

The boy was almost unconscious, the right hand smashed, a couple of ribs broken, the shirt totally torn off held only at the cuff of the smashed hand, the eyes swollen shut, a deep gash on the forehead where one of the halwais engaged for the kirtan had hit him with a khunti.

A couple of the younger merrymakers, all in their teens and early twenties, now pick up the boy by his arms and legs and take him to the children's park where each evening and on Sunday mornings Ritwik plays cricket with his friends. There is a huge banyan tree flanking one corner of the park where in the cricket season one end of the cricket net is tied. The boy is now tied to the base of the tree. Ropes around his neck and waist, head lolling on to his chest. He doesn't whimper now, not even when some young twelve-year-old kid gingerly walks up and kicks him in the stomach, or pokes him with a wicket. Ritwik stands there at his watchtower transfixed, the beacon of his mind locked on to the smashed face of the boy at the base of the banyan tree.

He wants to move from the window, but can't, and neither can he close his eyes. He isn't even sure whether it is a dream or reality anymore. He has had till now in his young life seen nothing in the past that could prepare him for this. Though he has seen violence, knife fights, Shantu Ghosh's ear sliced off by a rangbaz from Subzi Baug, Harryda slapping a rickshaw-puller for demanding a higher fare from Mrinal Babu, and once or twice even the random firing of pistols in the air during a confrontation, he has taken it all as the normal course of life. But this present incident is the first time he comes up close with inherent middle-class Indian mohalla cruelty and the casualness of it, the social sanction of it disorients him. He knows each one of the perpetrators. These are the people he meets each day, boys who sometimes include him in their cricket teams, uncles who buy him comics and chocolates, who come to his house and have food there. The coordinates in his mind shift forever altering the way he looks at things; what frightens him the most is not the fact that he knows them but that he will know them for the rest of his life. This is what he comes from.

Suddenly Ritwik opens both his eyes and Mother can't stifle the scream that rises in her throat. The eyes unfocussed and dilated look awash in tears of blood and drops of it fall on the pillow, staining the chikankari red.

Sudama Pathak and the Patna Good Food Guide

TIKKI CHAAT

There is a soft slowness in the Patna air which affects all of us in some way or the other who have grown up slouching at the corners of its myriad streets. Kadam Kuan, Patna, in the late eighties was a place of genteel shabbiness, large colonial houses with peeling paint, peopled with once aristocratic families come down in life. Mostly upper-caste Bengalis, Kayasthas and Bhumihars, with Yadavs and Banias on the fringes. Here Austin Minors, Chevrolet Impalas and Standard Heralds still abounded and were mostly rented out as the bridegroom's car during the marriage season. The logic being that driving down in an ordinary Maruti or a Fiat would dilute the grandeur and drama of the occasion. Since in Patna, not yet corrupted by western mores like Calcutta or Delhi, you still marry only once in a lifetime, the more outlandish the car, the better. For my own wedding a couple of years back I drove out in a mint-green Pierce-Arrow chauffeured by Saifuddin Mian, a retainer of a once flamboyant zamindar, but I drove back in a sky blue Maruti Omni which my father-in-law had generously provided for his daughter.

It is a somewhat insular place where everybody knows everybody else and nothing remains secret for long. Ambition and upward mobility are looked down upon and the trading classes frankly distrusted. Part of it is envy and part of it comes from the general semi-feudal ambience of the place. It is in many ways still a pastoral society where the barter-economy is strictly followed.

Most houses have retainers who haven't been paid in years but since there is no discernible difference between the condition of the owner and the retainer, there isn't much talk of class struggle either. I myself sometimes mistake one for the other and I have lived here all my life. One patrician looking elderly man with a striking resemblance to the old fifties movie actor Rehman, who I was convinced for years was a scion of a once illustrious Bengali family actually came to it as a cook in the forties. The young son of the family took him up to be his friend and even gave him the bedroom next to his, where he has continued to live till today. The Buicks and the Studebakers are gone but their friendship remains strong.

Even the girls, all kohl-lined and with round dimpled cheeks in Rani-coloured salwar suits and American georgette saris which makes sweat gather around their necks and waists, eating tikki chaat along with their mothers in the mind-bending Patna heat, do not get married until they are twenty-eight. They sulk, waste and pine away, convinced their good-natured ignorance is some kind of virtue. The only excitement in their lives, the three days from Saptami to Navami each October during Durga Puja, when decked out in their six sets of new clothes, they sit imperiously like princesses in the forecourt of the Ramakrishna Mission on Nala Road every morning, afternoon and evening, waiting to catch a longing look from the similarly lovelorn Kaushikda, Shubhojitda,

Shomuda, Ritwikda and yes even yours truly Sudamada, and all the other das, a look which would carry them on to the next Puja. In the meantime, if lucky, something serious could develop like a shared plate of tikki chaat—served in a chipped white ceramic plate along with the mandatory aluminum spoon—like between the famed coquette of Khaderan Singh Marg, Rukmini Mishra and Sudamada slouching by the side of Arvind Mahila College. Unforgettable. The watery sour-boiled kabuli chana, thinly sliced green chillies, the crisp tikkis, the smell of the sewer flowing nearby, Rukmini's watery eyes and the bent aluminum spoon which kissed and sucked at both our lips. That was the most fun I ever got from a five-rupee note. Unforgettable.

GULAB JAMUN

In Kadam Kuan, across the street from the Hindi Sahitya Sammelan building, painted a bright Gelusil pink—where in my childhood in the very same august halls that Dinkar and Renu had read their works, every few months a hosiery fair would take place, and whose prime beneficiaries and customers were our servants and maidservants—lay one of the few Sardar establishments in the locality: Peshawar Sweet House. Est. 1949, Proprietor Randeep Singh Chandumajra.

There, once when I, Sudama Pathak, was ten years old, I had the best gulab jamuns of my life. The earlier night we had slept late, as it was 25 June, 1983 and India had just beaten West Indies to lift the Prudential World Cup. The whole of India was in a euphoric daze. So when the next morning my servant Munna with a wide smile on his hydrocephalic face, woke me up around noon and announced, 'Sardarji ka barah baj gaya,' I knew it was going to be another memorable day.

Sardar Chandumajra in his pomp and happiness, in a white safari suit which made him look like a bandmaster of Patna's famed Master Musa Band, with a bhangra troupe for background music was doling out small clay handis full of gulab jamuns to each and every passer-by on the main street. The whole community was out thronging the street, the rich, the poor, the young, the old, the lame, the robust, and there was much singing and dancing going on. In the midst of all the gaiety stood Sardar Chandumajra, the very soul of rectitude and generosity humbly doing his bit for God and country.

In each handi, the mouth covered by pink gauze, nestled four huge gulab jamuns, as perfectly formed as donkey balls. As my eager teeth bit into the spongy softness and the syrup dribbled from my lucky lips I thanked Sardarji and God (in that order) a thousand times. From there we went on to the old area of Kadam Kuan near Park Road where a local rangbaz by the name of Harvinder Rai had organized a similar party and there we had some sumptuous rosogollas. It was truly a happy day.

JALEBI

2 November, 1984. 10 a.m. The back courtyard of Students' Scientific High School, Kadam Kuan, Park Road. Two days

after the assassination of our beloved leader, Mrs G., Munna in his hydrocephalic pomp doling out jalebis from huge containers seized from Peshawar Sweet House. Jalebis: huge, orange, with latticework patterns, and supremely satisfying. I again thanked Sardarji and God (in that order) a thousand times. Though I do wonder now if it was a truly happy day.

GOLDEN LOLLIPOP

The ten best years of my life between the ages of six and fifteen were spent at St. Xavier's High School, Patna. Whose magnificent cement-grey neo-Gothic building is flanked on one side by Golghar and on the other overlooks the Gandhi Maidan. Whatever its many detractors may say, for me it was and still is the best school in all of Bihar. It was started in the early forties by Irish-American Jesuits who to their eternal credit created a unique institution which for the next sixty years would, as they say in Patna, provide its 'cream' with unparalleled educational development. Their good work has been continued by the pious Indian Brothers and Fathers who now run the school. Hopefully every Friday after the extended assembly in the morning, the boys still march along to the soul-stirring strains of the 'Star-Spangled Banner'.

Since my father Nalin Vilochan Pathak 'Vidyarthi' taught the senior classes Sanskrit, my admission to that prestigious abode of learning was a mere formality. I was also the regulation poor boy in the class.

Even though by the time I enrolled in the late seventies, the medium of instruction had changed to Hindi, proficiency in the English language was a much sought-after accomplishment for both the students and the faculty. So while you, dear reader, were trying to measure out the length of a wavelength I was doing the same to a tarang-dairdhya in my bhautiki class.

But 'spoken English' was important and to augment our learning we had compulsory elocution classes twice every week. And when I was eleven years old I, along with my good friends Lucky Arora and Diwakar Sahay, was recruited to join the elite group of honey-voiced choir boys who were members of that legendary Xavier's fraternity, the Glee Club. Apart from the three of us there were also Manish I, Manish II, Rajiv IV and Amit I in the group.

Miss Vera Mookerji with her rainbow-coloured skirts and Parveen Babi profile was the music teacher and moderator. On the stage she wielded a mean Spanish guitar to complement her high contralto. The club used to have its practice sessions on the first floor of a building next to the handball courts where we played an indigenous strain of handball called 'liner' with skinned-off tennis balls during the tiffin-break.

We would sing at all the school functions, the annual sports day, the school fete, start of the inter-house drama competition—there were four houses: Lions, Tigers, Leopards and Panthers. Needless to add I was a 'Tiger'. We also sang each Friday before the march-past. Just as the Glee Club would end its performance with a flourish, the opening bars of the

'Star-Spangled Banner' would waft out through the public address system.

We usually started with 'Lead Kindly Light', continued with 'We Shall Overcome', and ended with a full-throttle 'The Joy of The Lord is My Strength'. There was no social occasion in the Xavier's calendar which was complete without a show-stopping Glee Club number. For variety we also sang Boney M's popular 'By the Rivers of Babylon', 'Brown Girl in the Ring' and ABBA's 'I Have a Dream' and 'Take a Chance on Me' which the convent girls absolutely loved. And it was outside the convent front gates one December evening after we had finished our life-enhancing repertoire of Christmas carols that Rukmini Mishra, a proud daughter of a proud Nala Road paediatrician, bought me an orange ice-encrusted lollipop from the Golden Ice-Cream vendor with his dinky little yellow cart for 50 paise and having a long teasing lick first passed on the bar to me along with her phone number. The taste of which needless to add I am sure even Nirula's of Delhi would not be able to top. Since we didn't have a phone at home I passed on Diwakar's number.

The years spent at Xavier's are like a dream. I know those days are irretrievably lost but still I attend all the alumni meets. Now with even Lucky gone, invariably I am the only one there representing my batch. I usually sit nursing a large whisky on the high diving-board and try to gauge intently the depth of the drained-out pool. The rest are all in Delhi. Manish I, Manish II, Rajiv IV, Amit I. Life since Xavier's has been a steady downhill ride.

KHEER

In mid-October 1990, I was once rushed to the emergency ward of the Patna Medical College Hospital with 50 per cent burns on my legs and torso. I was then a seventeen-year-old student activist and a couple of days before had tried to immolate myself outside the Patna University Vice-Chancellor's office during a gherao against the Mandal Commission recommendations. As an upper-caste boy from a middle-class background I had very strong reservations about the Mandal Commission recommendations. I still do. But that morning as I left with Diwakar Sahay to participate in the demonstration and stand up for my rights, self-immolation was certainly not on the cards.

Everything is a blur after that. I guess heroism is a spur-of-the-moment thing. You can't plan for it. When I opened my eyes a day and a half later I was in the burns ward of PMCH with a victim of bride-burning on the adjacent bed who, after driving me crazy with her small animal-like groaning throughout the afternoon and evening, finally died around midnight.

A couple of days later I was out of danger but chest down my body was fully bandaged. I remember Father brought a new janeu for me to wear but it itched so much that I tore it off as soon as he went home. The smell was terrible and due to intense pain I wove in and out of consciousness all day. It was a largish L-shaped room with only four of the beds occupied.

With mind-altering pain, if one is lucky, one sometimes gets transcendent lucidity as a complimentary offering. Like a gold coin in a bar of soap.

It was in that state of hallucinatory delirium I think I had the best kheer of my life. In one of my lucid moments, I forget whether it was afternoon or evening, I found Ritwikda and Miradi sitting beside my cot and looking at me anxiously. Since I barely knew them I was much surprised to see them. Ritwikda was a scion of an old head-in-the-clouds Patna Bengali family and I knew him from Kadam Kuan. He worked for a national daily and sometimes covered the local cricket tournaments for it. He is some kind of a writer now. Perhaps a poet. An ex-Xaverian himself, he once had my picture published when I had hit a century against our traditional rivals St. Michael's at Gardanibagh Stadium, playing in the Mohit Mohun Bose Tournament. As the Man of the Match I had received the 'Sunny Tonny', a cricket bat endorsed those days by Sunil Gavaskar. About the only prize I have ever got in my life.

Miradi of course was my friend Diwakar Sahay's cousin. I had seen Miradi many times at Diwakar's house and had admired her from afar. She had the remote beauty and serenity which one usually finds in upper-class Patna girls who never have to worry about anything in their lives.

I am sure it was the first time she had ever entered the general ward of any government hospital but by her mere presence she transformed it into an air-conditioned private room in an upmarket nursing home in Patliputra Colony where nurses usually have two separate sets of towels for wiping one's face and arse.

The one week that I spent recuperating in PMCH was the most despondent of my life. Alternately ranting against the world in general and feeling suicidal. I didn't want to live anymore. At night the cool breeze from the Ganges provided the only respite and lulled me into sleep. One night I dreamt of the Glee Club performing beside my cot ABBA's 'I Have a Dream'. We were all there: Diwakar, Lucky, and even I, Sudama Pathak. For some reason Diwakar was woefully out of tune that night.

And then one day Miradi wafts in like an angel and feeds me a spoonful of magical kheer and everything changes. She wipes the darkness clean with her smile. Just to look at Miradi was such a pleasure. In another flash of lucidity I realized that if beautiful upper-class Patna girls started smiling more often, there would be less crime in Patna.

As shc left with Ritwikda I started hearing from afar the 'Star-Spangled Banner' again, slowly building up in tempo. Always a good sign for me. I wanted to live again. Do kadam-taal again. Left, left, left-right-left.

CHILD BEER

CHILD BEER SOLD HERE. The legend printed in bold betel-spit red. Over the side entrance of the hole-in-the-wall theka run by Manager Sharma, right opposite Annapurna Café in Kadam Kuan. A place where at the ripe old age of fifteen, the day we finished our Bihar Secondary Board matric examinations, Diwakar Sahay, Lucky Arora and I had our first bottle of super-chilled Thunderbolt Strong Beer sweating under the April sun. Before we went home we each ate a mixture of Pan Parag and Tulsi to kill the smell. The resultant hangover lasted for two days. In retrospect we shouldn't have had the Tulsi.

Once we had recovered, we felt like new men, and over the years increasingly patronized Manager Sharma and his democratic theka for its incomparable child beer.

DAL-ROTI

The best ever dal-roti I have had and the taste of which like lichen is embedded on my tongue is that which Dular Mandal, MLC (on a cultural seat as he had one thin volume of self-published verse *Meri Gyarah Kavitayen* to his name), ex-minister, history-sheeter (extortion, rape, murder, rape, land-grabbing, rape) served to me at Beur Central Jail. Beur Adarsh Kara to be exact, where I a couple of years back once went to pay him a ransom demand on behalf of my old school friend Lucky Arora who, unfortunately, had to be abducted by Dular Mandal since he had opened a Toyota Qualis showroom but had not bothered to send one gratis to the Prince of Patna.

So Lucky (my classmate of ten years and fellow member of the St. Xavier's Glee Club) was now tied to a stake in a Danapore khatal and I was at Beur Adarsh Kara with a grocery bag full of 500-rupee notes and a spanking new wine-coloured Qualis at the gate. We sat on wooden benches in the forecourt of Beur. It was a winter afternoon and the sun felt nice on my face, though I must say my mouth was as dry as chalk. Dular Mandal, squat, of medium height but with tremendous arms and shoulders and very short legs, in an off-white Sandow ganji and stone-washed jeans, was having his toenails cut by the head constable. The arms, thick and sinewy, were from the wrist to the elbow totally covered in swathes of bright coloured strings and amulets. No god or place of worship was left unacknowledged on those arms.

Since it was lunch, we all had lunch. Dular Mandal, I, and Manager Sharma, Bhumihar theka owner from Kadam Kuan, purveyor of the legendary 'Child Beer' and sharpshooter, who habitually wore white leather sandals and white terry-cotton trousers, and had soft brown eyes and a thin brown moustache. The head constable served the meal. Very simple stuff as Dular Mandal is a very austere and pious man. His only vice being ganja, which makes his eyes look as if they continually shed tears of blood. I must say I was a bit taken aback when I saw the meal but nonetheless pleasantly surprised.

We had dal-roti and Dular Mandal informed me that he could not eat any kind of meat as he had turned a pure vegetarian ever since he became an MLC, 'though Sudama Babu there was a time when I liked nothing better than a well-roasted field rat on a blustery winter night in my village'. Now, as a true son of the soil, he preferred only dal-roti and in Beur it was brought daily by his oldest acolyte around noon. The dal was masur, thick and cadmium yellow, with a garnish of coriander leaves. The rotis softened by ghee. As I expressed my gratitude Dular Mandal pointed towards Manager and said with a wink, 'He has a Marwari girlfriend. Convent-educated. She makes this dal-roti for me each day. Such devotion, one day I must reward her for this service.'

'Bhaiya, you have to perform the kanyadan when we get married,' Manager with reverence dripping from every pore said to his patron.

'Arrey just fuck and fly,' Dular Mandal said and roared his famous Dular laughter.

'I love her,' Manager Sharma said in a small voice and I could see the eyes of the sharpshooter glaze over. On second thoughts they were perhaps double-glazed like a Patliputra colony window. Dular Mandal did too so he said, 'Fine, get married. I will do the kanyadan.' To me he said with a baffled shake of the head, 'Manager gets very sentimental sometimes.'

I left the keys of the Qualis near Dular Mandal's chillum and stood up to take my leave. Dular Mandal opened the bag and took out two stapled wads of 500-rupee notes and threw them at me like I was a Moti.

'Next time bring me the mailing list, e-mails and phone numbers of all the Lion's Club and Rotary Club members of the Patna Chapter. Without communication I feel lost.'

I caught an autorickshaw for Hardinge Park where as agreed Lucky Arora was waiting for me.

'It was not too bad, Sudama, only the cow next to me had dysentery these past two days, so that was a bit of a bother. I hope she gets better soon,' Lucky said to me in the rickshaw on the way home, as I picked a coriander leaf off my teeth and wondered if the poor bugger was not suffering from Stockholm Syndrome. Apparently not, as overnight he sold his business and shifted to Dehradun.

Six months later as I read about Manager Sharma and his fiancé's twin suicides—their half-naked bodies with bullet wounds were found in Manager's white Maruti parked at an abandoned state guesthouse a stone's throw from Beur on the outskirts of Patna—the smell and taste of the simple meal I had enjoyed at the behest of Dular Mandal wafted into my consciousness as I inadvertently picked at my teeth for the mythical coriander leaf.

PANEER STROGANOFF

Now alas a dish I have never had. And all because of my ignorant in-laws. At my wedding a couple of years back as my close friends and relatives, after being on a liquid diet (rum, whisky, desi) for close to three days, sat down to eat, one of my inebriated uncles from the village, a legendary troublemaker who at my parents' wedding pacing to and fro in agitation after watching the Baiji's nach and consuming a bottle of Solan No. 1, a turn of the century muzzle loader slung on his arm, promptly stumbled and fell, and almost took the groom's head off, now inquired imperiously of my saala, 'Do enumerate the paneer dishes on the menu. I am a vegetarian.' For my wedding he had reluctantly agreed to leave the muzzle loader at home.

'Matar paneer, shahi paneer, karahi paneer, paneer butter masala, palak paneer, paneer pasanda, paneer pulao.' Saala Babu answered like a seasoned waiter, which I guess all ideal saalas must become at a sister's wedding in Patna.

'No paneer stroganoff? What an outrage. I won't eat.' Uncle kicked the chair pulled up for him. My friends though somewhat surprised, in their macho baraati pomp quickly rallied behind Uncle and they all kicked their chairs and demanded that either paneer stroganoff be served immediately or off they sail carrying the bridegroom on their shoulders so what if the bugger is ninety kilos. Uncle then staggered off and sat in the new Maruti Omni van parked near the mandap for guests to admire and rallied his troops from there, sorely missing his trusted muzzle-loader.

All the famous Patna hotels and restaurants were searched, but to no avail. Later I heard even the halwai threw a fit and threatened to quit. So chaos all around but no paneer stroganoff. The wedding resumed after a recess of three hours, and much hectic parleys and negotiations, all of which I spent like a batsman waiting for the green light after a direct hit run-out. A new bottle of Peter Scot was ceremoniously presented to Uncle by the bride's Mama, and Uncle promptly took out a straw from his kurta pocket and inserted it into the bottle. After this conciliatory gesture everybody hugged each other, Uncle budged from my Maruti Omni and the wedding started. That was a close one.

These days I hear the Maurya Hotel near Gandhi Maidan serves a killer paneer stroganoff during Sunday buffets. But can't eat there. Too bloody expensive.

LITTI

With baingan ka bharta. Everyone who came that day was shocked at the choice of the menu. But I stuck to it. It was what she would have wanted. Rukmini loved litti with baigan ka bharta. I could hear the gentry of Kadam Kuan accuse me of being a tight-fisted bastard but I knew what I was doing and choked back the tears. Only Dular Bhaiya, the true son of the soil, who came early in the evening and stayed till late, understood my true sentiments and consoled me by eating twenty litties. He would take each of the baseball-sized litties, crush it in his powerful ring-encrusted fist, dunk it in a katora full of fresh hot ghee (sent over in a stainless steel degchi very generously by him from his Danapore khatal), smear it with bharta and put it straight into his Lord Krishna-like mouth, where if you were not as myopic as my weak-kneed neighbours you would have seen a whole new universe. The whole past, present and future of Bihar could be glimpsed in a tableau between the rows of sparkling white teeth if you looked closely enough. He is such a comfort. But very soon he had to return back to Beur for the night. Alas.

As an event manager I have managed countless functions, marriages, birthdays, product launches, political rallies and kavi sammellans but I never thought that managing Rukmini's shradh would be the hardest yet.

GLASS OF MILK

Patna in 2004 is an open city, like Sarajevo in 1992, likc Baghdad is right now. All that matters is whether your will is strong enough or not. If you have a strong will you can just stop someone on posh Bailey Road and ask him to hand over the keys of his Maruti Zen and he will if your will is reinforced by a Mauser. You can drive into a house you like in Kadam Kuan, like the magnificent Hriday Kutir whose sole occupant is a crazy Pathan, in your new Zen, and start living there, regardless of the original inhabitants, who will take the hint eventually and move out. So now you have a house and a car, what you want is a bit of money. Easy. Just call up any doctor, lawyer, professor, trader, paanwala, just anyone who is stupid enough to work for an honest living when you would rather not and ask him to deliver the money each month at your feet. But I guess one shouldn't blame anyone. People who live in a war zone do act differently. The coordinates of one's perception alter diametrically. The weak should bloody well move out. There is no law, no morality, no friends anymore. No fences, no bloody neighbours.

So yesterday evening after I watched Mr and Mrs Sahay drive out in the evening to Bankipore Club like they do every Saturday, I scaled our common boundary wall and entered their house after breaking a ground floor window. Their son Diwakar had been a special childhood friend till one day Dular Mandal facilitated his admission to BIT Mesra and he migrated to Silicon Valley in the late nineties where he now wears baseball caps to hide his baldness in the living room.

This is a house I have visited a million times since childhood yet yesterday as I walked through their home everything looked new to me, the collective memory of twenty-five-odd years seemed remarkably erased. I sat on the sofa for ten minutes and thought about many things. Mostly about Rukmini. My wife. On the blank TV screen I could see her twisted, curled and charred body, the bone split by the fire. Exactly the way I found her on the kitchen floor nine months back. I closed my eyes and concentrated. I asked myself questions. Was Sudama Pathak a good husband? Was Rukmini a good wife? Would things be different if I had a regular job? Would she still be alive if her heartless father had booked a flat in Patliputra Colony as he had promised to? Who knows?

Then I needed to piss, so I walked over to the bathroom in the master bedroom where Uncle and Auntie slept and which I had never used and pissed into the bowl. The doors wide open. On the way back to the living room, I opened the fridge and took out one of the two glasses of milk which I knew would be there and again sat down on the sofa, gently sipping the sweet cold liquid, and brooded some more about sweet Rukmini. A cold glass of milk is always good for the nerves.

Waiting for Godard

Fall 1990. I am back in Patna now. Except there is no 'fall' in Patna ever. It is still summer here. But the evenings have grown cooler. Yesterday, night, sitting on a rattan chair, in the lawns of Bankipore Club, the breeze from the Ganges felt wonderful. In the past five years the river has moved a couple of hundred metres from the walls of the club. White sand has overwhelmed the shoreline. A carcass of a steamer is marooned in the middle. Upstream, one can see the Gandhi Setu Bridge which connects Patna to Hajipur and Sonepur. Before it was built in the late seventies, we used to cross the Ganges in a steamer during Durga Puja holidays when we went visiting our maternal cousins in Lalganj. Gandhi Setu finally opened up Patna to the whole of Bihar.

The doob grass felt soft and cool beneath my bare feet. The dew had wet the aanchal of my ochre chiffon. Tiny blades of monsoon-lush grass remained stuck between my toes as I curled them.

The river still has the power to make me leglessly nostalgic. Though I must admit the Golden Eagle beer helped. The women in Patna still stare at another woman drinking in the 'open'. Some things never change. Samar was having a reunion of sorts. All his old Xavier's buddies were there with their overweight wives and petulant self-assured children.

The fact that the wives were all at least ten years older than I perhaps made them feel solicitous about me. They were sweet about our marriage. And the beer helped. A few of them to their credit were drinking Blue Riband Gin topped with Limca. But they, as good Patna women, were cautious about it in the 'open'.

Samar Sinha as the Patna wives phrase it is my 'hubby' and he of course was in the centre of it all. Never fails to amaze me how this innate charisma of his never dims and in the midst of an adoring sorority, whether Arts Faculty Building, North Campus, or Low Memorial, Columbia, or Bankipore Club, Patna, it burns and soars brighter and higher. Like Edna St. Vincent Millay's fucking candle. How Ritwik would jest about it, my liking Edna St. Vincent Millay. How square and 'conventish' in my taste I was. Ritwik was cool and ironic. He liked Philip Larkin and sucking my toe. Though perhaps not in that order. Sweet Ritwik.

Samar Sinha, my fabulous 'hubby' is perhaps a bit of a folk hero to his friends in Patna like he was to us when were undergraduates. Brilliant subalternist scholar who wrote the definitive insider account of the Emergency days in Patna. Tall, slightly stooped, a full salt and pepper beard, bit of a skirt-chaser who actually took part in the JP Movement and was shot in the leg for his zeal. Sixteen years back. On 16 March, 1974 when the Chhatra Sangharsh Samiti activists were fired at in Patna.

Sampoorna kranti ab nara hai
Bhavi itihaas hamara hai

It is a nubby one-rupee-coin-sized wound just above his left knee. He likes me to bite it, roll it under my tongue like a nipple when we make love. The limp though is a bit of an affectation. I guess with all that charisma one can't help but be a showman. Half the women here have been in love with him at one time or another it seems.

'Laloo Yadav is the best thing that has happened to Bihar in fifty years. For the first time we have democracy here,' Samar proclaimed about the man who had recently become the chief minister of Bihar with an unprecedented 'backward' support.

'In a year he will turn all of Patna into one big khatal,' one chiffon-clad wife observed very softly.

Samar dismissed the opposition with an impatient wave of his hand. 'It is just your generations-old upper-caste Kayastha prejudice talking, Mona. I know Laloo from the days of the Emergency. He is all right. He will change Bihar. He is a man with a vision.' Samar gave his no-objection certificate.

So that's Mona Srivastava. Samar's first girlfriend and erstwhile neighbour. Before Ila Lytton-Mowbray, the doomed light-eyed Marxist ideologue from Kadam Kuan and Ritwik's mentor, whom Samar met just before the JP Movement when she was fifteen. Mona is now married to a close friend of Samar's. Opened the batting for Xavier's with Samar in the Sukhdeo Narayan Tournament played every April–May at Gandhi Maidan. I forget his name. Something very Bengali-sounding like Tiku, Piku, Pikai, Tikai. With the large number of Bihari Kayastha and Bengali upper-caste marriages taking place in Patna, soon there might be a need for a new caste altogether.

Mona, the princess from Pirmohani, now a junior counsel at Patna High Court, was very gracious, and since all Kayasthas in Bihar are related, it turned out that we too were second cousins. As she explained to the group, 'Turns out Mira's grandmother and my nani were first cousins in Ara. If nothing else we are practically "gotias".'

Samar Sinha laughed and squeezed her hand which he had been holding for the past three minutes. Noticed that. Samar the charmer.

Cut to the present. It is a Thursday evening today. I stand leaning against a faux Corinthian pillar on the verandah of the Indian Medical Association building opposite Gandhi Maidan. Samar's at home nursing his hangover. I am here waiting for Godard. And Ritwik *le fou*.

The Patna Cine Society regulars have started arriving in their twos and threes. Mostly middle-class Bengalis with a seasoning of upper-middle-class Biharis. They speak a strange argot of Bangla mixed with Magahi Hindi punctuated with English words for emphasis. Everyone speaks English in Patna. Across class and caste borders. Even the rickshaw-wala who, when I enquired why he was charging an almost double fare of ten rupees for Nala Road to Gandhi Maidan, shrugged his shoulders, wiped his brow with his linseed oil-coloured T-shirt and said, 'Sir, hum log gareeb type hain na.' Right, so I gave him the ten bucks. If he were with Lintas he would have got ten thousand. I guess I am the rich type.

They are showing *La Chinoise* today. Godard's barricades movie of 1967. According to Leonard Maltin's movie guide, 'Five young Maoists share an apartment and try to apply their politics to the reality of their lives. Godard aficionados will be fascinated; others may be bored.' Sounds wonderful!

Though I must admit I am more of a Truffaut girl than a Godard moll. I am a sucker for love stories.

I remember Ritwik and me outside the Miranda House Hostel gate having a shared anda-parantha bought from the PG Women's Hostel and deciding with the solemn certainty of youth that we will name our first born Antoine. Come what may.

The previous evening we had seen *Stolen Kisses* at the weekly 'Celluloid' cine society showing at the University. To quote Maltin Baba again: 'This alternately touching and hilarious film about an inept but likable jerk-of-all-trades is possibly Truffaut's best movie and one of the best treatments of young love ever put on screen. Third in his Antoine Doinel series, followed by *Bed and Board*.'

Ritwik was a long-haired nineteen from Hindu College and I a resolute eighteen then.

We had met for the first time at the screening of *Pyaasa* at Gwyer Hall a month before. Ritwik was the volunteer usher. Collected the subscription for the cine club and along with it my willing heart. He started coming over each evening to the

Miranda Hostel. Hand in hand we walked the length of Chhatra Marg a lot. Sometimes up to Kamla Nagar, a shared Thums Up at Chacha's and back by 7:30. Promptly fell in love. I liked the intensity in his eyes as he explained the 'auteur theory' to me. Appreciated it more when he put his arms around me, tilted my head and kissed me in front of the deserted University Cooperative Store. He summarily explained that this was how James Dean had kissed Natalie Wood in *Rebel Without a Cause*. Loving Ritwik was all about getting a higher education.

It was strange how for seventeen long years we stayed in Patna but only to meet in Delhi. We did stay in opposite directions of the town though. I in Patliputra Colony and Ritwik in Kadam Kuan. I attended St. Joseph's Convent in Bankipore and he went to St. Xavier's. It was at Convent I met Ila Lytton-Mowbray for the first and last time. I was in the fourth standard then. She came to our class one day bearing a huge jar of bubble gums. We stood up awestruck and curtsied and said 'thank you didi' as she distributed the bubble gums. A day before she had been crowned 'Miss St. Joseph's Convent'. In retrospect it is easy to see why she had such an influence on both Samar and Ritwik. Her austere beauty commanded you to be better than you could ever hope to be. And yes you could slice a lemon on that cheekbone.

I remember hearing Ritwik's name at gossip sessions during 'tiffin' with the senior class didis whose fan I was. It seems Ritwik had quite a thing for Lopamudradi, who was three years senior to me. At one of the last socials that the Convent girls had with the Xavier's boys, where all the ninth and tenth standard girls in white shirts and navy blue skirts accompanied by three nuns and a moderator would go over in a blue and white minibus right up to the Xavier's auditorium, around one corner of which would range the boys in white shirts and trousers spit-setting their Amitabh Bachchan pompadours hemmed in by a couple of burly Malayali Brothers in white cassocks and Bata loafers, it so happened that Ritwik and Lopamudradi disappeared for twenty frantic minutes only to be discovered near the swimming pool exchanging eternal love along with their phone numbers.

It was a big scandal and as Ritwik told me years later in Delhi, 'I never kissed her, let alone cop a feel. Just about managed to touch her hair. It smelled of Lakme Egg Shampoo. It was new in the market then. Not even five minutes and the moderator, Veronica Furtado, barges in teary eyed. I could have drowned her in the pool.'

Ms Furtado was quite a character. An authentic Goan from Mapusa who would, among her various other academic duties, also relish taking moral science classes where one memorable afternoon when I was in the sixth standard she brought a table lamp to the classroom, held out the plug and proclaimed, 'This is the male', then pointed out the socket and revealed that this was the female. Then she plugged it in and switched it on and we knew all about 'sexual intercourse'. It had the desired effect. For years Kanupriya Bhaskar, my maternal cousin who was a year older to me, thought that she would be electrocuted if she ever had sex.

A few months after she published a vicious diatribe on Amitabh Bachchan, long hair and the effect it had on the morals, to say nothing of the hormones, of impressionable Patna boys in Th*e Indian Nation*, Ms Furtado was finally asked to pack her bags for Mapusa. The school authorities had had their fill of her ever-escalating craziness.

Lopamudradi was such a glamorous figure to us. A classic half-Bengali, half-Nepali beauty from Naya Tola with flawless skin, light green eyes and whose skirt always rode a good two inches above her well-rounded knees. I totally believed Ritwik that he never ever kissed Lopamudra, because in Patna all love is conducted over the phone. Reportedly there have been cases where a couple has gone steady for five years and never even met. When you actually kissed a girl, the girl rightly assumed that the time to elope had finally arrived and marriage would soon ensue. There were a lot of elopements. Twenty-five-year-old men and fifteen-year-old girls whom they taught how to ride bicycles among other things, usually.

So even though we had never met I knew about Ritwik Ray. He had quite a reputation. By Patna standards, someone who my mother would routinely describe as 'characterless'. But then she was temperamentally biased against Bengalis. She felt that they were too 'free'. Whatever that meant.

I have a faint memory of sex-deprived Kanupriya, a close friend of Lopamudradi, pointing out a long-haired boy in a maroon shirt, cream-coloured flared Avis Jeans and Travolta boots during the annual Bankipore Club fete and saying with a nudge which was more of a shove, 'Ritwik Ray, the one who messed up Lopamudra Ghosh-Dastidar', and I with my trademark disdain, 'Is that him? Too babumoshai, don't you think?'

Kanupriya loved boys. Never actually met them for dates or anything. That would be too subversive. But always had a steady string of phone boyfriends. The secret of her success being her beautiful singing voice. Her signature song was Geeta Dutt's immortal 'Mujhe jaan na kaho meri jaan, meri jaan' from *Anubhav*. She sang that song incredibly well and it never failed her. Once for a month just before her Senior Cambridge exams she had so much phone sex with her twenty-one year old Pathan boyfriend from Subzi Baug that she was convinced she was pregnant. That month she even skipped her period. On some days she also had morning sickness. When she started feeling a heaviness in her breasts, freaked out of her tiny mind, she came to me for advice. I to my eternal credit told her, 'May you have twins. You could then name them Ram and Rahim.'

The weekend evenings when I was growing up were usually spent at Bankipore Club. It was fate again I think that didn't let Ritwik and me meet till we were both at Delhi University.

The Bankipore Club was founded in 1865. Just after the turbulent Mutiny years. It was then known as the European Club. Popular legend has it the peepul tree in one corner of the courtyard was used for hanging the rebels by the British. Sarju, the head-bearer of the club, swore on his mother's name that on each full-moon night the peepul tree lit up, festooned with the dangling bodies of the mutineers. It was common knowledge that Sarju was perpetually in an opium-induced daze. I would often dream about that tree lit up like a lighthouse as I swam frantically across the Ganges trying to reach the shore. In the dream I would usually drown. I still get that dream sometimes.

Ritwik as he told me later was also a regular at the club till he turned thirteen and then under his mentor and next-door neighbour Iladi's Marxism he took a principled stand and refused to be a part of all the decadence.

'What bloody decadence are you talking about Ritwik? We only played housie and watched Amitabh Bachchan movies every Sunday evening in the open-air auditorium, while our fathers played bridge or had whisky and soda at the bar. Do you remember the potato chips in the small oil-stained brown paper bags, washed down with a bottle of Fanta which we clasped with both our hands, eyes glued to the screen as Amitabh beat Ajit to a pulp in *Zanjeer*.'

'Mira, you have to remember that Iladi was a severe ideologue. Once she issued a whip, I had to fall in line. She left for JNU around that time and once in a while I would get a letter. More of a reading list than a letter. Wherein for example I would be instructed to go to a particular rack and take out Joyce's *Dubliners* and Orwell's *Down and Out in Paris and London* from the third and fifth row in the Hriday Kutir library. I stopped going to the club on the weekends. Part of the reason could be that I had more friends in Kadam Kuan to hang out with now. My defiance was a source of much amusement to my parents and only once in a while they would force me to attend, like during the Spring Fair or a New Year's Eve ball. Usually I would register my protest by wearing a khadi kurta and jeans, and sit brooding, looking intensely at the Ganges. A man apart. With a bottle of Coca-Cola in his left hand. Regret to inform that nobody ever noticed.'

'Everybody must have presumed that you had your dates confused. Thought it was the annual fancy dress party. Believe me they noticed you and pitied you, only also had the grace to say nothing to you.'

'I usually dressed up as an RAF pilot when I was a kid for the fancy dress parties at the club and at Xavier's. It was a serge blue uniform brought by Iladi's mother on one of her whirlwind visits to Patna. All I had to do was march smartly across the stage and salute. Absolutely hated it. Did that for four years till one fine day the trousers came up short at the ankles. There are still some friends from Xavier's who call me Biggles when we meet.'

'I quite enjoyed the fancy dress parties. Usually dressed up as a doctor with my father's stethoscope and a white coat which my mother had specially stitched and big oversized glasses, with Kanupriya's two younger brothers as my patients. I had a good routine and more often than not won a prize. I loved the attention and really wanted to become a doctor. Of course, then I grew up and realized one had to study science for it. No can do.'

'I wish you were studying medicine. Then you could take my pulse.' Ritwik bent and kissed the top of Mira Verma's head, which was trying to burrow into his chest. We were under Ritwik's duvet in his Model Town barsati. A chilly December afternoon. The colleges closed for Christmas vacations but we had stayed back. For joint studies. We did a lot of that those days.

Usually I would take a Mudrika bus from the Mall Road bus-stop and after a five-minute's ride get down near Alpana Cinema Hall in Model Town. Then a brisk five minutes' walk to Ritwik's barsati in Tagore Park. A classic example of Punjabi baroque, the house had yolk-yellow bathroom tiles adorning the whole of its facade. On summer afternoons it would shimmer from afar in a blonde haze.

It was my very own Sonarkella and at the top waited the laconic prince of Patna in his book-strewn lair. There were books all over. In rows of small sagging three-tier bamboo shelves bought from Kingsway Camp. The few hardbacks in the bottom and paperbacks everywhere. Even on the floor, piled neatly on newspapers. Ritwik's M.A. English course-books were kept piled up on the writing table. Early mornings he would work on his stories before leaving for his classes at the Arts Faculty Building. In the afternoon I would read them reclining on his deck chair, a gift from the landlord.

Sunday mornings we would invariably drive down in Ritwik's Yezdi to Daryaganj and scour its pavements from Golcha cinema hall to the overbridge for old books and back issues of the *The New Yorker*, *Sight and Sound* and *The Times Literary Supplement*. There, once, in a single morning's haul, we found a split-spine hardback of Hubert Selby Jr's *Last Exit to Brooklyn* and Martin Amis's *The Rachel Papers*. Later panning would dredge up such treasures as Osip Mendelstam's *Journey to Armenia*, the complete

Clearing House and Praxis poetry lists, Lillian Hellman's *Pentimento* and the collected plays of Clifford Odets.

Somedays if we were feeling especially affluent we would walk down the narrow galis leading to Jama Masjid and have rice and mutton stew at Karim's. Otherwise it was back to Sonarkella, and after a quick bath together in Ritwik's tiny bathroom, we would share Ritwik's 300-rupees-a-month three-tier dabba with its five rotis, rice, peeli dal and a seasonal subzi, with kheer on Sundays. I usually had the rice. After that we would read the books we had bought in the morning till it was time for me to go back to the hostel in the evening.

It was at Daryaganj during another Sunday book-hunt when Ritwik finally introduced me to Samar Sinha. Ritwik was in M.A. Previous and I was in my final year of History Honours. Samar was a couple of stalls ahead, squatting by a pile of old *Marg* volumes.

I knew about their shared history. Ritwik and Samar's. How Ritwik had tagged along with Ila and Samar everywhere and how crucial an influence they were on his life. Ila and Samar for me were not real persons but were more like elusive literary characters that I couldn't ever hope to meet. Like Holden Caulfield and the French lieutenant's woman. Part of it could be because of the way Ritwik would speak about his childhood with its mythic undertones. I knew about Ila's Irish father who disappeared into the Purulia wilds, and her uncle, the erstwhile zamindar from Manbhum, Mrinal Thakur-Chowdhury, who brought her up in Hriday Kutir, Kadam Kuan, Patna, where they were next-door neighbours to Ritwik. Ritwik, how he spent more time in Hriday Kutir than his own home and how they were both looked after by Saifu Mian, Mrinal Babu's ageless Pathan retainer. Ila and Ritwik's shared world of books. The love story of nineteen-year-old Samar and fifteen-year-old Ila. How they drifted apart when Ila followed Samar to Delhi. The violent death of Ila Lytton-Mowbray when she was attacked while performing her protest play on the outskirts of Delhi.

There was, I believe, some element of hero-worship in the way Ritwik looked up to Samar. Samar Sinha of course was a legend to us budding historians. I had borrowed his book *Patna 75: Total Revolution and JP* recently from Ritwik and read it. I had seen him often in the Delhi School of Economics cafeteria surrounded by fawning M.Phil. scholars, smoking Navy Cuts, drinking coffee. He would then walk back with some of them to Gwyer Hall where he had his rooms. I guess he then took their tutorials.

For all the shared history there was some unspoken barrier between them, one could sense it from Ritwik's behaviour. He wouldn't visit Samar that often and nor would he talk about him much. Whenever I suggested to Ritwik that we should visit Samar sometime, he found some excuse not to. That day I practically dragged Ritwik to where Samar in a crouch was flipping through the *Marg* volumes and demanded to be introduced.

'You know, Mira, I've known Ritwik since he was nine years old. He was the most well-behaved kid in all of Kadam Kuan, perhaps the whole of Patna. He did exactly what his elders told him to do.' Samar it was apparent was genuinely pleased to see Ritwik. He was terribly good to look at and there was no donnish pomposity about him. He wore his fame lightly.

'Well, he is not very well-behaved now.'

'With you, Mira, that would be a sin.' Ah, the legendary charm.

He took us to Karim's and ordered biryani. Ritwik couldn't articulate a single sentence, only smiled his shy smile once in a while and looked distractedly around. I knew that Ritwik had a propensity for withdrawing from the world of conversation sometimes when articulating even a single a word like a 'yes' or a 'no' could become a deeply traumatic affair for him. I knew he didn't want to accept Samar's invitation but since I had already said yes, he didn't have an option.

'He was a voluble little fellow but it seems he has grown quieter over the years. I have a theory about that. I believe we all have a similar quota of words stuffed into us at birth. How quickly we spend it is our lookout. I myself was a very quiet child but these days I can't seem to stop. Once in a while Ritwik Babu comes and visits me at Gwyer Hall but won't give his address to me. Though now I know why.'

'It is nothing like that, Samarda.' The first sentence that Ritwik uttered. Must have come as a relief to him.

'Call me Samar, told you so many times.'

'I can't, am still too provincial. Sets my teeth on edge.'

Samar and I both chose to ignore that.

'Ritwik was Ila's little lamb. Sorry. Ila was a friend of ours when we were young.'

'I know all about Ila Lytton-Mowbray. So tell me, Samar, were you the big bad wolf?' As usual Mira Verma couldn't resist shooting her big mouth off.

The Cine Society regulars in Patna are a curious bunch. Each time I encounter them I feel a bit strange. The men coming from offices in their sweat-soaked and defeated shirts, working long hours in small crowded offices packed with bare glass-topped tables, worn out rexine-backed chairs, solitary coloured glass paperweights and ancient Godrej typewriters. It just didn't synchronize. Seems frighteningly incongruous that they should come and watch Godard, or say Truffaut, or Resnais for that matter, thrice a month. On the other hand one can see it as a transcendentally hopeful sign for Patna. Did they really love the movies that much or was it something they just did, like eat mutton religiously on Sundays. A kind of middle-class conformity. The regulars are mostly Bengalis. Something I would never imagine my middle-class Bihari relatives indulge in. To them it would be too subversive even to contemplate going to see a subtitled French movie.

On Sunday afternoons when Doordarshan telecasts award-winning Bengali, Kannada, Malayalam and other regional language films with subtitles, they keep their TV sets religiously switched off. Biharis are more practical that way. They know what is good for them. They realize that telling Jean Paul Leaud and Jean-Paul Belmondo apart won't necessarily make them better secretariat clerks. Or for that matter knowing what 'Rosebud' meant to Charles Foster Kane make them successfully clear the

Bihar Service Commission Exams. In their hearts they are sure that this 'culture' thing is a big fraud.

Most of them don't even have a single novel in their homes. If one looks very closely one might find a copy of Gorky's *Mother* or Agyeya's *Shekhar: Ek Jivani* buried under *Competition Success* guides bought from the pavement booksellers of Apna Bazar opposite Gandhi Maidan. A stone's throw from where I am standing right now.

The raging topic these days is the Mandal Commission reservations which all my relatives feel has finally disenfranchized their children. 'It is better to be a Kurmi now than a Kayastha.' 'What is the point of reservation,' they wail, after all not even 'Yadavs and Kurmis would go to a Yadav or Kurmi doctor if they were ill.'

Some good old-fashioned prejudice from the upper-castes as they see their citadels crumble one by one.

One foolish eighteen-year-old cousin of mine got his new North Star sneakers burnt while he cheered another student on to immolate himself outside the Vice-Chancellor's office during a gherao in protest of the Mandal Commission recommendations a couple of days back.

'I didn't step back in time, Miradi. Some amount of kerosene probably spilled on to my shoes while I was pouring it over Sudama Pathak,' the monster explained when I went to meet him today in the morning, surrounded by his five fawning sisters, sundry relatives, the bandaged toe cradled in his mother's lap.

Sudama, of course, is still at the emergency ward of the Patna Medical College Hospital with fifty per cent burns.

But my Mamaji had the last word on his son's doing. Sitting outside on the veranda, in his planter's chair sipping tea and watching George Bush Sr. bully Saddam on CNN, he said quite plainly, 'Donkey hai.' Then he shook his head twice, the thin proud face suffused with the vital knowledge which many fathers at different times in their lives get, that their sons will never come to any good.

It is four years since I last saw Ritwik. He was going back to Patna that day. He had vacated his Sonarkella and his two cartons of books and a writing table now adorned my little mezzanine bed-sitter at Outram Lines. I implored him to stay back.

'Stay in Delhi and do your M.Phil. There is no point in going back to Patna. What will you do over there?'

'I will get some kind of job, maybe journalism, and I will finish my book of stories. Once I get a job we can get married.'

'What is the rush Ritwik? I still have a year of my Master's left and I would like to do an M.Phil.'

'Once we get married you can do anything you want. For that to happen, Mira, I will first have to get some kind of a job. I can then speak to your parents about our marriage.'

'Get a job here in Delhi.'

'I want to stay in Patna. I am sure of getting a job there. I know people there. Later we can come back to Delhi. In a year or two I will finish my book too.'

'I don't want to stay in Patna and perhaps teach at Patna Women's College or Arvind Mahila College. I want to go out and see the world. Samar says I might get a scholarship to study at Columbia. He is joining their faculty next semester. You would too if you only tried. Samar would recommend you, if you only asked him.'

'I don't want to go out. Perhaps it is hard for you to understand but I never had that desire and I would certainly not ask Samar for anything, let alone a recommendation.'

'He said he would. He thinks you are quite talented and should do an M.F.A. in creative writing. I showed him your stories.'

'You met him again, didn't you?'

'He is my teacher. Of course I met him. He is an extremely nice person and he keeps asking after you. What is between you two?'

'He broke Ila's heart, Mira.'

'Who is being provincial now, Ritwik? People move on. Samar and Ila were so young. They were barely out of their teens. You can't have a commitment for life at nineteen.'

'He broke her heart. She followed him to Delhi and they beat her to death here. He was there and he couldn't even save her. He broke her heart. If you can't be constant, you shouldn't love.'

'Nobody could have saved her. You are being unfair. Everybody ran to save themselves. Nobody realized she was left behind. We all read it in the papers. There was chaos all around. Perhaps he did break her heart. How does it matter to you?'

I know I shouldn't have said that. I knew how much Ila meant to Ritwik but couldn't stop myself. Usually I am not the jealous type but Ila had even after her death cast her austere shadow over Ritwik's life, his very thoughts. Every decision he took in his life, his first concern would always be 'what Ila would have done in a similar situation'. She was his touchstone.

Ila must have whispered in his ears, 'Go back to Patna, Ritwik. That is where your work lies. Let Mira feel lonely and abandoned. Let her mope and cry her heart out in Outram Lines.'

Since Ritwik didn't say anything for a long while after this, I realized it would be prudent to change the subject. We had only three hours till Ritwik boarded the Magadh Express from platform no. 10. I knew he wouldn't let me come to the station to see him off. He hated goodbyes.

'You don't need my parents' approval, and I don't need yours. Even if you got a job, Ritwik, my mother still wouldn't like you much. If you come to ask for my hand in a white Ambassador with a red light on top, all sirens blaring, she might relent. Barring that nothing. Even if you wrote ten books it wouldn't matter. The only book she has read in its entirety is Vimla Patil's *The Working Women's Cookbook*. The fun of it is she hasn't ever worked and she doesn't cook.' Tears flowed down my eyes. Just couldn't stop myself.

Ritwik put his arm around me and wiped the tears away. But they wouldn't stop. I held on to him. I can count on my fingers the number of times I have cried in my life. They would barely exceed the digits of my right hand.

We were down on the floor. The coir mattress soft beneath my back. Ritwik took my shorts off. Kissed the line of soft hair from my belly button to my pussy. Parted the labial lips down to the perineum with his inquisitive tongue. I arched my back. Held his head in place with one hand and with the other fished out a solitary condom from under the pillow.

The sheer delight I felt in his body I have never felt with Samar. Even the sight of Ritwik just sitting there and reading a book with his heavy black glasses on would sometimes give me goosebumps.

He was not conventionally good looking like Samar, with not one feature that was remarkable, but his eyes could bore into mine and catalogue all my thoughts with their intensity. There was something inherently melancholic about him but whenever he did smile it would light up any room he was in.

There would be days when we would be naked the whole time and couldn't take our eyes off each other. One of the first letters he wrote from Patna contained this poem. He had joined a national daily by then.

ANTICIPATION

It is evening now
And I am back from work
Slightly tired but happy
The eyes hurt
I put the glasses away

Have subbed enough shit today
The newspaper rubber bound
sits still on the window sill
The words swim away
In a sea of print, I know
For I have no energy to
Reel them in today
Like yesterday
So let it languish and
Tomorrow shall it join its brethren
under the kitchen shelf
Unbroken, unread.
I pour some whisky
About two inches worth
And unlatch the door
For if I am lucky
Any moment now
You shall enter
And make this bare
Weary room come alive with poetry again.
The whisky blond and mellow
Makes this waiting a slow pleasure.

'Don't drink too much. Certainly not two inches worth and lay off Larkin till we meet. Read Betjeman if you wish.' I wrote back to Ritwik trying to be brave and flippant when the poem in its clumsy way had articulated all my longings, my very loneliness.

Ritwik rides into the IMA Hall driveway on his Yezdi. He still looks the same. Four years haven't changed him a bit, except he has shaved off his moustache. He wears old Wrangler jeans, faded blue, with an olive green twill shirt. The shirt is untucked and it makes him look leaner than he is. I remember the shirt clearly. We had bought it together from Sarojini Nagar with the money that came from *The Sunday Statesman* after they had published a short story of Ritwik's. I remember I had bought a white cotton top that day. Later that evening we had watched Ketan Mehta's *Mirch Masala* at Alpana in Model Town.

Ritwik is wearing frayed delicate Kolhapuri chappals which accentuate his beautiful thin feet.

'I heard you were in town.'

I am glad to see he is not surprised that I am here. I can't discern any resentment either. Though it is bound to be there. No surprise after what I did.

'How have you been? I saw the Cine Society programme in the newspapers today. So here I am, waiting for Godard.'

Mira Verma. The love of my life. Here she was, on a cool October evening in Patna, at IMA Hall, looking as young and unaffected with the world as the day four years back when I kissed her for the last time and left for Patna promising to meet over the winter vacations. She wears an off-white cotton sari with a red border, a red sleeveless blouse and a red bindi made with sindoor, Bengali style. Not much of a surprise really, since Samarda, though a

Bhumihar, is in many ways more of a Bengali than I am. He certainly speaks and writes better Bangla than I.

Mira's hair is cut short, really short. Making it look like the hair of an impish schoolboy and not a mature women in her mid-twenties. She doesn't wear any make-up except for kajal, which makes her eyes look deep set and brings out her cheekbones. The New York sun has considerably lightened her skin tone. Though always fair for a Kayastha girl, she now has the complexion which one comes across in some Bengali Brahmin and Bhumihar girls. She is finally a convent-educated gori girl.

I knew she was in town. Samarda was on a sabbatical from Columbia, working on a new book, the influence of the Bihari bhadralok (Brahmin, Bhumihar, Kayastha, Rajput) in post-independence Bihar politics. From Sri Krishna Babu, Anugraha Babu, K.B. Sahay to Jagannath Mishra. He gave a lecture on this topic at A.N. Sinha Institute of Social Sciences a couple of days back. A colleague of mine covered it for the paper. There was a photograph too, arms wide apart, a half-burnt cigarette smouldering in his left hand, tortoise-shell glasses dangling on a chain at his chest, black denim shirt. Samarda in his 'prachar' mode. He spoke for over two hours. Without notes.

I wrote the caption beneath the photograph: 'Columbia University luminary and local lad, Dr Samar Sinha back in Patna after six years.' I am sure he would have been irritated by the 'local lad' bit. Though prone to playing an exaggerated 'Bihariness' among his non-Bihari friends, there is nothing provincial about him. He would be at home equally among peasants of rural Sasaram, the faculty parties in North Campus and sipping claret high up in a Central Park West apartment.

The report on the A. N. Sinha Institute lecture mentioned,

> Accompanying Dr Sinha was his wife Mira, an aspiring novelist. Mrs Sinha is also a Patna girl, daughter of the eminent Patliputra Colony neurologist Dr Shyam Nandan Verma. She has done her schooling from Patna. A product of both St. Joseph's Convent and Notre Dame Academy. She did her graduation and Master's in History from Miranda House, the elite Delhi University college for women and the dream destination for many Patna girls. After her Master's she got a scholarship to Columbia, where she was one of Dr Sinha's graduate students and the rest as they say was history. "I was only a half-bright scholar," Mrs Sinha replies when asked about her time at Columbia. Dr Sinha standing beside her laughs and looks with affection at his wife. They were married two years back in New York. This is their first visit to Patna after their marriage.

Two things: she is an aspiring novelist and more importantly she hasn't lost her sense of humour.

When we were together, she didn't write much. Occasional satirical essays for the hostel rag *Pig Tails*. She has a keen eye for detail and I valued her comments on my stories very much. She has an instinctive feeling for structure which born writers and few editors have and which can't be learned. She was to me for a long time that extremely valuable commodity, the first reader.

Even though she didn't call I had a premonition that she would come for the Cine Society screening. She is many things but a coward she is not.

'Have you seen *La Chinoise* before?' We walk towards the small park where a statue of Subhas Bose has recently been installed. A massive black stone structure, baton in hand outstretched and pointing towards the big maidan named after Gandhi and which the old timers simply call 'the lawn'. There were some street children playing around it and a dog was sleeping at the foot of the statue. The surroundings, garden and the lawn were relatively clean by Patna standards.

Long back when I was a young boy, around thirteen-fourteen years old, there used to be a small pond in the same place, 'pokhar' we called it, and each morning as I walked past its side on my way to Xavier's, a ten-minute walk across Gandhi Maidan, the grass-green moss-covered water would beckon me, as if inviting me for a dip. The pond was polluted, slimy and choked with water hyacinths, but still in the early morning when there would be very few people around, the place looked calm and almost beautiful. I would without fail throw a small stone and watch the splash and ripples leap up through the weed and bright green leaves every day.

Along the edges of the pond on the path leading to Kadam Kuan, there used to be bamboo sheds of artisans who made clay idols of Durga, Kali and Saraswati for the respective pujas and all through the years the idols in various stages of completion would provide me with indelible images of the perfection of the female form. I would usually stop and watch them at work. Many of them were from Bengal and were contracted to provide murtis for hundreds of puja pandals around town. They were extremely poor. Some years back all their sheds were dismantled, the pond was filled up with tons of garbage and soil and the space cleared for the memorial to Subhas Bose.

'I think the show will start late today. The film hasn't arrived from Calcutta yet,' I said to Mira as she shooed the dog away and sat at the foot of Subhas Bose.

'Do you get it from Nandan?' she asked me.

'Yes, sometimes also from the film archives in Pune. The train was supposed to reach around eleven in the morning. I went to the station in the morning, they said it was running four hours late. Saifu Mian, our projectionist, is there at the station now. Most of the trains are running late. Some have been cancelled. All because of L. K. Advani's Rath Yatra. It is supposed to enter Bihar today. It is strange how quickly the RSS which was just a stale joke to us in our childhood has attained a pan middle-class respectability.'

'About a year back Mother ordered fifty bricks with Lord Ram's name embossed on them from our village kiln. Our pujari

Vidyarthiji—you would remember him from Xavier's—had the bricks ritually consecrated, and then wrapped in saffron cloth personally took them to Ayodhya for the shilanayas. In lieu of the bricks he brought back with him a handful of the earth dug up from the sacred ground, around the janamsthan. It is now kept in the Wedgwood teapot that Samar sent last year.' Mira smiled and then as an afterthought continued, 'Vidyarthiji is quite sweet actually. He quite innocently reported to Mama that in Ayodhya one errant (actually the word he used was 'uddand') langur broke twenty of the bricks as soon as he had deposited them with the mahant-in-charge. He is now in disgrace.'

'The langur?'

'No, Vidyarthiji.'

I leaned against the statue and lit a Gold Flake.

It was surreal, watching her sit so close beside me and I could in my mind also see myself watching her. I felt as if I were watching a home movie of Mira and me shot years before. If only the statue of Subhas Bose were changed to Swami Vivekananda's, it would be the Arts Faculty Campus in DU again.

I was surprised that her physical presence could still have such a strong effect on me. I had rehearsed this scene over many times in the last four years where we would meet accidentally somewhere, and I convinced myself that I would be cool and sophisticated, make small talk and move away unaffected. I had taken it on the chin and moved on. I was over her. Sometimes even a week would pass before I thought of her again. I was definitely over her and there was even a pretty Vaidya girl who worked in the features section whom I had taken out for a movie once. Probably *Top Gun*.

But now that Mira was before me, my only wish was to hold her tightly and never let her go again. My heart wanted to shout, 'All is forgiven. Let's erase the last four years and start anew.' I realized sophistication has got nothing to do with love. Even if a hundred years passed by, I still wouldn't be over her ever. It was pathetic; I could smell the Johnson Baby Shampoo scent of her hair. It was unbearable to realize that I couldn't ever touch her again, to kiss her again. She who I had known so intimately, who was almost an extension of myself, now each morning woke up beside someone who was not me.

'You are really involved with the Cine Society now, aren't you?' Mira asks me softly after a while.

'Every few years the Cine Society here winds down and then a new group comes and they revive it again. The old Bengali and Kayastha aristocrats are all gone. There is hardly any money but we have survived on the enthusiasm for the past couple of years. The membership has dwindled but the people who remain are committed folks. I enjoy managing things and this is something I really love. To remain connected with movies in some way is wonderful. We have our meetings every Thursday evening in the Hriday Kutir library. That is the Cine Society office now.

'Sometimes when there are only handful of members we have the showing in the library itself, like last month when we screened *Arvind Desai ki Ajeeb Dastaan* and only six people turned up. In

Hindi movies Saeed Mirza is probably the only auteur that we have. We pay a nominal rent to Saifu Mian. He now also doubles up as our projectionist. The Cine Society pays him Rs 50 for each show. Two months back we had a Guru Dutt festival. You would have loved that.'

'Didn't Saifu Mian used to ferry you and Ila around town when you were young.'

'He practically brought us up. Now there is no one in Hriday Kutir except him. Many of the artefacts are sold, the paintings, curtains, chandeliers, the Burma teak furniture, the Murphy radiogram. When Runu Debi, Ila's mother, was last here, she sold almost everything she could sell, except for the books in the library because Saifu Mian told her that Ila even now sometimes in her peach-coloured pinafore comes to read her favourite books in there.'

'Have you ever seen her?' Mira asked me, a slight edge to her voice. Mention of Iladi always did that to her. But I played along.

'No, but I am sure Saifu Mian is right. Ila wouldn't be able to keep away from her books for long. They were her life. In the evenings after I come back from work, I go straight to the library and work on my stories there. One of these days I am bound to meet her.'

Some of the Cine Society members amble over to the park, talking and smoking in groups of twos and threes. I wave to some of them. They wave back, notice Mira sitting by my side and keep their distance. Some of them know Mira as Samar's wife. Perhaps they have heard stories about us too.

For ten minutes we do not say anything to each other. There is so much to say yet we can't articulate our innermost thoughts. We both pretend as if nothing has happened. I am under no illusion. I know she hasn't come back to me but finding her in such close proximity makes me hopeful.

'Kanupriya sent me your book of stories, *Harryda and Other Stories*, last year,' Mira said after a while.

'More of a booklet than a book. It is barely fifty pages.'

'You should have sent a copy but you didn't. Anyway I enjoyed all the stories. Some of them of course I had read over your shoulder as you wrote them.'

'The Cine Society paid for it. We did 250 copies. About twenty-five are left.'

'The stories are good. You could have found a mainstream publisher in Delhi if you had tried.'

'It was for a week-long Satyajit Ray festival that we had organized last year. We started with *Company Limited* as Ray had shot some scenes for it in Patna. Most of the stories as you would remember are about the magic of movies. The copies were given free to the members and others who wanted them. Perhaps now I will send it to a publisher in Delhi. No hurry though. I am happy it reached the people it was meant for.'

'I would like a few more copies if you can spare them. I will send it to my editor in New York.'

'I will give you the copies. Give it to your friends. I would prefer if you didn't show it to your publisher. There is no point, they wouldn't know anything about Patna.'

'Precisely why you should let me show your work. Maybe they would like to know about Patna. True it is not Bombay but they are not as insular as you think them to be.'

'What is your novel about? I read about it in the paper.'

'It is about a young girl from an unnamed small north Indian town who goes to the university in Delhi and gets educated in the ways of life. Later she falls in love with a visiting American writer who takes her home with him and she escapes her provincial destiny.'

'It is a good theme. Of the hundreds of Bihari students who land up in Delhi University each year, I have always felt the girls cope with the pressures better than the boys. They assimilate better. They are less chauvinistic. They make friends with the Punjabis, the North-East students, the locals. They make friends with everyone. They are open to new ideas. While we boys just transplant the feudalism of our culture, the caste affiliations, the mohalla mentality, the servant, the cook, the dhobi, and try and make one corner of Indira Vihar or Mukherjee Nagar into the Patna, Ranchi, Chhapra that we left behind. The boys won't mix with the Punjabis because they are 'locals' and have more money, the North-East guys are 'chinks' and they too have more money, plus the mandatory girlfriends, and the Jats are of course an extension of themselves. But the Bihari girl has no prejudice, she will date a 'local', a 'chink' and very often a Jat, though in Patna if she is a Rajput she would rarely know a Bhumihar boy well. Delhi is the place where the Bihari girl finally blossoms. It could be a big theme.'

'They know that after three years of bliss, they have to go back to their hometowns and get married to the prototype of the same boys who sit at Kake da Dhaba, wear hawai chappals, dream of Ambassadors with red revolving lights and stare at them. So the motto is "have fun while it lasts".'

'In the coming decades there are bound to be more divorces in Patna. Perhaps sociologists should study it.'

'I have written 10,000 words, have to complete 30,000 more by next July.'

I turn and look at Ritwik. He must be wondering why I have come today. What do I want? Quite simple actually. I have come for closure. Four years back I left without explanations, without even a goodbye. For the first couple of years I thought I would gradually forget him. I was so much in love with Samar and living in New York was like a dream come true. The theatre, the music, the second-hand bookstores where Jack Kerouac and William Burroughs must have once browsed, new friends at the University, it was just wonderful. But Ritwik, try as I might, I couldn't leave him behind. I realize now that Ritwik will always be a part of me. Patna and Delhi I didn't miss even for a day but Ritwik and I are indissolubly linked together. So it is better to be friends with Ritwik and so for that I had to ask his forgiveness. Face to face. I can't go on living thinking I let down the trust of the one man who loved me more than anyone. Is it possible to love two persons at the same time? Perhaps it is. Men have done it for centuries.

'It might be some time till Saifu Mian arrives with Godard. Would you like to go someplace and have a coffee perhaps?'

Ritwik asks me, aware of the surreptitious looks we are getting from the Cine Society regulars. This is one of the things which so annoys me about Ritwik; he is too cautious, too worried of what strangers might be thinking. There is something exasperatingly proper about him.

'Let's go to the British Council Library and browse, look at the back issues of *Sight and Sound* like we used to do earlier,' I tell Ritwik as he pulls me up from the steps. When we would be back in Patna for our summer and winter vacations, we usually met at the British Council where we both were members.

'Mira it is quarter to five. They will be closing up for the day soon.' We walk towards Ritwik's Yezdi.

'You know what, let's go and climb up Golghar. I have never done it. They say you can take in the whole town from the top,' I say to Ritwik and for the first time he really smiles and yes it can still light up any room that I am in.

'Mira, it is like the Statue of Liberty. Only for tourists. For villagers during the chhat festival who come to the Ganges for the holy dip or for political rallies at Gandhi Maidan. One of the few attractions this ancient town holds for them. It is only for the transients, not the residents.'

'I am transient now. I want to climb up and see Patna. Will you take me there?' I feel the mood has shifted and after a long long while I feel lightness again. The awkwardness of the past twenty minutes has left us.

Golghar of course is the late eighteenth century granary built by the British to combat famine. In one of his stories Ritwik describes it as 'a huge black pyramid-like structure built by the British to store foodgrains by the side of the Ganges and now one of the few tourist sites in town. A huge coiled staircase runs the full length of the outer walls, right to the top, and from where one can have a bird's-eye view of the entire city.' Actually it looks more like a massive inverted beehive than a pyramid. It is so oddball a structure that I am glad it was built in Patna.

I run up the 'huge coiled staircase'. There are 200-odd steps. I don't feel gloomy anymore and am back to being a twenty-six-year-old girl who likes laughing a lot. Ritwik sprints up the stairs after me. There is nobody here. We are totally alone. Not even one tourist from Ara, Chhapra, Siwan today. We try and race to the top. We are friends again. I don't feel like a fugitive anymore. It is exhilarating, this crazy run. Around midway I stop, exhausted. Sweat pouring from every pore. I sit down on the step, leaning against the wall. Ritwik comes up and looks at me laughing. He takes the aanchal of my sari, leans over and wipes the sweat off my face and then wipes his own. I hold his hands and then he gently kisses me on the lips. Just touches his lips to mine. Surprised, I smile. Embarrassed, he pulls away. I don't let go of his hands. He pulls me up. We walk slowly hand in hand to the top.

The view is spectacular. I am glad I did this. There is Ritwik's old school St. Xavier's almost at the very foot of the monument. In the swimming pool, boys are having their swimming lessons. A boy the size of a butterfly dives off a high board. In the 'baby field' nets are being held. This being the cricket season. In the Gandhi Maidan two barefoot teams play a football match. Probably State Bank versus Patna Secretariat. A hundred onlookers watch. Across the street the Ganges flows past the A.N. Sinha Institute, St. Joseph's Convent, the Bankipore Club. On the banks of which, around fourth century B.C., Megasthenes must have taken his morning walks all the while contemplating the next folio of his magic-realist chronicle of Patna.

Up further one can see the Secretariat building, the Patna Museum and the bustling commercial hub of Hira Palace, Dak Bungalow Crossing and Fraser Road. BISCOMAUN Bhavan on our left further down the street from St. Xavier's whose employees haven't been paid for months by the state government. On the ground floor of which lies Hsin Long, the best authentic Chinese restaurant in Patna but now closed for a couple of years. People preferring to eat from the Matador van-faux-Chinese food dhabas that dot the newly opened Maurya Lok shopping complex in front of Hira Palace. Across the Gandhi Maidan, one can make out the IMA Hall building, the statue of Subhas Bose in front of it looking the size of a pebble. Behind IMA Hall, Ritwik and Ila's sprawling Kadam Kuan.

From the top of the Golghar, it seems as if a giant map of Patna has been spread before us and we can chart out the course of our past through it. Ritwik lights two Gold Flakes and passes one to me. He remembers that I like to smoke once in while. This is the moment I want to savour and take back with me to New York. I wish I had brought my Hot Shot automatic. A man and a woman who choose to remain friends as the sun sets gently on Patna. Click.

As they reach IMA Hall, Ritwik and Mira find Saifu Mian outside the gate having an animated discussion with a bunch of Cine Society members. He comes forward when he sees Ritwik.

'Lal Krishna Advani has been arrested in Samastipur. Laloo didn't let his Rath enter Bihar,' Saifu Mian with a broad smile informs them and embraces Ritwik. The train from Calcutta bearing Godard has been further delayed.

So there they remain locked in a freeze frame straight from the Master's ouvre, Ritwik, Mira and Saifu Mian, and tomorrow again they will play their respective parts under the indulgent gaze of Subhas Bose, endlessly, ceaselessly waiting. Waiting for what? For Godard of course.

Acknowledgements

This book would still have been written without the support of the following people but devoid of their friendship and trust, it would have been a lonely and joyless task.

My parents, brother Sanjay, sister-in-law Sharmishtha and nephew Rohit for being there.

Pankaj Mishra and Amitava Kumar for their faith and generosity.

Palash Krishna Mehrotra for being a friend when I didn't have many.

Bhola Varma and Ramesh Jain, my two gurus in publishing.

My childhood friends who continue to be friends, in spite of the fact that, to their horror, I suddenly turned a writer on them: Manish, Brajesh, Anuranjan, Ritesh, Bunty, Gyanant, Abhishek, Anupam and Shubhojeet.

My cousins Saraswati, Shantanu, Sharmila, Sanghamitra, Debapi, Sharmistha, Debesh, Kaushik, Ipsita and Sudipto.

Team Picador: Rajdeep, Joseph and the incomparable Shruti Debi, a team to die for.

In the end, Pragya Sinha Chowdhury.

Day Scholar

For Sanjay and Sharmistha

Contents

Shokeen Niwas

The first time I saw Zorawar Singh Shokeen was through a small gap between doors that connected my room in Shokeen Niwas to the adjoining one. He sat astride a large, naked Punjabi woman in her late thirties who had buttocks that even Asha Parekh would be proud of. She was on her knees, at the edge of Jishnu Sharma's (M.A. Previous, English, Ramjas) cot. Jishnuda, meanwhile, was in my room looking as usual philosophical and tragic. His left hand was in his loose, discoloured Tweety Pie Bermuda shorts, which he never washed. In fact the shorts were so stiff with profligacy that the story was that once during an argument in the hostel over who was supposed to pay for the Old Monk khamba that Friday night, Jishnuda in anger had taken off his shorts and thrown them at Farid Ashraf's (third year History Honours, KMC) face. Though Farid managed to turn his face in time, he cut his fingers on the razor-sharp edges of Jishnuda's shorts. The next day Farid had to take tetanus shots.

So right now with his left hand, in his own immortal words, Jishnuda was making 'baingan bharta'. Mashing his aubergine, if you would so prefer. Eight to ten boys from the neighbouring rooms were clustered around in mine, their faces shining with barely repressed lust, the air dank with sweat and Navy Cut smoke. It was two o'clock in the a fternoon on a hot July day in 1992 and I had just come back to my room after my first day in Zakir Husain College. A week earlier, I and my friend Pranjal Sinha had arrived in Delhi from Patna and landed up at Shokeen Niwas. Pranjal had taken admission in Hindu College reading Economics while I got English in Zakir.

'He has taken her once in the chut, then in her mouth, now he is doing her ass,' Pranjal informed me in a cool matter-of-fact way after taking a long Navy Cut drag.

He added as an afterthought:

'Jishnuda too is on his third shot.' Then he bowed and beckoned me to the slightly ajar door.

Zorawar Singh was holding on to both of 'Madam's' breasts with their large purplish nipples for balance, and was anally fucking her with much gusto.

Her real name was Mrs Midha and she was a section officer in Delhi University but everybody called her 'Madam' because once, about a year back, Jishnuda, along with Farid Ashraf and Ramanuj Ghosh (third year B.A. Pass, Ramjas), was standing outside Shokeen Niwas when Zorawar Singh drove up with her in his white Gypsy.

Zorawar stopped the car and asked Jishnuda whether he had got the admission for one of his candidates to Ramjas College, which he had been asked to follow up on.

'Uncle, you don't worry. The boy will be taken in through the sports quota after the third list. I have spoken to the teacher-in-charge. He was being uncooperative at first but I *convinced* him in the end.'

'Very good. Keep following it up, though. These Ramjas people are bastards. Remember this is for the Kaana.'

'Uncle, it looks like it will rain tonight. We are all feeling a bit chilly,' Jishnu smiled ingratiatingly and pointed to Farid and Ramanuj.

'Toh, Madam ki le le.' Zorawar Singh pointed towards Mrs Midha, who with her large white plastic-framed sunglasses on was looking stonily out of the other window. To emphasize his point, Uncle gestured with his fist, moving it back and across rapidly. Jishnu and the boys didn't know where to look. Then Zorawar Singh, laughing at their discomfort, had taken out two hundred-rupee notes from his shirt pocket and given them to Jishnuda. 'Buy a bottle of Old Monk Rum. You know what rum is, don't you? Regular Use Medicine. It will take care of the chill.'

So, from then on, Mrs Midha was universally known as 'Madam' in Shokeen Niwas.

Zorawar Singh looked as if he was concentrating hard on some faraway problem. His eyes were closed. From time to time Madam would turn her face away from the pillow and look back and loudly say 'oye' as if she was hailing someone from the balcony. She too was concentrating hard it seemed. After five minutes of this Zorawar Singh suddenly opened his eyes and shouted 'Jai Mata di'. From the bed Jishnuda commented 'game over'. Now his eyes were closed. With a loud plop Zorawar withdrew his dark, rapidly shrinking cock that a donkey would be proud of, and Madam slumped to the bed with a last feeble 'oye'. A thin watery stream of semen trickled out of her anus.

Zorawar Singh Shokeen, mid-level political broker and property dealer, was our landlord. A strapping six feet-two inches tall half-Jat half-Gujjar from Chandrawal, full bearded, with a dandy's studied taste in clothes, he usually wore deep pink or lemon yellow bespoke silk shirts with gold cufflinks that brought out his peaches and cream complexion. The colour of his eyes was light brown to go with his beard. He was forty years old and for the last ten years had been the terror of Chandrawal, Shakti Nagar, Roop Nagar, Kamla Nagar, Vijay Nagar, Maurice Nagar, Mukherjee Nagar, Indira Vihar and other areas adjoining Delhi University, North Campus. He was rumoured to be close to H. K. L. Bhagat, still then the undisputed New Delhi Congress boss, whom he called 'Kaana' with the proud contempt that only close familiarity breeds. An obvious reference to the vain Bhagat's damaged eye.

Sometimes Zorawar would be picked up from Shokeen Niwas in a white Ambassador car with a red flashing light on the top, tinted windows, and a Black Cat commando in the front seat. Zorawar would quickly get into the back beside a small gnomelike silhouette, and then the Ambassador would reverse in full speed and turn towards Bungalow Road. All sirens blaring.

Jishnuda was the de facto caretaker of Shokeen Niwas. In his first year itself, Jishnuda had endeared himself to Zorawar Singh, showing great presence of mind one evening when the enraged Sikh husband of a 'Madam' Zorawar was screwing quite frequently at the time arrived at the doorstep of the hostel with a Matador van full of sword-wielding sardars. Zorawar was at the time doing his thing to 'Madam' who was on her knees at the edge of the bed with a mouthful of pillow. In Jishnuda's room, of course. Hearing the commotion Jishnuda peeked out from the balcony and, gauging the situation correctly, locked his room from the outside. He then gathered a couple of boys from the other rooms who were there at that time of afternoon and went downstairs to meet the sardars who were trying to break open the front gates.

After instructing the boys, young kids from Chapra who had arrived only a week earlier, to just stand behind him coolly and not say a word, Jishnuda draped his cotton checked towel over his shoulders. Like a warrior's mail. Then, showing enormous pluck he opened the front gate, yawned, rubbed his eyes and demanded quietly, 'Madharchod, what the fuck do you want?' or something to that effect, of the sardar who was banging on the door with the steel hilt of his sword. Taken aback by the sight of this emaciated five feet-five inches tall rangbaz in a Sandow ganji of indeterminate colour and Tweety Pie Bermudas, not to mention the selfsame checked towel, the sardar replied, 'Where is Zorawar Singh Shokeen? He has kidnapped my wife.'

'Is that the problem? Then rest assured, he is not here. Haven't seen him here for weeks. Actually no, come to think of it, he did come here with a sardarni a couple of weeks back, but she was very friendly with him. Couldn't have kidnapped her. Probably some other sardarni, not your wife,' Jishnuda informed the sardar in an indifferent manner and kept rubbing his eyes and yawning. At this, unable to contain his rage any longer, the sardar slapped Jishnuda and he in turn latched on to the sardar's luxuriant beard with all his strength. Farid Ashraf and Ramanuj Ghosh, who were behind Jishnuda, joined the fray along with the other sardars. There was a lot of wild shouting, murderous threats, but very little actual violence.

'I am telling you,' Jishnuda shouted still hanging on to the sardar, 'that uncle is not here, screwing your wife. If you don't go away, all the twenty-five boys I have upstairs will come down and break your asses.' He then shouted to the only boy upstairs, looking down from the first floor balcony. 'Tell Panday and Mumtaz to take out the kattas.'

The sardars, confused by the bluster, deciding that Jishnu must be telling the truth after all, slowly retreated. After the Matador had backed out of the lane, Farid and Ramanuj almost collapsed with relief in the doorway. Jishnuda wiped the sweat from his armpits with his towel and then dramatically tied it around his head like a peasant and lit a Navy Cut.

'Boss, what were you trying to do, get us killed?' Farid Ashraf inquired after a while.

'Never under any circumstance back down in a fight or have a dialogue or compromise. No fight lasts more than five minutes. Remember that always. Never try to have a rational conversation with anyone who is trying to fuck you. He will then fuck you. But if you call him a motherfucker and offer to cut his throat, he will respect you. But when you say those words you must mean them from the bottom of your heart. Just like in the song.'

Farid and Ramanuj looked at Jishnuda with profound incomprehension but thought it better to nod their heads in agreement.

'Both of you did good.' Jishnuda passed the Navy Cut to Ramanuj. He then went upstairs and opened his locked room. Just as he triumphantly pushed open the door, a deafening roar erupted from inside the room. Zorawar Singh had opened fire with the Mauser that he always carried in his trouser pocket. For a second there Jishnuda caught a glimpse of the petite sardarni sitting by the edge of his cot, languidly putting on her scarlet lipstick. Though the bullet just grazed his hair, Jishnuda collapsed to the floor and fainted.

A close bond was forged that day between Zorawar Singh and Jishnuda, and it had continued unabated to the present times. From that day onwards Jishnuda had lived rent free at Shokeen Niwas and was given carte blanche as to the running of the place, the vetting of tenants, the collection of rents. He was the hostel president for life, so to say.

'Uncle has just one condition. The boys should primarily be Biharis. He seems to think that we are just like Gujjars. Tough and callous. No need to disillusion him. So never in any circumstance prove yourself to be otherwise. Be tough, stupid and callous always. Once in a while a Matador van will come and you two will have to accompany all of us to some colony somewhere in Delhi where you stand outside the van in a group for an hour or so, smoke a cigarette or two. Usually a property dispute somewhere. Nothing major. It's a show of strength, then you can go home.'

This was another of the things that Jishnuda had told Pranjal and me during our first week in Shokeen Niwas and I had solemnly promised him that even though I was a Bengali I would do him proud.

'I do not like Bengalis. They think too much. You cannot trust such people.' Jishnuda made his stand clear to me on the ethnic question. In childhood all his close friends had been Bengalis and somehow or the other they had all 'hurt' him eventually. Poor bugger. But his alleged prejudice was just an old Patna trick to throw people off balance at the start of a new relationship. The very next day he informed Pranjal that he didn't like Rajputs either, as they were usually of dark complexion and yet they thought themselves to be so superior to everyone else. This was fairly rich coming from someone like Jishnuda, himself what we in Patna routinely called an IAS. Invisible After Sunset.

After he finished his story about the sardars and their swords, Jishnuda took us out to the balcony where, on the wall diagonally opposite our rooms, a hideous calendar-art framed painting of Hanumanji on one knee baring his heart with both hands to show the images of Lord Ram and Sita embedded there, was hung. Pranjal and I thought that now Jishnuda would ask us to seek Hanumanji's blessing as another rite of initiation into the rarefied world of Shokeen Niwas. But no.

Jishnuda simply removed the painting from the wall and showed us the round, smooth hole made by that epochal Mauser bullet. The bullet itself could be touched by wriggling in one's little finger.

'It is just like a chut, it gets bigger as you go deeper,' Jishnuda said philosophically as he filled ganja into an empty Wills Navy Cut cylinder.

It was whispered among the boys of Shokeen Niwas, usually the senior ones like Jishnuda, that at the age of twenty-five Zorawar had committed his first murder. He was then a student of Satyawati Co-educational College in Ashok Vihar, and in the evenings he would visit Kamla Nagar from Chandrawal, where he lived with his widowed mother.

One day while having tea at the corner of Hansraj College, he saw a very pretty girl come out of the mandir that was across the street. In fact it was the same mandir where on Tuesdays Jishnuda and Ramanuj Ghosh offered their prayers. Ramanuj always carried a large cotton towel wrapped around his neck, and the joke was that after offering prayers, he would come outside, wrap the towel like a shroud around himself and sit with the beggars that lined the boundary walls. Come to think of it, he always did pay for his share of the Old Monk khamba with 25 paise and 50 paise coins. When the news broke out that all over Delhi images and idols of Lord Ganesh were drinking milk, it was to this very same mandir that Jishnuda and Farid Ashraf went to investigate, carrying a litre between them. Later that night in his room as he measured out the rum, Jishnuda told us ruefully that when he had offered milk, Lord Ganesh had spit it out and it had trickled down to the floor, but when Farid had offered the milk, Lord Ganesh had had no problem, and had imbibed it like a ravenous baby. Jishnuda was quite disturbed by the fact that Lord Ganesh had rejected a devout Hindu like him and had chosen to drink milk from the hands of a Muslim instead. 'Mera nahi piye, Musalman ka pee liye.' Even Farid, who believed that all Hindus were basically chirkuts, looked philosophical and overcome by the incident that night.

Anyway, Zorawar, totally smitten, left his friends and followed the girl to her home. I like to imagine that Zorawar was perhaps intrigued by her bare feet. The delicate arch of her ankle partly uncovered by the border of her petticoat. He did this every day for fifteen days. The girl had noticed him and once or twice while coming out of the mandir had smiled at him. On the sixteenth day, just as she unlocked the latch of the front gate, Zorawar caught hold of her from behind and slowly tilting her head, kissed her full on the lips.

'I am married,' she is said to have whispered to him. 'I know,' Zorawar said before parting her lips with his tongue again. The girl's name was Sunita Khandelwal and her husband worked as a lower division clerk in the Shakti Nagar branch of the Punjab National Bank. I visualize Sunita as short and delicately built, in American georgette and leheriya print sarees, with straight hair, the pallu wrapped tight over both shoulders like many Bania girls before the fat finally catches up with them.

Each afternoon after lunch when Suresh Khandelwal had returned to his bank, Zorawar joined Sunita in her marital bed. A couple of months of this and one evening Suresh comes home early and his fourteen-year-old saali Lado lets him in and leads him straight to the bedroom, where he catches his wife sucking Zorawar's cock. Such is their passion that they continue with their love-making even though poor Suresh is right there, one foot on the wooden choukhat, poised to enter his own bedroom, watching his young wife's mouth fill gradually with semen. Zorawar takes a hand towel and wipes the edges of Sunita's mouth, all the time smiling at Suresh Khandelwal. A mild-mannered man, Suresh then turns, retraces his steps to the front door, and carrying his rexine-covered briefcase walks into the sunset.

The next afternoon his body, cut in half by a slow goods train, is found near Sarai Rohilla station. Suresh's father and younger brother arrive from Sikar to arrange his funeral. Within a month Zorawar moves in with Sunita. A couple of neighbours who object have their faces rearranged and at nights windows broken. No one complains to the police. Zorawar Singh Shokeen settles in. He loves the house. Sure beats his narrow two-room heat-trap of a hovel in Chandrawal. He enjoys the old-style expansiveness of the courtyard and the high-ceilinged rooms on the three floors that surround it. Ground plus two. He especially loves the dark red flooring from which intricate patterns made with bits of broken china float up. In summer he likes to walk on it barefoot as it is so cold.

A true Bhumihar if ever there was one, Jishnuda describes Zorawar's love for his new acquisition, the joy of being finally a man of property, with telling detail. From the terrace Zorawar can see the whole of North Campus and the areas adjoining it. Kirori Mal and Hansraj College at a stone's throw. Beyond loom the dense kikar-encrusted Delhi Ridge and Bara Hindu Rao, where in 1857 Zorawar's Gujjar ancestors fought their last stand against the British and their Sikh mercenaries and forever lost the land on which later North Campus would be built. Hindu College, St. Stephen's College and the back gate of Miranda House. The teeming Bungalow Road is just outside the lane, with its bookshops, cafés, juice corners and glittering shops catering to all the needs of students who came to the university from faraway places and bring to it their own tribal customs and rituals. If Zorawar turns his head he can see Roop Nagar, Shakti Nagar, Amba Cinema Hall and outside it Darvesh Dhaba which serves wonderful frontier food, and finally Malkaganj where Mrs Midha, his future paramour, lives with her homeopath husband and fourteen-year-old daughter, who bears a striking resemblance to the Bollywood starlet Divya Bharti, complete with round applefed cheeks and rounder tits. If he strains his eyes he can also see the vast spread of Chandrawal. But try as he might he can't locate his own house where his mother still lives. It is too small. Too insignificant.

Six months pass. For Sunita it is a blissful time. A time of full sexual awakening. She never realized the amount of pleasure that could be had from the male body, to say nothing of her own. She constantly surprises herself. She forever wants to keep looking at Zorawar, keep touching him, have him three-four times a day, anywhere, anytime, if he is willing. 'Uncle is a heavy choder,' Jishnuda explains. Sunita can't have enough of her Zorawar. She doesn't care for household chores anymore, nor for the views of her neighbours. She realizes that Zorawar is a criminal of some kind but she couldn't care less. She would give up a hundred Suresh Khandelwals for one Zorawar Singh Shokeen gladly, every time. Meanwhile, it is Lado who cooks and takes up housekeeping. She stops going to school and Sunita and Zorawar do not force her to. Lado has always hated school and studies and for her too this is a time of liberation. Sunita and Lado have money of their own, provided by their father, a prosperous Kamla Nagar cloth merchant, before his death. Their mother had died during Lado's birth. It is Sunita who has brought up Lado like a daughter and now Lado, at fourteen, has finally come of age.

One night around 3 a.m. Sunita wakes up languorously, wants to curl up unto her gorgeous Zorawar but there is no Zorawar anywhere. Her bed is empty. Mildly alarmed, she pulls on her black kaftan and comes out of her bedroom to look for him. 'Black kaftan? How do you know it was black?' I interrupt Jishnuda's narrative flow but he does not mind. 'Would you rather, Hriday, that it was pink?' Jishnuda lights a Navy Cut spiked with prime Bhagalpuri ganja and carries on. Stepping outside her room in her black kaftan Sunita finds the door to Lado's room ajar. Even before she enters the room she knows in her heart what she will find there. Her fate is sealed. She can turn back, return to her room, pull off her black kaftan and wait for Zorawar to slip back beside her and all will be fine. But she does not do that. Mesmerized by fear and loathing Sunita walks into her sister's bedroom, only to be assailed with the very scene that led Suresh Khandelwal to kill himself. With a slight role reversal. This time it is Zorawar who is between the girl's legs and not the other way round.

Sunita screamed, ranted, and told Zorawar to clear out of her house. Right then, in the middle of the night. Then with tears streaming down her face she ran to her bedroom and bolted the door.

Her charred-to-the-bone body to which flesh still clung in places like sludge was recovered by the police the next morning. The entire room reeked of kerosene for years afterwards. 'If you sniff deeply, you can still smell Sunita off the walls,' Jishnuda said and took a deep breath.

It is true, the room had a funny smell come to think of it, a mild one no doubt, but certainly one redolent of an abattoir, of small animal flesh, bone and fear, which no amount of distemper and room freshener can do away. The room which was once the pride and joy of Sunita Khandelwal was now mine and Pranjal's for a rent of Rs 900 a month.

Within a month of Sunita's death, Zorawar married the fourteen-year-old Lado and the house was finally his. He named it, quite expectedly, Shokeen Niwas. He was finally a man of property. Full and proper.

About seven years back Zorawar had moved out of Shokeen Niwas with Lado and his two daughters, Goldy and Shiny, to a plusher house in West Patel Nagar that he had captured from a Sikh Major in the aftermath of the 1984 riots. He converted Shokeen Niwas into a student lodge. There were twelve rooms. Four on each floor. Usually two or three boys in each room. On weekends more, as friends from the hostels of Ramjas, Stephen's, Hindu, Hansraj, Kirori Mal would join in for drunken revelries. Across the street there was a small grocery store run by a man called Mehendiratta who lived there with his family. Mehendiratta catered to all our needs.

Even though Zorawar had moved out of Shokeen Niwas, he still preferred it for his romantic trysts, about once every fortnight. He usually used Jishnuda's room as it had been Lado's bedroom in the early days.

'Pranjal, you and Hriday do not have to worry at all. He usually walks by your room with averted eyes. He would never barge into it with a randi,' Jishnuda reassured Pranjal who had deep misgivings about living in Shokeen Niwas and was thinking of moving out. But I, Hriday Thakur, had no such qualms. I loved the wanton amorality of the place. Its chanciness, its far remove from respectability. I wanted to be a writer. It would be here I knew that I would start to write like one. I had finally found my material, if not my voice. Even though later Pranjal would be proved right (as always), I was deeply grateful to Jishnuda for introducing me to the magical world of Shokeen Niwas and the kerosene-suffused bedroom of the late lamented Sunita Khandelwal.

Fuselage

In 1990, when I was fifteen years old, I cleared my matric examinations in the lower depths of the first division. A 2 per cent grace mark which was awarded to NCC cadets who completed two years in the corps gave a semblance of respectability to my marksheet. At St. Xavier's, Patna, we were in the air wing of the National Cadet Corps, the No.1 (Bihar) Air Squadron to be precise, where once every Friday a sergeant called Sridhar Basu tried to teach us the finer points of different aircraft components. Years later the first thing I remember about Sgt. Basu is his meticulously maintained Raj Kumar moustache and a high hectoring voice full of cosmic despair asking me almost at the end of the two-year term just before our matric examinations: 'Hriday, do you even know what is meant by "fuselage"?'

Usually, after a fifty-minute somnambulistic lecture, we would go out of the large airy classroom into the Xavier's forecourt, where in our thick, slightly faded denim-blue cotton uniforms, with brass wings pinned above our hearts, we would do kadam tal for five minutes. After a few desultory savdhans and vishrams we would start our march-past, for which two drums to give our rebellious feet some synchronicity would be lugged out from the principal's office. Usually on those days, the principal, a nervous Mangalorean padre, would retire to his cloister early and after plugging in the requisite cotton wool, put on his bifocals and dip his eclectic mind into his vast Beatrix Potter collection.

For twenty minutes we would do our march-past. From the forecourt to the portico and then back again. Sgt. Basu would bang the drums with a furious, sweaty, clenched-teeth passion. Left, left, left-right-left. About turn! Peeche mudh! At the end of the twenty minutes a shiver of lightning would pass through Basu's spare and erect frame. With his light air-force blue half-sleeved cotton shirt drenched in sweat, eyes popping from the concentration, he would have one last spasm of convulsion and the drumstick would fall from his hand. He would then light a Charminar. That was the signal for visarjan. We could disperse. Basu would put on his black Aviator sunglasses and ride into the sunset on his Vicky moped.

But not before the mandatory 'tuck' that Shankar, our canteenwallah, distributed from his cavernous oil-stained bamboo tokri. Each brown paper 'thonga' contained two crisp samosas and a boondiya laddoo.

Six months before the Board Examinations it was suddenly announced that all NCC cadets of the air wing from schools all over Bihar had to attend a camp at the air force station near Bihta, about fifty kilometres from Patna. The camp was a wretched place to be. We were supposed to sleep on the ground in large, overcrowded garages where the smell of engine oil hung heavy in the air and seemed to permeate our every pore, on a bed-sheet that we were each supposed to carry and which I conveniently forgot; get up early around five and shit in the rice fields since there were no toilets; bathe every couple of days under an open tap near the officers' quarters since there wasn't much water and about 1,000 cadets were in the queue; eat inedible vegetarian food whose main ingredient was sand, so we only had dinner because by that time we were so exhausted by heat and hunger we could taste nothing. All this, according to Basu, was supposed to toughen us up. 'You won't fall ill again in your life.' Then there were the interminable march-pasts in the sticky September heat and mandatory lectures of the 'What is a Fuselage' variety in the afternoon. I don't know if it toughened us up or not since all of us suffered from headaches and fevers most of the time we were there. We just walked around bored and dazed from the sun and saluted the officers with desultory clicks of the heels and in unison the epithet betichod hissed out at them in an undertone. 'Betichod' was the preferred choice of verbal abuse when we were growing up in Patna. No one minded it a bit when anyone called them a 'betichod', a daughter-fucker, since firstly it was all in the future and secondly there always was a chance that one (hopefully) wouldn't have daughters. A sister or a mother was more immediate. Most of us had them. So calling someone behenchod or madharchod was serious business because then the brother/son would be forced to defend his honour. So one only called someone behenchod, or worse, madharchod, when one was really prepared to fight, razor blades and cycle-chains ready in the pocket. Because there was no getting away from it then. This is why some Punjabi boys in DU would suddenly get their faces slashed when all they thought they were doing was kidding around. In time they would learn that in Delhi there could be a profusion of sisterfuckers and motherfuckers but in Patna there were only daughterfuckers. In time the officers too learnt to give us, the Xavier's boys, a wide berth when we walked by. But we never forgot to salute.

Some of our doings probably got back to Basu and he was given hell for them but he wasn't unduly harsh on us. It just underlined his belief that upper-class boys were all fuckers and that he had been right all along. After the first week we got used to eating that one meal, not taking baths regularly though it was a bother for the Brahmin boys because it made the janeu chafe against their skin, and we rather enjoyed community-shitting in the open. One was almost in commune with nature. Even I admit it had a kind of bucolic charm, if you go for that sort of thing. After that two-week stint I suddenly realized why Munna, a servant we had when I was a young boy and who was only a couple of years older than me, invariably asked for the car to stop on the return to Patna after a winter picnic at Maner or Rajgir. The continuous rice fields would stretch for miles on both sides of the road and finally Munna, overwhelmed by all the greenery and open space, would ask the driver to stop the car and disappear into the fields. When he returned after a leisurely fifteen minutes, the serenity on his face could rival the Mona Lisa's.

A week before the study leave for the matric board examinations started, two names were announced by Basu. These were of the unfortunate boys who wouldn't be awarded NCC certificates. One was Chandragupta II who was the class topper and the other of course was me. One could understand the logic of failing Chandragupta II as he had never stayed back for the classes and the parades and he had also run away from the camp. After the second day, he simply got up around 3 a.m. and disappeared into the night and kept walking till he came to the main highway and boarded a truck carrying vegetables to Patna. We admired him enormously for the feat. Later he also stole a .303 cartridge when we were taken to the rifle-firing range near Bazar Samiti. A world authority on the Bhumihar caste, he was related to all the famous ones in history. From Parashuram to Sunil Dutt.

But when I remonstrated with Basu and pointed out to him that I, on the other hand, had attended every single class, he looked at me a trifle sadly and replied, 'Precisely the reason for not awarding you the certificate. You never missed a single class.' It was okay for Chandragupta II, he would get an 85 per cent anyway, but I desperately needed the 2 per cent which an NCC certificate entailed. I wasn't going to let go of that 2 per cent without a fight. I had shat for two weeks in an open field for the privilege. There were times when I could still smell brake-fluid in my sweat, which no amount of my mother's Cuticura would suppress.

The very next day, which was a Saturday, I picked up Chandragupta II from Nala Road and we cycled to Naya Tola, where in a cramped two-room flat near Ramna Road Basu stayed with his family. The two-room flat was on the upper floor of a huge colonial-type mansion. Most of the large bedrooms of these mansions, where the centrepiece once used to be a four-poster Burma teak bed, were subdivided into smaller rooms, and the four-poster now took up most of the space in the first room. The second room usually contained a small kitchen among other things. This mansion had been bought by Basu's grandfather in the early decades of the twentieth century when, along with other members of the Dhaka bench of judiciary, he was relocated to the newly formed Patna High Court. My father knew the family.

On the ground floor of the mansion there was a furniture shop selling ornate wedding furniture, a bookstore specializing in university textbooks which did good business as nearby there were many student lodges and the Patna University colleges just a ten-minute walk away, and a medicine store specializing in cough syrups, in which a man who looked like a younger version of Basu (the same Jaani moustache) sat reading *Mayapuri*, a Hindi film gossip weekly that one rifled through sullenly in barbershops while waiting for a haircut. The end pages of the magazine were quite interesting as they had stills from the climax or an intense romantic moment from a current Bollywood blockbuster with unintentionally hilarious dialogue coming out in a bubble from the mouths of the hero and the heroine.

We asked the man in the medicine store, who of course turned out to be Basu's younger brother, the way to the sergeant's home. He looked at us indifferently and, after a while, gestured in an upward motion with his *Mayapuri*-clasped hand. It could either mean that Basu had finally died and gone to heaven or that he lived upstairs. We decided to go with the second option. Perhaps the brothers were not on speaking terms.

Basu, in the Bengali national dress of thin cotton Somwari-mela polo T-shirt and white wide-bottomed Aligarhi pajamas, was sitting outside his rooms in a cane armchair, smoking a Charminar and listening to BBC World Service on a Bush transistor kept by his side on a small, round table. His ten-year-old daughter, Mamoni, was reading an Enid Blyton Secret Seven novel sprawled on the Burma teak four-poster wearing a navy blue skirt and a white cotton half-shirt. I found it slightly unsettling that she was wearing her St. Joseph's Convent uniform at home on a holiday. She glanced at us once and went back to her reading.

If he was surprised to see us, he didn't let on. He smiled and beckoned us to sit on a slightly crumbling rexine and foam sofa-cum-bed that had on it a cover made of thick cotton cloth usually used for making curtains. It was placed diagonally across from his chair in the corridor. The corridor was his living room.

Chandragupta II and I did a 'pranam sir' before sitting down. Basu knew what we were there for and perhaps he was expecting us. After all pairvi is a very revered Patna tradition and this was our initiation into it. Whatever you want to get in Patna, you have to do a 'pairvi'. From getting your son admitted to the right school, to getting a loan sanctioned from the local bank, to having a ration card made, getting a telephone connection and then insuring that it works properly for a few months at a time, procuring a gas connection and then another, getting your passport made without police verification, getting a driving licence when you can't distinguish a clutch from a brake, you do a pairvi. Metaphorically press the feet of your benefactor while he grants you your wishes as you sit in supplication. There was no shame involved. Everybody did it in Patna. Sons would say very proudly of their fathers that they did pairvi with a professor at Patna Science College to get them admission there through the sports quota. In a pairvi one didn't pay a bribe. It was more noblesse oblige than anything. It was about whom you knew and how good your own caste network was and whether your caste was in ascendance or in decline. A man's position in Patna society is inextricably linked to his capacity for coercing and granting pairvi. Pairvi has nothing to do with financial status, only class status.

Chandragupta II was certain in his mind that we would get our proficiency certificates and the requisite 2 per cent as I and Basu, though of different castes, were both Bengalis. In Patna, Bengali is also a caste. I, on the other hand, was not so sure about the outcome. Chandragupta II, the bright, worldly Bhumihar was cool about the whole thing: 'Just speak to the bastard in Bengali,' he advised. More of a Chanakya than a Chandragupta, that one. And then Basu, as if to nullify the language advantage, spoke to us in English, 'So Hriday, do you even know, what is meant by "fuselage"?'

'Yes, I do, sir. It's the framework ...'

'Never mind that, of course you know what a fuselage is. It's the least one can expect from someone from an educated Bengali family,' Basu cut me off. Chandragupta II bowed his head and sniggered. Basu didn't even look at him. As far as Basu was concerned Chandragupta II wasn't even there. In that corridor were ranged only two persons. Basu, the benefactor, and I, Hriday Thakur, supplicant and black sheep of the community. It was a role I had been chosen to play many times before. You could even say it was an author-backed one. I was then, some would perhaps say, a drifter of continental proportions. I was bad in studies, with no particular talent for anything artistic, whiled away my time playing club cricket in Patna, frequented tea shops in the evenings with certified 'bad characters', had started smoking, was sullen and rude to elders and generally did my own thing. I was everything a good Bengali boy from Kadam Kuan in Patna wasn't but what galled most people was that my parents were as unconcerned about my reputation as I was. But then for my parents, fortunately, other people's opinions never meant much. They realized I was only fifteen years old and they were a bit concerned about the smoking but of course they were not going to broadcast that concern to the community at large. They realized it was too trivial. My father dealt with the problem in his characteristic forthright manner: 'From now on you can smoke in your room. Here's some money, buy Gold Flake Kings. You don't have to smoke Charminars.' A diktat I happily follow to this day. But at fifteen one must only slouch at street corners and smoke cigarettes. That's the whole point of smoking, isn't it? So that when the St. Joseph's Convent School bus passes through Thakur Bari Road in Kadam Kuan, and Sadaf Khan Abdali looks out of the window, loosens her tie and straightens her hair, I, at that opportune moment, might light the cigarette stuck in my smile. For a second there, for a full year, our eyes would meet. On some mystical mornings I even had a Walkman clamped at my waist while the boy band Bros blasted 'When Will I, Will I Be Famous' from the headphones. The single was from their cult classic album *Push*, a CBS tape that I had bought for thirty-five rupees. It was either that or Bruce Springsteen tapes bought from the local pan shops near Hathwa Market and Fraser Road all through that year. I would follow the blue and white bus on my ancient red, appropriately named, 'Hero' sports cycle, as it would turn towards Bakargunj Road and then towards Gandhi Maidan. We would part company in front of the twin cinema halls, Mona and Elphinstone. On good days Sadaf would look back and straighten her hair again. As the bus turned towards Ashok Rajpath I would press the rewind button on the Walkman and listen to 'When Will I, Will I Be Famous' again and again and peddle furiously towards Xavier's on the other side of Gandhi Maidan.

In the evenings after I was back from school, at 4:30 p.m. on most summer days, it would be time to cruise Hathwa Market with Pranjal Sinha, fellow Kadam Kuan gallant and childhood buddy. The shops in Hathwa Market were spread in a large rectangular space with the parking lot at front like the GK-I M-Block Market in Delhi. Pranjal and I would just keep going around from one end to the other, walking indolently in the shade of the awnings and billboards, looking at the high-price shops selling branded garments, watches, electrical goods, furniture, books, toys and cassettes. It was from one bookshop in Hathwa Market in my childhood that my mother bought me Amar Chitra Katha comics and read them out to me. It was from that shop that I bought my first Tintin comic book for fifteen rupees on my seventh birthday. It was, I believe, *Prisoners of the Sun*, on which my mother later that evening put a cellophane cover so that it wouldn't get spoiled. It was from that shop that, while on one of my interminable cruises with Pranjal, I rescued *Vanity of Duluoz*, the bittersweet Jack Kerouac novel of his golden football-playing childhood, with twenty rupees. Pandey, the shop assistant who earlier had sold me Amar Chitra Kathas and Commando comics, told me that the novel had been languishing in that shop for the past twenty years. So it was one rupee for each year spent in Patna. It had already spent more years in Patna than I. To this day it remains one of my favourite American novels and Kerouac an abiding influence.

Pranjal and I would stand and look through the window showcases displaying new brands of jeans and t-shirts and discuss the merits of each novelty item like fashion acolytes but we would rarely ever buy anything. It was what in Patna parlance we called a 'timepass'. We did a lot of it that year and when a beautiful girl with her once beautiful mother passed by, our heads would swivel automatically in their direction as if on ball bearings and we would feel 'glad' inside. Around 5:30 p.m., about three times a week on an average, Yamini Sahay, along with her elder sister Rukmini, would stroll in from Kadam Kuan for the chaat and gol-gappas sold near the market entrance. Time for the cigarettes to come out. Pranjal and I would stand in front of the bookstall, light our Gold Flakes and just stare at the Sahay sisters as they tucked into massive quantities of gol-gappas. The secret perhaps of their architecturally perfect behinds. After the gol-gappas, the sisters would take a leisurely stroll around Hathwa Market and we would follow them ten paces behind, passing a Gold Flake back and forth between us. The sisters too were doing 'time pass'. Of the nine months we followed them around Hathwa Market every couple of days in the evening, we never spoke. But they knew us and we knew them. Talking wasn't important, we communicated through gestures. Through signs. Through lighted Gold Flakes, through a dainty hand with which Yamini Sahay fluffed her Madhuri Dixit locks, through the rani-coloured salwar suits that Rukmini wore whenever she was merry, which was quite often, through the imitation Wayfarer sunglasses that Pranjal wore even at twilight because they made him look like Aamir Khan and my black denim North Star shirt and jeans which I flogged all that year because I thought I was Jim Morrison. Pranjal and I would escort the sisters till the front gate of Hathwa Market from where they would go back to their home, their ample behinds gently rolling, while we crossed the road over to Lalji Market for a well-deserved glass of tea at the Ding-Dong tea shop, whose cramped wooden shack was plastered with posters of coming attractions torn from *Screen*, the film trade weekly, and *Mayapuri*. There was always a crowd of gallants from Kadam Kuan at Ding-Dong, from different generations and sometimes it seemed even centuries. There were a lot of two-handed handshakes: 'Kaise hain, boss?', 'Theek hain, boss', 'Padhai-vadhai?', 'Chal raha hai, boss'. In fact, one could centre it and set as verse.

Kaise hain, boss?
Theek hain, boss.
Padhai-vadhai?
Chal raha hai, boss.

Variations of this ditty are still heard in all tea shops from Patna to Delhi University where Bihari gallants meet to philosophize.

The USP of Ding-Dong was—the rumour floated decades back and which generations of Kadam Kuan 'bhaiyas' had helped sustain—that a pellet of opium was mixed with the tea leaves for every pot and hence once one had had a Ding-Dong cuppa, he would keep coming back for more and more, till the day he got married and turned respectable. Sometimes even then.

'Hriday, you are probably the single-most uninterested cadet in the history of NCC that it has been my misfortune to train. You are listless in the classroom, listless on the parade field, listless everywhere. Listlessness is the condition that defines you fully. From top to bottom. You have no ambition at all. But I am not failing you only because of that. I am failing you because you are a Bengali and you should have known better.' Basu poured a cup of tea and passed it to Chandragupta II and then he poured a cup for me.

'You are failing me because I am a Bengali?' I looked incredulously at Basu and repeated the statement. Chandragupta II was having it hard keeping a straight face and sipping his tea at the same time.

'You were the only Bengali boy in the group and I had high hopes for you. Don't you feel any responsibility towards your family, your community?'

'I have never thought about it that way. I am an average student, granted, and that is the reason I am here. I need that two per cent on my mark sheet that NCC provides. I am sure there are thousands of Bengalis here in Patna who are as average as I am. Why drag my family into it? They do not even know I am here doing pairvi with you.'

'Average. Of course that is where the problem lies. The Bengalis nowadays are all average. They don't have any spark. No ambition. They are happy with the small average lives they lead. Earlier in Patna most of the doctors, the engineers, professors and government officers were Bengalis but now … (Here Basu made a sweeping motion with his Charminar-clutched hand) nothing. Look at my brother.'

'Your brother?' Chandragupta II finally got a question in edgeways.

'Yes, my brother (again that sweeping motion of the Charminar-clutched hand), younger than me by twelve years. You probably saw him downstairs. He runs a medicine shop on the ground floor. I had him admitted to the best schools but he just wouldn't ever study. I wanted him to join the army. Put him in Netarhat military school when he was ten through my army contacts. He ran away from there in a month. Later I got him enrolled in St. Michael's and he failed twice in the sixth standard. They threw him out. Then I sent him to the Sainik School in Tillaiya. I bought him a brand new red-coloured VIP suitcase for the journey and his stay there. He was back in Patna within a week. He just wouldn't study. No drive at all. His only passion in life was to read Hindi detective novels. Pulp fiction. Surendra Mohan Pathak, Rajan-Iqbal, Colonel Ranjit. Disturbed by this, once I spent a hundred rupees on a Father Brown anthology, G. K. Chesterton, the great British novelist, but my brother never even opened the book. He can't read English. Can there be anything more shameful for a Bengali boy? I became so desperate after that I put him in the Ram Mohun Roy seminary which, as you would know, is only a five-minute walk from here. He survived there for two years. I had to arrange for him to take the matric examinations privately. He just barely passed. He didn't want to study anymore and I didn't pressurize him. But I will tell you I was disappointed. I had great expectations. Have you read Dickens? (Before I could reply, Basu continued on with his monologue.) Of course you haven't. Bengalis only read James Hadley Chase nowadays. They have stopped reading Dickens. Very disappointed. I wanted my brother to become an army officer. Join the National Defence Academy and, barring that, the civil services. But such a dullard! One day he comes up to me and says, "Dada, I want to open a medicine shop. Please have a shop vacated on the ground floor." I tried to reason with him, told him, "Montu, these things are for Banias. There is no need for you to go into business," but he wouldn't listen, so I got the shop vacated, borrowed Rs 50,000 from a Sultanganj Pathan and opened the shop for him. But I was disappointed. I had great expectations. And for all that I did for him, Montu these days doesn't even speak to me.' There was the same animated passion on Basu's face as when he beat the drums for the Friday evening march-past. All through he kept chain-smoking Charminars. Halfway through each unfiltered stick, he would light a new one.

'But medicine shops usually do well in Patna. My mama runs two shops in Kankarbagh.' Chandragupta II tried to assuage Basu's fears with sincere eagerness. He wanted Basu to be in the best of humours. In a charitable state of mind. Everything depended on that. A pairvi would never work if the benefactor was in a foul mood. Here Basu had gone off on a tangent and Hriday was of no help at all! It seemed that he was hell-bent on antagonizing Basu. Bengalis! He would never understand them. They were a different nation altogether. I shouldn't have come with Hriday. I should have brought my chotte mama, the pairvi specialist. Yes, the very same one who wears white patent leather sandals and moves around town in a chauffeur-driven rickshaw.

'Of course. Medicine shops do good business in Patna. Almost every second person is suffering from some ailment or the other. Maruti service stations and medicine shops are the safest business propositions in Patna. Montu is doing well, financially that is, I hear. But that is not the point. The point is that he has let life pass him by. He had the privileges. Even though my father died when Montu was very young, I never let him feel any kind of want. He had the options but he chose not to exercise any of them. He is indifferent to options. He doesn't have any ambition. He has never known what it feels like to be really poor. None of us do. And it makes us soft. It makes us weak. Saps the drive. Montu is a "scion" of a good Kayastha family. He should have been in administration. In government service. But he chose to be just a dukandar.'

'He didn't want to study. That too I suppose is an option. Running a business requires much more intelligence than being a clerk in the secretariat, I am sure,' I said to Basu. The old Bengali and Bihari prejudice against businessmen which, though getting milder since the mid-eighties, was still fairly prevalent.

Basu continued as if he hadn't heard me. 'One must not ever forget what one comes from. The family, the community, the caste. Whatever one does in life, in the end it is through these networks that help finally arrives. And our actions affect these networks. One must never shame one's family. Montu forgot his grandfather was a judge, his father a magistrate. He doesn't have any pride. And nor do you, Hriday. If you do not have pride, you won't ever do anything. You had no business to be in the NCC. You only enrolled because at the end of the two years you would get a certificate that would ensure a two per cent increase in your final aggregate. When I first saw you and learnt which family you came from, I had, I must admit, great expectations from you. You were the only Bengali who had enrolled and I thought I saw an officer there. I could see you in a MiG-21 flying over the border towards Lahore. But your mediocrity and studied indifference to everything worthwhile in life caused me great pain. I felt for your father, your family. What they must be going through. In the NCC camp both of you conducted yourselves abominably. Where did you think you were going? To a holiday resort in the hills? A boot camp is supposed to make you tough. But money has spoiled you. Eroded your pride and made you soft. You all resented the fact that you had been taken to a camp, away from your retinue of servants, chauffeur-driven cars and air conditioners and abundant food on the dining table which you can waste. Chandragupta II, you then did the ultimate thing. You went AWOL from an air force base! You could have been arrested for that. Do you realize the amount of pleading I had to do with Wing Commander Verghese so that no action was taken against you? But, of course, these things are of no concern to the youth.'

'I am very sorry, sir,' Chandragupta II, with a genuine quiver in his voice and eyes brimming with tears, said to Basu.

A regular thespian, I thought, looking at him. More Jeevan than Dilip Kumar.

'You have been right about me. I had no business to be in the NCC, but so didn't 99 per cent of the boys who enrolled. Everyone did it for the easy two per cent grace marks. You are right, I was indifferent and a disgrace, but so were the others. All we did was a lot of march-pasts in the afternoon sun. How that was ever going to toughen us or build our characters is beyond me. I am sure, from a distance, we cut a dashing picture, but it was no more realistic than a song-and-dance sequence in a Hindi movie. No one confuses it for real life. I am sorry that I have disappointed you and will probably have to pass on that opportunity to bomb Lahore in the near future. And you know what? I am glad that these two years in the NCC have not toughened me one bit. I don't even like tough guys. I get a terrible urge to beat them up when I accidentally bump into them sometimes. One more thing (here I stood up), please leave the Bengalis alone. They certainly do not need you. You should learn something from your brother. I am sure he is much happier than you. Namashkar.'

I went quietly through the corridor and down the stairs. As I waited for Chandragupta II to join me in the street I noticed that my hands and legs were shaking ever so slightly. Chandragupta II joined me after a couple of minutes.

'Are you crazy? What made you say all that? He offered us tea! He is crying now. I have apologized for your behaviour.'

'You shouldn't have. It doesn't concern you.'

'Of course, it does. I want my 2 per cent, don't I? Will get my chotte mama and a large handi of rosogollas and fall at Basu's feet tomorrow.'

'Suit yourself.'

We both mounted our cycles and went our separate ways.

The next day, late in the evening, I received a call from Chandragupta II. He sounded quite despondent. 'Went to see Basu with my mama. The bastard refused to meet us. Almost physically threw us out. Shut the door on our faces. All because of you. What do I do now?'

'Didn't you take the rosogollas for him?'

'Of course, I did. Full two kgs of it.'

'You and your mama can eat them now.' I laughed and put the phone down.

But the surprising thing was that when, a couple of months later, the NCC 'A' certificates did arrive at Xavier's, both Chandragupta II's and mine were included. For some reason Basu had decided against withholding them.

I never met Sgt. Basu again. Though about six months later I did see him in Hathwa Market buying comics for his young daughter. Pranjal and I as usual were stalking the copper-bottomed Sahay sisters. He saw me but quickly turned and started speaking to his daughter. Even I did not stop to greet him. It was quite evident that he didn't want anything to do with me ever. But as our eyes met, by reflex action almost, I took out the newly lighted Gold Flake from my mouth and stubbed it beneath my feet.

Brilliant Tutorials

At the age of seventeen in 1992 when I came to Delhi University to enrol in the B.A. English (Hons.) course at Zakir Husain College, I had vague ambitions of becoming a writer someday. Now from where that ambition took root in my heart I have no way of rationalizing as I had written nothing in my life till then. Not even a ten-line love poem tucked inside an Archies Valentine's day card to Sophia Rai and Yamini Sahay, two Kadam Kuan girls I was keen on once upon a time.

Even at St. Xavier's I had never contributed anything to the school magazine, Xavier Life, an eight-page stapled affair that was published every two months and where poems, short stories and moralistic essays with titles like 'Whither Love' were routinely printed. At Xavier's, cricket was my life. That was what I lived for. I had made the school team while still in the eighth standard and regularly played for them in local tournaments like the Sukhdeo Narain and the Mohit Mohan Bose Cup without ever doing anything spectacular. I had the ambition but not the requisite talent. To my credit I realized this quite early and from then on just played the game to enjoy myself. I remember the preparations on match days, when we played Loyola or St. Michael's at Gandhi Maidan. The early morning dew, the whole team carrying the green mat, the stretching of the leather hoops at the edge of the mat so that the curved nails hammered through it would keep it in place through the day. The ropey slipperiness of the mat itself, the way it shimmered in the early morning sunlight. The putting of whitener on our Power keds and sometimes on the collars and cuffs of our shirts and the groin area of our allegedly white trousers. The anticipation of the match, the slight fluttery sensation in your stomach while you took guard and Ashraf Imam of St. Michael's ran in to bowl, his fast swinging toe-crushers in a bowling action patterned on Imran Khan. The moment of stillness in the mind just before the ball is delivered and then the sound of the mat as the seam kisses it and zips past the hastily withdrawn edge of your bat. You are beaten fair and square but you project that you 'well left' it. It is about the only thing I have learnt from Sunil Gavaskar, how to do a good well left. The second ball, the same thing happens and your mind starts playing tricks. In it you can see yourself returning back to the pavilion, or in our case to the edge of the ground where the Xavier's team sits watching the game. The bat dragging on the ground and a sheepish smile on your face as the coach refuses to look at you. But next ball, you lean forward with the arc of the bowler's arm, keep your wrists steady and move with your bat in line with your pad. You hear the zip of the mat and then the solid whack of the ball hitting the middle of your BDM bat. There is no sound sweeter in the world than that. You connect and cross over to the other side for a single. This is how life is. More often than not you are beaten but then you are bound to connect. If you don't get bowled first, that is.

I was mediocre in studies, with no aptitude for the sciences, an affliction which was of great worry to my family. My father, a professor of English in Patna, probably wanted me to read medicine and become a doctor like my grandfather but he never said anything to me. I knew fully well my not being good at studies was a disappointment to him. Realizing that, during my two years of Intermediate course at Commerce College Patna, which was not a front rank college, to put it mildly, I had taken the science stream with the Biology option. I started preparing for the medical entrance examination. I even made my father pay for long-distance Brilliant Tutorials, which were highly recommended. Every month or two, when the guide books came through the post, wonderfully packed, printed in A-4 format, I felt a tremendous sense of purpose. Through those shiny white guide books I felt connected to the lakhs of ambitious middle-class boys and girls who similarly wanted to do well for themselves and also make their families proud. I wanted their goodness, their belief in themselves, their lack of despair, their unquestioning love for their parents, and above all their seeming normality.

But I was fooling no one. Least of all my father. He went along all the same as fathers generally do. I hated physics, chemistry, biology and rarely attended my classes at Commerce College. Those two years of Intermediate after my matriculation were spent in a daze. I wasn't apprehensive of the future. I just never thought about it. It was strange how a part of me wanted to conform to the idea of middle-class achievement and another diametrically opposite one was totally indifferent to it. This part wanted to be left alone, to do its own thing. Utterly self-absorbed. This side of me was way way stronger than my other conformist 'Brilliant Tutorial' side. It was just that there wasn't anything special I wanted to achieve. I was drifting along. At Commerce College, which had along with Anugrah Narayan (AN) College in Patna, a reputation of being a tough, dangerous place, I naturally gravitated, as was my wont, towards boys who like me had no purpose in life whatsoever.

Most of them came from an economic class much lower than mine and there was, I realize now, a desperation in their tough callous way of life. One of the students who sat beside me for a time in the Biology and Chemistry classes in the first couple of weeks was a boy named Vishnu Rajak, a dhobi by caste. His father was a chaprasi in the nearby Nalanda Medical College Hospital. In the mornings Vishnu would come for his classes and in the afternoon would go over to the hospital where he worked as a temporary ward boy. Vishnu must have been at least four or five years older than me and lived in a two-room brick house in the Kankarbagh slums. In the other room lived his uncle's family which carried on the family profession and still worked as dhobis. The two families were not on speaking terms. We had cycled over to Vishnu's house after the morning classes. We sat outside on folding chairs while his younger sister sent out tea and Glucose biscuits. Vishnu talked about his uncle's family in a dismissive way. It was evident that he considered himself and his father to be much superior. As a way of emphasis he added, 'We are vegetarians. My uncle eats everything. Last year we went all the way to Vaishno Devi.' Vishnu's ambition was to become a doctor and part of his interest in me was because of my 'Brilliant Tutorial' guide books. The first batch of which that day we were having photocopied. He told me about his work and the reason why he wanted to become a doctor. There was a beautiful young Brahmin junior doctor in the paediatrician ward, with whom Vishnu claimed he was in love. He wanted to become a doctor so that he could win her heart and hand.

'I am willing to wait centuries for her,' he claimed dramatically as we collected the photocopies.

But apparently he couldn't. When Vishnu didn't appear for a week soon thereafter I asked one of the boys who lived near him and he informed me that 'attempt le liya doctorni pe.' Vishnu had kissed the doctor on one of her rounds and then was soundly thrashed by all the doctors, nurses and patients around before being handed over to the police. The upshot of which was that his father too lost his coveted position of chaprasi.

One of the other friends I made at Commerce College and who would have a far-reaching effect on my life was Sudama Pathak. Pathak was a couple of years senior to me in Xavier's and was also from Kadam Kuan. He was someone I knew vaguely at Xavier's as the son of the Sanskrit master. Back then he was a shy, unassuming boy whom his friends called 'tikki' on account of the long rat-tail that he sported, but in the intervening two years he had blossomed into a tough little bastard. Six months back he had tried to immolate himself during the Mandal Commission riots in Patna and from then his reputation had grown. His hands were badly burnt and from afar they looked as if decorated with intricate patterns of mehendi, like on the hands of a bride on the day of her marriage. Up close they were wrinkled, scaly and cold to the touch.

Always clad in a cream-coloured safari suit, he held his court outside the main college gate, where there was a tea shop. From morning till evening each day he would sit there with his understudies. He kept a katta in a small black rexine handbag, the kind that secretariat clerks in Patna carry, hanging from their wrists. Apparently these bags were voluminous, accommodating everything from one's lunch, to a meticulously folded copy of Navbharat Times, a 'hand towel', a board of Ludo with dice, a pack of cards and, yes, sunglasses. I once even saw a group of clerks playing carrom in the fast passenger from Gaya. When Sudama saw me admiring his rexine bag one day he presented me with an identical one the next morning. In it I carried my shaving kit all through my college years.

Ever since a couple of months back when Pathak had shot the administrative officer at the college, Ramavatar Gupta, in the leg over the admission problem of a candidate of his, he had been barred from entering the college by the authorities. Gupta, meanwhile, had refused to testify against Pathak. According to legend Pathak always gave a choice to the person he was 'chastising'. Like to an erstwhile acolyte of his who had slapped the tea shop owner Bhandari for not giving him a pack of Navy Cut gratis, Pathak had given him a choice, whether the punter would like to be beaten with his own rubber Hawaii chappal or Pathak's more upmarket shiny white leather Bata buckled sandals. The boy had sagely pointed to his own rubber ones. Similarly, according to legend, Pathak had inquired of Gupta while keeping the katta an inch from his face, 'Sar mein ya pair mein?' And Gupta had pointed to his fleshy left leg and closed his eyes.

But Pathak didn't fully comply with the ban imposed on him, he would every morning roar through the college on his Rajdoot, take a tour of the college, shake hands with some of the students, wave to some of the staff, Ramavatar Gupta among them, and then park the motorcycle at Bhandari's tea shop and start his day.

Sudama Pathak's affinity for me was not because we came from the same neighbourhood but because we were both from the same school. A few weeks into my first semester, Pathak had sent word through one of his acolytes Mukhia (the same who would soon be chastised with his own Hawaii chappal) that I should meet Pathak the next day in the morning at the tea shop. 'Pathak Sir bulaye hain.' Between 10 and 12. The immediate thought in my mind was, 'Oh, just like a morning show,' but prudently I didn't say it aloud to Mukhia who didn't look very bright anyway. At the mention of Sudama Pathak's name most of my classmates had moved discreetly away I noticed. The next day I was there at the tea shop sharp at 10. I was carrying an astura in the front pocket of my jeans. At 11:30 a.m. Pathak arrived at the tea shop.

'Were you at St. Xavier's?'

'Yes, I was. But how do you ...' and it was then that I recognized him, by his rat tail, as the Sanskrit master's son.

'I was there too. '88 batch.'

'Of course, I remember you. You are Vidyarthiji's son.'

At the mention of his father Pathak looked at his acolytes and a reverent smile spread across his face. Pathak only wanted to meet me because he wished to extend his patronage to a fellow Xaverian. I felt foolish for carrying the astura but then that was part of what I was then. Pathak felt extremely proud to be a Xaverian, a feeling which didn't come naturally to me. For Pathak St. Xavier's was the place where he had spent the best years of his life. He told me that many times during that period. He felt it was a huge comedown in his life that after St. Xavier's he found himself in a place like Commerce College. A feeling that I myself didn't identify with as it simply didn't matter to me where I was enrolled or not. But I was glad to learn that Sudama Pathak was a Xaverian and a snob. And that he was not going to 'chastise' me. Only he was a bit concerned for me because he had received intelligence of my visiting Vishnu Rajak's home and inquiring about him a couple of days back.

'You do realize that he is a chutiya, don't you? You know what he has done.'

'Yes, I heard.'

'But then what can one expect from a bloody dhobi. I was surprised when I learnt that you had visited his home. I was concerned, that is why I called you. As Xaverians we have to uphold the tradition. For God and country and all that.'

'For God and country,' I reiterated.

'You need anything, you come to me. I am usually here between 12 and 3.'

'Like an afternoon show.' I couldn't resist.

Taken aback for a second Pathak looked at his court and smiled to reassure them.

'Housefull always.'

Sudama Pathak proved to be a true friend when at the end of the Intermediate course he helped me clear it. And in the upper half of the first division. I didn't take the examination with the other boys in the classroom, but with some of the other bravos whose patron saint Sudama Pathak was, in the tea shop. Bhandari, God bless his soul, had arranged for a desert cooler to beat the stifling April heat and Pathak, a young master he simply called 'Babaji,' to facilitate the answers. 'Babaji', whose real name I never learnt, was from a place called Ghosi near Jehanabad and was related in an obscure way to Pathak. Babaji was a thin, very fair, slightly effeminate young man who was the Patna University topper for M.Sc. in Physics a few years before. He was enrolled for a Ph.D. and was also preparing for the civil services. He stayed in a small room on the terrace—which in Delhi would be called a barsati—

of Sudama Pathak's house. Babaji subsisted by giving tuitions. I visited his room one of those days between the papers, and was shocked by his poverty. His room though large was completely bare except for a rope cot that we call khatia in Patna, with two thin cotton mattresses and a pillow which seemed to have been carved out of stone. There was a musty smell of boiled potatoes and wet towels in the room. The other bit of furniture was an old discoloured hardwood table and chair. On the shelves above the table, built into the rani-coloured wall, his study books, civil service guides, were stacked. He had been sitting at his table reading the Manorama Yearbook for the year 1991. The only book of general interest or fiction was a Raduga press edition of Gorky's *Mother* and if I remember correctly Cheiro's book on astrology. He very shyly asked to see my right hand. He held it softly like he were holding a bone china teacup and brought it close to his myopic eyes.

After a while he said, 'You will fall in love many times,' with an embarrassed smile. Not exactly breaking news, if you know what I mean, as I was born on 14 February. Hundreds of Archies cards, carefully perused over the years, had already informed me as much.

After we had completed our papers in the tea shop, Sudama Pathak would collect them himself and take them back to the invigilator. I now realize how crucial that Intermediate examination was for my life. If I had not got a first division I wouldn't have got admission in a Delhi University college. Left to myself, I think I would not have passed at all. I still sometimes get nightmares in which I suddenly realize that the Intermediate examinations are just a month away, and I haven't opened my physics textbook even once. When I do wake up and realize that part of my life is over, the relief is immense.

After the results came out, I visited Babaji again, carrying with me a navy blue Graviera safari suit length as a kind of guru dakshina. He touched the cloth between his delicate fingers and his eyes closed for a moment or two. Then he said 'Thank You' in English. As I was leaving he offered to look at my hand again. But this time I demurred as I already knew I would fall in love many times.

Continuing with my aimless wandering, I didn't even sit for the Bihar Medical Entrance Examination. My examination centre was in Ranchi. By that time the glamour of the shrink-wrapped packages of Brilliant Tutorials was past its sell-by date for me. I hadn't even opened the packages for the past five months. I went to Ranchi with a bunch of other boys, including Pranjal Sinha, in a Bihar Tourism bus that we caught from Serpentine Road. Pranjal, who had been with me in St. Xavier's, had done well in his Matric Board examinations, scoring in the high eighties, and had gone to the prestigious Patna Science College for his Intermediate.

While I indulged in my aimless wandering Pranjal as usual had been his prudent, ambitious and hard-working self throughout these two years. He knew exactly what he wanted to do. He would study hard and take various medical entrance exams and if he didn't get through he would go on to Delhi for his graduation and there start preparing for the civil services. He wouldn't ask his father, a senior paediatrician in Patna, to pay for a capitation fee college in Bombay or Mangalore. If he didn't crack the medical examinations on merit, he didn't want it at all. This kind of idealistic behaviour was totally alien to me, as you can very well imagine. But we had been friends from time immemorial. We loved each other for what we were. I his Bihari clear headedness and he my Bengali propensity to dwell in uncertainties.

We started out in the early morning and reached Ranchi in the evening. The next day while Pranjal took his exams, I spent my time wandering in and around Firayalal Chowk. In the afternoon I watched Aditya Bhattacharya's *Raakh*. I liked the movie so much that I caught the matinee show too. He was young, talented and cool as hell. Aditya Bhattacharya had been twenty-four when he had written and directed *Raakh*. To boot, he was married to Sanjana Kapoor, possibly the prettiest girl in India then or ever. Whatever residual guilt I had for not taking the medical entrance exam and wasting my father's money simply vanished after watching that landmark movie. One day, I promised myself, I would write something as dynamic as that. A few days later I started my story about a girl in Patna who was named after a famous painting by Da Vinci and the effect it had on her life. I finished the story a couple of months later in Delhi in my hostel room in Shokeen Niwas. I still remember writing that first page of 300 words, which took me two days. It was the first glimpse of any kind of self-discipline in over two years.

Pranjal, on the way back, in the bus, reiterated that I was a fool and that I owed my parents to at least sit for the exams. I didn't say anything; he was right. I did wonder sometimes whether he ever got bored of being right always. Then, I went back to sleep and only woke up when we reached Patna early in the morning the following day.

When my father before leaving for the university asked me, 'How did it go?', I replied, 'Not too bad.' He nodded. But he probably realized that I was lying. Fathers have a way of knowing things. A couple of days later I asked him, 'If worse comes to worst, will you send me to a capitation fee medical college in Mangalore?' and he said 'Of course not' like I knew he would.

So when the Intermediate results came out and I scored a high first division, he didn't have any problems when I said I wanted to go to Delhi. In fact, he probably breathed a sigh of relief.

In Patna if I were doing arts, it would be said that I was a 'good for nothing', but Delhi was far away and one could always be studying for the 'civils'. The best thing about my father was that unlike most fathers he didn't actually have great expectations from his son. Also, the fact that Pranjal was going to Delhi helped. My father instinctively trusted him more than he trusted me. And rightly so.

A week before leaving for Delhi I carried my Brilliant Tutorial workbooks and guides to a bookseller in Ramna Road and sold the whole lot for one thousand rupees. From that loot I bought two Graviera safari suit lengths from Patna Market. One cream and Babaji's navy blue. With the money left I bought a copy of

John Cheever's collected stories with the now iconic bright red cover from the wonderful bookshop tucked in the back of Patna Market for myself.

Sudama proudly passed the suit length to his acolytes to have a look at. 'Touch kar ke dekho' he told them.

'When you reach Delhi, go and meet Jishnu Sharma. Here's his address. I have already spoken to him. He will arrange a room for you.' It was the day before Pranjal and I were supposed to leave for Delhi. So with the address so thoughtfully provided by Pathak, I landed up at Shokeen Niwas and began the next phase of my life.

Great Expectations

Jaishankar Sharma aka Jishnuda came from proud Bhumihar stock and his family owned quite a bit of land near Nadaul in Jehanabad district, where the joke in some enlightened circles in Patna was that whenever on some winter night it got unbearably chilly, the upper castes gathered together and went to the nearest untouchable and landless labour settlement and set it alight. The upper castes could then warm their hands on the spreading heat. But with the recent spread of CPI (ML) activism in the district much of the joy of living, simple everyday pleasures like rape, beatings and bonfire, had suddenly been denied to the upper castes, especially the Bhumihar majority and the Rajputs. Now even for their weddings the upper castes crept out of their houses like fugitives, so that CPI (ML) cadres didn't attack their homes while they were away. The days of five hundred baratis, three-day revelries, the dances of nautch girls from Calcutta and Benaras, indiscriminate firing in the air of double-barrelled shotguns and Lee Enfield Rifles were over. Upper caste weddings in villages in the 1990s were clandestine affairs. Barely thirty to forty people from each side took part in the festivities.

Though only five feet-six inches tall in his thick-soled Chinese flipflops bought from the Tibetan Monastery bazaar near ISBT, I had once seen Jishnuda slash a six feet tall Jat boy's face with an astura outside the Miranda House hostel gate on Chhatra Marg. Most fights, 'compromises' and shows of strength those days took place outside the Miranda hostel. Between 4 p.m., when the girls came out slouchingly in their 'angrezi', crumpled, unwashed jeans and equally woebegone T-shirts after their afternoon cat nap, each carrying a huge mug of lukewarm tea, and 7:30 p.m. when they finally retired for the night. The ice-cream wallah and the bhel puri wallah would leave soon after.

Chhatra Marg was the preferred open-air auditorium for all sorts of 'tamasha' and 'nukkad nataks'. Some elaborately mounted and performed but most hastily improvised. The discerning audience, largely female, quite appreciative of the talent on display. It has been my good fortune to discover that nothing quite captures the female imagination as male conflict. An astura thinly coated with dried blood will always get more attention than a white rose wrapped in cellophane.

Like in most small towns of Bihar, when evening descends and people saunter off to the nearby railway junction for entertainment, so in Delhi University Biharis came out of their boroughs in Kamla Nagar, Vijay Nagar, Indira Vihar, Maurice Nagar, Mukherjee Nagar, Hakikat Nagar and myriad other nagars and vihars, and set out for Chhatra Marg. There they would dawdle for a couple of hours, have tea at Jai Jawan dhaba, meet their girlfriends at Miranda, or PG Women's or Meghdoot hostels, and thrash out 'compromises' without any group coming to real blows. 'Compromises' were usually about imagined slights to one's dignity concerning a girl who was a 'sister' even though the girl may not have known the guy but was from the same town. Or over some remark in some drunken party which had filtered back to the person concerned a month later with much mirch-masala added. Or better still, during July-August with election fever in the air, which candidates to support, whom not to support, and which lucky bugger would have to be forced to withdraw his candidature. When two groups were close to a major fight, the side which got hit or threatened first would look for a suitable 'compromiser'. A kind of amicus curiae who was always a village elder. Say someone like Jishnu Sharma. The other side would then invite someone who was a duplicate of Jishnuda in stature. Then drumbeats and alarums. The two Jishnudas would meet outside Miranda hostel while the warring groups smoked Navy Cuts and waited on either side of Chhatra Marg.

Usually in ten minutes flat most 'compromises' would be over. Then the leaders of the two groups would be summoned and asked to 'shake hands karo' and then everybody would have tea at Jai Jawan. All very proper and civilized. So what did the two Jishnus talk about during the all important 'compromise'? 'More often than not, cricket scores. But if it is really important, we drop names of people who will back us in an out and out fight. Like someone names Santoo Singh of Kankarbagh as an ally, I mention the great Sudama Pathak of Kadam Kuan. Or from Delhi, if one cites Mahendra Fauji of Najafgarh, I let slip Uncle Zorawar Singh Shokeen of Chandrawal's name. It is all about naming names. One instinctively knows who is telling the truth and who is just showing off. Usually two minutes of this and then visarjan. "Shake hands karo."'

A couple of days previous to the incident involving the Jat boy, a friend of Jishnuda's from Kadam Kuan, Paritosh Bhattacharya, had written him a letter. Jishnuda had ambled over to our room bearing the registered letter aloft like a flag, wearing new Minnie Mouse Bermudas with his trademark Sandow ganji. On the portable Panasonic Springsteen's mellow and brooding *Nebraska* was playing. Pranjal had bought the CBS tape on his way back from Hindu in the afternoon. Since then we had played it back to back a couple of times, especially 'Highway Patrolman' and 'Used Cars'. Jishnuda switched the stereo off. He didn't much care for rock music or the Boss. His favourite song was that legendary torch song from *Waqt* about sexual inadequacy, 'Aage Bhi Jaane Na Tu, Peeche Bhi Jaane Na Tu'. On Friday nights, invariably after the second peg he would demand the song be played and a special cassette called 'The Khamba Collection' that a girl from Kadam Kuan had made for him would be fetched from his room by Ramanuj Ghosh. The cassette featured the entire soundtracks of *Arth*, *Saath-Saath*, *Ghar* and *Bazaar*, among many other love songs from Hindi movies.

I closed *A House for Mr Biswas* and looked expectantly while Pranjal put aside his macroeconomics textbook with a world-weary sigh. Jishnuda sprawled on Pranjal's cot, put on his round wire-frame Mahatma Gandhi glasses and read out the letter to us. The ever present ganja-spiked Navy Cut smouldering between his left forefinger and thumb and his left ball peeking out of his Bermudas, right in my eye-line. To change the angle I got up from my desk and sat down on my cot on the other side of the room. In a while Farid and Ramanuj also joined us.

The Jat boy, according to the letter, was 'harassing' Paritosh's rakhi sister from his Science College days, an 'ex-Miss St. Joseph's Convent' chick called Vinodini Khan, now in her 3rd year doing English Hons. at Miranda House.

The letter, which came with a group photo with Vinodini Khan's face circled in red felt-tip pen, also gave the Jat boy's name and description. The letter implored Jishnuda in no uncertain terms to take care of the matter and save sister Vinodini's good name from getting 'besmirched'. I dutifully looked up the meaning of the word in Pranjal's Concise Oxford and read it out to the gentry.

'Hriday babu, just like every door has a dwarpal every chut has a chutpal. A chutpal never gets the chut just like the dwarpal rarely gets to sleep in the master bedroom. Every good girl needs at least one chutpal, to run errands for her and listen to her bitch about her mother. Paritosh is a classic chutpal, a maha chutpal, if ever there was one, but he is also a friend, so we will have to take care of the matter,' Jishnuda said to us after folding the letter carefully and slipping it into his pocket.

That very evening Farid and I accompanied Jishnuda to Miranda hostel on his ancient Rajdoot 175. I remember everything vividly, like it was yesterday. The Jat boy was wearing a red checked shirt with tight flared black jeans, the kind one bought quite cheap from Tank Road in Karol Bagh. He had a cleft chin, a deep pumped-up chest and shoulders fit for lifting sacks of potato. He was good-looking in a wholesome, rustic manner and looked about five to six years older than me. He leaned against the iron railing outside the hostel, one stylish boot-clad foot on the lower railing, the other on the ground. A slim pretty girl in a white chikan kurta with a red bandhini chunri was talking to him and once in a while ruffled his hair like a pet dog's. This was Vinodini Khan, the sister, and to all purposes it looked to me that she was harassing the poor boy instead. Jishnuda looked at the couple for some time, and after making sure that no white Gypsy was patrolling the street, took off his glasses and handed them to me. Once in his first year, some boys from Siwan had attacked him in the Mansarovar PG Hostel forecourt during Saraswati puja. One well-aimed nanchaku blow had shattered his glasses. His left eyelid got detached. The upshot of it was that his left eye was now permanently lower than his right and he became quite particular about taking his glasses off before a fight.

There was no going back now. I watched all this from the seat of the Rajdoot, parked by the gate of PG Women's Hostel across the road. The engine was running. Farid, the getaway driver. I was only to intervene if perchance the Jat boy fought back. 'No one ever does. The first reaction is always to run.' When Jishnuda had asked me to accompany him as a backup, I had said yes immediately.

Alone in our room after the mandali had gone downstairs for tea at Mehendiratta's shop, Pranjal after keeping the Concise Oxford in its proper place on his desk, pushed me against the wall roughly by my neck.

'Do you really want to do this stupid thing? Are you absolutely crazy?'

'Yes,' I said truthfully and went down to join the others for tea and matthi.

I very well could have said no to Jishnuda and Ramanuj would have taken my place gladly but it just never occurred to me to say no. It seemed like a community thing to do. Like a group of friends going out to see the night show at Batra in Mukherjee Nagar.

We saw Jishnuda walk purposefully towards the couple, the astura gleaming in the orange glare of the street lamps, and as he reached the 'sister', he pushed her gently away and swung his hand from left to right and back like a wide X mark, in a controlled arc. The boy looked surprised for a second and then covered his face as blood gushed out. Farid put the Rajdoot in gear, Vinodini Khan ran back into the hostel. The red bandhini chunri swirling in the air like a long-tailed kite.

The local boy whose name was Rajkumar Sangwan didn't lodge an FIR with the police but his family we heard was close to Sajjan Kumar, so while Zorawar Singh Shokeen brought about a compromise, we went on a week long pilgrimage tour to Haridwar, Rishikesh and Badrinath. We stayed in a small ashram owned by Zorawar Singh in Haridwar and each morning had a holy dip in the Har ki Paudi. Pranjal had reluctantly agreed to accompany us after much persuasion. He hardly said a word during the entire bus ride of five hours to Haridwar, preferring Naipaul's company to ours, but on the first evening as all five of us sat on the steps leading to the Ganga at Har ki Paudi with the aarti going on and thousands of diyas flowing past us swiftly, cleansing us all of our sins, Pranjal gradually came out of his blue period and even offered me a Gold Flake on the trek back to the ashram. He was all right after that.

'What a bitch,' Jishnuda said to us while we were taking turns drinking neat from a half bottle of Old Monk right in front of the theka at Kingsway Camp, minutes after the Miranda 'kaand', the raging testosterone coupled with raw rum making us gasp.

'Should have done a bit of enquiry.' Jishnuda finished the rum and then tried to bounce the bottle off the Ring Road. We could see he was intrigued by naughty Vinodini. He had liked what he had seen in those few close seconds. Like me. The thick shoulder length hair with auburn streaks in it, made by henna, the glowing Maithil Brahmin skin, the colour of freshly washed grain of wheat spread out to dry in the winter sun and an ass, the size of it, just right for my hands to squeeze gently.

About ten days later, right after we were back in Delhi from our holy tour, unable to wait anymore, one evening I put on my lucky North Star black denim shirt, black jeans slightly flared, the exact same kind that Rajkumar Sangwan had worn on the fateful day, and walked briskly from Bungalow Road via Kirori Mal hostel on to Chhatra Marg, towards Miranda hostel. To meet the sister. I didn't know what I would say to her once I was standing in front of her. But I didn't care. It just felt like a grown-up thing to do. To call on a girl at Miranda hostel. I had to see naughty Vinodini once more. It was already dark by the time I reached the hostel. Across the street, I spied Jishnuda's black Rajdoot parked a little way off the Miranda hostel gate. Jishnuda leaned against the railing outside the hostel, one foot on the lower rails, the other on the ground. On his feet, I noticed, were Pranjal's prized Power joggers. Vinodini Khan once in a while ruffled his hair like a pet dog's.

Then one day Pranjal and I came back in the evening after having bread-omelette at Jai Jawan and found Jishnuda's room locked from the inside. A red bandhini chunri was draped over the thick glass window giving it a stained glass effect. We decided it was better not to knock.

Then for weeks after that Vinodini Khan would come over to Shokeen Niwas on her turquoise blue Atlas mountain bike and run up the stairs shouting 'fore' at the top of her voice, making all of us lounging in our underwear run for cover.

In the evenings sometimes she would make coffee for all of us on Jishnuda's electric heater. A more life-affirming cup of coffee I am yet to imbibe. I would stand at the doorway sipping coffee watching Vinodini chatter incessantly, pulling everybody's leg and I would wonder what does she ever see in Jishnuda, who at the very moment was probably calculating the cost of the community coffee and whether he should charge us for it or not. But I was young then and I didn't know that women always went for men who were totally unsuitable for them. On the other hand there are things about men which only a woman would notice and appreciate and which would always be invisible to the male gaze. The same perhaps is true for the female gaze too.

'I am like Amrita Sher-Gil. I am polyamorous,' Vinodini once told me after reading part of a story I was writing in which the female protagonist I realize now was modelled on her. Then suddenly one day she stopped coming to Shokeen Niwas. It was over between her and Jishnuda. A year later, after her graduation she left for Magdalen on a Rhodes. Later on she would come back to India and join the Indian Foreign Service. I once asked Jishnuda why they had stopped seeing each other. He looked at me in a bemused manner and I realized then that he knew all the while that I had a massive crush on Vinodini Khan. He put a Navy Cut into his smile and said simply, 'She was turning me into a chutpal.'

An only son after three daughters of a middling Ayurvedic practitioner in Kadam Kuan, needless to add there were great expectations from Jishnuda. His father's dream was that his only son should enter the civil services and preferably become an IAS or IPS officer. Even the revenue services would do. The foreign service though prestigious was not of much use, if you were posted in Timbuktu, was it? Jishnuda's father would often say to him while on the topic of the civil services that once he became an IAS officer 'the whole profile of the family would change'. Jishnuda liked to quote that 'Boss, the whole profile of the family would change. Yes, no one can touch you then.'

For Jishnuda, like many other Bihari students in Delhi, whether in DU, Jamia or JNU, the white government Ambassador car with the red beacon light on top and all sirens blaring, was the ultimate achievement. To have that kind of power, which they perceived as invincible, the leisurely feudal ambience with five or six servants attending to all their demands and the unimaginable riches which came with the job, not to mention the dowry which would automatically catapult them into the 10–15 lakh category. It would in a single stroke change the 'profiles' of many. Their families back home in Patna, Gaya, Ranchi, Bhagalpur, Darbhanga and other small towns in Bihar made great sacrifices for them while they studied sometimes fifteen hours a day to change their 'profiles'.

Jishnuda's room in Shokeen Niwas was filled with civil services guides, ready reckoners, magazines, history and public administration textbooks and the mandatory chest expander. In his zealousness Jishnuda's father had got his son's age reduced by five years during matriculation, as a result of which Jishnuda was officially twenty years old when he should have been at least twenty-five. He was now finally eligible to sit for the civil services exam. After his graduation, each year he would enrol himself in the M.A. (Previous) English course but he never sat the examination in all the years that I knew him. Though he made it a point to attend classes at the Arts Faculty building a couple of times a week. He loved the fact that he was doing an MA in English literature and that in his classroom girls outnumbered the boys 10 to 1. It was probably another of his 'profile changing' things.

He liked reading the novels prescribed for the course. His favourite was *Tom Jones* which he read once every year. 'Each year I think I will take the exam, but then on the day the first paper is due, I decide not to take it. What's the use, I don't want to end up as a bloody professor of English literature, do I? I am an existentialist. I want my white Ambassador. But I am glad Hriday you too have chosen English literature. If you have any problem with Plato, you know who to call on.' Later on I got to know, in fact he himself let on one day after a strenuous ganja session, that he had graduated with 41 per cent marks from Ramjas College.

Like most of the other boys at Shokeen Niwas, who didn't regularly attend classes, Jishnuda would wake up around ten in the morning. He would spend fifteen minutes brushing his teeth, wearing his trademark ganji and Bermudas, a thin cotton checked towel wrapped around his shoulders. Sometimes in peak summer when he ventured out of Shokeen Niwas in the afternoons for campaigning in the DU elections he would wrap the towel around his head like a peasant. Along with a couple of other senior boys like Chaitanya Mishra and Abhinav Srivastava, who too were preparing for the civil services and doing their M.Phil. at the Delhi School of Economics, he would go across the street to Mehendiratta's shop on the ground floor of the yellow house for the succulent bread-omelette that Mehendiratta's daughter Dolly cooked for them, to be washed down with a glass of sweet milky tea. In a year's time Chaitanya Mishra would leave for London to do his Ph.D. at the London School of Economics and Abhinav Srivastava would clear NET and join Zakir Husain College (Evening) as an ad hoc lecturer in Economics. They would both give up their civil services dream but to me it seemed they didn't do too badly at all.

There was a bench right outside the shop, on the street, where they would sit and talk about life, Delhi University politics and the state of the nation, while having their breakfast. Soon Farid Ashraf and Ramanuj Ghosh would join them. Once in a while lacking for anything better to do, they would flirt with Dolly, who was fair but not lovely and somewhat a dimwit. Farid would regularly steal packets of Navy Cut from the shop when Mehendiratta wasn't there. Dolly was easily distracted. After dawdling around for half an hour or so they would go back to their rooms. They would read the morning papers, usually *The Hindustan Times* and *The Hindu*. The latter because it was highbrow and was considered de rigueur for the civil services. Jishnuda usually went to sleep while reading *The Hindu*. In fact he had a theory that reading *The Hindu* was a better soporific than Bhagalpuri ganja itself. If per chance *The Hindu* failed to put him to sleep he would usually pick up the mammoth civil services general studies guide which in half an hour or so would do the trick. He would then get up from his study table and chair made of wood and weaved with plastic strips (he made me and Pranjal buy an identical set from Mehendiratta) and crash on the wooden folding cot. Jishnuda would be fast asleep at 11:30 a.m. and would wake up only when our lunch arrived at about 1:30 p.m. in the afternoon from Hakikat Nagar. I too would arrive back from my college around that time. We usually had lunch together in Jishnuda's room. My tiffin box, along with the boxes of some other boys whose rooms were locked, was kept in Jishnuda's room. His room like his heart was always open. Soon Pranjal would join us, and sometimes Chaitanya Mishra and Abhinav Srivastava would bring over their tiffins and join us too. Chaitanya and Abhinav usually kept to themselves and even Jishnuda who was their contemporary was deferential to the duo. According to him they were 'scholars' and not to be disturbed.

The tiffin boxes were usually four-decker dented steel affairs. The upper box contained five rotis, the second rice, the third peeli dal and the fourth, the vegetable curry of the day. Usually curried tinda or arbi. On Wednesday nights there would be chicken curry and kheer. The charge was Rs 450 a month for both lunch and dinner. The owner of the tiffin catering business was a Bihari gallant from Hazaribagh named Satyabrat Ojha, an alumnus of Netarhat Military School. Satyabrat Ojha had come to Delhi University as a student in the early eighties. A short dark man with closely cropped hair and a pencil-thin moustache, he habitually wore thick khadi kurtas with faded denim blue jeans. His thick calloused feet were always shod in delicate Kolhapuri chappals. Perhaps the mode of dressing was his way of not severing his link with the recent past, when he too had been a student of the university. In fact all around the university, in Mukherjee Nagar, Vijay Nagar double-storey, Dhaka, Model Town, Indira Vihar, Kamla Nagar, one would come across these relics of the past. Ageing students, some in their late twenties and thirties, others hitting forty, who refused to leave the university area or go back home to Bihar. They clung to their tenuous connection as if it were a lifeline. Most would be preparing for the civil services or the state services as these were the only jobs worth doing and when age finally caught up with them, they couldn't go back home again as there would be 'great expectations'. Many would join the Law Faculty in their thirties so that they didn't have to leave the university. Sometimes even the parents were glad that they didn't come back home as they could then say to everybody that their sons were still 'preparing' in Delhi. Some would even get married, take up a job teaching in those very civil services study centres where only a few months back they too had been students, but the majority continued to subsist on money sent from home. One would see these 'danasurs' at tea shops all around the university in the evening, with their Hawaii chappals and Navy Cuts, arguing passionately about some obscure feud in Mukherjee Nagar or Indira Vihar, the chances of NSUI against ABVP, or gossiping about some girl who for a while studied with them at Rao's or Mishra's study centres and was now DM of Ara or Gaya and how she didn't seem very bright at all. 'You know she was the English type from Jamshedpur, Hi, hello, cool type.' 'Must be because of reservation.' If a girl or a backward caste boy ever got through to the civil services, it was always because of 'reservation'. It was a truth universally acknowledged across all tea shops in Delhi University at twilight. Never because of merit.

Along with his khadi kurta-jeans ensemble Ojha also affected thick black plastic prescription glasses, the kind that writers and intellectuals used to wear in the seventies. Jishnuda told me that the glasses were plain, 'power nahin hain', just a part of the uniform. He would come to Shokeen Niwas once a month accompanied by his large, friendly Labrador named Dunkel, a defrocked police sniffer dog who had apparently got too fond of opium, usually on the first Sunday, to collect the tiffin charges from us. If our money orders and bank drafts had arrived by then, we paid him.

Ojha had done a Masters in Sankrit from St. Stephen's and stood fifth in the university in his M.A. (Previous) examination. An achievement of which he reminded us each time he came to visit. He liked coming to Shokeen Niwas and holding forth on his 'Residence' years at St. Stephen's. His father, a much decorated Bengal cadre police officer, too had read at St. Stephen's in the early sixties. Since Satyabrat's marks were not that high in his plus two examinations, the only honours course he could get at St. Stephen's was Sanskrit. His father had laid down the condition that he could study at Delhi University provided he got into St. Stephen's. So he took up Sanskrit and stayed in the St. Stephen's residence for five wonderful years. Proficient in the language at school, he found that he had a natural aptitude for its complex grammar and precise syntax. As was his father's wish, he prepared for civil services too while he was doing his M.A.

Once I asked him about his rank in the M.A. Final examination since he never talked about that. Only about his fifth rank in the M.A. (Previous) examination. He kept quiet for a while and then with an indeterminate shake of his closely cropped head explained, 'Love'. Which needless to add was explanation enough to us Biharis. Love was a dangerous thing. We all knew that. It was a life-altering experience. The girl's name was Aparajita Chowdhury and we knew she was SP of Begusarai at the moment. Home Cadre.

After his M.A., Satyabrat Ojha, in keeping with his father's diktat, had indulged in the national pastime of Bihar, the civil services, till he exhausted his three 'attempts' and became a 'danasur'. It was around the time of the Mandal agitation and he became an active campaigner. Alongside many others he fought pitched battles with the police outside the Law and the Arts Faculty buildings and at the soon to be renamed Kranti Chowk during those months. He was arrested twice. The last time he was at the Maurice Nagar thana he, along with others, was badly beaten up. He had been caught while trying to flee after torching the sedately parked white Ambassador car of a senior police officer with a petrol bomb outside the Law Faculty building. By the time it became known that he was the son of a senior police officer, the SHO Joginder Tyagi had long had him hanging upside down from the ceiling and had really gone to work on him. Jishnuda had heard his screams in the next cell. Even now in the winter, on a December afternoon when it was cloudy and a stone cold wind blew from the north, Ojha found it hard to get up from his cot. All the joints in his body acted up then. 'Mutne mein bhi dikkat hota hai,' he added as an afterthought, holding his crotch delicately. At this Dunkel stopped licking himself and howled in assent.

After that ordeal he had borrowed money from his mother and set up his catering business. He knew he couldn't go back home. So he stayed in the University, where he felt comfortable and had some sort of standing as a Mandal hero. He was also much in demand as a 'compromiser'. Even now he could be seen at Law Faculty and DUSU elections, quietly sipping tea like an elder statesman.

Even though he was running a successful business, his links with literature and scholarship were still strong. He informed me when he found out that I too nursed an ambition to become a writer someday that he was writing an epic novel about the Mandal agitation in Sanskrit. 'Ek adbhut upanyas.' The working title roughly translated sounded something like 'Love in the Time of Mandal.'

901

The first time we met, Anjali Nalwa asked me to stand up on a desk and sing 'Jana Gana Mana' at the top of my voice. It was my second day at Zakir Husain College. Anjali, a third year student of English Hons., along with other second and third year students, was ragging the freshers. I readily obliged as she was very pretty in a plump, gori Punjabi sort of way. Long mehendi-burnt hair, light blue eyes and a full butter-fortified figure. A week in Delhi and I was already undergoing metamorphosis. If a senior had asked me to sing the national anthem in Patna, I would have politely asked the person to bugger off. But here in Delhi I wanted to blend in and try and do the regular things that regular students did. The last two years during my Intermediate at Commerce College had been chaotic, to say the least, and I had made a promise that I would apply myself better in Delhi and not drift like before.

I sang the national anthem at the top of my voice and when I faltered in some of the places, Anjali joined in and helped out. Soon the other students too joined in. We stopped when Dr Uday Chowdhury arrived to teach us *A House for Mr Biswas*. At Dr Chowdhury's arrival the senior students trooped out of the classroom laughing. The first year classroom was on the third floor and rather secluded and we found to our delight that if we arrived quite early in the morning or late in the afternoon for our classes we were bound to startle a couple of lovers from other departments at least once a week. The girls would scramble off quickly from the boys' laps and walk out straightening their kurtas, and the boys, usually overage toughs from Delhi 6, would swagger out straightening their elaborate gravity-defying hairdos and pulling on their faux Ray-Ban aviator sunglasses. The predominantly female contingent of my class couldn't stop giggling whenever this happened. During recess, most of the English department students, from all three years, would hang out on the wide steps that led towards the sports ground at the back. Most of the boys incessantly smoked Charms or Navy Cuts and gossiped with the girls. Anjali would usually be in the middle of a largish group, holding forth on some subject or another of global interest. The topic that day was her ever-continuing crush on Dr Chowdhury or Lord Jim, the name that Anjali had given him. I sat at the edge of the group listening to her chatter. According to Anjali, Dr Chowdhury, Joyce scholar from Corpus Christi, was hot stuff. 'He is one of us. Absolutely,' sighed Anjali dramatically, one hand folded across her face in a feigned swoon.

I found the freedom and casual frankness with which the boys and girls spoke to each other on Delhi campuses exhilarating.

Unthinkable in a place like Patna Commerce College, where the girls at the start of each new period would walk from the girls' common room together, in single file, like relief workers in a war zone, and walk back the same way after the class ended. There was no hanging about the classroom or any other place. Though outside the college they would be fine, laughing and joking like normal girls and would acknowledge your presence and walk across Hathwa Market to talk to you, inside the college a kind of tense rigidity gripped them. In Commerce College the front two rows of desks were reserved for girls, where they sat together listening to lectures. At Zakir Husain, even the teachers were extremely accessible and knew each student by name. These things were not much to go by, but after two years of Commerce College Patna, they were good enough for me.

'I think one of these days I will wink at him. Let us see what Lord Jim does.'

'He will do nothing. He will ignore you,' I said to the group in measured tones. Anjali turned her head and looked at me. One always remembers the moment when one had first fallen in love. For me it was that moment, the half second it took Anjali to turn her head and look at me. I still remember the way the light caught her hair, making it seem auburn. She was wearing a pink silk kurta with a white silk churidar and her feet were bare. Her tan buckled Bata sandals were kept one step below, like a still life.

'And, fresher, what if I wink at you?' Again the teasing Anjali laughter but there was slight uncertainty in it now.

'I will accept,' I said in all seriousness. There was much laughter and in a couple of minutes the bell for the next period rang and Anjali and some of the other third year students left for their classrooms.

I kept sitting there lost in myself. Chain-smoking Gold Flakes. It was a strange kind of happiness I was feeling. Though nothing much had happened, a girl had spoken a bit flirtatiously, regular boy-girl skirmish, not a big deal; but yet something had. Some tiny levers somewhere in my heart had shifted on their own.

I remember that evening I bought a pint of Old Monk and Pranjal and I polished it off while watching the night show of *Vishwatma* with some campus friends at Batra Cinema in Mukherjee Nagar. The Old Monk making the wretched Sunny Deol and Divya Bharti movie somewhat camp and bearable. After the show, instead of taking the bus, we walked all the way to Shokeen Niwas in Kamla Nagar. We took a grand tour of the university. Seeing friends off at Ramjas, Hindu, Kirori Mal hostels. I didn't tell Pranjal about Anjali that night. There was nothing to say. Only rapture.

A couple of days later, while returning to North Campus from Zakir Husain College on the 901, I felt a light tap on my shoulder. I looked up and saw Anjali standing beside me in the aisle. In a second our roles were reversed. Now she was sitting in my seat and I was standing beside her in the aisle.

At the Chandni Chowk roundabout, there was a bomb scare as someone had left behind a steel tiffin box in the bus.

The day before in Tarn Taran fifteen Hindus had been shot by Sikh militants. We all got off the bus while the puny Bihari conductor laughingly disposed of the tiffin box using a long iron rod. I still remember the splash of the sulphuric yellow dal as the tiffin box opened on impact with the street. When we got back on the bus, I finally managed to sit next to Anjali. It turned out that she too lived near North Campus, in Mukherjee Nagar, and she caught the 901 for her return journey. I made a note of this fact and from that day onwards waited forty-five minutes in college till Anjali finished her classes. She told me everything about her family, her life, her aspirations, on those long, dusty bus rides. It usually took us an hour to reach North Campus. Her father Sardar Baldev Singh Nalwa ran an electronic goods store in Kingsway Camp and had come to Delhi after partition from Peshawar with two elder brothers who now owned a prosperous auto parts shop in Gaffar Market. 'Though originally we belong to the village of Jhang Siyal in western Punjab. The very village that the legendary Heer came from and where she fell in love with Ranjha. Who knows we might even be related.' Anjali's grandfather died on the train that brought them to Amritsar because of heartbreak. The loss of his beloved wife and the North West Frontier Province had proved to be unbearable.

'You know, we think of ourselves more as Pathans than Sikhs. Though we do hate the Muslims bitterly,' Anjali had informed me the first day we had taken the bus ride together. 'Partition to you means nothing, Hriday, like it means nothing to most of the Indians who are not from East Pakistan or Punjab but you have to realize that it was worse than the Holocaust. No one ever recovers from that.'

She was right. Coming from Patna the partition of 1947 was just a chapter in the modern history textbook and her story just another episode from Ramesh Sippy's *Buniyaad* to me. Anjali told me about the hardships her family faced but in a very matter-of-fact manner. No sentimentality at all. 'For a while, my father also worked as a grave digger at the graveyard in the Christian colony in Vijay Nagar.'

Even though her family was quite affluent now, she was the only person who had studied till graduation. Most of the male members had left studies by the time they reached the eighth standard. All of them preferred to join some family business rather than a routine 9-to-5 job working for others. This was true of many Punjabi refugee families in North Campus. But the daughters usually graduated, sometimes even doing their Masters, and they would be wed to a boy who sold inverters but had studied only till the fourth standard. In the older generation alcoholism was rampant. Usually by seven o'clock in the evening, small clusters of middle-aged and old people would be sitting outside their houses in Hakikat Nagar, Mukherjee Nagar, Indira Vihar, swapping stories of Lahore, Multan, Gujaranwala and Peshawar, and getting increasingly drunk.

From the mid-eighties they had started getting prosperous because of the heavy influx of Bihari and North East students to the Delhi University. With hostel seats being limited, most residents of these refugee colonies bordering the university had converted their modest homes into hostelries. In each house at least two rooms (usually barsatis) were occupied by students from Bihar or the North East. With the coming of liberalization in the early nineties, their fortunes would rise further as real estate prices in Delhi soared. But so unfortunately would the alcoholism.

Students were a big business in these colonies. Many residents had overnight become property dealers, charging one month's rent as commission, others provided the students with food, some gave them furniture on rent. There was a grocery shop, STD booth-cum-photocopying centre in every other home. And they all ran profitably.

In the bus, after a week, Anjali let me hold her hand. Yet, at the college she would show deliberate indifference towards me. It did rankle a bit that I could not speak with her at any length, sit next to her or hold her hand when we were in a group. She didn't want anyone to know about us.

In Shokeen Niwas I would usually get up quite early in the morning and work on my stories. I would set the alarm for 5 a.m. and try to write for two hours before it was time to get ready for college. Even if I partied till 3 a.m. the night before and consequently had a hangover, I made it a point to stick to my schedule. Usually by the time I reached 300 words, the hangover would magically disappear. My target was 500–750 words each day till the story was finished. My stories rarely exceeded the 5,000-word count even in the final draft.

I would write on ruled A4 size spiral-bound notebooks with pencil, so that I could erase and make new corrections and there would be less of a mess on the page. I always wrote on the recto side so that on the verso I could write insertions and ideas for the next draft. I would switch on the table lamp and make as little noise as possible so that I didn't disturb Pranjal sleeping blissfully in the far corner of the room.

I would sharpen the three Natraj pencils nestling in the chipped coffee cup, where I kept my pens and pencils, my writing tools. I would read over the previous pages of the story to get into the rhythm of it, and also to enter anew the alternate world that I had created. I followed Hemingway's advice in *A Moveable Feast* (a farewell gift from my father as I was leaving for Delhi) to stop each day's writing at the point just before exhaustion, so that one knew where to begin, what to write the next morning. I usually had a paragraph, or at least a long sentence which would advance the action, ready when I started my writing each morning. After that I would let my instincts take me anywhere they wanted to. I would go off on tangents and discover new contexts in my story and also venture into areas one didn't know anything about, but yet remain plausible within the confines of the story was a good exercise for the imagination. With practise I found I could wriggle out of any storytelling jam and always land on my feet. But I always used things that I knew about as the takeoff point. Also, I felt a storyteller should always trust his instinct and never hold back. Certainly not in the first draft. But authenticity was of paramount importance.

While teaching *A House for Mr Biswas*, Uday Chowdhury would point out how even though he absolutely loved the novel, he still had issues with the name that Naipaul had chosen for his most famous protagonist, Mohun Biswas. According to Chowdhury, it was inauthentic as Biswas was neither a Brahmin surname, nor was it commonly found in Uttar Pradesh or Bihar. 'Why couldn't it be Mohun Misir? That would have been pitch perfect.'

My stories would be quite short, at times only anecdotes about people I knew, about my childhood and life in Patna while growing up. I wrote about playing cricket for St. Xavier's and the deep satisfaction of scoring thirty-odd runs in a twenty-over match against St. Michael's and how that made me happy for months. I only had that 'happiness' as the starting point but when I wrote the story it had a long description of cycling ten kilometres to St. Michael's from my home and in the evening cycling back ten kilometres the same way, in my cricket whites, with runs behind my name. The story had about a paragraph on the actual cricket played that day, the rest was on the bicycle ride to and from the cricket ground. It is not a great story but it is in some strange way about the happiness I felt that day. And writing it in the barely awake morning after the day Jishnuda slashed the Jat boy outside the Miranda hostel, I felt calm and somewhat justified in my parents' trust and expense in sending me to Delhi. For higher learning. I also realized that if I wrote consistently I would be all right. I wouldn't go to pieces. I wouldn't drift like before. This urge to write, to create stories, was a consuming passion those days, like it is even now. But then I was starting out. I didn't have any grand ambitions. I wanted to write stories that I and my friends could read. I didn't worry about publication, just that I should write about places and things I knew in a simple matter-of-fact manner. Concrete specificity and not long-winded waffle. I wrote about my friend Vishnu Rajak from Commerce College and his passion for the Brahmin doctor and his disdain for his cousins because they ate meat. About Sudama Pathak's sidekick Mukhia, who had once asked me to accompany him to a posh shop in Hotel Maurya for a premium pair of jeans. 'Nothing much happens in your stories. But they are readable,' Pranjal would say to me once in a while when he read something by me that he actually liked. But the first drafts he always called 'rubbish'. So I stopped showing him the first drafts. Readers should only see the sixth draft and thereafter.

After I'd written a page and a half, I would switch on the tiny immersion rod used for sanitizing surgical instruments but which we used for making tea. The immersion rod would be put in a steel tumbler and in a minute or two the water would be boiling. I would then pour the water into two tea cups which had sugar, Anik powder milk and two Taj Mahal tea bags each. After the tea was made, I would put Pranjal's tea on his table and gently shake him once. He would be up in the next five minutes after much groaning. Meanwhile, I would go back to my story and while sipping the tea read what I had written that morning. It was a good satisfied feeling to drink strong tea and go over the story in the morning. After that I would try and write another page.

There were no writers in my family. But then why only my family, there were no writers in any of my friends' families either. Nobody knew writers, at least published ones. A lot of people claimed to have written poetry in their youth—certainly women—but it was just one of the things that you did when you were young like the year you wore a ponytail and took part in a nukkad natak. One simply outgrew it in one's twenties. I had still not shown any of my stories, the finished ones, to my father as I didn't want to disappoint him, but he had seen me write every morning in Patna just before I came to Delhi. And he was pleased for me. In the two years since leaving St. Xavier's I had in some ways gone off the rails, as they say, and passed through territories which were not on the map that my father had loosely constructed of my life. But he didn't stop me from anything as he believed, he later told me, that I would in the end pull through. And when he saw me working on my stories every morning in Patna, it reassured him. He told me he didn't want to read the stories and find out how untalented I was, he was just happy that I couldn't be all that bad if I wrote every day. As a professor of literature the printed word was of paramount importance to him. If there was one temple he had regularly entered, it was the published book and the idol he worshipped was the printed word. 'I had promised myself I would only read a story by Hriday if it were printed somewhere. I have read enough undergraduate and postgraduate poetry and fiction to know that 99 per cent of all such writers have no talent. And I didn't want to be the one to tell you that. But I must admit, the fact that you suddenly started to write gave me great joy. I know you won't ever be a Narayan, but you can't be that bad if you write. There is hope for you yet.'

So every Sunday morning when I called up home he would in the end always ask, 'How's the bildungsroman coming along?' and I would always say, 'Fine'. It was the least I could do for him. If he ever came to Shokeen Niwas and actually saw the surroundings he would be horrified and part of the horror for him would be how naturally his good son fitted in there. How totally at home I felt at Shokeen Niwas.

It wasn't entirely true that I didn't know any writers in Patna. I did know Ritwik Ray. Rather I met him in March at Sudama Pathak's on Holi. A friend of Sudama's, he was in his mid-twenties and a reporter with a national daily in Patna. He also had a slim book of stories *Harryda and Other Stories* published by the Patna Cine Society. A copy of which I had borrowed from Sudama and read. Sudama was quite deferential to his Ritwikda and offered him glasses of bhang-spiked thandai every couple of minutes. Ritwik carried his one glass of thandai through the evening. 'I don't like the taste of it. Too fucking sweet. And it makes you slow. And as we already are from Patna, we don't need more of slowness.'

When I told him his stories were 'nice' and that I too harboured hopes of becoming a writer someday he said 'oh dear' and after waving a hasty goodbye to Sudama made quick his escape. I thought he was terribly superior and rude.

By 7:30 a.m. my writing for the day was done. After a quick bath, I would wear one of my two jeans, one charcoal black and one denim blue. The shirt usually was a white cotton half-sleeved one. By the time I was getting dressed Pranjal would have tea and thickly buttered toast ready. Pranjal would read *The Times of India* while having his breakfast. He would leave Shokeen Niwas at 8:45 a.m., as it took him fifteen minutes to walk to Hindu. As I left Shokeen Niwas, I would see a bleary-eyed Chaitanya Mishra brushing his teeth while Abhinav Srivastava did his surya namaskar. By 8 a.m., I was at the Bungalow Road bus stop and at 8:10 a.m. I would catch the 901 from Kingsway Camp, on my way finally to Zakir Husain and Anjali Nalwa.

Once a week, usually on Fridays, we would catch a matinee of any old movie that was playing at Shakuntalam in Pragati Maidan. The tickets were ten rupees each and usually the auditorium was empty except for a couple of other lovebirds. As soon as the lights were switched off, we would start kissing slowly. Her ardour was no less than mine, if not more. Gradually she let me put my hands into her salwar while she played with my penis and masturbated me gently. Afterwards I would light up a Gold Flake with pussy fingers. Fingering her pussy was like picking up a mango leaf drenched in the summer rain, feeling the well-defined ridges between one's forefinger and thumb, as the sun comes reluctantly out of the clouds. Her smell would linger on my fingers for days and at unexpected moments would remind me of her passion.

For all her ardent intimacy in the darkened auditorium of Shakuntalam, she would studiedly ignore me while at the college and also there was never any declaration of love from her side. Not that it mattered much to me but I did feel that if we were a couple then we shouldn't have to hide anything from anyone. I wasn't afraid and surely she shouldn't be also. Even in college whenever I had a free period I would want to spend it with her but she would be surrounded by her classmates and she wouldn't have time for me. Everything in her life was compartmentalized. Hriday was strictly after college hours it seemed.

Probably she shied away from the gossip that if made public our affair would generate among the faculty, not to mention the students. The faculty, barring a few young lecturers, was quite a conservative one. Even though they taught of love every day in its myriad ways, very few it seemed would actually welcome it in their lives. But then this is true of English departments anywhere. Teaching literary love each day would make anyone wary of the everyday variety.

Though only a couple of years senior to me in college, Anjali was three years older. She was twenty to my seventeen. The difference in age didn't matter to me and, come to think of it now, it was probably an added attraction. The mythical older woman. But psychologically, if not chronologically, I felt we were equals. I was even perhaps more practical and mature than she was. She had a tendency for depression, and there would be days when returning from Zakir in the 901, we would hardly exchange a single word. She had topped both her B.A. first year and second year examinations and the faculty had predicted great things for her future. Her short stories were published in the college literary review, *The Rambler*, and a few months back in March her first story in a national newspaper, *The Sunday Observer*, had been published. There were, I knew, great expectations from her. Something that she would fulfil in a spectacular manner with her searing 2000 novel *Adrift, Aloft* on the 1984 Sikh carnage in Delhi. A size-zero novel with a big heart, it would firmly establish her as one of the brightest novelists of her generation.

I had read the story in Patna and, unlike other short stories published in newspapers and magazines, one actually remembered it. At the time I myself was beginning to write. Her biography at the end of the piece simply noted that 'Born in 1972, Anjali Nalwa reads English at Zakir Husain College, New Delhi'. I had been impressed by the fact that a girl only a few years older than me had written a story that was published in a national newspaper. It was also the first time I heard of Zakir Husain College. I started reading the story expecting it to be a poor one.

It was called 'Bonsai' and much to my disappointment was quite fluently written. It told in simple unaffected tones a story about a young unmarried Punjabi girl in her late twenties who lives with her tradesman father and two younger sisters and looks after them. Her mother had died when she was seventeen and from then on she had shouldered the burden of the entire family just like her mother before her. On Saturdays she attends classes on bonsai-making in south Delhi, conducted by a society matron. She starts growing bonsais at home and is fascinated by their miniature perfection. Lemon, orange and apple. But soon she realizes it is an artificial perfection. Actually real things are never perfect. It is the flaws which make them interesting. A man who lives in her neighbourhood in North Campus and works as a property dealer wants to marry her but her father refuses him. He refuses all proposals that come for her. Nobody is good enough for her. The girl realizes that she will remain unmarried all her life. She has become a 'bonsai' of her own mother. It was a short 2,000-word piece and there was a lot packed in it. I asked her to expand it. There was material there for a 5,000-word story at least I felt. She was thrilled by the fact that I had read the story in Patna and then a few months later we had met in Delhi. She liked the happenstance, the structure of this episode. 'These are things which happen only to writers,' she said to me on the 901, shaking her head ruefully one day as we were returning home from Zakir.

Sometimes in the evenings we would go to a book launch at the India International Centre or the British Council where the atmosphere I found to be infinitely fascinating. The gulab jamuns and coffee afterwards for someone like me who was perpetually half-starved were attractions added to the fact that we were gatecrashers. The throwaway sophistication, the studied poise, the unimpeachable self-assuredness of the people attending these soirees were what we minutely observed. Anjali would study the writers reading out from their works, the way they carried themselves, the kind of clothes they wore, and she would note the details in a small notebook that she carried in her black and red, silver mirror-work jhola. She would always make it a point after the reading to go and meet the author, whereupon she would introduce herself as an aspiring writer. Usually at such times I would keep back, sipping my coffee. I found it to be excruciatingly embarrassing to meet someone who was a total stranger. But no such worries for Anjali. She would ask them all sorts of questions, about literary life, about publishing, about the kind of books they read and she would note down everything in her notebook like a reporter. Anjali wanted to know everything about the writerly life. On Sundays we would try and find the books that the various authors had mentioned at the second-hand book market in Daryaganj. If lucky we would find a couple.

It was at a book launch in British Council Library that I met Ritwik Ray again. It was the launch of an anthology of love stories by young Indian writers. Ray read from his soon to be classic story, 'The Truffaut Girl', which was anthologized in the volume. Most of the young writers who were part of anthology read from their stories and Anjali and I watched them perform with awe and envy. This was what we both wanted: to be published within the hard covers of an actual book that would be displayed in bookshops. After my earlier experience with Ritwik Ray I was reluctant to meet him that evening. I was sure he would snub me again but it was hard to dissuade Anjali, who took me by the hand and marched me over to the fountain in the Charbagh where Ritwik was talking to Mira Verma, excerpts from whose forthcoming debut novel were also anthologized in the volume. Mira Verma too was from Patna. Ritwik was sipping his whisky on the rocks and Mira looking striking in a Garad sari which complemented her Sinead O'Connor crew cut, held a tall glass of beer in her hand. They seemed to be having an intense conversation. Mira was explaining something to Ritwik who kept laughing, saying something quite witty and brief to her. It seemed a pity to disturb them. But then they had not reckoned with Anjali Nalwa and her reluctant sidekick Hriday Thakur. Surprisingly it was Ritwik who greeted me first after both he and Mira had signed Anjali's copy.

'Mira, this is Hriday Thakur. He is from Patna. From Kadam Kuan, in fact.'

'Well, the next thing you will tell me is that he too is a writer,' Mira Verma smiled and said to Ritwik.

'Well, he too is a writer,' Ritwik said to Mira while I smiled embarrassedly and wished I could suddenly disappear into thin air.

'At this rate, we will soon have a Patna school!'

'God forbid.' Ritwik finished his whisky and laughed out loud.

Both Mira and Ritwik were wonderful and they answered Anjali's queries with care and genuine warmth. There was none of the superior attitude in Ritwik that I had felt the last time round. He gave good advice about writing and how to get published. 'It does not realy matter whether you get published in *The Hindu* or *Femina*. A *Hindu* won't make a bad story better nor *Femina* turn a good one rotten. The story remains the same. It does not matter where you get published so long as you get published. It is foolish to be snobbish about these things. When one is starting out it is very important to get published once in a while. No use keeping your stories in your cupboard. Send them out. Always send them out. Learn to deal with rejection as early as you can.'

'That's the same thing he told me when I was starting out. I have learnt about writing mostly from observing Ritwik from our college days.'

'Yes, Mira was my Truffaut Girl.'

'Ritwik has had a lot to drink. As usual. There's Samar.' Mira kissed Ritwik lightly on his cheeks and went over to rejoin her husband Samar Sinha, a flamboyant historian from Columbia who was holding court near the bar.

Later in the autorickshaw Anjali asked me 'Do you think they have a bit of history, Ritwik and Mira?'

'History? Darling, what they have is pure chemistry. Like Guru Dutt and Waheeda Rehman.'

Anjali was much taken up with Mira Verma. 'Isn't Mira absolutely marvellous?'

'She is very pretty.'

'I saw you checking her out.'

'Only her haircut.' I lied but it was required.

Anjali was trying to get an education and she knew that Indian English writers usually came from a social milieu totally different from hers. But she would be damned if something as inconsequential as that would stop her. She would figure them out. She would do a social makeover for herself. Though I personally believed that her USP was that she came from a class which didn't write fiction in English, I did admire immensely her single-minded dedication to her dream. I wished I could be as pushy and resolute.

In those months that I knew her, I saw her transform herself almost on a weekly basis, if not a daily one, from someone of the Punjabi trading classes to a member of the ethnic-chic arty crowd at IIC and British Council book launches. Gone were the dressy well-tailored salwar suits in bright colours and in came Cottage Emporium and Khadi Gram Udyog cotton salwar-kurtas and tops bought from Janpath. She stopped using the light pink lipstick that she wore, which was a relief since I hated its taste. She bought a lot of white cotton T-shirts which she would wear with her faded denim blue jeans bought from the Tibetan Monastery. She went on a diet, lost 10 kg and in the bargain found her cheekbones. Generally, she started affecting a more studied dishevelled appearance that she copied from the south Delhi arty crowd that she wanted to emulate. Little by little, piece by piece, she mastered the 'looking like nothing matters' look. But then one day she cut her thick shoulder-length hair to a very short wedge cut and we had our last fight. 'You know before they killed my grandmother, they cut her hair off. My father saw them do it. He escaped while they tortured her. All night he lay hidden in the ditch behind our house in Peshawar and heard his mother scream and scream. He was twelve years old. Though my father does not say it I imagine they raped her through the night before finally slitting her throat.'

'But what's that got to do with you cutting your hair almost fifty years later?' I asked Anjali, unable to comprehend any link with this bit of family history.

'Nothing. Absolutely nothing. You will never understand.' We both got down at Kingsway Camp and she rapidly crossed the road to catch a shared auto rickshaw for Mukherjee Nagar.

I had loved the way she wore her hair before. It gave her face a softness, an air of vulnerability with which I fell in love. The new hairstyle made her look troubled and edgy, which perhaps could be quite attractive to many boys but was not to me at that time. As I stood looking at her cross the road that afternoon, I suddenly realized that it was over. We had known each other for less than three months. None of my friends knew about her. Certainly not anyone at Shokeen Niwas. Not even Pranjal. She had all along refused to meet my friends and this furtiveness was not something that I was enjoying anymore.

For days after that we couldn't meet because every day she had a new engagement, a new artist, a new author, a new gallery to visit, and I told her that I couldn't tag along anymore. I got stupefyingly bored in such surroundings. It wasn't entirely true but it would do.

By the time Pranjal and I caught the Poorva Express for Patna in the first week of October during the university autumn break, I knew my first real love affair was over. All through the twenty days that I spent in Patna I thought constantly about her. I felt a deep physical craving for her but I knew I would only be a footnote in her life and the earlier I distanced myself, the less heartbreak I would suffer. Anjali did call me twice at home but we spoke for a few moments only. A weary note had crept into both our voices. She had never given me her home number. She asked me when I would be back and I gave her a date but actually returned about a week later.

By the time I was back in Delhi in late October, my mind was made up and I didn't wait for her at the 901 stop again. We met in the campus, of course, but we were now reserved with each other. I started hitting the books. In the three and a half months since the term had started, I hadn't read a single book in my course except Biswas. It was time to make amends. I started with *A Farewell to Arms*.

Metal Fatigue

February 1993. It was 11 a.m. on a Sunday morning and Jishnuda strolled into my room wearing his Tweety-Pie Bermudas and Farid Ashraf's black leather jacket from Kanpur which was flaking at the elbows, and asked me to accompany him to the Oriental Hair Cutting Saloon near Chacha's off Bungalow Road.

As we entered the barber shop I saw that Zorawar Singh Shokeen's white Gypsy was double parked outside it. Zorawar Singh was getting his underarms done. He was wearing a white Sandow banian and black single-crease terrycotton formal trousers with turn-ups. On his feet were two-tone patent leather golf shoes. His shimmering lemon-yellow silk shirt was hanging from a white plastic clothes rack near the entrance along with his thick fleece-lined, custom-made, caramel-coloured leather jacket with epaulettes. His trusted Mauser, reputedly a gift from H. K. L. Bhagat, lay sedatedly on the white sunmica counter beside Emami hair dye, combs, scissors, Lakme egg shampoo sachets and other hair care paraphernalia.

Jishnuda and I sat down on the golden-brown velvet covered sofa, on which Ramanuj Ghosh had recently spilled slick the size of a quarter plate. The sofa was just behind Zorawar Singh and he acknowledged our presence by slightly tilting his head, like a potentate, and smiling to us in the mirror. His hair was wet and gleaming, the dye making his thick wavy hair look as if painted on and carved freshly from wood. The beard was trimmed and dyed and it made his cheeks appear pinker than ever. If one didn't know Zorawar Singh better one could even make the mistake of thinking that he was blushing.

The deal was this. Mrs Midha aka 'Madam', Zorawar's paramour, was worried about her daughter's education and needed a tutor for her. Zorawar Singh had asked his Man Friday Jishnuda to find one and after Chaitanya Mishra, Abhinav Srivastava and Pranjal had declined his offer, in desperation Jishnuda turned to me. After much deliberation I said yes but told him that I was hopeless in science and mathematics and Jishnuda said that this was perfect because then Mrs Midha would dismiss me within weeks and they would have to look for another tutor. Jishnuda would be off the hook then but for now he had to produce someone. So, like the fool that I was, I volunteered to be the rabbit that Jishnuda would pull out of his hat. I thought this project would take my mind off Anjali Nalwa once and for all and I would be able to concentrate on my writing and studies. I hadn't written a single line since our inexplicable break-up. Even though I had successfully ignored her and didn't meet her anymore, the sexual craving I felt for her was almost like an addiction. The smell of her cunt, the salt of her skin, the wet of her mouth was constantly on my tongue. I had to forget her and I would and this 'project' would do just nicely. Also I was intrigued by this whole Zorawar Singh-Madam situation and wanted to observe it from close quarters. Their behaviour was so removed from my own life that to me they were almost like characters in a pulp novel with a lurid cover that I was reading by the dim light of a train compartment, unable to sleep.

His underarms done, Zorawar Singh Shokeen looked deeply into his reflection in the mirror. From the frown of intense concentration on his face, it appeared as if he were trying very hard to locate something that he had recently lost, his broad left thumb constantly flicking at his moustache ends making it curl upwards. After he had surveyed his face from all possible angles and Nizam the barber had stood behind him with a smaller hand-held mirror so that Zorawar could see how his hair shaped up at the back, his face relaxed. It seemed that he had finally found what he was looking for. Nizam then massaged his arms and pummelled his head with his fists and with a final violent crick of his neck gave a short but fulfilling demonstration of his chiropractic abilities. In the evenings Nizam, under the title of Chowdhary Jarrah, had a lucrative practice as a bonesetter in Chandrawal.

Zorawar gave him two hundred rupees for his efforts and Nizam's vulpine face was lit by an effulgent smile which refused to die till the time we stepped outside. Zorawar sent Nizam to Chacha's for three glasses of hot badam milk while we leaned against the Gypsy and talked. Kamla Nagar was slowly coming to life, the shops were opening, the displays were being dusted, pooja was being done by the lalajis. Students from nearby hostelries ate their breakfast of tea and bread pakoras, sitting on steps leading to swanky shops, in woebegone tracksuits.

'Jaishankar tells me that you are a merit scholar and no one in the hostel reads more than you. Your nose is always stuck deep in a book, he tells me.'

'That is correct, uncle. We ask him to come with us to Kamla Nagar, go out for a movie to Batra, but he has a standard answer to all that: "My parents have sent me to Delhi to study hard and do well. Crack the civil services. And that is what I will do one day." He is absolutely amazing, uncle. Never has been a scholar in Shokeen Niwas with such dedication, ever.' In his hardsell Jishnuda made me appear as if I were Tagore and Einstein rolled into one.

'That is all very well, Hriday, but I do hope you will not try to suck the bachi's alphonsos once in a while,' Zorawar said to me in his inimitable eye-squinting manner, with his special ability to go from the ribald to the chilling in a blink.

'Of course not, uncle. I do not like mango lassi. It upsets my stomach.'

'That is very sensible of you. Because if you do, you won't have the stomach for anything, the rest of your life. Jaishankar, I thought I told you to get someone older and less chikna.' For a second Zorawar Singh looked at me appraisingly, like I were a shiny new pair of boots, unbroken and stiff. He then finished his badam milk and gave the glass to Jishnuda to hold and put on his gold Aviator sunglasses. He started the Gypsy and said to me, 'Remember, the father should not know that you stay in Shokeen Niwas or that you are associated with me in any manner. Tell them you stay in the Ramjas hostel. You start from tomorrow. Five o'clock in the evening. Jaishankar will take you to the house.' After that he backed the Gypsy with flourish and obligatory screeching tyres and sped down Bungalow Road towards the university.

At fourteen Sonya Midha still had the puppy fat which once shed in a few years' time would make her the knockout she desperately desired to be. Her best feature was her nose which was sharp yet not too long, and when she opened her shoulderlength hair and looked at you with her big startled doe eyes, she looked just like an Alsatian. Albeit an overfed one. Though, according to her, she looked just like Divya Bharti, who was all the rage that year. All her friends told her so.

After Jishnuda dropped me at Mrs Midha's place in Malkaganj and pointed out the first floor flat, I smoked a Gold Flake standing outside the pink-coloured building in which the windows and ledges were painted green. I was a bit nervous. It had finally kicked in the previous night around 9:30 p.m. as Pranjal and I were coming back from the Hindu hostel mess after dinner, there was no delivery of tiffin that evening as Dunkel was not feeling too well and Satyabrat Ojha had taken him to a vet near the Batra cinema hall in Mukherjee Nagar. All of a sudden

Pranjal said to me, 'What is your life's ambition? To turn into another Jishnuda? Is that it?'

'It is just a matter of a couple of days. Then it will be over.' I tried to reassure Pranjal but the fact was that I was only trying to reassure myself.

As I smoked my cigarette, the image of Zorawar Singh and Mrs Midha rutting in Jishnuda's room flashed across my mind. Her blotchy face down on the pillow and those magnificent buttocks up in the air, the thick shadow of her sweat-soaked cunt hair barely visible beneath her dilated anus. The cigarette trembled in my hands and I wondered whether my hyperactive imagination had conjured up the scene straight out of *Mast Ram*, but no, it was only eight months back that I had seen them both and it was for real. It would remain the emblematic image of my initiation into North Campus life. My mind was certainly playing tricks. It was for real. One evening, about a month back as I was going up the stairs in Shokeen Niwas, I saw Mrs Midha kiss Zorawar fully on the lips, her arms all around his broad chest, holding on for dear life. Zorawar saw me and winked and I hurried back down and waited at Mehendiratta's store, to come back only after ten minutes when the white Gypsy had left the premises.

With the cigarette finished and the nicotine fix calming somewhat my kinetic fingers, I slouched up to the first floor and pressed the calling bell. The thin lilt of the first few bars of 'Twinkle Twinkle Little Star' rang out from inside the house. The legend outside in stencilled brass read Dr Satyakam Midha.

It suddenly struck me that the reason I was there was to observe Mrs Midha, the legendary 'Madam' in her own home. I knew even then that I would write about her in the future and people look and behave very differently when they are in their own homes or with their families, relaxed and at ease. Like Sgt. Basu, who offered me tea in a cotton polo T-shirt and pajamas while his daughter Mamoni lay reading Enid Blyton in her St. Joseph's Convent uniform. The transformation could be quite startling, just like meeting the Maurice Nagar SHO Joginder Tyagi, out with wife and twelve-year-old sullen-faced daughter, watching the night show at Batra wearing a bottle-green polo shirt and eating buttered popcorn, when only a week back I had seen him smash a fifty-year-old Punjabi man's face in Shokeen Niwas with his baton for not selling Zorawar Singh his two-room flat in Vijay Nagar double-storey. Zorawar and Joginder had picked up the man right outside his home and kept him locked in a vacant ground floor room in Shokeen Niwas for three days till the poor man's son brought the property papers to Zorawar.

Mrs Midha opened the door wearing a mauve-coloured chiffon sari with a black blouse. As middle-class Punjabis wear saris only on special occasions, like party wear, I got the impression that she wasn't much used to receiving guests in her home. On the other hand it could be trepidation mixed with nervousness. She knew I was a resident of Shokeen Niwas, the site of her occasional debauchery. I noticed how small in stature she actually was. Not more than five feet two inches in her off-white Liberty sandals. In my mind she was much bigger, the face harder, the hair shorter, the movements brazen. But in reality she was delicately built and in profile bore a striking resemblance to Lado, Zorawar Singh's wife who came once a month to Shokeen Niwas to collect the rent from Jishnuda. On these visits Lado would sometimes be accompanied by her elder daughter Goldy who studied in a boarding school near Mussoorie. Goldy then was in her mid-teens.

I guessed Mrs Midha must be around thirty-two years old, and her face was unlined. A few pimples on her chin, for which I was sure she used a face pack of Multani mitti at night before going to bed, accentuated her youth. Her arms were slender and bare except for thin gold bangles on both wrists. A thick smudge of sindoor adorned her widow's peak. As a kind of security measure. Long back in St. Xavier's, Patna, when I was in the sixth standard, our Hindi teacher Mrs Kaul, who was also the class teacher that year, had explained the significance of sindoor. 'It is like the red traffic light. When a woman puts it on, it means halt. Don't you dare go further.' Halt! Never forgot that. It seemed a reasonable enough explanation.

The flat had two rooms, a small kitchen carved out of the sitting room, and a toilet-cum-washroom. The furniture was quite threadbare and shabby, the cover of the sofa-cum-bed was watery pink when once it must have been deep maroon. There was a small study table with Sonya Midha's school bag kept on it. Alongside were two chairs. One presumably for me. On the table was spread a freshly laundered yellow bed-sheet, folded in two, with blue sunflowers.

After five minutes of chit-chat, the doorbell rang again and a breathless Sonya burst through the front door. The room was so small that I could smell clearly the mild sweat mixed with vanilla cream bar effluvia that came off her skin. It wasn't a disagreeable smell. She was wearing a faded bottle green pinafore, one size too small for her, and a denim jacket over it which had a yellow rose embroidered on the left pocket. She was carrying a skipping rope in her hands. The frock was a gift from her aunt in Chandigarh who had brought it for her from London. The frock was quite a prized one she told me later. She had been wearing it since she was ten years old. It was two sizes bigger then and now at fourteen, though she had outgrown it and it was tight across her slightly distended belly and rode much above her knees when she was sitting down, she loved it so much she couldn't give it up. Also, it was the most expensive dress that she owned and none of her friends had anything like it.

Sonya Midha was in the eighth standard at Queen Mary's School near Kashmere Gate and was repeating the year. I was to teach her English, mathematics and science mainly. Five days a week, from Monday to Friday, and for my troubles I was to receive a remuneration of Rs 1,000 a month. A sum, going by the look of the household, they could ill afford. Mrs Midha wanted her daughter to do well and she was saving money for her to do an MBA later on. What with economic liberalization and the markets opening up, India would need thousands of MBAs to manage all that wealth. 'Just when I thought reservation would make paupers of us, God has given us liberalization so that we as upper castes can hold our head high for some time more. Till they eventually catch up.' Mrs Midha let me know that she too was upper caste and middle class. Her job as a section officer in the university wasn't a high paying one and her husband's homeopathic practice in a Jain mandir charity clinic in Shakti Nagar wasn't doing too well either. All this Mrs Midha told me while making tea in the five to ten minutes before Sonya made her appearance. And when Sonya came and sat beside me on the sofa-cum-bed, Mrs Midha told her softly that she must do well and that she should obey 'Hriday Sir' and do her lessons diligently. 'You have to become a manager one day.' Then she turned to me and said, 'Do speak to Sonya only in English. I want her to become absolutely fluent in it.' Sonya looked at me, bit into her sugar encrusted Nice biscuit and giggled.

We started with English composition that day. Sonya showed me the essay 'My Favourite Person' that she was supposed to write and she was halfway through with it. She had already written about 300 words and I wrote the remaining 200 for her. Apparently her favourite person in the whole world was the Bombay starlet Divya Bharti. Sonya told me about the whole filmography of Divya Bharti and what she wore in each song sequence, and most importantly for the song 'Saat Samundar Paar', and her meteoric rise and then her affair and subsequent fairytale marriage to the film producer Sajid Nadiadwala. Sonya knew everything that there was to know about Divya Bharti and then some. She had gleaned all this from old copies of *Mayapuri* and *Stardust* magazines which she borrowed from a magazine vendor outside Amba cinema hall. He charged her two rupees for each new magazine. 'I read *Stardust* cover to cover in the night and return it the next day. That is why my English is so good.' She whispered, constantly worried that her mother might overhear her. 'Do you watch movies?' she asked me as I tried to describe Divya Bharti's histrionic range on paper. I kept looking down, a mask of intense concentration on my face to avoid chit-chat and project gravitas. I nodded 'yes' to her question. 'Oh good, then we two will get on fine. I do not like people who do not watch Hindi movies. I wish I could go to the cinema hall and watch on the big screen but I have to make do with cable TV at home. It is all right but it is not the same thing. There is more glamour in cinema halls. Last year on my birthday my father took me to Chanakya to watch Amitabh Bachchan and Kimi Katkar in *Hum*. Jumma Chumma. It was very glamorous. I had buttered popcorn and fountain Pepsi. Have you ever been to Chanakya?'

I remember this conversation even now almost word perfect because of the way she used the word 'glamour/glamorous' twice during her chatter rendered otherwise in perfect Delhi Hindi with liberal use of the female gender, a whole lot of strilings thrown about the place.

'Yes, I have been to Chanakya,' I answered Sonya's query.

'Will you take me there one day?'

'No.'

'Why not? Do you have a girlfriend?'

'Here, your essay is done. You can copy it out in your own handwriting now.' I couldn't keep a stern face any longer and smiled and passed her the notebook. My smile reassured her and she happily started making a fair copy of the essay in her English composition notebook, all the while humming the tune of her favourite song 'Saat Samundar Paar' for logistical support.

While she wrote I observed her closely for the first time. At that time following Hemingway's advice, I was training myself to observe better, to notice things only a writer would. To start seeing as a writer, to get an insight into a person's personality from her clothes, her physical appearance and her surroundings. I was training myself to look at everyone as a potential character, to try and see what they would do ten pages later if I were writing their story. But over the years I have learnt, after many mishaps, that it is always safer to just make things up.

It was during the 'observation' that I noticed that she looked like an Alsatian, which in my family was a great compliment. When my grandfather used to say that someone looked like an Alsatian, it meant that someone had a regal bearing and took himself or herself, for that matter, quite seriously. It was something that was bewildering to outsiders and was often misconstrued as an insult. My grandfather reportedly, when he saw my mother for the first time when she had come to his clinic with her father who was suffering from gastritis—'vayu' she called it, 'wind'—exclaimed in wonder, 'Professor Sen Sharma, your daughter looks like an Alsatian straight from the Rhineland.' My maternal grandfather, a Chaucer scholar from All Souls, was deeply affronted and left seething from my grandfather's chamber. Even though the 'vayu' was killing him and going out of the chamber he, according to my father who had just walked in, inadvertently farted once. My mother denies the farting. The very next day my grandfather went to Prof. Sen Sharma's house in Naya Tola with medicine for his ailment and a marriage proposal for his daughter. So my parents got married because the family was dog crazy. We had a series of Alsatians over the years at home and stories of these magnificent creatures were recollected and retold as if they were family members. There was Jim who had once bitten an Englishman on his rump in the 'Lawn', which is now called 'Gandhi Maidan', as his Aryan sense of order was violated by the man's corpulence. The fact that their two countries were at war might have further aggravated the stituation. Jim's wife Manda, short for Mandodri, loved caramel pudding and like a good Bengali wife ate only after her lord and master Jim had had his chopped liver and rice. Their son, a never-do-well called Scotch, had a strange fascination for postmen and indigenous bitches. On a regular basis, half-chewn copies of the *Lancet* were retrieved from his den, which was under the four-poster in my grandfather's room. It was usually a rolled up copy of the *Lancet*, which was used for his chastisement. Hence, his deep-seated anger for the 'weapon' and the arms dealer, poor postman Langat Ram Kesri. His son Hercules was my boon companion in childhood and his death when I was ten by food poisoning was a defining moment in my life. For years after that we didn't have an Alsatian at home but then young Raffles came in and started a new dynasty.

So it was that when Sonya Midha's appearance struck me as reminiscent of an Alsatian's, my mind was already forming a favourable impression of her. Also the fact that Mrs Midha had instructed me to speak to her daughter in English helped matters. In our family we always spoke to our dogs in English. Sonya's fascination for Bollywood movies was another plus in my evaluation of her personality. It told me that she had yearnings for better things. This shabby two-room flat was not for her and if she could escape her mother's taint she would make something of her life. She had inherited her mother's elegant yet hardy bone structure and would be quite good-looking by the time she entered college. Perhaps she could be another Divya Bharti. Like she blatantly desired.

Suddenly she stopped writing, turned towards me and asked, 'How old are you?'

'Seventeen,' I replied.

'I am fourteen. We are like Romeo and Juliet.'

'Actually I will be eighteen next Sunday.'

'That is Valentine's Day! How exciting.' Sonya clapped her hands in glee.

'Do concentrate on the essay and finish it quickly.'

After she had copied the essay I looked it over once more and corrected the few spelling mistakes. As I was leaving for the day, the doorbell rang and Sonya, showing off, danced to the door before Mrs Midha could come out of the other room and opened it. A middle-aged man wearing a grey pullover over a red checked shirt and shiny black terrycotton trousers walked in carrying a battered brown rexine satchel like the one that Lal Babu, my grandfather's compounder, used to carry and which always gave off a whiff of surgical spirit. Lal Babu, later on in his life after his daughter Chitra drowned in the Ganges on her sixteenth birthday, got somewhat addicted to drinking spirit which he now preferred to his desi elaichi and narangi.

'It has more body, a better flavour,' he explained to me one day, as if he were talking of some premium single malt and not sterilizing surgical spirit.

Sonya affectionately hugged the man who was obviously her father, and introduced me to him. He looked at me once and said 'Namaste' and then, somewhat flustered, with an embarrassed smile quickly went into the bedroom and pulled the curtain.

As Mrs Midha came out of the kitchen, drying her hands on a Charlie Brown towel, I took my leave. Standing outside the house I fished out a Gold Flake from my pocket, somewhat bent but still smokable and lit it. The way Sonya hugged her father and his obvious affection for her made me miss home. Home where father would be reading his heavily annotated Collected Auden in the study while listening to Billie Holiday LPs, and mother pottering around in her vegetable garden. In ten minutes she would make a large pot of tea and take it to the study. I felt a desperate need to speak to my parents and connect to a life that was so different from the one that I was leading in Delhi. Whenever I spoke to them, usually on a Sunday morning from the Mehendiratta store, I felt a bit guilty. After the whole Anjali episode I had started feeling I wasn't keeping my end of the bargain. The thought always played on my mind that perhaps I was wasting their hard-earned money but then after a while this depressive thought would pass away. If they came to know that all of a sudden I had started giving tuitions, they would be quite hurt as they would feel that they were not sending me adequate sums of money, and that I had to sacrifice my studies to earn that extra bit. When the fact was that I always had a fair bit of money in my account at the Shakti Nagar branch of the Punjab National Bank, where long back Sunita Khandelwal's husband had been a lower division clerk. My parents were generous and on the thirtieth of every month a demand draft of Rs 2,500 would be waiting for me in Jishnuda's room as the postman usually deposited all the mail there. I knew no one in Shokeen Niwas got as much as Pranjal and I did. Ramanuj Ghosh received about Rs 1,200 and Farid about the same. Jishnu got about a thousand but then he lived rent free. Only a week back I had asked and got an additional Rs 1,500 so that I could buy a rather expensive black leather jacket with quilt lining from the Chankaya shopping arcade in south Delhi that had caught my fancy and an Everyman edition of Arthur Miller's early plays.

I stopped at Mehendiratta's shop, where Dolly was playing Ludo with herself, and called up home. Father picked up the phone and we spoke in a general way about home and Delhi. He said Patna was a bit tense in the aftermath of the Bombay riots, a fallout of the Babri Masjid demolition. There had been a couple of days of curfew in December and January but nothing major. I reassured him that everything was just fine in Delhi. He said that he would be sending a thousand rupees for my eighteenth birthday and that I should buy a good fountain pen with the money. Preferably a Sheffers. I reminded him that I had already got my birthday present. But he wouldn't listen. He only said that he hoped that I wasn't smoking too much. I said I wasn't. He then reminded me that my first year exams were due to start in April and he hoped that I had read all my primary texts at least once. I lied again and said yes. He also informed me that a friend of mine called Vishnu had come asking for me and had left a number where I could reach him. He told me the number which I didn't note down. Father then passed on the phone to Mother who complained once again that I had not come home for the winter vacations in December and January and then started talking about a wedding reception recently where they had met Pranjal's parents. She said that Pranjal's mother was complaining to her that Pranjal didn't call home that often and I said that I would ask him to do so more frequently. I knew she was talking about me and not Pranjal. Pranjal called home every few days. I called, well, whenever I needed money. Mother then instinctively asked me whether everything was all right and I said 'of course' and kept the phone down. After this somewhat mundane conversation with my parents which cost exactly fifty rupees, I felt much better. The depression faded and I even rolled the dice for Dolly a couple of times. Always thrilled by any kind of attention that she could get, she gave me a great big smile that I could carry with me to Shokeen Niwas. For all my posturing I knew I wasn't so tough. Like a small boy I needed the reassuring presence of my parents ever so often.

It was around 6:30 p.m. when I entered my room and Pranjal was already dressed for the evening. We had been invited to the Miranda Hostel Night by Rukmini Sahay, the elder half of the famed Sahay sisters of Kadam Kuan whom Pranjal and I used to follow around Hathwa Market in our not so distant childhood. Rather Pranjal had been invited and since he didn't want me to feel left out, Rukmini had graciously invited me too. Any fortunate day where one could escape a Satyabrat Ojha dinner was a cause for celebration. In the past months while I had been so absorbed in various extra-curricular activities, Pranjal and Rukmini had become something of an item. They had, of course, known each other from Patna, but it was a chance meeting one evening at Jai Jawan dhaba while having banta that their friendship rekindled and soon settled down to a steady rhythm of evening walks on Chhatra Marg, bhel puri and stolen kisses in the university garden. They were in love. As strong and true as a summer cataract. When during the autumn break Pranjal was in Patna and Rukmini had stayed back in the hostel, he wrote a five-page letter to her every day. Pranjal in true Patna courtly style, where once you give your word to a girl, you honour it throughout your life, had already started talking of marriage. Even his clothes were now laundered at Miranda House. They had a good dhobi there who would, at a little extra cost, starch and iron your cotton shirts to razor-sharp perfection. Once in a while I too would slip in a couple of shirts, a jeans or two. If Nehru's clothes could get laundered in Paris, mine could at least be washed in the hallowed precincts of Miranda House.

Rukmini was a ferociously bright and forthright girl and I liked her very much. There was a natural warmth and concern in her manner and she was quite like Pranjal in many ways. In fact, they were the male and female version of each other. They were made for each other and by the time they actually got married, they had even started to look like each other. Rukmini was reading History with an eye on the civil services.

Pranjal was wearing a new suit that he had got stitched from the Varieties shop in Hathwa Market during the autumn break. It was a dark blue pinstripe double-breasted affair which he wore over a black crew-neck cotton pullover. He was freshly shaved and his moustache was trimmed to perfection. He looked dashing and very much in love. Since I was letting my beard grow around that time, I was saved the hassle of shaving. I only borrowed Chaitanya Mishra's ancient Herringbone tweed coat with frayed leather patches on the elbows and cuffs and took off Pranjal's Power joggers and put on Abhinav Srivastava's freshly buffed Bata Oxfords. I wet my comb under the tap and ran it quickly over my hair. I was set for the evening. We caught a rickshaw outside Kirori Mal College and in ten minutes were standing outside the Miranda back gate on Chhatra Marg.

On the way there, Pranjal asked me about Madam Midha and my first day of tutoring. He was curious about Sonya and her father, the kind of house they lived in and whether I could sense any discord in the air.

'I get the feeling that Dr Midha knows about his wife and Zorawar Singh but he has made his peace with that. He looks about ten to fifteen years older than Madam Midha and I didn't sense any discord between them but then I only observed Dr Midha for about five minutes,' I told Pranjal while we passed a Gold Flake back and forth between us on the rickshaw. 'She must have been our age when she married him,' Pranjal added after a while. The air was still cold and clean, though the winter in another week or so would fade away. It felt good to be on that rickshaw, moving gently towards Miranda House. On the way we passed other students from KMC, Hindu and Stephen's dressed in borrowed blazers and neckties. Some walked carefully on the curving sidewalk alert to the pitfalls of dogshit and puddles of muddy drain water and the peril of getting it on their borrowed shoes. Some carried in their hands coloured polythene bags inside which would be a small bouquet of half a dozen white roses wrapped in cellophane. As soon as they reached the hostel gate they would discard the plastic bags and finally feel bold enough to declare their aspiration to love in public.

Even then they would pray fervently that no acquaintance saw them on the street clutching a posy of flowers so it became a favourite topic of conversation at the mess table for the next couple of days. Till the time some neophyte tough guy committed an even greater faux pas, puked in the corridor washbasin after a strenuous night of drinking and then, to make matters worse, got caught cleaning the basin, trying to suppress the evidence of his frailty. Very few boys ever lived that down. It would keep recurring every time that particular set of friends sat around a khamba of Old Monk.

Being observed carrying flowers to Miranda House could seriously dent a hardboy's credibility and make life suddenly very dangerous for him. Like it happened with Haidar Pehelwan of Dehri-on-Sone, former vice-president of Zakir Husain (Evening) and a master with the astura with two attempted murder cases registered against him in Dalluchak, Gaya and, in Delhi, a much respected arbitrator and compromiser for the Nawada-Gaya set. It was a chance sighting by Farid Ashraf and Ramanuj Ghosh on a regular evening recce on Bungalow Road that finally did the great Haidar Pehelwan in. They saw him with Agnimitra Batabayal, a very portable item number from Bokaro Steel City who was in MA (Previous) Sociology at the Delhi School of Economics. She lived in Hudson Lines with friends from Bihar and the North East and her large second-storey flat was known all over North Campus for the wild parties that she threw. She moved around the university in a Morris Minor that she had bought from one of her professors. Her mother was a judge in the family court in Ranchi. And here she was, right in the middle of Bungalow Road, walking hand around the waist with Haidar Pehelwan who looked as if he had never washed in his life and wore cheap shiny synthetic shirts, the collars of which would be rimmed by dirt and sweat. He was thinner than even Jishnuda if that was humanly possible, hence the legend 'Pehelwan'. In front of the Vidyarthi Clothes and Tailoring Shop, bang opposite the KMC backgate, Farid and Ramanuj saw Haidar stop and buy a white cellophane-wrapped rose from the flower seller who set up his shop there every evening and present it demurely to Agnimitra who laughed and then to Farid and Ramanuj's eternal glee kissed Haider quickly on the hand that held her own.

It confirmed to Ramanuj and Farid something that they had always suspected, that this ferocious rangbaz from Dehri-on-Sone was as fake as his legend. He was about as hard as a soft-boiled egg. Farid and Ramanuj raced each other laughing and panting to Shokeen Niwas and promptly apprised Jishnuda of the strange sighting.

The enmity between Jishnuda and Haider was of a recent provenance and had started, when during the Delhi University Students' Union elections in September he had gone to Haider to seek support for Prachi Jindal, an independent presidential candidate Jishnuda was supporting that year. He was her unofficial campaign manager for North Campus and Haider was said to control two hundred and fifty votes from the Nawada-Gaya-Jehanabad belt. Realistically it couldn't have been more than fifty votes but Haider refused and said that he had taken an Akhil Bharatiya Vidyarthi Parishad contract that year. They were sitting in one of the upper storey suites in Jubilee Hall where Haider had lived rent free for the past five years ever since he was admitted as an MPhil scholar in the History department.

Things would have been fine if Haider had refused and left it at that. But then he cast aspersions on Prachi Jindal's character and hoped that Jishnu was doing her 'Mobil palti' regularly. He then added for good measure that he would mobilize the votes if the 'chut' spent a weekend with him in Jubilee Hall. By the time Farid could stop him, Jishnuda had toppled Haider onto the floor, scattering steel tumblers full of Old Monk and Thums Up, his trusted astura, stolen from the Oriental Hair Cutting Saloon, stretched straight taut behind Haider's left ear. It took three of Haider Pehelwan's boys and Farid to prise Haider out of the stranglehold.

Jishnuda had vowed revenge that day and had waited for any sign of weakness from Haider. 'One of these days I am going to cut that campy miyan's balls and stuff them into his rouged mouth.' And now suddenly a month after the elections, during the autumn break, the opportunity had presented itself. The first sign of weakness had come to the surface. The miyan was in love.

Each year in August and September Jishnuda like most 'compromisers' in North Campus, milked both the National Students' Union of India and the ABVP during the students' union elections. There would be the regulation white Ambassador taxi which Jishnuda would hire each election season and which would be parked outside Shokeen Niwas, and at eleven in the morning all of us would board it. Jishnuda's chelas from Indira Vihar and Mukherjee Nagar would also join us sometimes. Most years Jishnuda would cruise around the university stopping at Ramjas, Hindu, Hansraj, Kirori Mal, Miranda and colleges off campus like Zakir, the windshields and body plastered with the posters and bunting of the party he was supporting that year. The open hand or the blooming lotus. The year before Jishnuda had campaigned for NSUI in the day time and ABVP at night. Though eventually he got votes for NSUI, I believe. But he got paid by both sides and every day there would be packed lunches from Bulawa in Outram Lines and packed dinners for everyone at Shokeen Niwas from All Heavens in Model Town at night. It was a bumper year, Chaitanya Mishra had informed me on the first day of campaigning as I was eagerly waiting by Mehendiratta's store for the white Ambassador car to arrive.

Jishnuda had been paid Rs 3,000 per day by each side the previous year. Along with the free lunches and dinners, he also accepted a bottle of Old Monk each evening. Elections in Delhi University had a carnival ambience, not like the drab, taking yourself too seriously affairs in JNU. The DUSU elections were in many ways the bonsai version of national elections. Enormous amounts of money were spent, with alliances and voting patterns forged and analyzed on caste and community lines. They were tremendous fun. The Jats usually won all the important posts but Bihari and North East votes were needed in the North Campus, as these two communities, especially the Biharis, turned out in large numbers to cast their ballot.

In the evenings we hit the residential colonies, Vijay Nagar, Maurice Nagar, Kamala Nagar, Mukherjee Nagar, Hudson Lines, Outram Lines, Indira Vihar, Model Town, Dhaka, Nirankari Colony, where most of the Bihari and North East students boarded. In the evenings a very tough Angami guy from Khonoma district in a Metallica T-shirt and ponytail called Samson 'Man to Man' Ratsa would join us. Samson had a wonderful sense of humour and would end each argument with Jishnuda with a 'Hey man, do you want to fight me man to man?' He was our point man for the North East set. His going rate was Rs 750 an evening. He rarely worked in the daytime as he usually woke up in the afternoon. This, according to Jishnuda, was because he lived with two Mauritian sisters of Bihari descent in Indira Vihar and had to do 'overtime' every night. I liked Samson very much and it was in his rooms that I heard the Boomtown Rats and The Clash for the first time. Not to mention Miles Davis, whose trumpet could be constantly heard from the street as you walked to his ground floor rooms. Even now whenever I hear 'Bitches Brew' I think of Samson 'Man to Man' Ratsa and his two sisters. He was the most content man I have ever seen. Later he would clear the state services and become a Block Development Officer in Nagaland.

The candidate that year whom Jishnuda was supporting was not from NSUI or ABVP but an independent one. Prachi Jindal, a five feet-nothing Punjabi spitfire, was the rebel NSUI candidate, supported by H. K. L. Bhagat. Her father was a prosperous caterer and tentwallah in Karol Bagh, who took care of the arrangements at weddings and religious functions in the homes of most of Delhi's politicans at that time. He was also an old friend of Zorawar Singh Shokeen from his Satyavati days. Prachi, an alumnus of Modern School, Barakhamba Road, and Kamla Nehru College, would sit between me and Jishnuda in the backseat of the Ambassador and listen with total attention to whatever wisdom Jishnuda was dishing out about voting patterns or 'hawa', as he called it. Once in a while she would lightly touch his hand while speaking and even in the dim light in the Ambassador I could see Jishnuda blush. 'Jishnu only campaigns with female candidates. He is a true romantic at heart,' Chaitanya Mishra had informed me. Jishnuda was totally smitten. And this at a time when Vinodini Khan's mountain bike would be regularly parked outside Shokeen Niwas. How does he manage it all the time, I would wonder looking at Prachi Jindal caress Jishnuda's thigh in the car as we sped along the North Campus streets.

'Prachi Jindal must win, Hriday.'

'Of course, she will win, Jishnuda.'

'We have to do something.'

'What?' I asked with a by then familiar sinking feeling in my heart.

'We must shoot her.'

'Shoot her? Are you crazy.'

'I mean, shoot at her, you Bengali chirkut.'

We were standing outside a three-storey house in Hudson Lines, where a dozen girls from Bihar and the North East stayed in two-room flats, connected one to the other like railway compartments, and mezzanine bedsitters, where the smell of Maggi 2-minute noodles cooked late in the night always hung in the air. Prachi Jindal was inside campaigning with Farid, Ramanuj and Samson. The sardar taxi driver had gone towards Kingsway Camp for his evening tea. Jishnuda pulled out Zorawar Singh's ancient Mauser, checked the magazine, slid the safety catch and then asked me to get out of the taxi. Then he fired two shots into the windshield. The noise was deafening. Instinctively I looked up and thought I saw a shadow on the darkened first floor balcony.

'Here take the gun and run to Shokeen Niwas,' Jishnuda said to me urgently as the overpowering smell of cordite wafted up around us.

By the time the girls came to the balcony, I was off through the proverbial patli gali, running onto the Ring Road, from where I caught a bus to Bungalow Road. I remember sitting at the back of the dimly lit bus, with my sweat-soaked shirt sticking to the rexine backrest and a hard on which would subside only fifteen minutes later in the ground floor bathroom of Shokeen Niwas after some tender loving care.

The tube light in our room was switched on and Pranjal was at his study table copying something from a red leather-bound library volume as I walked in breathless from my sprint up the stairs. He looked at me once as I took out the Mauser from my satchel and hid it between some old newspapers stacked in the corner, and said to me 'Your tiffin is kept outside the door. I have had my dinner.' But his eyes full of despair said something familiar and increasingly frequent: 'You are fucking up your life.' Pranjal didn't ask me anything about the evening as I ravenously ate my four rotis, rice, dal and egg curry. The next day our little nukkad natak made front page news. 'Poll violence grips Delhi University: Presidential hopeful Prachi Jindal shot at in North Campus.' There was a grainy black and white head shot of a visibly shocked Prachi, in a white khadi kurta and black jeans with her trademark pink leheriya-print dupatta and Chanel sunglasses, being escorted by a grim Jishnuda to a Model Town nursing home where she spent the night recuperating from her brush with death. Prachi Jindal won the elections by a landslide.

Soda, Lemon
Gingerpop
Prachi Jindal
On the top

A week later as I returned from Kingsway Camp, after spending the better part of the morning getting a new short story of mine called 'Vishnu Paswan' typed up by a fine typist who worked on an electronic typewriter, I saw the leheriya-print dupatta draped over Jishnuda's window. I didn't knock of course.

Soda, Lemon
Gingerpop
Prachi Jindal
On the top

It was a month since election day, during the autumn break when Pranjal and I were in Patna, that the strange sighting of Haider Pehelwan and Agnimitra Batabayal was reported to Jishnuda. Two days later, after extensive surveillance and recce carried out by Farid and Ramanuj, the hit took place. At around ten in the night as Haider was returning from Hudson Lines after dropping Lady Batabayal on his Yezdi, three masked men on a Hero Honda chased him and, where the Hudson Lines main road meets the Ring Road, crashed into his Yezdi from behind. As Haider fell down, the men pounced on him and started kicking and stomping on him as if he were a field mouse. Then they coolly sped away. Amulya Bharti, a third year Ramjas history student who was walking hurriedly towards the Ring Road Kingsway Camp theka before it closed, saw it all happen before his own eyes. He recognized Haider Pehelwan and helped him get off the ground. Haider's knees were rubbery and he kept falling down but after a while he wiped the blood off his broken nose and started his Yezdi. His parting shot to Amulya Bharti was not a thank you but a whispered 'kisi ko bolna nahi yaar' and he was on his way.

'The bastard didn't even offer me a lift to the theka, I told him I was going there. Of course, when I reached it was closed. I had to go all the way to Majnu Ka Tila for my khamba. "Kisi ko bolna nahi yaar."' The very next day Amulya reported the story to everyone in the Ramjas hostel mess during lunchtime. By dinner everyone in North Campus knew. The upshot of which was that Haider and Agnimitra's love grew ever stronger and in a couple of years they would get married and live happily thereafter.

At the larri-batti encrusted Miranda hostel, lit up like a marriage hall for a change, while Pranjal took to the dance floor with Rukmini Sahay, I sat with her sister Yamini and felt like a charity case. Earlier in the evening the girls had put up a wonderful variety show, full of skits, lampoons and choreography, but now they were out on the dance floor, celebrating the end of another academic year. All around us there was the din of loud carefree voices that girls affect when they are showing off. Yamini had grown quieter since the time we used to follow the sisters around Hathwa Market and she now didn't fluff her Madhuri Dixit style locks once every two minutes. She stayed somewhere in Hudson Lines with a few other girls from Patna and was a day scholar at St. Stephen's doing Economics Honours. She wore a sky blue-coloured Baluchari with a simple three-quarter length blouse which I noticed was cut deep in the back. Her eyes were light brown and she wore a tiny diamond stud in her left nostril, which gave off sparks whenever the disco lights from the dance floor caught it. She wasn't wearing a cardigan, nor was she carrying a shawl. I noticed that none of the girls wore any warm clothes to ward off the outdoors February chill, while the boys were decked out in jackets, sweaters and three-piece suits.

I promptly reported this profound observation of mine to Yamini who looked at me shyly and informed me, 'Since you are so interested in women's welfare, I am wearing thermal pajamas under my sari. So are most of the other girls. It is not as if we are freaks. We do feel cold.' Then she lifted the hem of her sari to her calves, so that I could have a closer look. That effectively shut me up for the next five minutes. I lit a Gold Flake and watched the boys and girls dance to old chestnuts like 'Summer of 69', 'Hold on to the Night', 'Simply Irresistible', 'Another Brick in the Wall', 'I am on Fire' and the entire *Saturday Night Fever* and *Dirty Dancing* soundtracks. In the middle of the dance floor there was a group of first year girls who kept butting into the couples around them trying awkwardly to slow dance to pop numbers, with the boys stepping on all the dainty toes that they could possibly find. But at least they got to hold the pliant waists of their beloveds for a few sweet minutes. Even though the boys had taken considerable pains to appear their best, the difference with the girls was glaring. While the boys still looked like boys, immature and slightly flustered, the girls looked poised and in control of the situation. Every last one of them including the imperious Yamini Sahay had been transformed magically into fine specimens of healthy Indian womanhood. Since my cigarette break was over I thought I should report this new finding to Yamini. 'It is the sari, you know. Even you will look mature in a sari. You should try it sometime,' Yamini said to me very sweetly while stifling a king-size yawn. So I did what I normally did in such situations. I lit another Gold Flake.

The dance floor was packed now and after a while we couldn't see Pranjal and Rukmini in the swirling crowd anymore. Everything was one wild blur of silk sarees and awkward hand and feet movements which encapsulated within themselves the entire dance styles of the world. Here the waltz turned into a Texan two-step and the twist into bhangra and then flamenco and then all five into an invigorating mishmash that Bollywood would be proud of. Some of the boys and girls it seemed, looking from afar, were jumping up and down, like puppets, a dance style that would be perfected by Aamir Khan a decade later in *Dil Chahta Hai*. The song that was playing was 'The Time of My Life' from *Dirty Dancing*. Again. When the song ended, a voice that I recognized immediately announced over the mike that 'This song is for Hriday Thakur. Will he please come up to the dance floor.' And as the opening bars of 'When Will I, Will I Be Famous' wafted from the jukebox, I got up and walked to the dance floor as if I was going to receive an Oscar. Yamini Sahay looked at me and said, 'I am impressed. Vinodini Khan is playing a song for you. Now hurry. Don't keep her waiting.' The way she spoke, one could gather that Yamini Sahay didn't much approve of a Vinodini Khan playing a song for Hriday Thakur. Then, to make matters worse, Yamini started clapping and all the boys and girls sitting around us in the lawn turned and looked at me. For some reason it made Hriday Thakur, an eternal fool for love, feel gloriously alive. For the first time that evening I felt I had a slight advantage over Yamini Sahay in our eternal boy-girl skirmishes. Vinodini Khan was a star and very few girls ever liked her. Among girls she had fans not friends. A fact that she very well knew and was quite thankful for. 'Pass me a boy any day' was her motto.

As I reached the dance floor I shouted 'fore' and the sea of adolescence parted to make way for me. Vinodini was standing in the corner near the jukebox surrounded by a group of kohl-lined acolytes, and as I reached her, she gave me a life-affirming hug and put into my hands a Styrofoam cup of fountain Coke, which was half full. It was spiked heavily with Old Monk. I, in turn, passed into her hand a tola of Bhagalpuri ganja that she had sent word through Pranjal she wanted. As Vinodini and I slow-danced to that legendary anthem of my childhood, passing the

Styrofoam cup of Cuba libre back and forth between us, it made me realize how far I had travelled from the time when I thought smoking Gold Flakes at street corners was the epitome of cool.

Those precious few minutes dancing and chatting with Vinodini made me feel the best in weeks. As the Bros song ended she said to me, still holding on to my hand, 'There is something different about you today. Something has happened to you over the past few months. Someone has taught you how to hold a woman. Yes, you have to be taught that. And then that someone has broken your heart. But she has made you better looking and I am not flirting with you. Now you go back to the Sahay sister. The poor girl thinks I am never going to return her boyfriend.'

'Vinodini, it is not what you think. We are not a couple.'

'Not yet.'

'Not ever. I don't think she even likes me.'

'We will see about that. You come and see me sometime, I have kept my first year notes and some "background" material for you. Also, do bring your stories, if you have written any new ones. Don't disappear again.'

Then Vinodini ruffled my hair and sent me on my way. The jukebox started playing 'Last Christmas' as I, slightly sweaty and flustered, went back to reclaim my vacant chair beside Yamini Sahay.

'Vinodini Khan is quite something, isn't she?' Yamini looked at me mischievously and said.

'That she is,' I accepted but didn't elaborate any further as I could see that she was intrigued about Vinodini and me.

Sometimes it is infinitely more rewarding when you do not satisfy a girl's curiosity.

Pranjal and Rukmini were still dancing, very slowly, with Rukmini's head resting on Pranjal's shoulders.

'I didn't know you were a dancer as well as a sprinter. I thought tough guys don't dance.'

Since I must have looked totally mystified by the sudden drift of her conversation, Yamini relented and spoke to me plainly once more.

'You know, during the elections, there was a shootout involving Prachi Jindal outside my home in Hudson Lines. I saw you running away and that monkey Jishnu Sharma looking on.'

'You were the shadow in the balcony! I thought I saw someone that day.'

'You ran quite well. Considering.'

'You are a very curious girl.'

'That I am. But I didn't tell anyone. Not even didi.'

By then the evening was winding down and as the hostel matron kept pointedly looking at her watch, soon the last number, Sinead O'Connor's already iconic 'Nothing Compares to You', was played and the dance was over. All the boys and girls walked towards the mess for dinner. Along the way Rukmini pointed to a dark room on the first floor and said that it was her room.

'Shall I sneak in and wait for you there?' Pranjal lightly touched her face with the back of his hand and asked her.

'Well, what about my roommate?' Rukmini said softly and held Pranjal's hand. Yamini and I walking behind them pretended that we didn't hear anything.

Then Rukmini trying to change the topic said, 'We are trying out a new caterer tonight. He is supposed to be quite good. Apart from his catering business, he is also a novelist. He is quite a character. His name is Satyabrat Ojha.'

Pranjal and I let out a collective groan. Sure enough Satyabrat Sir was near the buffet table, looking proprietorial in his mustard-coloured khadi kurta and faded blue jeans, but thankfully the food was not bad. Perhaps Dunkel had forgotten to piss in it that night. Pranjal and I somehow managed to elude Ojha and we had a lovely dinner with the sisters and their inquisitive friends at the farthest corner from the Mandal hero. I was glad that Pranjal and Rukmini had invited me to the party. It was good to move out of the misanthropic atmosphere of Shokeen Niwas for a few hours and not think about Anjali Nalwa at all. I had promised myself that I would try and lead a disciplined life in Delhi University and seven months down the line I wasn't sure whether I had kept my word. Yes, I went to Zakir Husain College every day, but not to study, to catch a glimpse of Anjali Nalwa. Sure I wrote stories but were they any good? The amoral atmosphere of Shokeen Niwas was fascinating at first but now Pranjal had asked me whether I wished to become another Jishnuda. And the answer, I realized, was an emphatic of course not. Pranjal on the other hand had done what he had always done. He applied himself to the task at hand to the best of his ability. He had his masti. He would sit with us, Jishnuda, Farid, Ramanuj and me, with a khamba of rum. When everyone had gone to bed, he would hit the books. Apart from his economics textbooks, he also had his medical entrance guide books to read, the Brilliant Tutorials that I had sold off with such relief. In the end he would get into Maulana Azad Medical College and also manage 55 per cent in his Economics (Hons.) first year exam. I, on the other hand, would limp off with a measly 48 per cent. My teachers at Zakir were surprised that I had even passed as they had hardly seen me in the classrooms in the last few months of the term. But all this was still some months away. Pranjal was a lot like Abhinav Srivastava and Chaitanya Mishra, he knew instinctively that he had to keep Shokeen Niwas at arm's length to succeed in life. At the other extreme were Jishnuda, Ramanuj and Farid, who were naturals in the world of Shokeen Niwas. And I fell somewhere in between the two ways of life. I was neither resolute nor callous enough. I was such a loser.

It was close to eleven when we came out of the Miranda House back gate and started walking towards Bungalow Road. At Jai Jawan, someone shouted out my name and we both turned and saw Jishnuda sitting on his Rajdoot 175, the smouldering tip of a Navy Cut aglow in the darkness. Apparently, for some reason, Zorawar Singh wanted to see me right away. He was waiting for us in a bar inside the Tibetan resettlement camp at Majnu ka Tila called Dimlight. The Tibetan camp was very popular with the North Campus students as it served liquor all through the night and often enough we would go there to buy a khamba of Old Monk or Aristocrat Whisky at 2 or 3 a.m. to replenish our stock. Most of these small-time bars were run by women but rarely any trouble was reported from there. No one picked up a fight in Majnu ka Tila. The Tibetans kept to their business and we kept to ours. Most of these bars also served good, inexpensive chinky food. Sometimes when there was something to celebrate like Abhinav Srivastava clearing his NET examination which made him eligible for a Junior Research Fellowship and an ad hoc lecturership at Zakir Husain (Evening), he took all of us from Shokeen Niwas to Dimlight for a treat. We had a khamba and a quarter of Old Monk and most of the mutton and chicken dishes on the menu along with fried rice and hakka noodles and the bill still came to under a thousand rupees. At night with its badly lit narrow alleys and the bright neon-lit legends, the Tibetan camp was a fascinating place to spend time in. It was a place that gave off a whiff of danger and forbidden pleasures but in its own way was quite safe. The night we celebrated Abhinav Srivastava's success, we had started at 2 a.m. from Dimlight and reached Shokeen Niwas exactly an hour later. High on ganja and rum and our stomachs adequately filled for once, we walked through the university singing Hindi film songs, stopping only to piss, standing in a row, on the walls of the PG Women's Hostel on Chhatra Marg. Needless to add, it was a memorable night.

Jishnuda dropped Pranjal near the Kirori Mal College hostel gate and we reversed and continued on our way to Majnu ka

Tila. Pranjal, sensing something was amiss, wanted to come with me but Jishnuda told him not to worry and to go home and wait for me.

'What is with Pranjal and Rukmini Sahay? Are they in love?' Jishnuda asked me.

'Looks like love,' I replied.

'Was Vinodini there?'

'Yes, she was. She danced with me.'

'Did she ask about me?'

'No, she didn't, but I told her that you were well,' I lied for no apparent reason.

'She was a good girl,' Jishnuda said a bit wistfully and then kept quiet for the rest of the journey, except for a bit of advice as he parked his bike outside Dimlight.

'If Uncle Zorawar offers you a drink, do not say yes.'

Zorawar Singh had Joginder Tyagi, the SHO of Maurice Nagar thana with him. The same Joginder who was the cause of Satyabrat Ojha's chronic urinary problems. The khamba of Aristocrat Whisky in front of them was down to the last quarter and a fresh bowl of chilli chicken and a plate of thickly sliced mooli doused in green chutney was brought to the table by a dainty but bored-looking Tibetan girl. Then she went back and sat behind the sunmica counter and continued with her Maths homework. She wouldn't have been more than fourteen. Joginder Tyagi in a police-issue black leather jacket over a crumpled khaki uniform stared drowsily at the girl all the while that I was at Dimlight.

Zorawar Singh offered us whisky and Jishnuda refused and then uncle offered us chilli chicken and mooli, 'roti khalo,' and Jishnuda said we had had our dinner. So then Zorawar came to the main point and asked me how my first day tutoring Sonya Midha had gone. I told Zorawar that it went all right and that Sonya seemed to be a bright enough kid. Before Jishnuda could say anything I told Zorawar that I wasn't sure if I was suitable for this job and maybe he could look for another tutor. The way he had me brought to Majnu ka Tila for this conversation, like I were some sleazy gang member, had upset my delicate sensibilities. That was the reason I told him I wanted out. I didn't want to tutor his paramour's daughter anymore. But Zorawar merely smiled at this and said that I was doing fine and that he now thought I was perfectly suited for the job and that I should continue with it. Then he asked me to wait outside while he spoke to Jishnuda. I went outside and lit a Gold Flake. It was reassuring to note that my hands were not shaking.

Jishnuda came out after a few minutes.

'Uncle is very impressed with you. He thinks you are a very sincere boy.'

'Sincere?'

'That's what he said. Here's something for Sonya from uncle. Give it to her tomorrow when Madam is not around.' Jishnuda gave me a small, brown paper-wrapped package to keep. On the way back to Shokeen Niwas, I opened the package to take a look. It was a 100 ml bottle of Charlie perfume.

That night sleep came to me very late. And when it did I dreamt about Anjali Nalwa. In the dream Anjali and I were again on the 901 which was empty except for the two of us and the driver who I couldn't see. Anjali was looking outside the window and was not speaking to me, while I held on to her hand. I said something to her, which made her start crying instantly, though I myself couldn't hear what I said to her. We passed the Red Fort twice and then Kingsway Camp. Anjali kept shaking her head at whatever I was saying to her and tears continued to flow. Later we were on my cot in my room in Shokeen Niwas, making love. I could see Pranjal, the table lamp burning, studying as usual at the far side of the room. I was between her legs, my tongue inside her cunt. Then she was on her knees and I was screwing her from behind but when she turned her head to kiss me I found I was kissing Madam Midha instead. She started to moan loudly and I became afraid that she would disturb Pranjal's concentration, and he would turn and see us together. I clamped my hand around her mouth to stop her from screaming but she wouldn't stop. She went on and on. And as we both came I yanked her head by her hair and it came off neatly in my hand. She was wearing a wig. Exhausted we slumped together on the bed. I rolled off her and Madam Midha turned on her back and faced me. Only it was not Madam Midha but Sonya, her hair cut close to her skull like Anjali's. Looking at me with a mischievous smile. I must have screamed then as Pranjal woke me up soon after. I lay awake the entire night after that, chain-smoking Gold Flakes.

The next evening as Mrs Midha went out for her grocery shopping after serving tea to Sonya and me, I took out the bottle of Charlie perfume in its deep red cover and gave it to Sonya. Lest she misunderstand my intentions, I quickly told her that it was from Uncle Zorawar. Sonya was not the least bit surprised and opened the package with a smile that lit up her eyes. She inhaled deeply from the bottle and then dabbed some perfume on her wrists and rubbed them together. And then, before I could stop her, she touched my nose lightly with her right wrist. The dank sweet smell made my head reel.

'Do you like it? Isn't it glamorous?'

'Of course. It is lovely.' I knew that this smell would never evaporate from my senses and that later on in my life I would encounter it at unexpected places, reminding me of the time when I had been a willing accomplice in the plot to ruin a young girl's life. The smell told me that I was not to be trusted. Not even by myself. I should always be monitored.

'Go and wash your hands before your mother comes back and open the windows,' I said harshly to Sonya. The tone must have startled her because she quickly put the bottle of perfume in her school satchel and went to the tap in the kitchen. Even though it was bitingly cold I turned on the pedestal fan which someone had painted a rich ferozi blue and gradually the stink went away.

'Don't you think uncle is very handsome?' Sonya asked me as she wiped her hands on a small towel, the kind I had taken to the NCC camp near Bihta instead of a regular one.

Sonya had met Zorawar Singh by chance about a month back outside the Bungalow Road Nirula's when she had gone out with her mother to Kamla Nagar. Mrs Midha had introduced Zorawar as her colleague and then Zorawar had insisted on treating them to pizzas at Nirula's. It was at that meeting that Mrs Midha had voiced her concern about Sonya's declining academic fortunes. Zorawar had promised that he would find someone suitable to tutor her. After that meeting—of which Mrs Midha had forbidden Sonya to say anything to her father as he didn't like Zorawar much, 'I don't know why'—Sonya had accidentally met uncle thrice outside her school and each time he had taken her to Nirula's in his white, gleaming Gypsy and treated her to pizzas and ice cream. Her favourite was tutti-frutti. About these meetings Mrs Midha didn't have a clue as she would scold Sonya for making Zorawar uncle spend so much money on her. 'Her constant refrain is that I do not know the value of money. I spend too much but, Hriday Sir, I never have any money to spend. I do not even get pocket money. All my friends do. Every time I have to make a phone call to a friend, I have to ask mother for two rupees to go to the corner shop. Did you get pocket money when you were in school?'

'No,' I lied.

Later on as I was leaving, she quickly wrote something on an Archies card, sealed it with her spit, and gave it to me for uncle. Mrs Midha was in the kitchen making rajma for dinner.

'Uncle is very sincere.' Sincere. Again that word. She must have learnt it from Zorawar I realized with a sudden chill in my heart. My mind which had slowly started disintegrating the night before, after my meeting with Zorawar, segued into a fast forward mode.

As I walked from Sonya's house to Shokeen Niwas, I thought about Mrs Midha and how blissfully unaware she was of the danger to her family. Here she was, in her early thirties, with a respectable middle-class job as a section officer in the university, a daughter who was pretty and bright, and a marriage that was all but dead. She had a lover, a somewhat dangerous man who provided security and physical sustenance. I am sure she loved Zorawar but she was never going to leave her family for him. Nor did she expect Zorawar to leave his wife and marry her. Marriage was important to her. Even though she perhaps didn't feel love for her husband, Satyakam Midha was still her husband and he was what kept her little world together. I saw it in the deferential way both husband and wife treated each other. They wanted the marriage to continue. It was the most extravagant thing they had bought together, even though it was not of much use to them. Like a crystal chandelier in a one-room flat. Sure, Mrs Midha was in love with Zorawar Singh Shokeen but the reverse was certainly not true. Her love for Zorawar was her only indulgence and it must have taken considerable courage to conduct the affair. But to be desired by a powerful and attractive man like Zorawar Singh Shokeen would have worked like a charm on someone who had lived a life of nil delights till then.

I do not know the circumstances of her first meeting with Zorawar or how the affair started but I certainly knew how it was going to end. In a tragedy. In the two days that I had observed her in her house, my previous impression of her as a woman of 'loose character' or 'randi' as Jishnuda had affectionately called her had taken a complete 360° turn. She was a regular middle-class mother with a somewhat complicated personal life. There was not anything glamorous about her. She was hardly a gangster's moll, like Helen, in a tight sequined dress and fishnet stockings. She cooked rajma in her small kitchen wearing a ragged orange cardigan over a faded floral-print cotswool nightie. And she cut recipes from *Woman's Era* and *Grihshobha*, which she kept meticulously in a brown Delhi University file. Recipes for Chicken a la Kiev, mince cutlets, devilled eggs and caramel pudding, dishes she wouldn't ever cook in her home as they were Arya Samajis. And then almost as a natural progression my thoughts turned towards Anjali Nalwa and I knew I had not done right by her. I had abandoned her because she was not of the right class, I realized, and that my friends and family members would make fun of her if they ever met her. It was not Anjali who did not wish to meet my friends but it was I who had always found a reason to avoid introducing her to them. I had used her sexually and then callously withdrawn my love when I realized I was getting in too deep. I was no different from Zorawar who used women in a calculated manner for his pleasure and then discarded them. I was a coward and a cad. This sudden realization of my behaviour fuelled by a rapidly splintering mind almost buckled my knees and I sat down on the pavement outside the mandir opposite Hansraj College to rest my legs. This was the very same mandir where years back Zorawar Singh had first seen Sunita Khandelwal and it had led to his acquiring Shokeen Niwas. The beggars looked at me sympathetically, as if they already knew that my condition was far more precarious than theirs ever would be. I instinctively looked around for Ramanuj Ghosh, and then I started to laugh. The beggars looked on indulgently. I sat there in front of the mandir for what seemed to me to be hours but could not have been more than half an hour in reality. Probably less. My life was at crisis point and I was close to a breakdown. What added to it was my fiction writer's imagination in which everything I had ever done was invariably connected to my present situation. I reviewed my whole life up to that point. My upper middle-class upbringing, privileged childhood, St. Xavier's, Commerce College, friends and the inexplicable ambition to become a writer one day, and in the end the move to Delhi and Shokeen Niwas. Somehow I had again created an author-backed role for myself. I lit a Gold Flake and took a deep drag. It being a Tuesday there was a rush of devotees for the evening aarti. I must have cut a strange and somewhat isolated figure sitting in the midst of beggars waiting for alms, chainsmoking Gold Flakes. They would have taken me for a charsi or afeemchi and the indifferent yet relieved middle class gaze of the devotees said as much. Relieved it was not one of their own, a son or a brother, who was sitting outside the mandir looking totally wasted. It is true that at that time I would have paid anything for a tola of Bhagalpuri ganja or even a pellet of charas. Anything that would make me escape my present reality.

When I eventually came down from the trip, I'd find everything to be just a bad dream, like the one about not being prepared for the Intermediate examination. I wake up back in my house in Patna, firmly centred in the security of my family, my father reading Auden in the evening while my mother tends to her roses. But this was no dream, it was my life. By the third cigarette I was calm again. The crisis had passed. What my mind was telling me was correct. Everything was connected. I had to take a stand now. I couldn't drift anymore. I had been unfair to Anjali Nalwa and in the last year and a half I had tried to lead a life of studied indifference to anything good and decent and veered more and more towards the callous and amoral. Things somehow had to change. I couldn't be a disinterested flaneur anymore. I had to show interest in things around me. I had to start being good once more. I was getting bored with being bad. Somehow I had to save Sonya from Zorawar Singh Shokeen. I had to redeem myself. I took out the card that Sonya had given me. It was a Valentine's Day card with a large maroon heart bound in pink ribbon on the cover and 'Will you be my Valentine?' written in bold italic inside. Beneath it was Sonya's childlike handwriting in red sketch pen, proclaiming a defiant 'Zorawar Uncle, I love you', and a hastily scrawled, 'Many thanx for Charlie. Love & Kisses. Sonya.'

A beggar in a threadbare Harris tweed jacket pointed to the pack of cigarettes in my hand and I offered one to him. We smoked in silence for a while. Before I left I gave the entire packet to him as a neighbourly gesture. Valentine's Day was the following Sunday. I had to see Pranjal and seek his counsel. As always he had been proved right.

The first time Zorawar Singh Shokeen hit me, it split my lower lip and I could taste my own blood. We were in Jishnuda's room, the same room in which about seven months back I had seen our legendary landlord for the first time. Only difference being, at that time he was screwing Mrs Midha and this time around it was I who was being screwed. Pranjal and I were held captive in Jishnuda's room. Till that day I had never taken a sustained physical beating in my seventeen years of life. And I found that after a while it alters your mind. Pranjal's hands were bound with his own belt and Farid kept a restraining hand on his shoulders to keep him sitting down on a chair in one corner of Jishnuda's room. Farid observed Zorawar Singh's interrogation methods quite keenly and it would stand him in good stead when he joined the police force and become an ASI a few years later.

They didn't touch Pranjal. He was there only for show. So that I would finally speak up and tell the truth. Pranjal kept staring at the floor, refusing to look at me. I don't blame him for that. I wasn't a pretty sight. In fact, I wouldn't ever be pretty again. My left eye had swollen up and was almost closed after Ramanuj Ghosh in a show of exemplary zeal had hit me with a pair of steel pliers before Jishnuda could stop him. My nose was cut and bruised on the bridge where it had connected with Zorawar's ring-encrusted right fist. My maroon sweater tore from the neck to the chest when Jishnuda pulled me off the floor using the sweater for grip, this after I had slid off Jishnuda's bed as a result of a well-directed kick in the stomach from Zorawar Singh. The pain goes away after a while. Your mind becomes numb with fear and what remains is humiliation. But I refused to think about humiliation and after a while I realized that if you stop thinking about the humiliation you can take any amount of physical pain. Though my eyes were filled with tears, I promised myself that I would not break down. But you can't ration an imaginative mind and the thought suddenly struck me, how utterly helpless and ashamed my father would feel if he saw me like this. Absolutely the very kind of thought one shouldn't be thinking when one is getting the shit kicked out of him.

The question that Zorawar kept asking me between the beatings was how did Madam Midha come to know about Sonya and him. I mostly kept silent but after he hit me on the forehead with the butt of his Mauser, I said I had no idea what he was talking about, and that when I had gone that evening as usual to the Midha household, Madam Midha had informed me that my services were no longer required. She didn't give any reason. And, yes, she had given me two hundred rupees for the two days that I had taught Sonya. At this, Zorawar, to my complete surprise, took out Sonya's Valentine's Day card from his jacket and threw it at my face. I knew then I was going to die.

The previous evening, looking for Pranjal in desperation, I had walked from the mandir after distributing my packet of Gold Flakes to beggars, towards the Miranda hostel. I found Pranjal at

Jai Jawan having tea with Yamini and Rukmini. He looked at me and knew in a flash that something was seriously wrong. Yamini asked me to have a glass of tea but I declined. To her credit she didn't ask if anything was wrong. I am sure anyone who saw me at that time would have known in an instant that everything was wrong with Hriday Thakur. You can't camouflage monumental ill luck. We quickly said goodbye to the sisters and started on our way back to Shokeen Niwas. I took out the card that Sonya had given for Zorawar and showed it to Pranjal. 'I can't take it anymore. I am not a bloody dalal.' Pranjal said after a while, 'You must let the parents know the kind of danger Sonya is in. Tell them tomorrow. But it will be dangerous. If Zorawar or Jishnuda comes to know about this, we will be fucked.'

'Certainly not the father. I can't tell him. He will be destroyed. I'll meet Madam Midha in the university and show her the card. My job will be done. Surely I can't be expected to do anything more.'

Pranjal agreed and then we made the plan. We discussed shifting out of Shokeen Niwas overnight, carrying whatever we could, but then gave the idea up as impractical. Pranjal said that it would arouse suspicion and we should stay at Shokeen Niwas for at least a couple of weeks and then move out, but that the next day while I went to meet Madam Midha in the afternoon, Pranjal would pack most of our clothes and books into two large bags and take them to Rukmini for safekeeping. Nobody would suspect anything as every couple of weeks it was a common sight to see Pranjal take the dirty laundry to Miranda. This strategem was only for the worst-case scenario. I was to apprise Madam Midha of the situation and request her not to divulge my role in it. I would come back to Shokeen Niwas around six and inform Jishnuda that I had been relieved from tutoring Sonya and that would be that. We were to act as if everything was normal. We knew it was going to be extremely dangerous but hopefully we would pull it off and nobody would notice.

So the following afternoon, as planned, Pranjal took two carrybags filled with our clothes and books to Miranda House, while I crossed the university garden to meet Madam Midha in her office. Seeing me standing outside her window counter Madam Midha was startled for a second but then she closed her counter for lunch and came out to meet me. We went to the university canteen next door. There, without any preliminaries, I gave her the card and told her about the bottle of Charlie and the Nirula's pizzas and footlongs that Zorawar was treating her daughter to. At first, as she read the card and listened to me, there was total incomprehension on her face, but then it crumpled slowly like a Styrofoam cup as the enormity of the situation hit her.

I told her that she should just leave with Sonya for Chandigarh, go to her sister's place, and at present say nothing to Zorawar about it, especially my role in it.

'Just go away for a fortnight, a month. Do not say anything specific to your husband and when you come back, break it off with Zorawar Singh. Stop seeing him. Everything will be all right then. But don't confront him at present. He is a dangerous man. He has killed before. He will kill again.'

As I left the canteen, Madam Midha was still sitting at the corner table, the cup of tea untouched by her side, looking with vacant eyes at the card that her daughter had written to her paramour. At Jai Jawan Pranjal was waiting for me. We had four hours to kill before six so we decided to take in a revival of Aditya Bhattacharya's *Raakh* at Shakuntalam. We reached Shokeen Niwas at 6:30 p.m. in the evening. Jishnuda, along with Farid Ashraf, was standing outside Mehendiratta's shop, looking tense. Dolly fluffed her hair and gave me a smile.

'Uncle is upstairs. He is waiting for you,' Jishnuda said to me.

Groggy from the blow to my forehead, I looked at the card, Sonya's innocent, flamboyant 'thanx', and tried to fathom how the fuck could that have landed in Zorawar's hands. Did Madam Midha double-cross me? No, that couldn't possibily be true. Later, from Chaitanya Mishra, I came to know the exact sequence of events as they unfolded that day. Mrs Midha had picked up Sonya from her school at three o'clock, and as they were getting into an autorickshaw, Zorawar drove up to them in his white Gypsy. Seeing Zorawar in such close proximity to her daughter, Madam Midha started screaming at him at the top of her voice and in a final flourish pulled out the card that I had given her only a short while before and threw it at him. As a small crowd of onlookers was starting to gather Zorawar quickly turned the Gypsy around and left for Shokeen Niwas. He had been waiting for me since then.

'I have not written this card nor have I seen it before. I do not know what you are asking me to admit.'

'Hriday, stop lying. Sonya gave you this card for uncle, why did you give it to Madam?' Jishnuda came close, absent-mindedly opening and snapping shut his trusted astura.

'Sonya gave me nothing. I agreed to tutor her only because you asked me to.' I kept denying the charge.

'Hriday, tell me the truth or I will slit Pranjal's wrist.'

Chaitanya Mishra and Abhinav Srivastava who were watching the proceedings of the last ten minutes (yes it wouldn't have been more than that) with growing alarm tried to intervene then.

'Jishnu, why don't you believe Hriday. I am sure he is telling the truth,' Chaitanya said to Jishnuda. At this Zorawar turned and looked at Chaitanya and Abhinav and motioned with his hands for them to disappear. To their credit they refused to go and stood their ground near the door.

I then decided to try out one of Jishnuda's own rules regarding the art of war, that of never backing down, of not showing fear, as I saw him place the astura on Pranjal's left wrist. Even though my harkat didn't have the desired effect, I did finally manage to find my voice.

'I don't care how much you beat me. I am not scared of you, Jishnuda. You are just a small-time crook. Do anything you want, but you will remain a crook all your life. There will be no profile change for you ever. Do your B.A., your M.A., even an M.Phil. if it strikes your fancy, and your pretense studying for the civil services, but nothing will change for you. You are not a scholar. Come on, cut my wrists. I dare you to cut my wrists, you moron.'

So Jishnuda did just that. He rushed over to my side and before Zorawar could stop him he had slashed my right wrist. As the blood spurted out in a jet and hit my eyes I screamed in pain. I probably passed out around that time.

When I woke up, two days had passed. I was in my room in Shokeen Niwas, in my own bed. My right hand was heavily bandaged and there were stitches on my nose and around my chin. A highly regarded general surgeon from AIIMS was brought by Joginder Tyagi within twenty minutes of Jishnuda's assault. He had patched me up properly and had visited twice to monitor my progress. He stayed nearby in Nangia Park.

Around my bed were Pranjal, Farid Ashraf, Chaitanya Mishra and Jishnuda. I asked for a cigarette. Jishnuda lit a Gold Flake and put it in my mouth. I never saw Zorawar Singh Shokeen again. As for Jishnuda, I would see him from time to time in North Campus. He made my prediction about him come true and in a few years' time he would become an event manager and a leading importer of blondes in collaboration with Zorawar Singh. He would never go back to Patna. After failing for two years in a row Ramanuj Ghosh would go back to Chapra to run his family sweet shop near the railway station. As for Madam Midha and her family, as far as I know they never returned to Delhi. I always avoided going back to Malkaganj but only once, when in early April just before my examinations started I read of Divya Bharti's suicide in Bombay, I gathered some courage and in a rickshaw went past the Midha house. The green windows were still fastened shut.

And by Sunday, Valentine's Day and my eighteenth birthday, both Pranjal and I would move out of Shokeen Niwas. In those two days I had become some sort of a celebrity. A constant stream of assorted tough guys from the different Bihari sets would come to visit me. Nothing like a sustained beating to really propel you through the popularity charts up north. Even if it was a case of friendly fire. In North Campus no one bothered about the truth anyway. They all had their own theories. They were all storytellers and I didn't feel like correcting them. Even Haidar Pehelwan came visiting with a few of his bravos and extended an invitation to the Holi celebrations in Jubilee Hall. All this must have alarmed Pranjal no end, as he told me that he had decided to shift to one of the servants' quarters in Mall Apartments that Satyabrat Ojha in his new avatar as a property dealer had arranged for him. Pranjal told me that he had made up his mind to shift out a month back but didn't know how to break the news to me. So when Satyabrat Ojha came to visit me that evening that I came to my senses, I asked him to find me a barsati, which he promptly did, in Hakikat Nagar, near Kingsway Camp. I moved in without seeing the room because I liked the name of the colony. I needed a reality check.

The barsati was splendid. The walls were painted a fungus green and it had a small kitchenette where Yamini Sahay would sometimes make bread-omelette and coffee while Dean Martin slouched in the corner and sang 'Amoré'. It was a good room. I would stay there for years. I wrote many stories there.

Some published, many unpublished. But I wrote and kept myself alive.

Soda, Lemon
Gingerpop
Hriday Thakur
Back on Top

Acknowledgements

I wish to thank my parents, my brother and extended family in Patna and beyond. Their unconditional love and support has been crucial to my survival.

Lima Kanungo and Anuradha Marwah, my two mentors at Zakir Husain College.

Colm Tóibín, Gish Jen and Pankaj Mishra for nominating *Day Scholar* to the 2009 Man Asian Literary Prize shortlist.

Amitava Kumar for being a star in a sky mostly obscured by clouds.

Palash K. Mehrotra and Hirsh Sawhney for keeping me on my toes and including excerpts from *Day Scholar* in their groundbreaking anthologies, *Recess: The Penguin Book of Indian School Days* and *Delhi Noir*.

Ramesh Jain and my colleagues at Manohar for making the past ten years an enriching experience.

The British Council, New Delhi, and the Charles Wallace Trust, London for the 2007 Writer-in-Residence Fellowship at the University of Stirling, where at the Polwarth Guest Flat, over half of *Day Scholar*, to the incessant chant of oystercatchers, was composed.

At Stirling: David Richards, John Drakakis, Ruth Evans, Rowan Cruft and the lovely Gemma Robinson for making my stay so enjoyable and productive.

Team Picador: The austere and wise Rajdeep Mukherjee and the still incomparable Shruti Debi.

In the end, Pragya Sinha Chowdhury, without whom, of course, all this would be pointless.

Author's Note

Diksha at St. Martin's was first published in 2002 and sank without a trace in no time. No stranger to bad taste or behaviour, I had even put my own face on the cover, hoping it would boost sales. The austere reception of course didn't cure me of my innate vaingloriousness. But it did temper my profound sense of entitlement somewhat. Then newly married, I said to my wife in despair, 'I do not know what I should do to get noticed.' 'Perhaps it would help if you wrote better and did not worry so much about getting "noticed",' Pragya said to me. It was sound advice, I felt. She then put on the soundtrack of the *Wonder Boys* on the tape deck and we danced slowly to 'Things Have Changed'. *Diksha* remains the blueprint, so to say, for all my writing.

Patna Roughcut followed in 2005 and it did slightly better. It was reviewed well and in time would become a cult book but the sales were as ever poor. But it was 'noticed'. Good enough for me. *Day Scholar* came out in 2010 and sold better than the earlier two books and ruffled a few middle-class feathers with its graphic description of some transcendental ass-fucking. But the performance could hardly be called spectacular. *Day Scholar* would also turn me into that strange pariah of the literary world: the writer's writer.

So when Diya Kar Hazra, my publisher at Pan Macmillan India, suggested an omnibus edition incorporating the three beleaguered volumes, I could hardly believe my luck. Books are rarely given a second chance in India and writers never. So it is with profound gratitude that I thank Team Picador: Diya Kar Hazra, Teesta Guha Sarkar, and Rajdeep Mukherjee—for ensuring that these manifestos of literary longing and despair are kept alive for a few more years.

For over twenty years I have written the same story again and again. There has been no variation. For me, every boy is called not Patrick but Ritwik. Or sometimes Hriday for that matter.

The Patna Manual of Style which came out from Aleph last year, continues the further adventures of Hriday Thakur and wherein Ritwik Ray also makes a guest appearance. So it would continue, hopefully every decade or so. The world of my novels is enclosed and exclusive and I would like to believe it is also universal. So dear reader, you needn't ever visit Patna or Delhi to get seduced or repelled by my novels. In fact, it would be an advantage if you never do so. Many readers who actually live in those twin cities of my imagination find my work to be, well, totally fictional. The world I create is a stylized one, and yet for the characters who inhabit it, it is I believe intensely real. But then, in my defence, I can only say that I never set out to write *The Rough Guide to Patna*, did I? Only *Patna Roughcut*. And *Day Scholar*. And *Diksha*. To me all novels are essentially rough cuts. The final cut is always with the reader.

Siddharth Chowdhury
Bhiwadi
May 2016